HERO'S LIFE

SONG OF PROPHECY
BOOK TWELVE

P.E. PADILLA

OLIVERHEBERBOOKS

The Great Prophet predicted you would want to read his story

Tsosin Ruus, the most renowned mage during the Age of Magic, wrote the Song of Prophecy to aid the world of Dizhelim as it would exist thousands of years after his life ended. But who was the Great Prophet, and how did he come to be the most important person in history...up until the present time?

And what of Erent Caahs, the most famous of contemporary heroes?

Get these two full-length companion novels to the Song of Prophecy and Hero Academy series for free and find out the fascinating stories that transformed ordinary boys into figures idolized by millions.

To get your free books and find out about upcoming books, please visit my website at https://pepadilla.com (Newsletter menu item or the bottom of every page). Thank you!

PARTIAL MAP OF
DIZHELIM

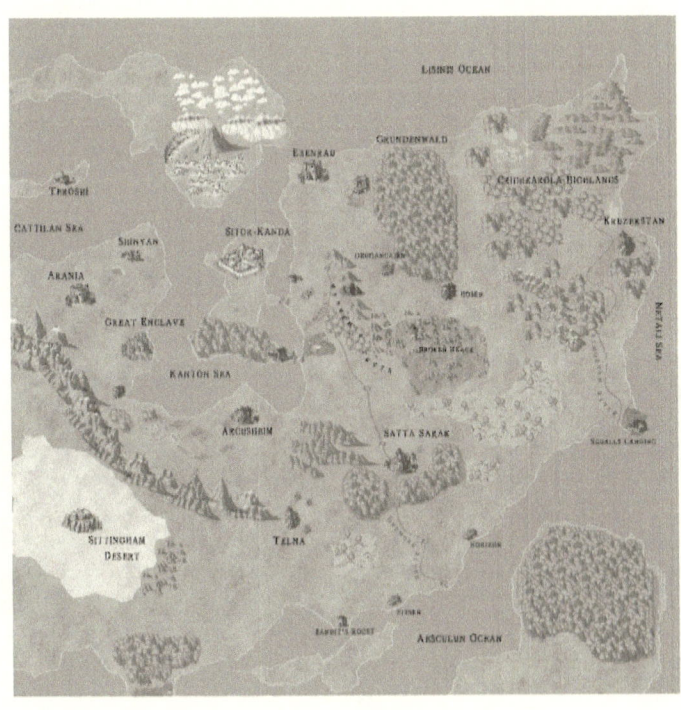

There are times when I'm sure life is one long, monotonous slog, that merely existing is my sole purpose. It's at those times I go out exploring, which never fails to make me realize I'm not as smart as I sometimes think I am.

Erent Caahs, in casual conversation with his friend Raisor Tannoch.

PROLOGUE

"It's a bad one this time," the woman said. "She's burning up with fever and she stopped breathing altogether three times in the last six hours."

"Did you send for Mother Sella?" the man asked.

"No. She's off in Drusca visiting family. She left some vials of the medicine she prepared for us in case there was an episode."

"All we can do is wait it out then, like always. She's strong, she'll make it through."

"Probably," the woman said. "I wish I could take all the pain and the weakness and the sickness from her onto myself. A child shouldn't have to deal with things like that."

"I know, dear. You know I would also take it all on myself if it were possible. We're not mages, not even healers like Mother Sella. We can only do what we can do. She will fight. It will be enough. It must be."

The small girl was in a pocket of consciousness within the current flare-up of her sickness. Most of time during her episodes, the pain and weakness were everything in the world, the only thing she recognized. Sometimes, though, she would have a minute or two where she could hear—and other times even see—what was going on around her.

Her mother and father were worried about her, like always. If she had to tell the truth, she was worried about herself. More, though, she was sorry. All she seemed to do was to cause problems. She never knew when whatever the illness was she had inside would come upon her and then she would be bedridden until it passed. In the meantime, her parents worried and had to spend money on medicine and watch her closely to see if she would finally die this time.

Sometimes she wished she would, just to be done with the pain, but also because then her parents could have a normal life, one where she didn't take up all their time like she did now.

She could feel the illness swell again, and with it, her own energy dimmed. Breathing became difficult, just because it took every bit of her strength to try to get air into her body. It would be easy to stop trying. If she didn't push herself to breathe, she could sink into the blackness and she wouldn't be a burden to anyone ever again.

Like so many other times before, she decided not to exert herself. She could relax and fall into the dark. All her troubles —and most of her parents'—would go away that simply. She only needed to give up.

The sharp pain of taking a breath despite her resolution made her want to throw up. If she could afford the energy it would take. No, her body would keep trying to breathe for as long as it could. Something seemed wrong about giving up and letting her sickliness win. With a whispered apology to her parents within her mind, she set her entire being to one task: breathe and fight and stretch her life on for another minute. If she did that enough, this time would pass, too, like all the others before it.

When the weakness, pain, and breathing problems passed, as she knew they would eventually, the girl rested more comfortably in her bed. Her mother picked up the plates that had held lunch and stood over the bed smiling at her daughter.

"You're feeling better, if your appetite is any indication."

"Yes, mama. I made it through another one. Can I go out and play?"

"No, dear, not just yet. Take some time to rest and eat so you can build your strength up again, okay?"

The girl nodded, her lower lip pouting out and her eyes sad.

"I do have a surprise for you, though."

"You do?" the girl said, the sad expression disappearing from her face. "Did you get me a present?"

Her mother laughed. "Not something you can pick up and keep. I think you'll like it anyway." She stepped through the doorway and jerked her head back toward the girl in her bed. A second later, a tall man with brown hair and a big smile on his face came through the doorway.

"Uncle Arten!" the girl shrieked.

"'Lo there, pretty one. I hear you were sick. Are you better now?" He stepped up to the bed to tousle her hair, but she grabbed him and pulled on his arm until he moved closer so she could hug him. He hugged her back, carefully so as not to squeeze too hard.

"I feel okay, but mama won't let me go out and play."

"Your mother's right. Better that you take some time to rest before going out and running around. If you weaken your-self, you might have another episode."

The girl made a point to turn her frown to him so he could see it full force.

"Oh, now, don't go glaring at me. It's not that bad. I can tell you a story, if you want. It'll help to pass the time."

Her expression forgotten once again, her eyes lit up. "Ooh. Yes, tell me a story."

"All right, then I will. How about a tale of Erent Caahs?" He looked at her as if he expected her to show some kind of excitement.

"Who?"

"Erent Caahs," he said. She shrugged. "You know, Erent Caahs, the most famous hero alive."

"Never heard of him."

"You never...what kind of child are you that you've never heard of the greatest hero in the world?"

"I'm just a little girl. I can't know about everything."

Uncle Arten blinked at her, then started laughing. "Fair enough. Well, take my word for it. He's a famous hero. Do you want me to tell you a story about him? I think you'll like it."

The girl yawned. "I guess so."

He tilted his head, narrowing his eyes as he looked at her. "Uh, okay. I will then. Since you've never heard of him, I'll tell you a short one and then you can figure out if you like the story. If you do, there are a lot of others. He keeps busy, he does.

"So, Erent Caahs is known for his skill with the bow. He can shoot better than anyone else and can even make his arrows curve around corners sometimes. He can do a lot of other things, too, but you'll just have to listen to some stories and you'll figure it out. He has a friend, another great hero, named Raisor Tannoch, one of the fierce Crow warriors that come from up in the highlands to the east.

"Now, Erent and Raisor were traveling, as they usually did, going from town to town to help folks who needed heroing done. As they passed through different communities in the area, they heard tell of a thief that took advantage of people who became sick. While they were weak with their illness, he took their purses and other valuables and ran off. They couldn't run after him on account of being sick and all, so he stole a lot of money.

"'It's just a silly rumor,' Erent told his friend. 'Who ever heard of a man who ran around finding sick people to steal from? I suppose people are saying that he eats children who are bad, too.'

"Raisor, who had a great booming laugh, rumbled with merriment. 'I don't know. We've seen stranger things, you and I. I can believe someone taking advantage of the sick, though finding himself in the right place at the exact time when someone is afflicted might be a bit hard to swallow.'

"They moved on, talking about other things as they reached the next village on the narrow road they were traveling. The two rented rooms at an inn and went down to the common room to have a nice dinner of mutton and roasted boar. After they ate, they sat and chatted for a time, since it was still early.

"A commotion from a part of the common room turned out to be two men who were making strange noises. When Erent Caahs went over to get a better look, he discovered that the men were of a strange color, almost greenish, and they had vomited.

"'Can't hold the ale they drank,' Raisor said as the two sat down again. A few minutes later, others showed signs of being unwell. By the time half a dozen people were complaining of discomfort, Erent felt the first twinges in his belly. A loud, gurgling noise came from his stomach and he put his hand on his middle.

"'Ugh. I'm not feeling so well. What about you, Raisor? Does it feel like anything is amiss with you?'

"'Aye. My middle is swirling. I...ach...something is definitely not right.'

"Before too long, nearly everyone in the common room, which was more than half the village, in Erent's estimation, was in a bad way. Some vomited, some were afflicted with cramps, and others...well, there was a high demand for the privy. All while this was happening, a man in dark clothes with a hooded cloak came into the common room. His hood covered his face and as he moved between the suffering patrons, his hands moved quickly.

"'My purse,' a man said weakly. 'He took it.'

"Soon, the call was taken up by several others. The man seemed well practiced, cutting the purses from peoples' belts with a small knife as he quickly passed through them. No one was in the condition to stop him.

"Raisor took a step toward the man, but sat down quickly and gritted his teeth as his stomach sent out a loud sound that Erent was afraid meant something bad was about to happen. He knew that he couldn't chase after the man himself because his belly was betraying him, too.

"As more calls went up that the thief had taken more money, Erent realized that this was who the rumors had nick-named the Privy Pirate. He also saw that the man knew what he was about. Even then, he was making his way toward the door, satisfied with what he had already stolen.

"Being a hero and all, Erent Caahs could not let the man escape, but he couldn't go chasing him down, either. Instead, he steeled himself, clenching all the muscles necessary to prevent something unwanted from happening. Then he picked up his bow, which was leaning against the wall next to him. He grabbed a handful of arrows and set them on the table, then nocked one and let it fly.

"Now Erent Caahs could shoot three or four arrows in a second, usually. He had to control his movements so as not to shake his stomach up, though, so he slowed it down to shooting five in eight seconds. The first few stuck into a post, the wall, or a table a few inches from the man, causing him to change his direction. He went exactly where Erent wanted him to go. The final arrow went through the hood of the man's cloak, not only revealing his face, but also securing the heavy cloth to the wall in one corner of the common room.

"By the time the man freed his cloak from the arrow and put the hood back in place on his head, several men who had heard the commotion came in from outside and wrestled the thief to the ground.

"It was soon clear from the statements from all those present that Erent Caahs had saved the day. The constable arrived shortly after to take care of matters.

"One of the men who had been robbed wiped spittle and vomit from his mouth and said to Erent, 'You kept him from getting away with my purse. I appreciate it, stranger. How can I repay you?'

"Erent set his bow down and closed his eyes as a particularly loud gurgling sound echoed from his belly. 'You can direct me to the nearest privy.'"

Uncle Arten stopped speaking and watched the girl for her reaction.

She laughed first at the silliness of the whole thing, but the more she thought about it, the more she realized that she had enjoyed the story. Not just for the humor, but because though sick, the hero still was able to help people and catch the bad guy.

"You have more of those stories about Erent Caahs?" she asked.

"Dozens of them," her uncle said.

"Maybe you can tell me some more?"

Her uncle smiled hugely at her. "I'll make you an expert on stories about Erent Caahs yet, Lily Fisher."

CHAPTER
ONE

"Are you sure you want to spend your time doing this?" Tere Chizzit asked. His white eyes seemed to lock onto her, but she knew they didn't. He couldn't see with them, but with his magical sight.

Lily shook back her long red hair and frowned at the man. "Yes. That's why I asked you to help me. Are you really going to tell me that you don't approve of training to become better?" She knew that would frustrate him. He was a bit more subtle about training constantly than Aeden Tannoch was, but not by much.

"Training is good, yes, but *this*?"

"Why not?"

"It's…I don't know. It seems silly. Why not practice your own unique movements, figure out something new to do? This is a waste of valuable time."

"Again," she said, ignoring what he'd said completely.

The older archer sighed and stepped back from the targets he had reset.

The two of them were in one of the training areas, one specifically designed for archers. Ahead of her, affixed to an ingenious mechanism, were six targets. When reset, they would swivel to one of many combinations of positions. Of course, they weren't meant to be struck nearly simultaneously. That was unreasonable, impractical, damn near impossible.

Yet Tere did it, time and time again. If there had ever been any doubt this man was Erent Caahs, the simple fact that he could duplicate what Lily had come to regard as his signature move over and over removed it all.

Sure, he had slightly flubbed using his technique when Lily had been one of a group—called a brace—of Falxen assassins after him, but that was an awkward situation. He and his friends had been in a jail cell for a time, then traveled through a dangerous living and thinking forest, only to be confronted by a large group of the elite assassins. He also didn't have his full faculties, having lost the ability to see the magic of the world. She'd give him a pass on missing with one of the six arrows he shot in under two seconds. He hadn't missed by much.

Now that he was rested and his magical sight was back, though, it was like he was better even than the stories about him she grew up loving. Just half an hour ago, he'd flawlessly nailed all six targets *three times in a row*. That had drawn a crowd of Academy students.

The move was relatively simple, but in no way easy. It started with three arrows being withdrawn from the quiver, nocking, drawing, and loosing. As the projectiles were released, the archer spun the bow, granting a unique trajectory to each. Almost before they struck, another two more arrows were loosed, and finally a single arrow followed the others. The archer was successful if he—or she—struck six different targets in the blink of an eye.

She had never successfully performed the move. Oh, sure, she did well enough, hitting four or—one time—five of the targets, but she slowed down with the second group of arrows and the last one, taking up to four seconds to make the shots. Lily knew she had a long way to go to be able to succeed at the insane technique every time she tried. Even after accomplishing it the first time.

The statuesque red-haired archer stood in a relaxed stance, taking several deep breaths to relax. Her limbs needed to remain loose or she would never be able to finish the complex actions at speed. Glancing over at Tere to make sure he was out of the way, she prepared herself, then sprang into action

Three arrows appeared on her bowstring almost like magic and she drew the string smoothly to her cheek, releasing them a fraction of a second later. As she did, she spun her bow with the exact amount of travel it needed to shoot the arrows off to separate targets. She didn't pay attention to where they went, focusing on nocking, drawing, and releasing the next two arrows. She spun the bow again, this time in the opposite direction while she shifted her stance and torqued her hips to aim at the next two targets. Finally, the last arrow left her string and rocketed toward the only remaining target.

Lily dropped her arm to hang loose, allowing the bow to swing like a pendulum. She narrowed her eyes to locate the targets and—hopefully—the arrows stuck within them. She saw immediately that one of the first three missed the target by less than two inches. It might as well have been two feet.

"Damn it!" She found that one of the arrows in her second flight had barely skimmed its target, as well, cutting a notch in the side of the tightly wound straw circle and sticking into the tree whose branch it was hanging from. One look at Tere's face also told her she had taken too long to launch all the arrows.

"I really don't see why you need to get this move down," he said as he went from target to target to remove her arrows. "It's really not that useful. It was something that came to me that one time because I needed to hit a lot of things in a very short period of time."

"You used that move a number of times," she told him, "if the stories can be believed at all."

"Generally, they can't, but okay, I did use it several times. I was young and arrogant and thought it made me look impressive."

She couldn't help but smile at that. "It did—does. I've always wanted to nail that move. Can't you understand that?"

He stepped up to her and handed her arrows to her. "You're not me, Lily. You don't have to be me. Hells, I'm not even me anymore, not that guy everyone expects from the stories. I'm not sure I ever was."

"Says the man who can perform that move in your sleep."

"Come on," he said. "That was the eighth time you tried it today. We're done. You'll only get worse each time and create sloppy habits. You don't have to train all the time, you know. Live a little."

"That's what I'm working toward. If we're facing dozens of animaru, this training may be the only thing that lets me live through the attack."

He chuckled, and put out a hand to her, which she took. She liked the feeling of her calluses rubbing on his. They were halfway back to Batido before they dropped each other's hands.

After depositing her bow and arrows in her room and changing into a different set of clothes, Lily went to the back of the building where she'd been working on a little side project. She had to admit that she mostly had started it to hush any talk that all she ever did was train.

She'd decided to take up gardening, planting and nurturing flowers and herbs in pots in the small yard of the dormitory. She was mostly feeling it out, trying to figure out what she should be doing, and she had to admit that it wasn't going all that well.

She had both hands in the soil of a large pot when Saevel, the arba woman from the Mellafond swamp, joined her.

"Hi, Lily."

"Hello, Saevel."

"Urun told me you're trying your hand at growing things. I

thought I'd come and see what you've got going. My people have a close connection with plants, you know."

Lily chuckled. With Saevel's auburn hair and her green eyes and skin, she looked almost like a plant herself. A tree. Lily was well aware that the arba were especially loved by both Mellaine and her daughter Osulin, nature goddesses both, because of the arba's connection to the natural realm.

"It's...not going great," Lily said, gesturing with one dirty hand. At least a dozen pots of various sizes were arrayed around her, all of them containing plants in some stage of death, ranging from wilted leaves to brown, dry, brittle plants that would break if one touched them.

"I see. Maybe if I sit and chat with you and watch what you're doing, I can help."

"Sure. I can use all the help I can get, I think. Master Chesaren has been giving me some pointers."

"Master Chesaren?"

"Oh, sorry. She's the Master of the College of Woodcraft. She knows everything there is to know about traveling and surviving in forests, but she also covers everything flora and fauna. There aren't any farming or animal schools, so all of it is lumped in together in her school."

"I see."

"She had me trying to communicate with my plants." Lily chuckled at the notion.

Saevel didn't seem to find it humorous. "Communicate how? Simply by talking, or actually trying to connect with them?"

Uh-oh. It suddenly occurred to Lily that Saevel might have similar views to the master. "Both. I think she's frustrated with me, mostly because of my attitude."

"Are you being difficult?" the arba asked, a smirk forming on her face.

"No, nothing like that. It's my viewpoint toward...certain things."

"Like?"

"Life. I have an unusual take on things, I think. To me, life is all about surviving."

"That sounds reasonable,"

Lily nodded. "I think so. But when I told her that, to me, life is all about surviving each day, that the sum total of one's lifetime is how many days they're able to survive what the world throws at them before succumbing, she wasn't pleased. She told me it's no wonder I couldn't connect to my plants.

"She said that generally, living things of all types find value or pleasure in simply being alive, not focusing on the struggle as much. Sounds weird to me. I mean, animals in the wild have to either exert themselves to eat and to protect themselves or another animal will eat them. Doesn't that sound like what my viewpoint is?"

Saevel sat down on a nearby patch of grass. "I can see your logic, but she's right that plants don't respond well to that type of attitude. Some water, good soil, and the sun shining on them and they're content."

"That's what the master said, too. So, I'm not a plant. Anyway, I've flummoxed her. Apparently, I have a highly developed ability to kill plants without really trying. Great for me, huh?"

Saevel laughed. "It's good to have a skill."

Lily continued her work as Saevel talked with her about her swamp home, the things she'd seen since leaving to bring Dob, the little arba, to the Academy to study, and how Urun still promised to bring her to the Grundenwald. She inserted some suggestions as they conversed and, though Lily wasn't sure she'd ever be able to keep a plant alive, she thoroughly enjoyed the time with the other woman.

"Uh, Lily? I have one question."

"Yes?"

"I understand why you wear what you do for combat,

keeping yourself free of restricting clothing and all, but why do you wear what you're wearing now to do gardening?"

Lily looked down at what she was wearing. She had what amounted to a tight undergarment covering her breasts, though it left her abdomen and much of the top of her chest uncovered. On her lower parts, she wore very short pants, the legs of which only covered the barest sliver of thigh and though tight enough to seem like her own skin, it allowed her free movement without binding.

"What? This is more material than what I wear for combat."

"Yes, it is," Saevel said. "Though barely. Do you have issues with being able to move when wearing something...ah, more conventional?"

Lily compared Saevel's snug trousers and tunic, which covered her lithe, athletic body more conventionally. It suited the woman, who was a skilled warrior in her own right.

Lily shrugged. "I don't really think about it. It's comfortable to me."

"Yeah, but not so much for every male student at the Academy. And some of the females. Haven't you noticed that they follow you around, staring at you? Or that no fewer than seven have stopped to gawk at you while I've been here conversing while you bend over to do your work."

"They do?" Lily scratched her head. "I don't mean for it to be an invitation."

"I know you don't. Some will take it that way anyway. As long as you're comfortable with it, though, I suppose that's all that matters. You're pursuing your hobby with gardening, so whatever you want to wear should be fine. I just throught I'd mention it."

Lily smiled at the other woman. "That's the way I feel about it, too. Now if I could only get these plants to pay attention to me like you say, maybe I could convince them not to die on me all the time."

The two women went back inside to the common room to find Urun entertaining Dob. The boy was awaiting the official start of his instruction at the Academy, so he was able to spend time with Saevel and the others he'd come to know when they'd saved the goddess Osulin in the Mellafond swamp.

"Dob!" Lily said when she saw him. She squatted and put her arms out. The green-skinned boy's eyes lit up and he ran into her arms, wrapping his around her and giving her a mighty hug.

"Hi, Lily," he said happily.

"How are you? Have you been preparing to start learning to be a hero?"

They released each other and he grabbed her hand to lead her back to the table he and the others were sitting at. Aeden, Urun, Jia, and most surprisingly, Tere, were there in a bunch.

"I got some books and I've been reading them to learn about what will happen when I start my classes. They gave me a room with another boy, but he's already going to classes, so I don't see him much."

"Ooh," she said. "It sounds very exciting. I know you'll do well and make everyone proud." She nodded to the others and smiled as Saevel sat next to Urun. "What about you guys?" she said, directing her attention to the nature priest. "Do you have plans yet to go to the Grundenwald?"

"I...uh, have been trying to find a time when we can go," Urun said. His dark hair was long and unkempt as always, but Lily might not recognize him if it were actually brushed. He'd promised Saevel he would show her the forest, but they hadn't gotten around to it yet. "Every time I try to plan a trip, some-thing comes up and we're sent off on some mission."

Saevel patted his hand. "I understand, Urun. Don't worry. The forest will still be there when we get around to it. The work you're doing is more important. Being a hero is a sacrifice."

"Hero?" he said with such surprise that Lily laughed.

"Of course, Urun," she said. "You've done just as many heroic things as anyone here. Well, maybe not Tere. If you put that label on any of the rest of us, you'll just have to accept that it's going to stick to you as well."

"Speaking of heroes and neverending work," Aeden said as he stood and went to the center of the room. With his auburn hair and blue eyes, he looked like the perfect example of a Croagh. His handsome face left no doubt he was related to Marla Shrike, his beautiful twin sister. "I have something I need to tell everyone. Well, everyone who is here at the Academy and not chasing after Marla. I was waiting until we were all in the room, but I can catch up the stragglers later. I saw Lucas Stewart a little while ago. As usual, he had a message from the masters. Master Qydus wants us to meet in the morning. He said there are some things that need to be discussed."

"We all know what that means," Tere said. "It's likely Urun is not going to be visiting the Grundenwald anytime soon, not unless the animaru have invaded it and are tearing it apart."

Urun shook his head at Saevel. "He's kidding."

Tere took a drink from a mug in front of him. "Am I?"

CHAPTER
TWO

In the morning, Lily was up early, as was her custom. She didn't rise as early as Aeden did, getting up when it was still dark every day to train, but she beat most of the group to the common room for breakfast, after training.

"Good morning, Lily," Mildred Farnsworth said. "You're looking as lovely as ever this morning. Would you like some eggs and ham, as normal?"

"Good morning. Yes, please. Thank you so much, Mrs. Farnsworth."

The kindly woman set to making Lily breakfast. She reminded the archer of her mother, though she didn't resemble her in any way. Her mother had been tall, with light skin and reddish hair, though not quite as red as Lily's. She'd also been one of those women whom other women envied, never really doing anything special for exercise, but keeping her figure slender and attractive. Mrs. Farnsworth, on the other hand, was nearly as short as Aila and wider than three of the princesses from the Great Enclave.

It was her manner, Lily figured. She treated everyone like they were her children and, like a good mother, watched out for them. Especially when it came to food. No one would ever go hungry on her watch.

She and one other woman, Elaith Tucker, had been assigned to Batido by Master Qydus himself to prepare their meals and generally take care of them. With an assistant between them—who mostly did the cleaning work but helped out in whatever way he could—the trio essentially ran the dormitory and treated all who lived there as one extended family.

As always, the woman whipped up the food in less time than seemed possible and set it down in front of Lily. "There you go, dear."

"Thank you. How are things, Mrs. Farnsworth? Anything exciting happening in your life?"

"Oh, aren't you just the sweetest thing to ask after me. Now that you mention it, yes, there's one development. My son and his wife just found out they're going to have a baby."

"Oh, that's fantastic. Is this your first grandchild?"

"No, no. I have three others. It's this son's first child, though, and honestly, first or hundredth, every one of them is special and a gift. Do you plan on having children, Lily?"

Lily coughed, choking on a bit of ham she didn't swallow right. "Oh, I don't know. Maybe after everything is safe. Right now, we're all focusing on trying to stop the monsters trying to kill us all. You know..."

"Of course, dear. I understand. You don't want to wait to long, though. Time passes so quickly."

"Especially for old women like Lily," a woman's voice said from the stairs.

Jia winked at Mrs. Farnsworth and sat down next to Lily, who swatted her arm.

"I'm not quite a year older than you," the archer said.

"Yep, a year *older*."

"Oh, hush."

Mrs. Farnsworth had Jia's food out before the room started

filling up. Aeden, freshened up after his training, Fahtin, Tere, then Saevel. Saria came down just before Urun and Conren filled out the group.

"Oh," Aeden said. "Saria, I forgot to mention it last night before you went to your room, but Master Qydus wants you to join us for our meeting this morning, if you would like to. He said you might be interested in what he'll be discussing."

"Me?" the astri said.

Saria was a relatively new addition to their group, but not to the Academy. She had been a guiding figure in Marla's and Evon's life before she'd left the Academy to do work out in the world. The woman was simply stunning, with her long blonde hair, her lithe form, and her pointed ears. Her every movement was grace personified and as she addressed Aeden, she drew all eyes.

"Of course. Why not? You're an Academy graduate, right? You're as capable as any of the rest of us, maybe more so. Isn't that why you came back, to help out with the war against the animaru?"

"Yes, though to be honest, I didn't know why I'd been called back. I thought the masters would have me doing what I did before, running messages, scouting, or doing other stuff like that. That's what Academy operatives typically do."

Fahtin put her cup down and leaned toward Saria. "Is that what you want to do?"

"I don't know. I want to help in whatever way I can."

"Wouldn't you rather go on missions with us? I mean, it's fine if you don't, but I would love for you to join us. It can be really dangerous, but...I don't know, it feels like we're doing a lot of good."

The astri laughed. "If even half the stories I've heard about what you've been doing are true, you have been doing more than a lot of good. This group—and your other friends who are off chasing Marla, as well as Marla herself—are going to be the reason the world survives this thing. The danger isn't a problem. I'm just not sure if I can stack up."

"What?" Aila said. "Sister, let me tell you something. Marla and Evon are in awe of you. Even without knowing anything else, that's enough for me to drag you kicking and screaming to join us. But that's not all. I think you've gotten even better since you left here and that you're even more worthy than those two know. You'll do fine. It's a matter of whether or not you want to run around fighting for your life every few days."

"Absolutely. If the masters will let me, I'd love to join your little group. It's obvious you're where the action is."

Aila formed a predatory grin on her face. "Good. We need someone lower on the ladder we can push around."

Lily pushed Aila hard, nearly sending her off the bench and onto the floor. "Be nice, Aila. We don't care if you're a princess."

After breakfast, the entire group walked to the administration area and into the reception room to the headmaster's office.

Aeden stepped up to the desk. "Good morning, Aletris. We're here for the meeting."

"Good morning, Aeden," Aletris Meslar said. "You'll be in Meeting Room Four. You can go right over. Oh!" The receptionist stood and stepped over to Saria. "I'm so glad you have returned, Saria dear. I missed you." She hugged the astri woman, who returned the embrace.

"It's nice to be back, and to see you again."

It seemed to Lily that the meetings they'd been having were getting larger and larger. True, some of their number were off with Marla at the moment, but sometimes Master Qydus brought in other masters and it was always nice to have enough room so they weren't sitting elbow to elbow with each other. Meeting Room Four was one of the bigger ones in the administration building and it had several nice windows in it. Lily appreciated being able to see the trees and the grounds during long meetings. It kept her from getting anxious from being cooped up.

They selected seats and sat down. Saria looked around in confusion.

"There aren't any assigned seats," Aila said. "Come on over and sit by me." She pushed on Conren's shoulder and he sighed, but moved over one seat so Saria could sit down where he'd been.

The knight was responsible for keeping Aila safe, but she didn't make his life any easier for it. They acted like brother and sister, which they almost were, having grown up together. Well, until Aila ran away from the kingdom her father ruled.

Master Qydus Okvius, the Headmaster of the Academy, swept into the room. Behind him came three other masters.

Master Isegrith Palus was a familiar face in the meetings. She and Master Yxna, who had gone to retrieve Marla, were at nearly all of them. Master Isegrith's stern face and perfect posture were set off by her formal master's robes, green with fringes of white fur over her typical darker green dress. Her long grey and brown hair seemed to lie exactly where it should be without having the look of being fussed over. She surveyed the room as she sat down and turned her head to focus on the headmaster.

Master Nasir Kelqen was also present. He was the Master of Research and Investigation, and was a regular fixture at the meetings as well. The marks, or tattoos, on the master's wrinkled face still tried to draw Lily's eyes, simply because she wanted to figure out if they were designs, pictures, or stylized words. She resisted the urge, though, and usually ended up focusing her eyes on the droopy knit cap with the tiny brim he wore often.

The other master wasn't familiar, however. If she was a master at all. Lily struck that thought out and replaced it with another. Of course she was a master. No one displayed hidden power and confidence like the masters Lily had met. She wondered who the woman was, but not for long.

"Thank you all for coming," Master Qydus said. His narrow face, all sharp angles and points, normally looked like he was scowling, but Lily had found him to be a compassionate and even-tempered man. "Saria, it is lovely to see you again. I am glad you decided to accept my invitation to join these others in the work they've been doing."

"It's a privilege, Master Qydus. I hope I can be of some help."

"You will, child. You will. So." The master clapped his hands together. It was so unexpected, Lily almost jumped. A few of her friends did. A shadow of a smile came to the head-master's lips underneath his bushy whiskers and mustache. "Most of you probably have not met Master Liluth Olaxidor. Please allow me to introduce her. She is the Master of the School of Firearms."

The third master nodded her head. She was quite a bit different than the other masters Lily had met. For one thing, regardless of their age, most of the other masters looked far too young to be a master of anything. Not so with Master Liluth. She was slender and looked hale enough, but her face held wrinkles—not quite so many as Master Nasir, but more than most masters she'd met—and her hair was grey throughout. Not the grey color of Master Yxna's, but the grey of authentic age, with a visibly course texture.

Her clothing was not so much strange—not to Lily—but different than what others at the Academy wore, especially other masters. It consisted of green quilted clothing, armor of a sort, on both the bottom and top half of her body. Over it, she wore what looked like short yellow pants that came down to mid-thigh with cloth that puffed out and a jacket with long tails. It hung almost like a cloak, and was the same color as the short pants. Across her waist wrapped a wide belt with many little pouches and what looked like animal horns made into containers. Most strangely, though, she also wore two pistols and a short sword on that belt.

Seeing the master's smiling face, wrinkles and all, brought back memories for Lily. Her heart ached for a moment, but she pushed the feelings away, determined to pay attention to what was being said.

"Firearms?" Aeden asked. "Those sticks that burn things and lob little balls at enemies? I didn't know there was an entire school dedicated to them."

"What are firearms?" Fahtin asked, looking back and forth from the master to Aeden.

Master Liluth drew one of the pistols at her waist. "This is one type. They're called pistols. I can explain the technology to you after the meeting if you'd like, but for now, I'll tell you what they do. When I pull this trigger, an alchemical compound burns and the pressure generated throws a projectile faster than an arrow at the target. If any of you would like a demonstration, let me know and we can schedule a time when you can come to my school and I'll give you one."

Lily chuckled at the reaction that brought to her friends, not the least of which was Aeden, who immediately blushed. Lily noticed that Aila didn't seem surprised at all, nor Tere.

"I take no offense, Aeden. There is little accurate information about firearms out in the world. There will be more soon, I think, but we can wait to speak of that."

"Thank you, Liluth," the headmaster said. "Now, on to business." At a look from Master Liluth, he shook his head. "Pardon me for my rudeness. I introduced Master Liluth, but not the rest of you to her. Allow me." He identified each so the master could greet them individually. When the headmaster was done, he continued.

"I understand that your companions are still on the move, trying to catch up to Marla," he said, the hint of a sigh in his voice. "You've no doubt seen the messages I have in the message tablet. Marla seems to be fine, though it is unclear as to when she will return. I assume no one else has any futher information on this? No? Very well.

"As you no doubt can guess, this meeting is not to simply bring you up to date. As so often as of late, I am afraid I must ask your assistance. First, a bit of background. One of our masters was traveling, on personal business, and was attacked by an organized group of people who seemed to know who she was. There were no significant users of magic, but there were seventeen of the attackers, all armed."

Fahtin gasped, causing the headmaster to pause and look at her sympathetically.

"Pardon me, Master Qydus," Saria said into the silence. "Which master was it?"

Lily hadn't been sure before, but this time it was clear that the headmaster smiled under all that facial hair. "It was Master Mitsuo."

Saria barked a laugh, then immediately put her hand to her mouth. "My apologies," she said.

"Not at all. It was my exact reaction when I heard who it was, despite it seeming on the surface to be an inappropriate response."

Master Liluth wore a wide smile and even Master Isegrith's mouth turned upward slightly.

Saria noted the frowns and looks of confusion on Lily's own face and that of her friends, and she explained. "Master Mitsuo Ishimi is the Master of Long Weapons. Besides being one of the few masters of strictly combat schools at the Academy, she is notoriously skilled at combat. When I was here, I saw her fight Master Yxna for nearly half an hour before she finally won the bout with a particularly beautiful and skillful combination of attacks. If there was double the number of non-magical attackers, I would still feel sorry for them."

Lily shook her head. The things she'd seen from the Academy masters were no less than miraculous. She'd never seen such skill before, and she'd been told more than once that she was the pinnacle of combat skills, sometimes by the leaders of the Falxen assassin guild.

"Needless to say," Master Qydus continued, "Master Mitsuo is fine. Her attackers are not. I bring up this occurrence because it has prompted me to put in place a new rule, ratified by the body of the masters. No one, even the masters, is to travel outside of the Academy grounds alone. Lucky for Marla, the rule came into place only two days ago, after she had already left, or she and I would be having a serious conversation. More serious than the one we will already be having when she returns.

"Because of this new rule, I would impose upon you to help with escorting another master on a journey important for our cause in preparing for the war. I would like some of you to go with Master Liluth to the city of Drusca, in Sutania. There, in the City of Firearms, she will attempt to secure powerful resources to aid the army against the animaru."

THREE

"I'll go!" Lily's hand was up and the words out of her mouth before she even realized the thought had crossed through her mind. Everyone else in the room looked at her and it seemed that they might have something going on behind their eyes. Judging, or at least analyzing.

Master Qydus took it in stride. "Thank you, Lily. I appreciate your enthusiasm. Perhaps we can wait for a few minutes to decide who will go? The second announcement I have might affect that decision."

"Of course, Master Qydus. I'm sorry for speaking out of turn."

"No, do not be sorry. I truly appreciate you putting yourself forward for this task. I promise, we will discuss it in a few minutes. First, the second thing I wanted to speak to you all about.

"We have gotten reports—rumors, really, at this point—of some organization that is apparently building its membership to carry on activities harmful to our cause. They claim the animaru can be bargained with and their desire is to make agreements with the monsters.

"We lost an operative investigating this group in

Arcusheim. He was working alone and disappeared even before the attack on Master Mitsuo. We still need information on this group, but seeing as it is a dangerous situation, perhaps even with animaru involved, we would like some of you to go and pick up the investigation where the operative left off, possibly even find him. We have nothing to track him, not like when some of you—Urun and Jia of those present—went to the Dark Pinnacles to find Emiliya Sterris."

Fahtin shared a look with Aila and both women turned their gazes to Saria.

"You have something to say, Fahtin?" the headmaster said.

"Umm, yes. My visions involved myself, Aila, and Saria near Arcusheim. I think we, at least, should take this mission. We're supposed to be in the area anyway. It seems too coincidental that there is a mission there right now."

"Very well. We must be cognizant of your visions and what they are trying to tell us. You three may go."

"I'll join them," Sir Conren Gardner said.

"And Scrapper will go, too," Aila added. The trebaxel bounced in his seat, but didn't chatter, as he was wont to do.

Aeden raised his hand. When the headmaster nodded at him, he said, "Master Qydus, I suggest that the rest of us go with Master Olaxidor. Tere, Urun, Jia, and I will join Lily. There's no good reason to leave one or two of us here when that won't be enough to safely go on another mission."

"I agree. Decide on who will go where and notify me before tomorrow morning. Since both of these missions are in Sutania, it would be advantageous for everyone to travel together and split up near Drusca. Not even a large group of animaru will be able to harm that many of you together."

All in attendance agreed and, after a few short discussions on other facets of the war preparation, the meeting was adjourned.

On the way out, Aeden caught up with Lily. "Is it okay with you that we go along to Drusca?"

"Of course."

"It surprised me when you volunteered so quickly."

Lily chuckled. "You want to know why. You could have just asked me instead of hinting about it." Aeden's downcast eyes told her she guessed his motivations. "It's pretty simple. I was born in Drusca. We left when I was young to go to Arcusheim, but I still have some family there and it would be nice to see what the place looks like now. I haven't ever gone back, though I passed within ten miles of it when I was doing work for the Falxen."

"Oh. That will be nice, to see your hometown, and to see the family that's still there."

"We'll see. In any case, Master Liluth needs to go there, so we'll be helping out. I think you might find the city interesting. You'll definitely enjoy learning about how firearms are made."

"Is it really that big an industry there?"

"Yes. It's their claim to fame. No other place on Dizhelim makes that many firearms. In fact, the technology was invented there and very little of the knowledge has made it to other places. There are a few isolated shops in other places that smith the weapons, but they are few and are all very small."

"I can't wait to learn all about it," Aeden said. "I'll see you back at Batido. I need to catch up to Fahtin."

Lily gave him a farewell and settled into her long stride, heading back to the dormitory.

"You've really never been back?" Tere said as he stepped up from behind her.

"Nope, never have. I will, though, in just a few days."

"Firearms. Psht. Too slow and too inaccurate."

"Don't go causing fights when we get there. I know there's a big rivalry between the users of the different weapons, but do me a favor and act in a civil manner."

"Me? I'm always civil, even downright polite."

Lily rolled her eyes at the archer as they walked.

Master Qydus had been generous enough to assign someone to gather the supplies for the journey, freeing the group to accept Master Olaxidor's offer to go to the School of Firearms and witness what the weapons were all about. Lily had seen them before, of course, but even she was impressed by the master's knowledge and skill.

"All firearms operate on a similar principle," the master said, in full lecture mode. She held up one of her pistols. "Like a crossbow, the trigger, here, is the initiating action for using the weapons. When the trigger is pulled back, the mechanism brings the striker into contact with the part of the chamber filled with the alchemical compound called flash powder. The striker itself is a magical device that, when it rams into the small striking plate, generates a spark to ignite the powder, which is quite sensitive to ignition. The powder releases products of combustion, which are trapped within the chamber. They have but one way to escape; through the barrel. This makes an excellent medium in which different types of projectiles are carried out at great speed.

"The most common projectiles are simple lead or iron balls, but more sophisticated missiles are sometimes used as well. I have studied different shapes extensively and make my own that are more triangular. I'll show you the difference when I demonstrate some target shooting."

The idea that a spark could cause an explosion wasn't novel. There were alchemical explosives that used different methods to ignite the flammable material and Lily understood enough to know that the trick was to confine that combustion. It wasn't as easy a concept for others to comprehend, apparently.

"Pardon me, Master Liluth," Conren said. "I am having trouble seeing why the powder would react so violently that it would push a projectile at a high speed. Things burn all the time, but they don't cause concussive damage. I've heard of explosive devices, but have never seen one myself."

"That's a fine question," the master said. "The key is pressure. If the powder is confined—let's call it squeezed, though that is technically not correct—and then ignited, the burning powder and the gases produced want to escape quickly. Sitting in the open, the flash powder would burn rapidly, the byproducts flowing out into the open air and flashing. Confined, however, it's like what happens when water is boiled in a sealed container, developing pressure. If the steam builds up and a hole is made in the container, what will happen?"

"Steam and maybe water will shoot out," the knight said.

"Exactly. Now, multiply that ten times. A hundred times. A thousand. That stream of steam and water shooting out is like the gases trying to escape, but they only have one way to go: through the barrel. Like that steam, anything caught up in the gases—or more precisely, in front of the gases—will be carried along at great speed and force. It's the same with explosive devices. The material to be ignited is kept contained enough so that when the pressure builds sufficiently, the container bursts and the concussive force explands all around. If the device has things to kill people in it, like bits of metal or blades, those items will speed away from the device and shred anything within its range."

"It sounds like a very dishonorable way to attack one's enemy," Conren said. "The explosive devices, I mean."

Master Olaxidor laughed. "I won't argue that point. As for firearms, the projectiles are no more or less honorable than a bolt from a crossbow or an arrow from a bow. Now, would you like to see some firearms in action?"

They moved to a range that looked similar to that for archery. Instead of straw figures, however, there were thick wooden objects in the shape of people.

Master Lilith drew a pistol from her belt and shot it, then did the same with the other pistol so quickly that that loud retorts sounded like they were one continuous noise. Chunks of the middle of the wooden target's face flew off, both projectiles hitting the same exact spot.

"Wow," Aila said. The targets were only fifty yards away, but still, the master's accuracy was impressive.

"Now, I know what people say about firearms. They're impractical because once they've been fired, the wielder is helpless," the master said, casualy glancing Tere's way. "The same thing is said about those who use crossbows. Some archers don't appreciate crossbows because there isn't as much skill necessary to point one and pull the trigger as to nock an arrow, draw it back, and release. I respond to those comments this way."

The master snatched one of the horns from her belt, poured a dull grey powder from it into the barrel of one of her pistols, fed a small object after it, then tamped it down with a rod she produced from its holder on her belt. Then she flipped the pistol up and fired, taking off a few more wood chips from the indentation she'd already struck twice. It only took her seconds, about the same time as a fair archer could loose another arrow. It was much faster than a crossbow could reliably be loaded.

"I don't try to compare my weapons to a bow, or even to a crossbow, no more than I would argue that a sword is a better weapon than an axe. They are simply different. I could never match the rate at which someone like Tere or Lily could shoot arrows, but firearms have some other advantages. I'll show you one. Give me a moment to load up again, this time with a different projectile."

The master repeated her loading procedure, slightly slower so the others could see what she was doing. When it came time to put the actual missile in, she chose one that looked more like a cylinder with a narrower end than a little ball. Like a target arrowhead. It appeared to be exactly the size to fit in the barrel of the pistol.

"Watch carefully," the master said as she casually brought

the pistol up and fired. The entire head of the target exploded in a shower of wood splinters. "I hear that Lily likes arrows that can do similar things, though my weapon doesn't burst into flames with fancy fire in midair. The projectile is a special one, with some of the flash powder inside, sensitive to hard shock. They can be useful.

"An even rarer form of firearm is the long gun, also called a rifle because of the ingenious way the barrel is scored to make the projectile fly straight." She picked up a strange looking contraption from a nearby rack and held it up for the others to see. "The advantage of this type of firearm is its range. Can you see the target out that way?" She pointed the long gun toward a small shape that had to be three hundred yards away. "Do you think I could hit it from here?"

Tere was paying more attention now, Lily noticed. He looked down range at the target, then back at the master. "Few archers alive could make that shot."

Master Liluth winked at the archer. She put the flattened end of the long gun to her shoulder, sighted down the length of the thing with one eye closed, then pulled the trigger.

The sound was louder than the pistols the master had used, so loud Lily jumped a little, but she didn't take her eyes from the target, small as it was. Almost instantly as the loud boom rang out, the top of the target disappeared, much like the one she had hit with the explosive projectile.

"Walk with me," Master Liluth said, putting the long weapon back in the rack and heading toward the target. When they arrived, it was easy to see that her attack had the desired results. The top portion of the target had been torn up, a surprisingly clean hole the size of a fist through what remained.

"How?" Tere asked. Was that respect in his voice?

"One can't use a simple ball, or even something like the explosive round I used earlier. The benefit of the rifle and the way the long barrel is designed, is that a suitably built projectile can travel straight to a target over long distances." She held up a piece of metal with a triangular head. "We have to worry about such things as the way the air passes over the projectile and how it reacts to being pushed through the barrel, but when we get everything right, well, you can see the result. This one didn't even have any of the powder inside it. This damage was caused by the extreme speed and the heft of the projectile. So? Would you think something such as this could be advantageous in combat?"

"Definitely," Aeden said. "I didn't know such things were possible."

"Granted," the master said, "one wielding such weapons has to train to be able to hit their targets accurately, and to load them more quickly, but imagine squads of our soldiers with these weapons. They are devilishly difficult to make and there is also the powder and projectiles that need to be produced, but manufacturing them with a bit of life magic thrown into the making and we have another sound weapon against the animaru." She paused and waited for any other comments. "I understand there are animaru that fly?"

"Aye, the aliten. Humanoid with large wings."

"Imagine, if you will, a small group of skilled and accurate shooters with rifles taking out the flying animaru during a battle. They won't have spies to communicate troop movements to their commanders and they won't be able to drop dangerous things, if that is even something they do."

"I'm sold," Tere said. "Thank you for the demonstration, Master Liluth. I can see the value in getting more of these and training people to use them. Though I think I'll stick with my bow, if you don't mind."

The master cackled her contagious laugh. "I don't mind at all. I would never suggest depriving our forces of a bow in your hands. Like I said, weapons aren't superior to one another, just different. I think we'll need all kinds to win the day. Now you know why we're going to Drusca, though. I need to speak with the makers of these fine weapons and see if they'll be willing to trade—some information we've devised here at the Academy for making us firearms in quantity."

"I don't know about the others," Aeden said, "but I'm happy to be going along. I never thought such things existed. I'd like to help any way I can."

The next morning, ten people, and one trebaxel, set out on horseback to journey south. They might have been able to make better time taking a ferry from the island down and around toward Arcusheim or one of the smaller coastal towns, but Master Liluth preferred taking the land route. It was just as well as far as Lily was concerned. She'd rather be on solid ground than on something floating in the water, anyway.

"Did you know," Saria Gilwenys said as they rode, "that the city was named after Charislev Pardruscan, a mage and great craftsman in the Age of Magic? He quietly worked on his craft as the War of Magic raged. As the story goes, he was in Arcusheim briefly, visiting friends, most of whom had managed to stay out of the war as he did. One of them, tiring of Charislev constantly talking about his work, told his friend that it would never amount to much. When Charislev argued that the things he created would have a lasting impact on the world, enough that he could build a city on the technology, his friend bet him a handsome sum he could never build a city from nothing, not one that would be viable for the long term.

"Charislev took the bet, choosing an undesirable patch of

land near the southeast shore of the Kanton Sea. It wasn't on the actual coast and there were no roads, but he set about building several structures in which he could experiment and perfect his inventions. He created the flash powder and the delivery system using it and over the course of several years, convinced others to join him in his work. When their number amounted to only ten, he formally named the loose collection of buildings Drusca. It was several more years before a reliable road that connected to the River Road was built and until the population increased enough that his friend admitted defeat in their bet, but it was a little thing for Charislev. He had created something new in the world and he knew it could be valuable.

"He never did introduce his firearms to any of the great powers in the War of Magic. His family and coworkers carried on his work after he died and they've been in the city of Drusca ever since, trying to improve on Charislev Pardruscan's invention."

"I knew some of that," Master Liluth said, "but not the bit about the bet. Fascinating. You always were able to tease the little details out of history, Saria."

The astri shrugged. "The little details are interesting to me. I enjoy hunting them."

"Speaking of details," Aila said, Scrapper sitting behind her in a saddle that was made for two to ride comfortably, "didn't you tell us that you were born in Drusca, Lily?"

The archer hadn't really been dreading the question, but she didn't welcome it with open arms, either. "Yes. I only lived there until I was fourteen years old. My family moved to Arcusheim after that."

"You don't have to talk about it, girl," Tere said, glaring at Aila. "We know the memories are difficult."

The look of surprise on Aila's face told Lily that the smaller woman didn't know, or didn't remember, the tragedy that had befallen the young Lily. "Oh! I'm sorry. I didn't know."

"It's fine," Lily told her. "I told some of the others when we were on our way to Ebenrau. You weren't there, off having fun with Jia and Evon."

Fahtin cleared her throat and her face flushed at Lily's words.

Aila continued. "Tere's right. You don't have to talk about uncomfortable things."

"I can tell you about it," Lily said. "We'll be going there. I still have some family that lives in the city, so it's going to come up anyway. I might as well get it out in the open. It's a pretty simple tale. Like you said, I was born in Drusca, though we moved to Arcusheim when I was young.

"Before I left, I remember thinking about the industry of the city, the making of firearms, but I didn't understand that it was not the normal thing for all cities. In my childish way, I figured every city had manufactories and celebrations, even contests, that involved the weapons.

"I...was a sickly child. Something within me made me weak. I would have episodes that included fever, weakness, difficulty breathing. I'd often stop breathing altogether. Those times were when my parents really worried. Even back then, I thought it would be easier on everyone if I didn't fight it so hard. Sometimes, I decided to give up, not push so hard to be able to drag the meager amount of air into my lungs, and just let myself quietly go into death. It definitely would have made my parents' lives easier. They had to watch me constantly and spent more than a little money on potions from our local healer, Mother Sella. The medicine didn't cure me, just lessened the effects of the episodes."

She laughed, a wistful look in her eye. "I remember after one bad episode—one in which I almost gave up and let death take me—my uncle Arten came to visit me. He was my favorite uncle and it meant the world to me when he visited. On that particular visit, he started what would be a regular ritual, one

41

that Raki would definitely approve of. He would tell me stories.

"My parents weren't big on storytelling. Sure, there were the common children's stories, but good, meaty tales or myths, not so much. Uncle Arten asked me what story he should tell, but I didn't know what to say. He offered one that changed my life forever.

"He told me the story of Erent Caahs and the Privy Pirate."

"Oh, no!" Tere said, putting a hand on his face. "Tell me he didn't tell you that stupid story. How embarrassing."

"He did."

"Let that be a lesson to you all," Tere said. "If you want to be famous heroes, you not only have to put up with tales that get everything wrong and exaggerate even the things that are partly right, but your entire life is opened up to the whole world. Even when you're sick, in the most embarrassing way possible, you're not spared."

"That story is true?" Aila asked. Her mouth twitched like it wanted to jump into a big smile, but Lily appreciated her control. She was sure Tere appreciated it too, though he glared even harder at the woman than he had earlier.

"Yes, it's true," Lily said, "but enough about that. The point is, Uncle Arten told me that story and I fell in love with Erent Caahs tales. He told me other fables, but every time he asked me what I wanted, I'd tell him I wanted to hear about Erent Caahs.

"From the beginning, I idolized the man. The story about him being a hero even when he was sick was a big motivation to me, who spent quite a lot of time being ill. It didn't matter that his was a temporary affliction of the stomach caused by poison, my child's mind only latched onto his body being in turmoil but him still acting like a hero should.

"That was the start of it. I convinced my parents to get me a bow, mostly with the tried-and-true part of a child's arsenal called *whine until they give in*. Once I got it, I taught myself to shoot it, asking every person I saw who carried a bow for tips and to watch me so they could tell me what I did wrong. It wasn't only the bow, though. My father caught me playing with his carving knife and carved me some crude wooden knives to play with instead. I still remember being punished for that little stunt before he gave them to me.

"More importantly, I trained my body. Jumping, running, acrobatics, anything I could do to increase my strength and my ability to move, I would do. I didn't realize then, and neither did my parents, but that self-imposed training is what hardened my body. As time passed, I had fewer of the episodes and even those I did have weren't as severe as they had been. My stronger body seemed to work better to fight against whatever it was that was within me. No healer they had taken me to had ever been able to identify what the ailment actually was, and I still don't know, but by the time I was ten years old or so, I stopped having the episodes altogether.

"Interestingly enough, Mother Sella, the only healer my parents had ever found whose medicine helped me, moved to Drusca when I no longer needed her aid. She had family there and I'm not certain, but I believe she'd put off moving until I was better. I never thanked her adequately for that.

"Anyway, when I was almost fourteen, my father got an opportunity to work a job in the Great Enclave for many times his normal pay, so we took a caravan and planned on staying for at least two months. There had been some reports of bandit activity, so the caravan was a better choice than trying to make the journey by ourselves.

"We had a small wagon, so we slotted in along with other wagons, carts, and even people traveling on horseback. On the way—in a location I think was close to where Tere found the Encali carvan that had been attacked when he was a boy—the caravan was assaulted by bandits.

"There were a lot of attackers, but they underestimated the abilities of the guards and the individual people within the

43

caravan because they ended up with a fight on their hands. My father and mother weren't fighters, but I had my bow and arrows, though only practice knives still at that point. As the bandits swarmed in, I helped out by shooting several of them with my bow.

"It was only a child's bow, lacking the power of a full-sized weapon, but the arrows could penetrate skin and I was good with it even then. I killed four of the bandits. While I fought, my parents gathered some of the other non-combatants and helped out with treating wounds where they could.

"Eventually, a handful of the attackers came at us and I wasn't able to hold them off. One of them got close and swung his sword at me. I froze, knowing I was going to die. Then my father leaped in front of me and took the sword in his belly. I managed to get another arrow off, putting it through the eye of the man who'd stabbed him.

"Right at that moment, the caravan guards rallied and swept the rest of the bandits away from us. They killed a few while the rest fled. My father died in my arms and I found my mother later, also having been cut down.

"The attack was over, but I was an orphan. One of the happiest trips of my life had ended in the greatest tragedy. My parents had shared some news with me and our family when we were on our last visit to Drusca. My mother was pregnant. I was going to have a little brother or sister."

Lily stopped, emotion welling up in her. She hadn't told Tere and the others that part of it when they were on the way to Ebenrau. In all honestly, she wasn't sure why she did now. She had to take a few breaths to regain control before she could finish off her story.

"Anyway, the rest of what happened doesn't involve Drusca at all. I obviously survived the bandit attack and got to the Great Enclave. I won an archery contest, lived on the streets for a while, and was eventually recruited to the Falxen, whom I made a deal with. I would join if they would help me find the bandit group who killed my parents and then let me kill them without interfering. It took a couple more years, but I eventually wiped out the entire bandit group and began working for the Blades.

"I never went back to Drusca. Maybe I should have done so, gone back to stay with my uncle's family, but the tragedy of my parents' deaths affected me strangely and for the longest time, I didn't want any reminders of what I'd had. Who knows what I would have done, what I would have become, if I had gone back to Drusca? I wouldn't be here now, I can tell you that. I'm glad I am, but that doesn't stop me from wondering sometimes what might have been."

Though there were a few towns and villages along the River Road, Master Liluth requested that they not stay in inns, but instead that they camp along the way.

"I know it may be an inconvenience," the firearms master said, "but I didn't have a lot of opportunity to camp while traveling when I was younger. I rarely left the Academy when I was a student and when I became a master and journeyed, I would stick to established paths and stay in an inn each night. I never really got to experience what you all have. Would it be too much to ask if we could camp at least a couple of nights?"

Jia greeted the question with a mischievous smile, one that Lily had seen often on the woman's face when she knew her during their Falxen days. "You're not missing out on much, Master Liluth, but if you want to rough it, I think we can accommodate you. It's all we've been doing lately." The others didn't seem to have a problem with it, either.

"I appreciate it. I'll take part in the watch schedule, too, and in doing whatever chores are typical. Treat me like anyone else so it's an authentic experience."

Jia laughed maybe a little too heartily at that, and Lily

thought she might take advantage, but thinking about who Jia was and the way she thought, those ideas went right out of her head. The dark-haired former Falxen was one of the most genuinely kind people Lily had ever met. For a former elite assassin.

When they settled down to camp the third evening on the road, the group was scattered around the fire they'd built, finishing up their dinner.

"How are you doing with the book the Prophet left you?" Fahtin asked Aeden.

"Wait," Saria said, before Aeden could answer. "What? Did you just say there's a book the Prophet himself left for Aeden?"

"Aye," Aeden said. "We probably skipped that part when we were trying to catch you up on all the stuff that's been happening."

Master Liluth sat up straighter. "I heard something about a special book, but I thought it was just one among the many you and your friends found."

"It was. Sort of."

"Many books?" Saria asked. "Hold on. You're going to need to back up and tell me what you're all talking about. You found many books? Where? What kinds? In the many you found one by the Prophet, Tsosin Ruus?"

Aeden chuckled. "You sound like Evon, who coincidentally was instrumental in us finding the books." He held his hands up as Saria opened her mouth to speak again. "Okay, okay. I'll give you the short version.

"We found a reference in a book written around the time of the end of the War of Magic, hidden in a pillar in the Academy's library, of all things. Before you say it, yes, we know the library burned down, but the pillar remained, with the book inside protected by some magic. It interprets common children's stories for the prophecies they are. Within one of the stories, the book pointed out that there was a cache of hidden information, squirreled away by the

Prophet himself, meant to be a backup for myself and Marla."

"The Malatirsay," Saria said.

"Aye, the Malatirsay. Evon figured out how to use one of Tsosin Ruus's original finders and we went searching for the books. We found them—after a few adventures involving Falxen assassins and some animaru—in a hidden cave in the Aruchul Mountains, now called the Aerie Mountains. We basically went through a gauntlet and, thanks to Evon, made it to the Well of Knowledge.

"It had been there long before Tsosin Ruus found the area, which is why it was so conducive to thought. In fact, it was in that place that he received the visions that became the Bhavisyaganant. As far as we can tell, he didn't know about the wells, only that the magic of the place seemed to be good for study and other intellectual pursuits.

"He chose that place—one of a few, according to what he wrote—to be a backup repository of knowledge the Malatirsay might need. He wisely foresaw that something could happen to the Academy's resources and he wanted there to be other copies of important information. As it turns out, a large amount of what we found are copies of books that were destroyed in that big fire at the Academy all those centuries ago."

"You found books that the Academy didn't have?" Saria asked, her voice getting higher pitched as her excitement grew. "From the records, there had to be at least a dozen or two books that were lost and that couldn't be found anywhere else in the world."

Aeden shared looks with Tere and with Fahtin. "Uh, try more than two hundred. I don't know what the current accurate count is, but it's many dozens of books that no one even has a record of."

"No way," the astri said.

Master Liluth snorted. "I haven't been paying that much

attention to it, but Aeden is correct. Many of the masters are in a tizzy, poring through the books and trying to absorb all the things we've been missing. What about the book left to you, Aeden?"

"Oh, right. So, according to Evon, the most valuable books in the collection are Tsosin Ruus's personal journals. Some of the things Evon had found in them so far have turned a lot of what everyone thought on its head. In addition, there was a book hand-written by the Prophet himself titled simply *For the Malatirsay*. It's set up like a personal letter from a good friend or relative. I've been going through it, but it's slow going since it's in archaic Alaqotim, similar to the language Khrazhti speaks. She's helped me with some of the words and I've learned a lot so far, though I haven't progressed as far into it as I would like. I told you about Khrazhti. She's the animaru who defected and is now part of our family."

"The book. Do you have it?" Saria asked. "Can I see it?"

"Sorry. I didn't bring it with me. It's the only copy in existence, as far as we know, and I didn't want to take it off Academy grounds. Master Qydus asked me if he could have it copied before we left and I agreed, of course. There will be several copies available when we get back and I'll be able to carry one with me wherever I go without worrying about anything happening to the original."

"The Great Prophet, Tsosin Ruus, wrote a book-length letter to you—"

"—and Marla," Aeden added.

"—to you and Marla with his own hand? What is it about?"

"Malatirsay things. It is hard to believe sometimes, but it's not like I'm the only one. He wrote Fahtin a book, too."

"He…he what?" Saria swept her hair over her pointed ears and pounded both palms on her forehead, then turned toward the Gypta girl. "The Prophet wrote you a long letter, too?"

Fahtin wrapped her arms around her chest like she was

hugging herself as she squeaked out a reply. "Yes. He wrote to help me get my vision powers under control, telling me that Aeden and Marla would need my help."

"He knew the Malatirsay was going to be two people?" Saria said.

Aeden eyed Fahtin and her reaction. "No. It doesn't seem so. When he received the original vision that gave him the Prophecy, it appears that it looked like one entity. Like I said, though, I'm not far into it. The part I'm reading right now seems to be getting to what happened when he got a barbarian high chieftain with a Gypta wife to agree to put in place some inviolable commandments for his offspring. I think it's going to tell me more about my people, the Croagh, but I'll have to wait until we get back to read more. I'm not sure how Fahtin is doing with her studies. Evon has been helping her."

"It's slow," Fahtin said. "Like with you, we have to work through each part, individually and slowly. Evon helps me with the Alaqotim, but I want to understand everything thoroughly before I move on to the next part."

Aeden put a finger up. "Oh, there is something that I've learned. Most of what I've read so far is background information, but part of it is about unorthodox magic. The Prophet wrote that the Song itself would be a type of this unorthodox magic and he gave some general tips about using such things, though he did admit that he didn't know if all or any of them would apply to my situation with the Song. Marla has the magic she's learned from the Academy, so she's not that interested in learning more about the magic of the Song. Her mood lately makes it even worse."

"What did the Prophet write about it?" Aila asked. "Will it help you to learn to use it better, to do other things?"

"Aye, maybe. One part really stuck with me. I repeat it to myself all the time. If I can get my head around it, I may be able to enhance some more of the spell of the Raibrech—the spells based on the quatrains of the Song—to make them more powerful."

"Can you remember it well enough to tell us what it said?" Tere asked.

"Aye. I've read it over so many times, I can nearly tell it to you word for word.

Conventional magical theory holds that the qozhel for use in any particular spell can be obtained from within the caster, from the environment around the caster, from another distinct source such as a person or item, or a combination of these. My studies have revealed that there are other types of magic, however, that have some way of generating the qozhel needed for the casting in other, rarer ways. It is thought that the gods are able to wield magic by several other methods. As a group, I will refer to these as unorthodox magical spells.

Though little information can be found about unorthodox spells, experiments I have personally performed and theories I have myself formulated indicate that, unlike conventional spells, unorthodox castings may utilize other universal power sources, the likes of which are not understood. Using these hypothetical spells, a caster would need to commune with the method of channeling the magic to actually increase not only the efficiency, but also the power. It is feasible that in growing to know the mechanism of the magic intimately, the caster might be able to stretch the bounds of an individual spell and create effects different than lesser versions. The key, I believe, is to dissect the very way in which the qozhel flows and is accumulated into the mass to be used by the spell. This is, of course, the subject of another work altogether, but it holds forth fascinating promise to the caster who manages to achieve this intimacy.

"I take it to mean that I need to delve deeper into the source of power of the Raibrech, the words of the Song and the Song itself. There is a cadence to each spell, in addition to but related to that of the Song. When I sing it, I know its rhythm, somehow. With the enhanced spells I have figured out so far, I learned how to move in concert with the lyrics and the music and created a situation in which my body itself is vibrating with the Song's magic while allowing it to move me as it will.

"The answer is just out of reach. I've stumbled upon it a few times, but only when I really understand what I'm doing will I be able to progress in making the spells more powerful. I'm going to need them to be as strong as they can be for what's ahead."

Saria's face went thoughtful as the others sat silently and took in what Aeden had said.

"I'll think about it, too," the astri said. "Music is my specialty, so maybe I can come up with something to help."

"I'll appreciate any help I can get," Aeden said. "I don't think my chances are good at convincing the animaru to wait until I figure everything out before they attack."

CHAPTER

SIX

The large group reached the road that wound off the River Road in the direction of Drusca. It was time for them to split up to accomplish their respective missions. They had seen no sign of bandits or any other hostile groups, but then they hadn't expected to. Who in their right mind would try to attack a sizeable gathering of obviously accomplished warriors? If their gear didn't give them away, anyone watching them move for any length of time would recognize there were much easier targets out there.

Lily hugged Fahtin, then Aila. She didn't know Saria well yet, but since everyone else was trading hugs and the astri was looking a bit uncomfortable, Lily opened her arms to the other woman and wrapped her in an embrace when Saria stepped forward.

"You be safe," Aeden told Fahtin. "I expect you all back safe and sound, with another successful mission under your belts."

"Just watch out for yourself, Aeden Tannoch," his adopted Gypta sister said.

"I think I'll be safe enough sitting around while everyone is talking in a city. But yes, I'll be careful doing that."

Aeden, Tere, Urun, Lily, and Jia headed down the road to

Drusca with Master Liluth while Fahtin, Aila, Saria, Conren, and Scrapper continued south to eventually make their way to Arcusheim. Only a few minutes after they had split, Lily could no longer see the other group of her friends. She stared out over her shoulder, feeling a slight pang, like she had lost something. When had she gotten so sentimental and sappy?

"You okay, girl?" Tere said from beside her.

"Huh? Oh, yes. I'm fine. I think I've gotten so used to being around everyone, it's strange when we split up."

"I know what you mean. Last year, I was happily living in the forest, not seeing another person but maybe once every few months. Now, I wonder how everyone is doing, stretched out across Dizhelim like we are. I didn't have a big family, didn't have any family at all for most of my life, but it feels like I do now. I'm getting soft in my old age."

Lily laughed. "Yeah, me too."

It was a few hours to the city and as they traveled, the group chatted.

"How did you get so involved with firearms, Master Liluth?" Tere asked.

"Oh, I've always been involved with them. I was born in Drusca. My father was a small manufacturer of the weapons and I spent a lot of my time in his shop. I already had a good basis even before I went off to the Academy to learn."

"You must have been the star student in the School of Firearms," Lily said.

"No. Actually, there was no School of Firearms back then."

"There was no school?" Aeden asked. "I thought the schools always numbered forty-nine. Seven times seven."

"They did, and do," the master said. "After I graduated and did some time working as an Academy operative while I continued to learn more and master other schools, one of the masters, Carlan Templar, died of an illness so suddenly, even magical healing and the Medica couldn't help him. He was the Master of Thrown Weapons. Because a master had to be raised, the headmaster and the council of masters decided it was a good time for a slight change.

"They combined the School of Launched Weapons—I always thought it was a silly name, anyway—and the School of Thrown Weapons into one school called the School of Ranged Weapons. They added the School of Firearms to the combat lycad with me as the first Master of Firearms. I've been in the position for over thirty years now."

"You're the first Master of Firearms?" Jia asked.

"I am. First and only. So far. My unique circumstances, having friends and relatives in Drusca that worked in the industry, and my knowledge and abilities with the weapons were seen as an asset. I think it was a good move. There is a lot of potential with the technology. Of course, I may be a bit biased." She flashed a big grin at that.

"I would have disagreed last week," Aeden said. "But after your demonstration, I think you're right. If you can work out something with the manufactories so you can start and train squads of skilled firearms users, it can have a great impact during battles, especially if the projectiles are infused with some life magic. I keep picturing the head of that training dummy being blown off and imagining it being an animaru."

"That's my hope as well. Some of the people I'll be talking to are a bit prickly, though. A few will appreciate the improvements we've made to the technology at the Academy, but some will have their pride bruised by such things. I don't expect it will be easy, but we can't produce enough weapons at the Academy to suit our needs. If I can get at least one or two of the bigger manufacturers on board, my trip will be successful. It's exciting to think about."

Lily thought about the master's mission for a moment. "I wonder if an endorsement from a famous hero would help move things along."

Tere frowned at her, but didn't come right out and say he wouldn't do as she asked.

"It might," Master Liluth said. "Word is spreading that Erent Caahs has returned. I don't know how far it has spread, but that name is highly respected. I could imagine that a manufacturer with a recommendation from a hero would have a feather in his cap that others wouldn't have."

"I'm not saying no," Tere said, "but why don't we wait and see if it's necessary. I'm not sure how I feel about coming out and saying I endorse a weapon meant to replace my beloved bow. It still astounds me that it would make a difference. The whole world is crazy."

Lily directed her horse toward his and reached out to pat his arm. "People need hope in all its forms right now. Heroes are more important than ever."

Tere grumbled under his breath, but Lily left him alone. Something else had caught her attention.

They had reached the city of Drusca.

As if by some agreement, everyone stopped their horses and looked out over the city. It hadn't come up in conversation if anyone other than Master Liluth and Lily had been there before. She assumed Tere had been there. He'd been every-where, though she couldn't recall a story where he was in Drusca. By the way Aeden gaped, he hadn't been there before, but Aila and Conren almost seemed uninterested.

She herself didn't remember much of the city. Strangely, her strongest memories—other than a few scattered remem-brances from when she was very young—were of specific places in the city, places she had visited that last time before her parents were killed. She tried to remember gazing out over the city from the outside like she was currently doing, but couldn't get more than a vague feeling that it had grown. It had been more than a decade, so there was no doubt it had, even if just a little. The buildings did look bigger than she remembered. Wasn't it supposed to work the other way, that they looked smaller now since she had grown up?

There was no real wall to speak of, at least from a security perspective. A low barrier, apparently made of dried and hardened clay with what may have been straw or some kind of reed within for strength surrounded Drusca, but that was more to keep animals in—or out—than anything else. Even from where she sat a few miles outside the city, she spotted higher and thicker walls around different manufactories. There would be more than walls within those compounds. The value of the weapons, and of the technology itself, was high enough that people would kill or die for it.

The homes were different than many places she'd been, squat buildings mostly of stone with slate roofs. The city had realized early on that the more fireproof everything was, the better. She understood that there were still accidents occasionally, but many times those involved actual explosions rather than fires burning. At a glance, Lily could tell the older part of the city from the newer. The roads and alleys of the original city, which had been rebuilt several times over the centuries, meandered around the mismatched structures with no apparent reason other than someone had decided to build a house or a shop in a particular area and traffic flowed around it. The newer section had straighter streets and at least some uniformity of the siting of the structures.

That, of course, was by far the minor part of how the city was laid out, though. The reason for Drusca's existence, and the dominating factor in where and how everything was arranged, was the manufactories. There were five major producers of firearms and the associated equipment. Two of those, along with two other factories, produced the flash powder itself. These seven families—for they were still arranged thus after all this time—were the jewels of Drusca.

Some had split their manufactories because they ran out of space where they had originally started, but others, the newer families, had the foresight to build their facilities on the outskirts of the city—or in one case, a fair distance away from the it—so as they expanded, they were able to keep all their buildings together within the walls they built to surround them.

"It reminds me of the industrial section of Coaltar in the Great Enclave," Aeden said. "I visited there with the caravan. The whole city seemed to be one big forge, with fires constantly going and the sound of ringing anvils at any time, day or night."

"I was thinking the same thing," Tere said. "Not with the fires, for Surus's sake. Fire is not something you want to see in this city. The last time I was here, some flame got to a store of flash powder and three buildings rained down over a large part of the city in small pieces."

"I remember that one," Master Liluth said. "I wasn't here, but I heard about it and saw the aftermath. That was, what, twenty-five years ago now?"

"Thereabouts," Tere said, and left it at that.

Lily checked off the box on her mental list next to Tere—or rather, Erent Caahs—visiting the city before.

"Shall we?" Master Liluth said, kicking her horse into motion. "I'd like to get a room, a bath, some food, and some sleep before I have to deal with meetings tomorrow. I sent letters ahead, so they'll be expecting me any time now, but it's too late in the day to worry about meetings."

"What happened to wanting to rough it and camp on the road?" Tere said with a smirk.

The master laughed and winked at him. "I did that and it was very memorable. Now I want to sleep in a bed."

There were plenty of rooms available at the Slow Fuse Inn. The master explained that she used the inn whenever she visited, so the staff all knew her and went out of their way to be extra helpful. After the aforementioned bath, the travelers met in the common room to eat.

"I appreciate you all escorting me here, though we didn't see any sign of trouble. You're all welcome to attend the meetings I'll be having with the manufacturers, though I have to warn you it will be as bad as a political meeting. It's the thing I hate most about my position, but I'll give it my best. If we can get some solid agreements, it could help change the course of the war."

The others seemed to find everything but the conversation interesting. Their food, the ceiling, each other. No one looked in the master's direction. Lily understood. Even the meetings she attended with the masters seemed to be too much sometimes, and there was little argument in those meetings.

"I'll attend," she said. Wide eyes greeted her statement. Even Master Liluth seemed surprised. "At least the first day. I have an uncle to look up while I'm here, but I'm interested in what your negotiations entail, if you don't mind me tagging along."

"You would be a welcome addition," the master said. "Having an ally present always makes things easier. It'll be the two Lilies, then."

It was Lily's turn for surprise. "Two Lilies?"

The master chuckled and waved the question away. "Oh, nothing. It's just that when I was younger, many, many years ago, my family and friends called me Lily as a nickname. Maybe it's just a Drusca thing."

"I was wondering about that," Jia said. "If you were anyone but a master, I would have already started calling you Lily, just to frustrate our Lily."

"Gods, no," Lily said. "Please don't. There are entirely too many Lilies in our past already." She looked at Tere as she said it, hoping her joking wouldn't be too inappropriate. His expression didn't change, so the reference to his murdered sister either passed unnoticed or didn't affect him too much.

"Don't worry," the master said. "It's been over forty years since anyone has dared call me by that name. You're safe as the sole Lily."

After dinner, before everyone scattered to their own rooms, Master Liluth laid out the schedule for the meetings the next day. She'd sent messages to notify the manufacturers when they first arrived in the city, so it would be a full day of negotiating.

"Get some sleep," Master Liluth said. "You'll need it. I'll meet you down here for breakfast and we can brave the meetings together. You be sure to let me know if you change your mind. You have no obligation to attend."

"I'll go," Lily said. "I am interested in the discussion. Hopefully I can provide at least a little support so it's not you against all the family heads."

"Oh, don't you worry about that. I know how to handle them. You just watch and see. You may actually enjoy yourself, at least a little bit."

SEVEN

After breakfast, Lily bade farewell to the only two of her companions who were awake and in the common room—Urun and Aeden—and accompanied Master Liluth to the place the meetings would be held. She was surprised to find a separate building dedicated to gatherings such as the ones she would be taking part in.

"With seven major families and several smaller families all in the same trade, they determined pretty quickly that there needed to be facilities for getting together and discussing things," the master told her. "It does make it nice that we don't have to meet in a barn or anything. The conference center has a full kitchen and they bring by refreshments during the day. We can eat lunch without leaving the area, if we are so inclined." She leaned in close to Lily. "I usually grab my lunch and bring it outside so I can get some fresh air and escape anyone wanting to get a few extra minutes of discussion in."

"I completely understand that. It sounds like the right thing to do. I'll follow your lead."

When the two women entered the meeting room, they found seven people already there waiting.

"Here we go," Master Liluth said to Lily, then turned to the others. "Good morning. Thank you for coming. We should probably get started." Once everyone was seated, the master remained standing but continued speaking. "My companion is Lily Fisher. Coincidentally, she was born right here in Drusca, but she is here as a representative of the Academy at Sitor-Kanda. As a companion of the Malatirsay and Erent Caahs himself, she is a hero in her own right and has been working to combat the dark monsters that you no doubt have heard about."

The seven eyed Lily, some with appreciation, some with suspicion, and one—the only woman among the family heads —with a bit of disdain. Lily was used to it. Her choice in fashion was not to everyone's liking, though she rarely found that men disagreed with it.

"As you know, I am Master Liluth Olaxidor, Master of the School of Firearms at the Academy. I only remind you because I know that at times, you see only an old woman who was also born in Drusca and who went away. Thinking of me as such is a mistake, as some of you no doubt remember." Her stern look transformed into a friendly smile. "Now, for Lily's benefit, please introduce yourselves. We'll start with you, Elmer."

A man who Lily placed squarely in his seventies cleared his throat as he swept his thinning hair across his scalp to cover the large patch of skin there. "I am Elmer Trensel, the head of the Trensel Manufactory. We are one of the three original families who produced firearms in Drusca when Charislev Pardruscan founded the city."

Next to Elmer was the woman, who was maybe a year or two younger than the man. "I am Fortuna Vandenbom. The Vandenbom Manufactory produces not only the finest firearms in the world, but the most effective flash powder as well. You have no doubt heard of us, if you know anything at all about firearms."

"Dorin Panalus," the next man said. It was hard to tell with him sitting, but he looked to be nearly six and a half feet tall.

The rotund man with a pinched face next to Dorin identified himself as Gardon Wessel. Lily had to exert her self-control, to keep from laughing. His name sounded so much like "weasel" that if she hadn't clamped down on herself, she would have laughed out loud looking at his face.

"Taristen Tracten," the next family head stated. "We produce the top pinnacle of firearms as well as the best flash powder to be found anywhere." A hissing scoff from Fortuna didn't break the man's smile. His clean-cut face, wavy hair, and younger age than most of the family heads set off warning bells in Lily's mind. He was no doubt a competent salesman and one to be watched during the discussions. She'd met men like him before, ones you always had to keep one eye on so you could see the hidden dagger.

"I am Flagon Fairbairn," the next man said. Lily was still analyzing Taristen, so the ridiculous name caught her off guard and a chuckle escaped from her. "Yes, yes, I know," he said. "My father was a...fan of good ale. And beer. Wine too."

"He'd have to be to try to match the smooth sound of my name with one such as yours," Taristen Tracten said.

Flagon cleared his throat. "You are not the sole recipient of an alliterative moniker. Your name does not, however, lend itself as well to your inferior products. Fairbairn Firearm Flash is known the world over as the highest quality flash powder, and it rolls off the tongue."

Finally, the last man, a hefty sort who seemed unwilling to make eye contact with anyone. "Brandon Simm. My family makes flash powder also."

Master Liluth looked at Lily and gave her an eye roll, tilting her head to hide it from the others sitting around the table. "Very well. Let me tell you why we are all here today..."

Master Liluth started by explaining the animaru threat. Most of the family heads seemed unaware of the danger, though Fortuna Vandenbom and—surprising to Lily—the shy Brandon Simm sat comfortably following along but obviously already having knowledge about the monsters.

From there, she continued to explain what kind of help she needed, that the Academy would need dozens of firearms, of both the pistol and the rifle types, and plenty of flash powder. When she explained some of the specific things she was trying to accomplish, though, that was when the individuals sitting around the table stopped idly listening and took part in the discussion.

Taristen Tracten was the first to voice his opinion. "There are no such things as what you're speaking about. The technology does not exist, nor will it. Dreams and fantasies. Did you come to have sport with us, Master Olaxidor?"

"I must say I agree with Taristen," Elmer Trensel said. "I am aware of nothing like what you speak of. Perhaps I misunderstand. Are you here to entice us to create new technology, to develop the weapons you specify?"

"No," Master Liluth said. "I don't think I've made myself clear. *We* have invented the technology of which I speak. Myself and some of my Academy colleagues. I am looking for partners to mass-produce what we've already invented and produced on a small scale."

"Ridiculous," Dorin Panalus said. "If such things were possible, the Panalus manufactories would have already created them...and perhaps one of the other families would have invented an inferior product similar to what you refer to."

Master Liluth picked up the case she had brought with her and, without a word, started for the door. When she reached it without anyone else but Lily following her, Lily took it upon herself to give the family heads the help they needed.

"Well, come on. The master is about to show you something you've never seen and that most of you don't believe exists."

Lily followed the master through the door, not caring if the others followed her or not. They did, one at a time, begrudgingly.

It was obvious the master knew her way around because she stopped at a range that was empty, for the most part. There were two official-looking people, one man and one woman, who were both shooting pistols and meticulously taking notes with each round they fired.

The master placed her case on a nearby table. She didn't even acknowledge the family heads that crowded around her to see what she would do. Instead, she drew one of her pistols and pulled the trigger exactly when it reached a horizontal position. A chip of wood blew out of the face of one of the target dummies. She hummed to herself and nodded.

"Okay," she said. "I will show you this one time and one time only. Pay attention or you will have to rely on the details the others have noted that you did not." While she spoke, she took one of her horns from her belt and fed powder from it into the pistol. As she had done at the Academy, she placed the ammunition in and tamped it down. She glanced at a nearby flag to gauge the wind, then raised her pistol once again.

When she pulled the trigger this time, Lily knew what to expect. She watched the dummy's head explode then shifted her eyes to the family heads standing nearby. As she did, she caught the master's small smile as she, too, watched the reaction.

"That's one of the two things I told you about, a combination of an improved alchemical flash powder and a shock-sensitive charge of a different powder within the projectile."

All of the family heads spoke at once, creating a mishmash of sound that was unintelligible. Master Liluth ignored them —and the two other people who were furiously taking notes with their mouths open—as she opened up her case and took out the rifle she had shown them at the Academy. She sighted down the barrel, apparently at a set of target dummies several hundred yards away. They weren't on the main range, but looked as if they were in a storage area.

"Is that storage area controlled?" she asked. The others stopped their deluge of questions and comments for long enough to look dumbly at her. "Is. That. Storage. Area. Controlled?" she repeated, enunciating every word.

"It is," Fortuna said.

"So there would not be anyone there right now, anyone that might get injured if, say, one of those dummies splintered and sent wood everywhere?"

The woman seemed at a loss about how to answer that question. Brandon Simm, of all people, spoke up.

"It's not accessed often. If someone were there, they would come through the gate off to the left, so we could see them. There are fences to keep people out, which should stop any... flying wood chips."

"Thank you. Again, I suggest you pay attention. Lily, if you please, there are enough looking glasses in the case for every-one, including yourself. Be a dear and hand them out."

Lily did as she was asked, putting the glass up to her own eye.

"The first row, third from the left," Master Liluth said. She brought the rifle up, apparently already loaded, and sighted. With a squeeze of the trigger, the rifle boomed and at nearly the same time, the chest of the dummy suddenly developed a fist-sized hole. When everyone turned back around to look at the master, she was setting down the smoking long gun. "And that is the second thing that, I have under good authority, is impossible. Now, I shall ask again, who would like to partner with the Academy to aid us in mass-producing weapons that could mean the difference between life and every living thing on this planet being destroyed?"

This time, seven hands went up without hesitation.

CHAPTER
EIGHT

"You really got their attention with your demonstration," Lily said to Master Liluth that evening as everyone sat in the common room for dinner.

The master chuckled. "That tends to happen when you do what they have told you to your face is impossible. Things played out predicatably. The only surprise was Brandon Simm. I haven't dealt much with him before and he strikes me as being more intelligent than his demeanor would indicate. I've already decided that if he is as I expect him to be now that I've observed him, his family will be making flash powder for us."

"That's great!"

"We're well on the way. You saw the most exciting part of it today. You're wise to quit now."

Lily grinned at the master. "I was thinking the same thing. Really, though, my reasoning is that I need to go and see my uncle. I haven't talked to him or sent any letters for years. I'll be spending the first hour apologizing to him repeatedly. I've never even met his wife, my aunt."

"I'm sure it will be fine."

Lily nodded, but wasn't so sure. What if Uncle Arten didn't

even recognize her? Maybe he wouldn't speak with her at all. It would be so easy to be too busy to go and see him...

She didn't sleep much that night, her mind going through all the different scenarios that could occur when she tracked her uncle down. After a light breakfast, one she hardly ate any of, she got up to go do her duty.

"Hold on there, girl," Tere said. "I'm going with you. If you don't mind, that is."

She could have kissed the old archer. Who could worry with Erent Caahs at their side?

"I'd like to meet your uncle, too, if that's okay," Aeden said.

"Urun and I were talking about it, too," Jia said. "Can we tag along as well?"

Lily stood there smiling at them, her eyes a little misty. Whatever happened, she'd have her friends at her side. That meant more than she could express. She settled for saying, "Thank you."

It didn't take too long to find where her uncle lived. She didn't remember the streets well enough to find it, partly because they'd changed over the years and partly because it had been so long ago. A few well-placed questions and she and the others were standing outside a house that she definitely did remember. She and her parents had been at the house the last time they'd visited, all those years ago.

Lily's stomach fluttered as her gaze lingered over the doorway and the front of the house. Around back, there was a small yard where she had played while the adults chatted. It all looked the same, if a little worn and aged.

Tere cleared his throat behind her and she realized she'd been standing in front of the house for some time without doing anything. She shook her head and stepped up to the door. It was the same wooden plank type, with the same green paint as she'd last seen it, if the fading and peeling were to be believed. She rapped on it with her knuckles and took a step back to wait.

From within, there came a shuffling sound and then the latch was drawn. A man poked his head out.

"Yes?" he said.

Lily recognized him immediately, though he had aged far more than he should have for the time that had passed. His dark brown hair had faded and was greying and thinning. His drawn face carried wrinkles that seemed to indicate he didn't drink enough water—and that maybe he drank something else too much—and even his posture was alarming. The strong, erect man she remembered, was stooped and radiated weakness and illness.

"Uncle Arten?" Lily said. "It's me, Lily."

The man blinked at her, then rubbed his eyes. Inexplicably, they filled with tears and he let out a little sob. "Lily? Little Lily?"

"Yes, it's me. I'm sorry I never came to visit after my parents—"

She ran out of air to speak as he grasped her in a hug and squeezed with strength that belied his appearance, forcing the breath out of her.

"No, no," he said. "No apologies, not from you. I thought you were dead. Part of me knew you weren't, though. I should have found you, taken you in. I...oh. Come in, please. Come in. Are these your friends?"

She gave him a final squeeze and released him as he retracted his own arms. "Yes, this is Tere Chizzit, Aeden Tannoch, Jia Toun, and Urun Chinowa. I hope it's alright they came with me."

"It's fine." He stopped and looked her over. "My, Lily, you grew to be such a gorgeous woman. Are any of these young men your husband?"

"No. I'm not married. There's no time for that right now..." She waved what she was going to say away. "Let's sit down and chat. About something else."

Arten led them into a living area and they all took seats. He excused himself to start water boiling for tea as Lily looked around. The place was unkempt, items lying around as if they'd been carelessly thrown down and there were plates of old food that had been sitting for much too long. She shared a look with the others, wondering what was going on with her uncle. He'd always been tidy.

When he returned and poured tea for everyone, he shuffled to a chair and sat. "Where have you been, Lily? After what happened with your parents, I was going to go looking for you, but the report was that the caravan was wiped out. Still, I almost went, but...others talked me out of it, told me that I was just making things worse on myself. I found out much later that those first reports were false and I went to Arcusheim to try to find you, but I couldn't. It's a big city, but with your hair, I thought I might be able to talk to someone who remembered seeing you."

"I left the city," she said. "Or to be more correct, never went back. It's a long story, but I ended up okay in the end. Now I have a lot of friends who are heroes." She waved her hand at her friends. "We do important work, mostly for the Hero Academy."

"The Hero Academy?" he said. "You must be very important."

"No, I mostly try to keep from stumbling around while I watch my friends do the work."

"Don't believe a word of it," Aeden said. "This woman has saved my life on more than one occasion. She deserves the name hero as much as any."

Arten looked at the floor and Lily thought maybe they'd said something insulting to him. He stared down for quite some time, the others remaining silent, probably not knowing what to say like her. Finally, he looked up, his eyes brimming with tears.

"She died, Lily. My wife died, three months ago. We were married for almost twenty years, since right after you left to live in Arcusheim. Do you remember her? You only met her once."

"I'm so sorry, Uncle Arten. About your loss and that I don't remember much about her. I was only a girl when we visited last."

"She wasn't here the last time you visited. She had to go and help her mother out. The time before, though, you met her briefly. Elenya was my life. I already decided that I would join her in death, after I finish one more thing. Something, it seems, I am not well-suited to do currently. Her death has ravaged me. I look like a sick, old man, and I feel worse."

For lack of anything she could think of to say, she went to him and put her arms around him. After a moment, she said the only thing she could come up with. "I'm so sorry."

He cried quietly for a few minutes, holding onto her as if she were a floating log in a flood. He finally straightened and wiped his eyes. "I'm sorry I'm such a mess. I'm sure this wasn't the reunion you had expected." His gaze turned inward and after a moment he continued. "Lily, would you do something for me?"

"Of course. What can I do?"

"I want you to do the one last thing that needs done, something I can't do because I can't travel in this condition. If you can do it for me, then I can quietly take my own life and be free of the constant sorrow I am weighed down with now."

"Uncle Arten!" Lily said. "I have always loved you, and still do, but I will not do something so that you can take your own life. If this task is keeping you from carrying out the foul deed, then no, I will not do it for you. Don't be ridiculous. Elenya wouldn't want you to take your own life."

"Compared to the pain of living, she would agree with my choice. The suffering is unendurable compared to..."

"Compared to watching your parents, your only family in the whole world, being murdered before your eyes when you're a child? Is it comparable to that?"

Arten's eyes widened and he flinched like he'd been struck. "Lily, I didn't mean it like that. I'm sorry, but I—"

"No," she said. "Don't apologize. I'm not trying to compare scars. It just came out. I only wanted to show you that I understand. I've been there. I know heartache and loss and despair. Running away from it, taking your own life, is not the solution." She took a few breaths to calm down. "What is this important task of yours, so important you won't do what you had planned to do until it's finished?"

He wiped his hand across his face. "It'll seem silly. I have some items locked away at a bank in Satta Sarak. They're not valuable in a monetary sense. They're memories, ones I want to see one last time before I go. There's also something in there I want to give you, now that I know you're alive. I was going to hire a messenger to go get it, but the things are precious to me and I need someone I trust to get them, since I can't do so myself."

Lily sighed. "You know I would go there, and farther, to retrieve the items for you, but I will not hasten you killing yourself. I'm sorry. If you promise me you won't go through with your plan, I will gladly go and get your things for you."

"I...I can't do that. The suffering, Lily. It needs to end. My health is declining. I'll soon die anyway, if things keep up the way they're going. What if I promise you that I will not take my own life until you come back with my things and we discuss the matter thoroughly?"

Lily narrowed her eyes at her uncle. That wasn't much of an agreement. He could get his items, talk to her, and still go ahead with his ill-conceived plan. On the other hand, he could always do as he had planned at any time. She couldn't watch him every hour of the day. At least with his promise, he wouldn't do so until she came back and they talked it over.

She didn't know what to do. Glancing at Tere, she noticed him jerking his head toward the door.

"Can you excuse me for a moment, Uncle Arten?"

"Of course."

She got up and went through the front door of the house. Tere followed her. Once they closed the door, she turned toward him.

"It's a hard decision," he said to her. "You look like you're having trouble with it, so I thought I'd give you my thoughts, if that's okay."

"Absolutely. I need help."

"Good. The way I see it, he can do the deed any time he wants. He says he doesn't want to without seeing his items again, but if the situation becomes too hard, he'll move forward with his plan anyway. If you can trust his promise—"

"I can."

"Okay, then agreeing to go and get his stuff will keep him from harming himself at least until you're back, at which point you can speak with him and try to talk him out of it. Throw in a stipulation that he has to take better care of himself between now and then to make sure he survives until you get back and it seems that it might be your best chance of keeping him from killing himself. Right now, he seems pretty set on doing it, but that was before he knew you were alive. Alternatively, you can give up everything else and live with him full-time, watching him every moment of the day to make sure he doesn't try to do it."

"That's a fool's errand, to keep watch like that. I'll have to sleep sometime. I think I like your suggestion. Do you think I can take the time to go to Satta Sarak, though? With all that's going on?"

"It's your uncle's life we're talking about. You can make the time. I will, too. I'll go with you."

Just like that, Tere had solved the problem. She leaned in and kissed him on the cheek. "Thank you."

"I didn't do anything you wouldn't have done anyway. I just shortened the wait time, is all. Make sure to put the stipulation in to take better care of himself."

They went back into the house and she explained the deal to her uncle.

"While I'm gone getting your things, you will do nothing to harm yourself, including asking or hiring others to harm you, and you will take better care of yourself. Do you have any relatives or friends left that can help?"

"It's been a hard year. With Elenya's illness and then death, I've chased away all the friends I had and I don't have any relatives left. Even Elenya's mother is gone, passed away six years ago. Oh, there is always Nadine."

"Nadine?"

"Yes, Nadine Dufour. You remember Mother Sella, the healer?"

"I do," Lily said. "She made medicine for me. Is she still alive?"

"Sadly, no. Nadine is her daughter, though. She took over being a healer when Mother Sella got too old to handle it. She and her husband Halden are kind to me. They've helped me out before. She might be willing to do what you want."

"I like it. Tell me where I can find her and we'll discuss it."

"She only lives a few doors away," Arten said. "Go outside and turn right. The fourth door you come to on this side of the street is theirs."

"I'll go right now. I'll be back shortly to let you know what we decide."

CHAPTER
NINE

Tere and Aeden stayed with Lily's uncle as she went to search for the healer, with Urun and Jia in tow. The house was easy to find, not only because Lily was able to count to four, but because, like Mother Sella's house when Lily was young, there were little planters and pots with herbs growing everywhere. She imagined that the yard behind the house had a multitude of other plants lined up in neat rows. The sight of it brought back memories and an ache crept into Lily's chest.

"You all right?" Jia asked.

Lily made an effort to smooth her features. "I'm fine. I was just thinking of Mother Sella, the healer. She was an amazing woman, and as caring as any person could be. I guess it goes with the territory of being a healer, but still..."

Jia made a funny face and shifted her eyes toward Urun. Lily had spent enough time with the woman to understand what she was trying to say. Yes, Urun was a healer, an actual priest of a goddess whose main role was to maintain and promote health, but he wasn't the most personable of people. He was easy to get along with, most of the time, but relating to others was not his strong suit. She kept herself from chuckling. No use in being mean to her friend.

She knocked on the door and a plump woman with a round face answered the door. She wore a simple dress and her light brown hair was pulled up into a messy bun. The relationship to Mother Sella was unquestionable. Lily unconsciously took a sharp breath in. Her mind scrambled for words and after an eternity of the woman staring at her, she finally got them out.

"I...uh, hi. I'm Lily. Fisher. Lily Fisher. I—"

The woman's face brightened and she aimed a huge smile at Lily. "Oh, my. Lily Fisher. Mother talked about you all the time. You're so pretty, and...healthy. If you don't mind me saying so. From the stories Mother told me, I wasn't sure what happened to you. You're done with whatever that sickness was, then?" She gave a little hop. "Sorry, I'm sorry. Where are my manners. Please, come in. I'm Nadine Dufour. Mother Sella was, well, my mother. For real, I mean. I'm her actual daughter. I took over her healing practice when she got up in years. My, Lily Fisher. How she loved you."

"I'm so sorry about your loss. I wish I would have visited to tell her I was fine. I should have."

"Nonsense. She understood. All she hoped was that you had gotten healthy and strong, and you are obviously that. Strong enough to carry around weapons, at that."

Lily's face heated immediately. She was so used to having her weapons with her at all times, she barely thought about it. Most folk didn't walk around in the city with a bow and with long knives and a full quiver strapped to them.

"Come, come," Nadine said. "Let me put on some tea. Are you visiting Arten? Poor Arten. He's in a bad way." She waved to seats in the room they entered. "Make yourself comfortable. I'll put on some water for tea and be right back.

Lily traded looks with Jia. Urun was busy studying some of

the plants that were growing in small pots along the windowsill.

"There," Nadine said, returning with a man following in her footsteps. "Lily, I'm so sorry for my rudeness. Seeing you has flustered me. May I have your friends' names. This here is my husband, Halden. Halden, this is Lily Fisher, the one Mother always talked about. Isn't she gorgeous?"

The poor man worked his mouth, as if he was trying to figure out if it was all right for him to say such a thing about another woman. His wife didn't give him an opportunity to answer, though.

"What's your name dear?" she said to Jia.

"I'm Jia Toun, and this is Urun Chinowa. He's the priest of Osulin and a healer also."

That started a whole new round of conversation as Urun and Nadine discussed different healing herbs and his ability to heal with magic. She dragged herself away to get the water and tea leaves, allowing Halden to get more than two words into a conversation.

After they all were settled and drinking tea, Lily broached the reason she was there.

"Nadine, there's another reason for my visit, in addition to paying my respects to your mother. Uncle Arten is having a rough time, like you said."

"He is. The poor dear. I've been trying to check on him, but his isn't a physical illness. He's heartbroken."

"He is," Lily said. "In fact, he told me that his plans are to take his own life."

The disappointment on Nadine's face told Lily she already knew. "I have learned a thing or two about people's attitudes from watching Mother and being a healer for so many years, but I can't crack that man. I've tried everything I can think of."

"Oh, no, it's not that. I wasn't asking for you to try to change his mind. He wants me to do something for him. To do it, I'll be out of town for a while and my main concern is him following through on his plans. He promised he won't, but part of that promise was to get healthier. He looks twenty years older than he really is. I came by to ask if you could check in on him. I'm not sure how long what I need to do will take and I think it would help to have someone call him to task, if that's not too much for me to ask. I'm sure you've inherited your mother's knack for cutting through the whining and excuses and telling people exactly how things are."

Halden, sitting next to his wife, nodded his head vigorously at that and Nadine patted his leg with a chuckle.

"I can do that. If he's promised to take better care of himself, that's something I can help with. Maybe once he's in better shape, he won't be considering doing what...well, you know."

"That was my hope, too. Thank you so much. I'll run his errand as quickly as I can and then maybe we can gang up on him when I get back and get that stupid idea out of his head once and for all."

"Now I can see why Mother loved you so much. So full of fire. Like your hair."

"If you only knew," Jia mumbled.

"Do you mind me asking, Lily, do you have any children? I know you're young yet, but I had my Iriam at a young age."

"I don't. I've never really had time. You have a daughter? How old is she? Does she help you with your healing?"

The frown that crept onto Nadine's face didn't suit the woman at all. "No. She's near eighteen now. She's been out of the house for a couple of years now. There was a blowup and some words and she's...I'm not sure where she's at now. It was Arcusheim, then Telna, of all places, but we've lost track. She doesn't write and we don't know where to send letters. Oh, I'm sorry. None of this is your problem. It's enough to say that we hope she comes around soon and realizes we only want what's best for her. Time has a way of teaching us lessons we can't get any other way."

"I'm sure she'll figure it out," Lily said. "She's from good stock, after all."

"Yes, she is."

On the way back to Arten's house, Lily shook her head and let out a long breath. "Sorry to dominate the conversation like that," she told her friends. "That woman is a force of nature. I'm tired just from the few words I could slip in now and then. I wasn't kidding. If Iriam is anything like her mom or grandmother, she's a handful. No doubt."

"Okay, Uncle Arten," Lily told her uncle when they returned, "Nadine said she'd check in on you and that she'd help you to keep your promise and get healthier. That means you need to do what she says, even if you don't want to. I suspect there will be a lot of advice on food and such. Are we still agreed?"

Lily had to give her uncle credit, he stopped to think about it. Making a promise like that wasn't one to be done on an instant. After he thought, he nodded. "Yes. I will not do anything to harm myself while you are gone and I will try to gain better health, even if that means quaffing Nadine's horrible concoctions."

"And we are going to have a long, long talk when I return."

"Yes, we'll talk."

"Good enough. I'll most likely leave in the morning. Give me the information I need and I'll be on the way as soon as I can."

CHAPTER

TEN

When Lily and her friends were all gathered in the common room of the inn later that evening, she explained everything about her visit to her uncle with Master Liluth. It was a little awkward since she didn't know the master well, but she needed to know what was going on.

"That poor man," the master said. "It's a hard thing for someone so dear to die, even more so if there is no one else in your life. This is the uncle you spoke of before, the one who told you stories when you were a child?"

"He is," Lily said. "My family wasn't big to begin with and now they're spread all over Dizhelim. Either that, or they've died, too. Time and circumstance hasn't been kind to the Fisher family."

"Maybe your presence will help to stabilize him," Aeden said. As someone who lost his entire family as well, Lily appreciated the thought.

"I hope so. After. Right now, he's got his items on his mind, whatever they are. That, and trying to end his own life. I believe he'll keep his promise, but only if I keep my part of it."

"It's strange to me how someone would contemplate

taking their own life," Urun said. "There is pain in life, but there is also good."

"I'm pretty sure you have to say something like that," Lily said. If her voice held an edge, well, it was just reflecting how she felt about what he'd said. "For a lot of people—including myself until recently—life is just something you do because the alternative is death. To some, surviving is the only life they'll ever have. I think that's what Arten is feeling right now. The difference is that the one thing that brought joy to his life was taken from him, so surviving looks like a lot of work for no reward."

Suprisingly, Aeden defied the shocked looks from the others. "I felt like that, when I watched my father die in front of my eyes. If it wasn't for my Gypta family, and the hope of exacting retribution on the monsters, slight as it was, I could see how that attitude could have grown into despair."

Jia raised her hand. "I understand the feeling, too. When my parents died, I was too young to understand it fully, and I had my grandfather to help me through it. But when my grandfather, the only person I had in the world, died...well, I understand."

"Fine," Tere said. "Despair is understandable. We've all felt it in one way or another. Do you really believe that there's nothing to life but just to survive for no apparent reason?"

Lily occupied herself with watching her hands as she wrung them in front of her. "I think that's what my uncle is feeling right now. I understand it. We've gotten off track. I have to go and do what he asked me. I'm sorry, but one extra archer isn't going to affect the ability of this group to protect Master Liluth on the way back to the Academy. If it seems like I'm shirking responsibility and dodging the task that Master Qydus set us on, I'm sorry, but I have to do this. He's the only family I have left. I'll leave tomorrow morning for Satta Sarak to retrieve his items."

"You're not going without me," Tere said. It was a simple

statement, but with the finality that said he would brook no arguments.

Jia looked back and forth between the master and Lily. "I want to go, too, but now we're talking about half of the protectors leaving. Master Liluth, how long will you be here for your meetings? Long enough for us to go to Satta Sarak and come back in time to escort you back home?"

The master smiled at Lily. "Don't worry about me. I brought my own message tablet to communicate with the Academy. I'll send a message to tell them to send more escorts. They should easily be able to arrive here before I'm ready to go."

"Thank you," Aeden said, "because I'm going, too. I doubt Lily will be facing dangers traveling the roads to Satta Sarak, but I'll stick with my friends if it doesn't mean shirking my duty to the mission and you."

Urun's head swung around the room, stopping on Lily, then Tere, the master, and Jia. "Uh. Is there room for one more? No use in breaking the group up, right?"

Lily leaned over in her seat and gave Urun a one-armed hug. "Thank you all. I could use some conversation to distract me from my uncle's plight."

Tere clapped his hands. "Good, then we're all in agreement. We'll leave for Satta Sarak in the morning. Thank you, Master Liluth. I hope we don't cause you too much trouble."

"Not at all. The trouble is dealing with these family heads, something which cannot be done by anyone else but me, unfortunately. Finding some guards to present the picture that I'm too protected to attack is a minor issue." She turned to Lily. "If I don't see you for breakfast, have a safe trip. I hope you'll be able to bring your uncle around. There is too much sadness and death in the world already, and things are getting worse. Every life we can save is a blessing."

The next morning, Master Liluth was already finished with breakfast and off to her meetings by the time Lily was up and about. Aeden had seen the master when he came inside after his morning training ritual and passed on the message to Lily that the master had sent a request for more escorts the night before.

"Thank you," Lily told him. "I hope it doesn't cause trouble that we're leaving our post like this."

"Don't worry. Our job was to keep a large group from attacking her while she was traveling. In the city here, with the city watch and people everywhere, no group large enough to daunt Master Liluth could gather together. I feel sorry for any handful of people that try. She'll be fine."

Lily chuckled at that, the image of the master and her pistols passing through her mind. Apparently, she was adept at fighting even without her firearms, though she hadn't ever seen the master demonstrate the skill.

Before leaving Drusca, Lily borrowed the message tablet from Aeden to send a message to the rest of their friends. Master Qydus would get it on his own linked tablet, too, but since the firearms master had sent her request the night before, it wouldn't come as s surprise to the headmaster.

HI EVERYBODY,

WE'VE HAD A LITTLE CHANGE OF PLANS. MY AUNT DIED AND THERE IS SOMETHING I NEED TO DO FOR MY UNCLE. THE OTHERS ARE GOING WITH ME TO SATTA SARAK TO HANDLE THE TASK MY UNCLE ASKED ME TO PERFORM. I'LL EXPLAIN MORE ABOUT IT LATER. I JUST WANTED TO LET YOU KNOW WE'LL BE HEADING SOUTHEAST.

—LILY

She handed the tablet back to Aeden, who stowed it in his saddlebags. They didn't need to delay their departure waiting for responses. They could check the tablet at their leisure as they traveled.

"Here we go," Lily said, guiding her horse out toward the edge of town.

"Satta Sarak," Aeden said. "The last time we were there, we got attacked by Falxen, the animaru almost attacked the city, and we ended up farther away from the Academy than ever, though that was where we wanted to go. I hope, this time, things will be a bit calmer."

Alloria Yurgen, the Vituma of the Dark Council, stood by her chair in one of the meeting rooms in her home. It was not the room used for the Council meetings—that one was reserved for only that purpose—but it was nearly as spacious. Her head servant Votior opened the door and followed two visitors in. He was, as ever, garbed in a fine black suit, tailored to perfection, with not one dark hair on his head out of place. As befit a servant of the head of the Dark Council.

"Lady Yurgen, will you be needing anything else at the moment?" he said.

"No, Votior. Thank you. We have what we need."

The immaculately dressed servant bowed and departed, closing the door behind him.

"Welcome," Alloria said. "Would you like something to drink, some food?"

"Tea, please," the woman said, as the two visitors sat on separate couches, both with good views of the doorway. The man grunted even as another servant poured the tea. Alloria assumed the noise meant he didn't want anything.

The people before him could not have been more different. The extremely dark-skinned man, as tall as Alloria—just under six feet—was solid. It wasn't so much that he was muscular, though he was. He seemed to be made of stone, a wall that even the most powerful force could not knock down.

With her slender pale form and his solid dark appearance, they were very nearly opposites.

The woman, on the other hand, though tall, was an inch or so shorter than Alloria or the man, and was slender, with strawberry blonde hair cinched in a tight tail at her back. She was not quite as thin as Alloria herself, though still willowy, like a breeze could move her, bend her. Not break her, certainly. She seemed flexible enough to withstand any type of flexing and twisting without damage. Even the way she brought the teacup to her lips was graceful, almost mesmerizing.

"I am Waterdancer and this—" she waved toward the man "—is Ironspike, for obvious reasons."

The man narrowed his eyes at her, and Alloria detected a slight hint of an eyeroll.

"We are on the Board of Direction of the Falxen," Ironspike said. "We speak for the Board and thus for all the Blades and have the authority to make decisions, should it be necessary."

"I thank you for coming to see me," Alloria said. "I would have been more than willing to go to you."

"The location of Vatheca, our headquarters, is not something we allow others to know."

"I see. Yes, well, I thank you for coming here. As I explained when I requested an audience, I would like to modify the relationship the Dark Council has with the Falxen. Increase it. In these times, we have need of more agents with the special abilities of the Blades."

Waterdancer took up the conversation, effortlessly slipping her thoughts into the moment of silence. "We have had a long and prosperous relationship, though it has had its disappointments."

Alloria was hoping the Falxen wouldn't bring up the fiasco with Blackshade and Firesnake. Blackshade was able to return from the mission with Cara Moore, but Firesnake had been killed by the Academy group Cara had been following.

"We apologize for the loss of one of your operatives," Alloria said, "but the foes that abound against us are powerful. All the more reason we need more of your skilled personnel."

Waterdancer took another sip of her tea. "Of course. What manner of work will you be assigning the Falxen assigned to you?"

"It will vary from working in an advisory role to hunting particularly powerful people and killing them. The same type of work we have been using the Falxen for previously. We find that there is more of such work that needs to be done."

"What type of arrangement are you requesting?" Ironspike asked, his deep bass voice sounding irritated.

"He's not mad," Waterdancer said, as if she read Alloria's mind. "With how deep his voice is and his...intensity, many confuse those qualities with anger. Think nothing of it. He's really very kind, when you come down to it." Her lips curved into a wry smile.

"I see," Alloria said. "We seek to have operatives assigned to us permanently. They will act as any of our forces do, taking orders and giving them, depending upon their position within our ranks. It is similar to the Blades we have used recently, but the delay between our need and their actions will be reduced, we hope."

"We can perhaps accommodate your requests," Waterdancer said, "though it will not come cheaply. How many Blades are you requesting?"

"At least twenty, possibly as many as thirty."

Ironspike made the first significant gesture since he'd arrived. His eyes widened fractionally, clearly evident because of the contrast of the whites of his eyes to his dark skin.

Waterdancer looked over her teacup at her companion, almost daring him to speak. With another expression that threatened an eye roll, he accommodated her.

"We can make such an arrangement within the authority

given us by the Board. Are you looking for specific Blades, or any with the particular skills you desire?"

"Both. We have a handful of names, but also a list of what abilities we'll need. Do you have a list of Blades you can refer to?"

"We do," Waterdancer said. Alloria noted that neither of the two carried anything with them. "Both of us have all the names and qualifications of every Blade memorized. As of a few days ago. It's possible someone has been killed during that time, but unlikely. We rarely lose Blades, other than recently."

Alloria's face threatened to heat, but the wave of Waterdancer's hand distracted her.

"I was not talking about Firesnake. Some time ago, two full braces followed a contract to kill a target. Of twelve Blades, only one came back to Vatheca, and he was so injured, it was not clear if he would survive."

"Twelve?" Alloria said. "I've never heard of two full braces banding together, even in times of war."

"You keep abreast of the Falxen," Ironspike said. "Your connections—some familial as well as members of your council, I understand—appear to be strong."

Waterdancer continued. "Not all of the blades were killed, which actually makes the situation worse. Two of them switched sides and joined the ones they were sent to kill. You know the targets well, I believe. Some of them were the same who injured Blackshade and your own council member, and killed Firesnake. I believe we can come to an accommodation. We have only to work out the details, and you will have your own corps of Falxen assassins."

~

THE LISTENER SHIFTED a body part slightly, relieving the tension from the awkward position that needed to be held. It had been almost a challenge to infiltrate the estate where the two members of the Falxen Board of Direction met with the tall, pale woman. She apparently led an organization. The Dark Council, they'd said in their conversation.

But that was not the only thing the listener heard as the three negotiated for a nearly unprecedented number of Blades to be assigned to one entity. All of it was interesting, as well as concerning.

The unknown visitor stayed in the awkward location long after the two Falxen had departed, waiting for the opportune time to leave. The conversation had not revealed everything about the relationship between the Falxen and the Dark Council, but it was enough. Enough to expend a bit more energy to search out more specific facts.

As to what would be done once the entire story was revealed, well, that would be decided at a later time. As all experienced Falxen knew, decisions should only be made after the research had been done. After that, of course, was the time for action.

With the Falxen, that usually meant someone's death.

ELEVEN

"I know it seems like we're going the long way around," Tere Chizzit said as the group traveled northeast toward the River Road, "and the truth of it is that we are. It'll be faster, though. If we tried to travel southeast from Drusca to meet the main road, it would take us a lot more time to go through the rugged country. We're going to backtrack a little to the River Road, then go south until it forks to the Genta Highway and the Trail of Sarak, and then we can head southeast."

Aeden waved a hand at the road ahead. "We trust you. You've traveled more than all of us put together. I agree that it'll be better to travel the bigger roads, even if it doesn't save time. There's no real reason to hurry."

Lily wasn't so sure she agreed with the Croagh. Her uncle promised her he wouldn't do anything to harm himself, but the sooner she could get this errand done, the better. Temptation only grew with time.

Travel *was* nicer on the big roads, though. As a frequent traveler herself when she was a Falxen, that became clear very early on. If there was no reason to hide, she'd take a wide, well-maintained road any day.

The group ate up the miles and stopped for the night after they'd reached the River Road. To Lily, it felt like they'd slipped back into their habit of travel that had dominated their lives since she joined the others. Moving through different areas, stopping to camp alongside the road at night, then repeating the same thing the next day. Thankfully, on the second day out of Drusca, there was the opportunity to sleep in a real bed again.

"Ten miles or so ahead is a small town called Simpton's Well," Tere told them. "It's a little place, but being on the Trail of Sarak, they have three inns, even though their total population is less than a hundred. We can stop there and sleep under a roof for a night."

"That sounds good," Jia said. "You timed it perfectly, too, so we don't have to stop too early or continue to travel after dark to get there."

Tere laughed. "Not my doing. It just worked out that way."

"Why do they call it Simpton's Well?" Urun asked.

"There's a large spring-fed well—more of a pond, really—and apparently the guy who started the town was named Simpton."

"No grand story, just some guy who found some water and then started building?" Jia asked. "That's the best you can do?"

"Yep. It's all I've got. If you want a story, ask the people who live there. Maybe they've got something more interesting to tell you."

"I just might."

Tere cocked his head. "Actually, there is one interesting thing about the town, though it doesn't have anything to do with why it's called what it is. This area is sort of a no-man's land. Technically, it may belong to Sutania or to the Saraki Principality. I seem to remember that Simpton himself was Saraki, but that doesn't mean much. Occasionally, there is some contention between the two nations, but there's not a lot of value, military or monetary, to the town, so it usually blows over without anything changing. It's not exciting, but at least it's mildly interesting."

When they reached the town, it didn't look to Lily like there was any kind of grand story attached to it. A scattering of small homes, three inns—two of which had two levels and one that had three—and a few assorted shops were all there was to be seen. With how spaced apart the homes were, it seemed even emptier than it might have, with only maybe a dozen people visible on the dirt streets.

The citizens were friendly enough, greeting the party or waving as they passed on the street. Jia had a fit of giggling and Lily thought the woman might have seen someone that caused her to laugh. She stared at Jia, uncomprehending, until the smaller woman told her what was so funny.

"There are three inns in town, right?"

"Yes," Tere said. "Three."

"They're all close to each other," Jia said, "so I can see all their signs from where I'm at. They're called All's Well, Well Wishes, and the Wishing Well. I've seen some silly names for inns before, but it seems the town conspired to use bad puns on all of them."

Tere shook his head at the chortling former Falxen and stopped his horse in front of the All's Well inn. He secured them rooms at the inn and they settled in for the night.

Lily approached the innkeeper, who was behind the bar overseeing the women scurrying around to bring food to the patrons in the common room. The seats were only half full, but with so few people in town and three inns to serve them, that was to be expected.

The man was taller and skinnier than many of the innkeepers she'd seen, though he did have a bit of a paunch, so the old adage about a skinny cook probably couldn't apply. Besides, he wasn't the cook, but the owner of the establishment. It was still nice to see that he appreciated the food, though.

P.E. PADILLA

"Good evening, miss. My lady?" He'd added that last part, but it was clear that he didn't know how to address her.

"Not a lady. You can call me Lily."

"Ah. Of course, Miss Lily. I am Tefford Pimms, the owner of this fine establishment. Is there something I can do for you?"

"Maybe. We're heading to Satta Sarak. Any news from that part of the world that I might need to know?"

He leaned in closer, conspiratorially. "You know the Saraki, holed up in their city with not much care for the rest of the world. That has not changed, of course, but there are things happening. Bandits are getting bolder. Not bold enough to attack a city, or even a small town or village, but travelers? It seems to be another surge in robberies. We have them from time to time. Your group looks to be able to handle themselves, so the bandits most likely won't bother you. They appreciate easy jobs.

"There's another thing altogether, though. Word is, the dark monsters that we've heard tell of have moved this far from wherever it is they're spawned. They've been attacking people as well. A few have escaped and told the tale of a horde of dark creatures with monstrous faces swarming them to slaughter and eat them. Those you might want to be careful of. Some outlandish tales I've heard say that the monsters can't be killed, though that doesn't seem right to me."

"Really?" Lily said. "Dark monsters? I've heard about them, but they're supposed to be over toward Kruzekstan and Artuyeska. If they've come this far, that's not good news at all."

"You have the right of it there. Why, one of our citizens, a tracker and guide by profession, saw the aftermath of one of the attacks. A dozen travelers, all cut up like they'd been torn to shreds. Not a valuable among the corpses. The damn monsters picked them clean, even took some of the clothing off bodies that were killed by injuries to the head, so as not to have rents and tears in their outfits."

"Wait a minute," a voice said from behind Lily. Aeden stepped up next to her. "Did you say that the monsters attacked a dozen people, killed them, then took their valuables, including clothing?"

"That's right, young sir. Old Forin Vess was the first to come upon them. He explained the scene to me in horrific detail. The mayor sent a group out to dig graves for the poor victims. Everyone deserves at least that much dignity."

"So Forin saw it for himself, right after the people were killed?" Aeden asked.

"He did. Some of the bodies were still bleeding. One was even warm, he told me."

"No one got to them before he did to steal the valuables?"

The strain of keeping a smile on his face was showing on Tefford, his lips slipping downward. "No, sir, not according to what he told me. He might be in tonight. You can ask him yourself."

"Thank you. If he does come in, will you let us know? I'd like to hear his tale firsthand."

The smile came back, with some effort, and the innkeeper nodded at Aeden and Lily. "Yes, sir. I'll do that. Can't be too careful when traveling. The more information you have, the better, I always say."

Lily smiled at him. "We agree with you, Master Tefford. Thank you for the news. The food is excellent, by the way. Thank you so much."

"You enjoy it, Miss Lily, and do be careful on the road. These are dark times, and no doubt about that."

"Truly," Aeden said, steering Lily by her arm back to where the others were sitting.

Forin Vess did not come that night. Aeden and Lily explained what the innkeeper had said and Tere saw what they had seen right away.

"That makes no sense," the archer said. "Animaru couldn't care less for valuables or for peoples' clothes. Either that tracker is dishonest and took everything himself or thieves or bandits got to the bodies before he did."

"He also said that he heard the animaru ate their victims," Lily said, "which we know they don't. I'm pretty sure Khrazhti is the only animaru who eats at all, and it's not corpses."

"The Academy needs to hurry up and spread the information about the animaru and what's happening," Jia said. "People will make things up to fill in the details in any stories or news they hear. It'll end up being worse even than reality and there will be widespread panic."

"There will be panic anyway," Urun said. Lily almost forgot he was there. He'd been very quiet the whole trip. Not quiet like there was something wrong, but just in a sense that he hadn't been taking part in most conversations. "Monsters from another world coming here to fulfill prophecy and try to destroy all life? I don't think rumors will add anything to those facts that will make it sound worse."

"Yeah," Aeden said. "I guess you're right there. Still, I don't like this news. If animaru have come this far west, we may be running out of time faster than I thought."

Tere slapped Aeden on the shoulder. "Don't go and panic yourself, not on a tale that you find in a common room. Stories have a way of changing as they're told over and over. Until we see more evidence, we should treat this as unreliable. We're already always on the lookout for animaru, so it won't hurt us to put this tale aside for now. We'll know the truth or untruth of it soon enough."

Soon enough turned out to be two days later.

CHAPTER
TWELVE

The travelers were making good time on the wide road called the Trail of Sarak. Despite its humble name, Lily appreciated the maintenance and engineering of the road. It was, for the most part, level and wide enough that the entire group could have ridden side-by-side, if that wouldn't have been an awkward and selfish way to travel. After all, there were others on the road, even if only occasionally, so they couldn't simply act like a moving wall taking up the whole roadway.

They passed through another town, this one called Redfield, but it was too soon for them to stop for the night. With several hours of daylight left, every one of them voted to continue on, even if that meant camping alongside the road when darkness finally came. It seemed that they were the only ones to decide that, because the road immediately became empty except for them.

In the late afternoon, when Lily's traveling instincts kicked in to start looking for suitable places to set up camp, she spotted movement ahead of them as the road passed through a heavy stand of trees. The road itself was clear, but to each side, huge woody pillars crowded in on it, even the spaces between them filling up with leafy green stuffing.

Lily blinked, then narrowed her eyes to get a better look ahead.

"Did you...?" she asked.

Tere shushed her. "Yes. I'm not sure who or what it is, but best for us to act like we didn't see anything. Keep your eyes open and let me know if you see anything else. I'll tell the others." He slowed his horse and dropped back to give the news to everyone else.

It was frustrating, riding alone at the front and watching for movement in a place that was custom-built for hiding anyone wanting to be hidden. Lily didn't catch any further flashes as Tere, then Aeden, joined her in the lead.

"I think we're coming up to where I saw the movement," she told them softly.

"Be alert," Tere said. "I don't see anything yet but...ah, there we are."

"What?" Aeden said. "What do you see?"

"Give it a moment. I can see them in the magical matrix. There are something like a dozen or a dozen and a half people. They're moving like they're preparing to jump into the road-way. It's hard to tell anything more from here. We'll know soon enough."

As expected, shapes leaped out from the trees, charging the party. Forewarned, they all had their weapons out and their feet on the ground before the first one even reached them.

"Are those—?" Jia started to ask.

"No," Tere said.

To Lily's eyes, they were being attacked by animaru. Ugly, bestial faces on dark bodies poured out from the trees, some of them growling or howling, though none speaking their own brand of Alaqotim. By the time one had gotten close enough for her to get a good look, she realized why they looked so awkward.

"They're wearing masks and costumes," she shouted as she neatly skewered one of the attackers with an arrow in its eye.

"They're human," Tere confirmed. "Bandits dressed like animaru to scare their victims into panic. Luckily, we know how to fight bandits *and* animaru." He proved the truth of what he said by loosing two arrows, each killing a bandit outright.

The bandits were almost to the party when more hidden in the trees started shooting their own arrows. To Lily's left, two arrows bounced off of nothing in front of Aeden, while another bounced off another invisible obstruction near Urun. Tere calmly stepped out of the way of another shaft and returned one in the blink of an eye.

Lily spotted the motion of another archer and released the arrow she had drawn, hitting the archer and ruining his shot, which spun off to the side and actually bore into one of the other bandit's legs.

Lily lost track of Jia until the blue-haired woman sprang up in front of two of the charging attackers, cutting them down so quickly with her daggers that they didn't even have time to raise their weapons.

Aeden finally got his chance at some combat when five of the remaining bandits reached him in a group. Lily moved to aim her bow at them, but Tere tsked and pointed toward the trees. "Let him have his fun. We need to take out the snipers. Keep your eyes open for arrows. I can see at least two hidden archers climbing down to flee. I'll take care of them."

She nodded and directed her attention to the trees ahead of her. Sure enough, a small movement that could have been a squirrel—but which she knew was not—telegraphed an arrow shot from that location. She'd been looking right at the spot when the projectile came at her and she was able to twist aside to dodge it while loosing an arrow of her own. Lily wasn't sure, but she thought she heard a grunt, then she saw a shape fall from the tree she had been looking at, confirming she'd hit her target.

After fighting groups of animaru for so long, the bandits fell quickly to the group. Just in the time Lily had spotted and dispatched the sniper, Aeden had carved through four of his attackers and was about to cut down the last one. Jia had dropped several bodies on the roadway, too, and Tere ghosted through the trees, hunting those trying to escape.

Then it was over. Aeden and Jia cleaned their blades on the clothing of the nearest corpses. A few minutes later, Tere emerged from the undergrowth, carrying Lily's arrows back to her.

"None of them escaped," he said, handing the shafts to her. "The grand total, including dead in the trees, seventeen."

"I guess that explains the story the innkeeper told us," Aeden said. "He spat toward one of the dead bandits. "Dressing up like animaru to more easily kill people to rob them. At least the animaru are acting according to their nature. I have no sympathy for humans that not only kill their own, but prey on fear and uncertainty to do it."

Tere shrugged. "Well, they won't be doing it anymore. When we get to the next town or to Satta Sarak, we can send a message to Redfield and Simpton's Well to let them know it was bandits who attacked the travelers and that they've been taken care of."

"If only all problems were so easily resolved," Jia said. "Are we ready to move on? I'd like to get a few miles from here before we set up camp. There's going to be a feeding frenzy of scavengers in no time."

~

AEDEN WAS TELLING Lily about the use of archery in the Croagh warfare between the clans as they got closer to Satta Sarak on the road.

"You have to understand," the Croagh said to her, "the clans do not put much stock in striking an enemy from afar. Even if they could use the Raibrech like I've learned to do, they would opt to get close and match blades with their enemies. Call it bravado or pride in their melee skill, no self-respecting traditional Croagh warrior would choose a ranged weapon over one they could use face-to-face. That being said, there are some fine archers in the clans, but they focus mostly on hunting, where the weapons are not looked down upon. I knew a warrior who..."

Aeden trailed off and Lily's head snapped up. She'd been listening, but her mind had been busy creating pictures to go with what her friend was saying. When she looked up and saw him leaning forward in his saddle to peer ahead of them, she turned to see what he spotted.

At the very edge of sight, where the road curved around to the left, a shape slumped at the side of the road. She copied Aeden and leaned forward to get a better look, thinking it might be the remains of someone who had met the bandits they'd killed the day before. As they grew closer, she thought maybe she was mistaken. Maybe.

Finally, when they got near enough to make out the details, Lily recognized that it was a man standing next to a horse, studying something in his hands.

"I don't believe it," Aeden said, and moved his horse up ahead of the others. "Dannel?"

The scrawny man pushed a bit of his light brown hair out of his face and casually rolled up the papers he had been reading—a map of some kind?—then raised a hand to the Croagh. "Aeden Tannoch. The winds of fortune put us in each other's path again. Well met. How are you?"

"How is it that you're always on the road somewhere when I see you, as if you're sitting here and waiting for me to pass."

The man looked at his horse, then at his feet, then back to Aeden. "I hate to tell you, Aeden, but I'm standing."

"You know what I mean."

The man smiled. "I do. You have some new friends with you this time."

Aeden seemed to take the hint. "Ach. Dannel Powfrey, these are my friends, Lily Fisher, Tere Chizzit, Jia Toun, and Urun Chinowa." He gestured toward each as he said their names. "Everyone, this is Dannel Powfrey." The horse snorted. "Oh, and that's Blennus."

Tere chuckled. "Blennus?"

"As I tell all who are surprised at the name, you should hear some of the things he calls me. It's all fair and in good fun. It is a privilege to meet so renowned a hero...uh, Tere Chizzit. Also, a great pleasure to meet one of the rare priests of Osulin. Lofty company you keep, Aeden, and the young ladies no less so than the men, though perhaps there has not been sufficient time for tales of their prowess to have leaked from the Falxen grip to spread throughout the land."

Lily started. "How do you know so much about—"

"Don't bother asking," Aeden said. "He knows a lot of things he shouldn't. Isn't that right, Dannel?"

"Who is to say who should know what? Knowledge is costly at times, but it truly belongs to no one. If I manage to scrape up some interesting facts here and there, who can tell me no?"

"Who indeed," Aeden said.

"Were you able to locate the book I told you about the last time we met?" Dannel asked.

"Aye, I did. It was exactly where you claimed it would be. There was another surprise hidden within it. A story, the translation of which helped us to find a secret cache of priceless knowledge and books, a compilation Tsosin Ruus himself set aside."

"Truly? You don't say."

"What's more, there were two special tomes within, one to me and my twin sister and one to Fahtin, whom you've met."

"Actually," he said, "I've met them both. Delightful women, both of them. I expect Marla's friend Evon was also on hand. I met him as well, when I met your sister."

"You...oh, never mind. You know, no doubt, that the Academy has declared both myself and Marla the Malatirsay. Collectively."

"Ah, clever, clever. Thus is solved the plurality debate. Fascinating. Congratulations? This book to you and your twin, is it helpful?"

"It was written specifically for us by the Prophet's own hand," Aeden said. "It's something of a guidebook on how to be the Malatirsay."

"Useful, then, indeed."

"Uh-huh."

Lily wasn't following everything the two were talking about, but she could see Tere looking intently at the strange man. It was like he was studying some new kind of life. She prepared to say something, but Dannel beat her to it.

"Have you heard the tale of the feuding families?"

THIRTEEN

"What?"

It was Aeden who spoke the word, but it was ringing through Lily's head at exactly the same time.

"Feuding families," Dannel said, as if it hadn't just come out of nowhere. "The story of the feuding families. Blennus likes to hear about them. Do you know of them?"

"Feuding...families?" Aeden said. "Dannel, what in the world are you talking about?"

"It's a story, an account, a summary of the things that happened between the two families who were feuding."

"I don't understand," Lily said, starting to think the man was more than half cracked. "Which families are you talking about?"

"The ones that were feuding, of course," Dannel said, patting his horse on the cheek. "Thus the name of the tale."

For a moment, she closed her eyes, hoping it would help her dispel the utter confusion she was feeling.

"Will it tell us something we need to know?" Aeden asked.

"Perhaps. Who can really say what one *needs* to know? Stories have a life of their own, to help or to harm. Some tales pass through lips and ears and do nothing whatsoever, while others change the course of history that might have been. Or that could be."

"Ooh," Jia said excitedly. "Which one is this?"

"Could be both, or neither," Dannel told her. "Often, it depends upon the listeners."

Aeden sighed and rubbed his hand over his face. "Fine. Sure, Dannel, tell us the tale of the feuding families."

"Oh. Really? That old thing? I've never seen the draw in it, though Blennus enjoys it. Have I mentioned that?"

"Yes, I believe you have."

"Good thing, because it's true." His eyes lost focus for a moment as if he were reminiscing. "So, the tale. There were two families—both very large, one dark and one light—and they were bitter enemies. Don't ask what their names are because it matters not and don't ask when or where the tale happens because no one knows. All that's important is that from the disagreement of a few relatively insignificant people, the two families became enemies and, as tales would have it, they both wanted the same piece of property.

"You can see the dilemma, I'm sure. Two families, each with a multitude of members, wanting the same place desperately. At first, it was only a few members of each who desired the land, and the heads of each family paid no attention to the little tiff. Such things happened often, even *within* families as large as these. But from the lowest members, the attitude spread. In a shorter time than anyone would have expected, nearly the entire membership of both families knew of the conflict and had taken their sides, supporting their family and hating the other family intensely.

"As is often the case in large conflicts, the more abundant lower class of members were sent off to fight each other. In the skirmishes, the darker family was victorious more often. That was when the lighter family sent more skilled and better trained warriors against the dark family. For the first time, minions of the darker family began to lose their lives. It made the lighter family happy, but as was to be expected, the dark family was furious. Predicatably, they brought out their better trained and more skilled warriors.

"This went back and forth, always small groups or individuals fighting each other. The family heads did not commit large numbers of family members to the fight, but whether that was because they didn't think the situation justified it or they were simply taking the time to plan for the larger campaign, it wasn't clear.

"Unbeknownst to the lighter family, the darker had a handful of family members that were skilled in disguise and stealth. These went off, usually alone but at times in pairs, and they infiltrated the light family, blending in with the numbers where no one would have expected them to be. From within, they were able to work against the lighter family, even killing when it was appropriate to their missions. The real reason they were within the lighter family, though, was to spy and obtain information on the secret strategies and abilities the family planned on bringing against the dark family.

"As the conflict escalated and casualties mounted on both sides, the family heads began to take the feuding even more seriously. No longer did they expect the lower members of the family to handle the problem. They became involved themselves. The family head of the dark family was off at some distance, so he sent his heir and successor to wage the war.

"This one was ruthless and efficient and clever as can be. He put in place a command structure and, using the information he had gotten from the spies—the ones who had disguised themselves so expertly that they were seen as important members of the light family—set about planning a campaign that would result in the complete annihilation of the other family. The lighter family made their plans as well, but much of their success still relied upon a small handful of successful heroes. The head of the light family struggled to prepare for what was sure to be a war unlike any anyone had ever seen.

"Oh my. Is it that close to sundown already? I'm sorry, my friends, but I think it's time for Blennus and me to go. I thank you for your hospitality and look forward to seeing you next time."

Dannel tugged on his horse's reins to start him moving.

"Wait!" Aeden said. "You didn't finish the story."

Dannel tilted his head, then said, "You're right. It is not done. Unfortunately, that's all there is. I'll be sure to tell you if I hear the ending between now and when we meet again."

"What is it supposed to mean? What do we do with what you've told us?"

"Mean? Do? It's a story, Aeden. Maybe it is meant to teach us the value of life or maybe to forewarn us about war and feuds. Think about it and maybe it'll make sense to you. If so, be sure to tell me the next time we see each other. It doesn't mean a thing to me."

Dannel and his horse strolled off, the man talking softly to the animal. Aeden sputtered, but seemed incapable of forming complete thoughts. Finally, when Dannel Powfrey walked out of sight, Aeden threw up his arms.

"That's a chunk of time we'll never get back. Come on, let's get to Satta Sarak before he decides to come back and waste more of our time."

"Nice guy," Jia chirped. "If a little strange."

"Is he always like that?" Tere asked.

Aeden shook his head. "He's difficult to define. Sometimes, he seems like an old, wise man, and at others like a man younger than he looks. This is the first time he's demonstrated scattered thoughts, though. I don't know what to make of it. His counsel and information have helped us in the past."

"I ask because I've never seen anyone quite like him with my sight," Tere said.

"What do you mean?"

"Every person has their own way about them and how they move through the magical matrix. Call it an aura or just each person's distinctive way they leave effects in the matrix, but I can use the differences to track individuals, some more easily than others. With him, it almost seems like he's invisible. He leaves only slight traces, like he moves through the matrix with stealth. I could hardly notice him unless I focused. It's like camouflage."

"What does that mean, though, Tere?" Lily asked. "Does it mean he's got powerful magic or that he's not human? Is he animaru?"

Tere shrugged. "I don't know. He's not animaru, I'm pretty sure of that. They have tracks as individual as humans or anyone else. It's almost like he's wearing a heavy blanket over him that blocks my vision of him. I don't get any bad feelings about it. It's just strange."

"Strange isn't necessarily bad," Aeden said.

"It's not necessarily good, either," Jia pointed out.

"That's a fair point. Regardless, he's not our problem right now. Let's get our task done. We can figure out Dannel Powfrey some other time." He mumbled something further about "spies" and "disguises," but Lily couldn't hear much of it.

Late the next day, they finally reached the city of Satta Sarak. Lily had been there before, of course. It was the largest city in southern Promistala and where there were a lot of people, there were always jobs for Falxen. In fact, her last job had originated there: the one to kill Khrazhti and her friends, including those with her right now. Well, except for Jia, who was in her brace, assigned to kill the others just like Lily was.

Shadows danced over the high wall surrounding the entire city when they approached, the stone blocks reflecting the reddish light of the setting sun. The Trail of Sarak ended—or started, depending on whether leaving or arriving—at the city, and it was its widest and most proud there. Traffic had picked up, with wagons, mounted riders, and people on foot going into and out of the city.

"Hopefully, there will be less excitement here than last time," Aeden said. "No animaru ready to breach the walls in their fervor, no assassins attacking us." He winked at Lily as he said it.

"Don't worry," Jia said. "We know all about Falxen. No one's going to get the drop on us. Besides, I heard that the two best Blades from that group changed their profession anyway."

"I can vouch for that," Tere said.

It was nice, the banter. Lily spent so much time with her friends in life-or-death situations, it was good to be able to travel for something so mundane—and safe—as picking up a box of items for her uncle. She could get used to things being a little more normal. For a little while, anyway. If her life consisted of nothing but ordinary things, she might be bored. It was definitely nice to have a break once in a while, though.

"How about we find an inn and relax. We can go to the bank tomorrow morning, get Uncle Arten's things, and figure out if we want to rest for another day or go straight back."

"I think that's a great idea," Jia said. "I might even do a little shopping. We were in and out of here so quickly last time, I didn't get a chance to go to the market section of the city."

"I know just the inn to go to," Tere said. "Follow me."

Tere led them to an inn named The Spotted Frog. Lily had never been there, but Aeden's mouth formed into a smile when he saw the sign above the door and even Urun, who didn't seem to be doing much of anything so far on their journey, nodded his head.

"I could really go for some of the bread made from the Stouth family secret recipe," Aeden said.

"What am I missing here?" Lily asked.

"It's nothing," Tere told her. "We stayed here last time we

were in Satta Sarak. I used to come here...before. The original owner, Bartle Stouth, has retired and his daughter runs the place now, but the food and the ale are still marvelous. You'll like it."

Jia was nearly bouncing. "Ooh, that sounds good. When we traveled as Falxen, we usually had to keep a low profile, which a lot of the time meant staying in places where people minded their own business. Places in the dangerous part of town. Inns like that don't go hand in hand with good food or nice beds. It's one of my favorite things about traveling now. You know, when we actually stay at an inn rather than to camp out on the dirt somewhere."

"Then you're in for a treat, Jia," Aeden said. "They have nice beds *and* good food. The prices are not bad either, which is a bonus."

Tere shook his head at everyone else. "Let's stop gabbing and get the horses taken care of and you'll all find out for yourselves. I'm hungry, could use a bath, and wouldn't mind a place softer than the ground with rocks in my back to sleep."

They did as he suggested and Lily couldn't argue with any of what they had told her. Jia was right, traveling was much better than it had been when she was a Blade. It might be a little thing, but she'd take it.

CHAPTER

FOURTEEN

Morning came, and breakfast was as good as their dinner the night before. Though she usually ate for convenience, Lily took her time and enjoyed the meal served at the inn's common room.

"We'll head over to the bank first thing," she told the others. "I want to take care of that and then we can go shopping or whatever else it is you want to do. That's assuming that you are going with me. You don't need to. It's a simple errand."

"I'll go with you," Tere said. "You don't know how much stuff your uncle has stored. You might need another person to help you if it's several boxes."

"I hadn't even thought of that. Thank you, Tere. That's very kind of you."

"Yeah, that's me. Kind." His smirk ruined his bluster, but it made Lily appreciate it even more.

"I'll go with you," Jia said. "The bank is near the market area anyway."

"We can all go," Aeden said.

Urun continued eating his breakfast. He didn't add to the conversation in any way, so she'd take that as agreement.

After a few minutes of silence, she couldn't stand it anymore. "Are you okay, Urun?"

He jerked upright in his chair. "What? Oh, me? Yes, I'm fine. I've been thinking a lot lately. The world feels...strange."

"Would you care to elaborate on that?" Aeden asked.

"I'm not sure I can. It's difficult, with all the changes in the magic of the world lately. Things seem to be a bit off. Not necessarily wrong, but not normal, either. I don't even know if we can use the word *normal* anymore, for anything. Maybe I'm having trouble adjusting. It's like a premonition or something, a faint feeling that something is wrong—or may go wrong—though I don't have anything concrete to point toward that makes me feel that way. I'm sorry I've been quiet. I've been going around and around in my mind about it and it's driving me to distraction."

"I understand that feeling," Tere said. "It seems like I have to learn how to see all over again with how the ambient magic in the world has been shifting. I get the feeling that some calamity is waiting right around the bend. I'm afraid all this stuff will take my magical sight away again."

"Aye," Aeden said. "Even I can feel enough of the magic that it puts me a bit off-balance. You're not alone, Urun. Eventually, it will settle down or we will figure it all out. The greatest minds on Dizhelim are at the Academy trying to make sense of it all."

The priest smiled at them. "Thanks, everyone. It doesn't bother me so much as confuse me. It's been keeping my mind busy. Preoccupying me."

Lily wasn't sure about all the magic stuff they were talking about, but she could understand having a feeling about something happening. As a Falxen, she'd developed her danger sense to such a high degree, it almost seemed to border on magic at times. Premonition, intuition, magic, she could see the connection in how they could make one feel.

"Well," Lily said, "we'll take care of the chore we came

here for and then we can enjoy a day of shopping or relaxing. Maybe you can buy a funny hat, Urun, and that'll make you feel better."

Jia opened her mouth, but Urun put a hand up to cut her off.

"No, I don't think that will help me at all. I appreciate that it would entertain some others, but I don't need a hat."

Jia frowned at him.

"It wouldn't go with my robes, anyway."

They left the inn with Lily not knowing if Urun had been joking or if he was truly affected enough by his musings that social cues were lost on him. More lost than usual.

The bank was easy to find, squatting at the end of the largest of the market streets and touching two others. The heavy stone block from which it was made fairly shouted strength and security. The heavy wooden doors, banded with iron and flanked by guards with both halberds and swords, only reinforced that impression.

Lily hadn't had much use for banks in her life. Before the Falxen, she never had enough money for it to stay in her purse for long. After she joined and began to do jobs, she accumulated a fair sum. Most of it she kept with her, changing up to larger denominations of coins when her purse got too full, and hiding it in little cubbies all over the world.

"I've never been in a bank," she admitted to the others.

"I went in one, once," Jia said. "For work."

Lily laughed. *Had Jia robbed it or did she kill someone in it?*

Aeden put his hands up. "Don't look at me. I grew up in the highlands and then with the Gypta. Banks are about as foreign a thing as I can think of."

"My parents had use of banks occasionally," Urun said, "but I never did. I left my small town when I was young and began living in the Grundenwald. The only banks there are riverbanks."

Tere stopped and turned around to stare at Urun, his mouth open. "Gods, Urun. Did you just tell a joke?"

The whisper of a smile on the priest's face gave the answer. Tere barked a laugh and continued toward the bank's doors.

"I do have a sense of humor," Urun said softly.

"I know that now," Tere said, still chuckling. "As for banks, I've been in a few. They don't just change coins and store gold for people. A large part of their business is keeping things secure, such as your uncle's items, Lily. They have dedicated strong rooms for such things, accessible by tokens like the one Arten gave to you."

Aeden scratched his head. "It seems strange to me to have so much stuff that you need to pay someone else to hold it for you."

"People do like *things*," Tere said. "I think a lot of them are items of sentimental value, ones they don't want damaged by accident or fire. I'm guessing Arten's possessions are items he's gathered during his life, meaningful trinkets that he wants home so he can let them stimulate his memories. People often think of such things when they're faced with death."

Lily and the others all looked to the archer. As if he could sense them doing it—he probably could—he turned back to them. "What? I've told you before, I've been alive a lot longer than you lot. I've learned some things."

Lily flashed him a smile and stepped up to interlock her arm with his. "We know, we know. Come on, let's get this over with."

Once inside, Lily had to wait in line for several minutes, another experience she hadn't had the pleasure of experiencing before. Once she made it to the desk of the bank worker, she placed the token on the desk as she greeted him to move the process along.

Lily put the man somewhere in his mid-thirties with

rather forgettable face under an uninteresting haircut. His dark trousers and tunic were nearly identical to other workers in the place, almost like it was some kind of uniform. She noted the dark rings under his eyes and his slow, methodical movements. She expected he worked long hours, though she didn't know if that was typical for a bank or not.

"Good morning. I'm Lily Fisher and I'm here to retrieve my uncle Arten Fisher's belongings."

"Good morning, Miss Fisher. I am Mikel Tonsend. I believe I can assist you. Give me a moment while I find where your uncle's items are stored."

He took the token and went through a door behind his desk.

"More waiting," Lily said, tapping her fingers on the wood of the desk.

Several minutes passed before Mikel returned. The expression on his face did not look like he had good news.

"What's wrong?" Tere asked.

"I am very sorry, Miss Fisher, but the items that belong to this token...they're no longer here."

"What do you mean they're no longer here?" The sharpness of her voice caused Mikel to flinch. She took a breath, then tried again, more softly. "What do you mean they're not here, Mikel?"

"I...uh, well, it is not too rare an occurrence. When items remain unclaimed for a long period of time, the bank disposes of them to reclaim space in the strong rooms."

"Dispose?" Aeden chimed in. His voice also held an edge, and if Mikel was flinching before, he was nearly cowering now.

"The account for the storage of items was paid for as a lifetime service," Tere said. "It doesn't bloody well matter if Arten *never* came back for them. Your bank was paid to store the items forever."

"Yes, sir. Of course, you are correct, sir." The man's eyes

were frantically going from place to place, usually stopping briefly on the weapons that the group was wearing openly. "I don't know what happened. I—"

"Do you have a superior bank officer?" Lily asked. "Someone higher up who might answer our questions? It's clear that this wasn't your fault, Mikel. For example, who is in charge of the strong rooms?"

The man snatched at the idea as if it were a rope and he was sinking in quicksand. "Yes, of course. Mister Tannis Edgar is the bank officer responsible for the strong rooms. You may talk with him. Pardon me for a moment. I will go and ensure he is in his office."

The frantic man left again, but returned more quickly this time. "Come with me, please."

He led them through the door he'd been ducking behind, down a hallway, to a large office with the door barely ajar. Mikel knocked and a voice from within said, "Come."

Tannis Edgar was an older man, a fringe of white hair ringing his mostly bald head. It was obvious by the belly that pressed up against his desk that he spent much of his time sitting. Drinking, too, if the prominent veins on his nose were any indication. The room seemed dim for someone who dealt with documents all day, with a few lamps and a scattering of candles throughout the large chamber. When he spoke, his voice was as Lily expected, course but with a confidence that could only be found in military commanders, supervisors of lowly employees, and bullies.

"I understand there is an issue with a strong room?"

Lily noticed he didn't bother introducing himself or asking who they were. She slapped the token down on the desk. "I want my uncle's things. He paid for the items to be stored forever. Since forever has not elapsed, you must still have them."

"Hmmm." Tannis acted as if he had no knowledge of the situation, but he was a horrible actor. "Let me check the ledger." The man got up from his seat with a grunt and stepped to a cabinet behind his desk. He thumbed through it for a moment before withdrawing a sheet of paper. "Yes, here it is. It appears there has been a mistake. That collection has been marked for disposal. You say your uncle purchased a forever plan?"

Lily took a deep breath, closed her eyes, and exhaled.

"You know damn well he did," Tere spat. "You'd better produce his things or we'll go straight to the constable."

The man gave Tere an oily grin.

"Oh, it's like that, is it?"

Tannis Edgar turned from Tere to Lily. "Listen, Miss Fisher, perhaps we can come to an arrangement. I might be able to locate the items if you were to give me some incentive?" The way his eyes roamed over her told her exactly what incentive he was talking about.

In a flash, she had her long knives out of their sheaths and at the pudgy man's throat. "Listen, you disgusting pile of manure. You will produce my uncle's things or they will find you in at least two pieces when they come in to check on why no one has seen you. You will get no other incentive but keeping your miserable life."

Tere was there in a blink, carefully pulling her arms to bring the knives from the man's throat. "Lily, hold on a moment." He turned to the bank official. "I don't know if you've heard, Mister Edgar, but a man who people called a hero has returned from retirement. That man is infuriated by people stealing others' belongings, especially when they turn around and try to bilk money—or other things—from honest people to get the things back. If you think our fiery redhead here is vicious, you have a surprise coming when this man decides the world is better off without you."

"What are you talking about?" Tannis said.

"Erent Caahs is back in the heroing business."

"Erent Caahs is dead."

Tere smirked. Then he shot four arrows in rapid succession, cutting the wicks from three candles on the other side of the room and impaling the center candle in the candle holder. "Is he?"

Tere held the door open for Lily as she carried the box of her uncle's things out of the bank.

"Do you think that's all of it?" Jia asked.

"Oh, I would bet it is. Would *you* want us to come back to complain about items being missing?"

Jia laughed. "Not me. That guy didn't seem too smart to me, though."

"Smart enough not to tempt fate when an angry Erent Caahs was staring him in the face, white eyes or not," Aeden said. "I believe the man almost soiled himself."

Even Urun had a smile on his face, though he didn't go so far as to laugh out loud.

"Thank you, Tere," Lily said. "Even if I would have carved him up, he wouldn't have cooperated as readily as with you."

"My pleasure. At least the name is good for something."

FIFTEEN

Urun Chinowa couldn't shake the strange feeling he'd been having lately. The insidious sensation was ever-present, but as much as he tried to focus on it, tried to identify what it was, it was as elusive as dandelion fluff in a breeze.

He ate dinner in relative silence. Confiding in his friends about what had been weighing on his mind bought him some time before they would question his reticence to speak, so he methodically chewed, only half-listened to their conversations, and excused himself when he'd had his fill of food and drink.

"I thought you'd bring the box of your uncle's things with you so we could see what is in there," Jia told Lily.

"No. I don't think he would mind me looking, or even showing the rest of you, but it's not something I'm comfortable doing in the middle of a common room."

"Oh, right. I guess I wasn't thinking. What do you think it contains? Books, old love letters, maybe paintings or pictures?"

"No," Tere said. "It's probably stuff from when he was

younger. Strangely colored stones, an eagle feather, curious bones from a small animal...that kind of stuff."

The two women goggled at Tere.

"Really?" Lily said.

Aeden, who'd had his mouth open, closed it quickly.

"What were you going to say?" Jia asked him.

"Nothing. Nothing at all."

Lily laughed. "After dinner, we can go up to my room and look at what's in there, okay? I'm curious, too, but I have no idea what he would hang onto for so many years. We'll find out as soon as we're finished eating."

Urun wasn't really interested in another man's keepsakes. "I'm going to go find a park or step outside the city to the forest so I can be more surrounded by nature," he told them. Aeden offered to go with him, followed quickly by Tere doing the same thing, but the whole point of going into the trees was to be alone with the natural world. "Thank you, but I'll be fine. I need to calm myself and soak up the natural energy of the trees and plants."

He looked for a park, but since he hadn't seen one of any great size since he'd been in the city and he didn't want to ask someone for directions, he took the nearest exit from the city to the forest that surrounded Satta Sarak. It was funny. The last time he had been in the city, he ended up in the Mellanor Forest by no intention of his own. They'd been fleeing the Falxen then. The brace that chased him, Tere, and Aila included Lily and Jia. How things had changed since then.

The forest was especially meaningful to him, as it had been named after Mellaine, the Goddess of Nature and Osulin's mother. That would make her his grandmother, in a way. That very nearly brought a chuckle to his lips.

The soothing energy of the forest went to work on him as soon as he crossed into the vegetation. He continued further in, hands brushing some of the bushes and grasses that grew in between the ancient, gnarled trees he encountered as he passed through the most domesticated border toward the heart of the forest. He wouldn't go that far, of course—he didn't have the time—but the shift from nature tinged with interference from civilization to a clearer reflection of the forest itself was like a cool breeze blowing over him.

The nature priest found a nice patch of soft grass and sat down on it, cross-legged. He closed his eyes and soaked up the ambient energy.

He lost track of time, so he didn't know how long he'd been there when a familiar voice spoke to him.

"Urun Chinowa, my beloved priest."

Urun's eyes immediately snapped open and he scrambled to reposition himself on his knees toward the voice. "My Goddess."

A warm pale light shone in front of him, though he heard no footsteps or any other kind of movement.

"Do not kneel, my priest. You are not a trained animal that you need to demonstrate your obeisance so. Look to me that I might see your face."

He raised his eyes to see her, standing a few feet in front of him. Osulin, Goddess of Nature. His patroness. She appeared as she always did, a beautiful woman with green glowing skin and shining green hair. Her emerald eyes sparkled, making his heart ache with her beauty. The last time he had seen her, she had come back from the brink of extinction in the Mellafond, only to show her power and bring life back to Saevel, the arba huntress and tracker who had died.

"My Goddess," he said again. "I had not expected to see you. I merely came to feel the peace of the trees. At times I miss my home in the Grundenwald."

"Does the task I have set for you chafe so?"

"No! I didn't mean it that way. I am...out of sorts of late. I came to erase the effects of being in cities so often. I had not expected the privilege of seeing you. Are things...well?"

Her laugh, a mix between tinkling bells and the burble of a

stream washed over him. "I have been keeping myself occupied in trying to determine the secrets the world seems to hold from me. I have learned little that makes sense or that I can share with you."

"I understand," he said.

"One thing, however, not only *can* I share, but I *must*. It is the reason I have called you to this place tonight. I have another task for you to complete. Not instead of your charge to help the Malatirsay, but in addition to it. In fact, doing what I will assign you will indeed aid those fighting on the side of light, life, and nature."

"I will do whatever you ask of me. What is the task?"

"I have felt a great disturbance that must be investigated and resolved. It is at the place called Life's Cradle."

Urun's eyes opened wide at the name. "Life's Cradle? Does it truly exist? I had thought it was metaphorical."

"It exists, and has done so for countless millennia. There is a corruption, something polluting that sacred place. I would that you were to go there, my priest. Investigate this corruption and remedy it, or I fear there will be dire consequences."

"Is it—"

"Like the Mellafond? No. It is not the same taint, though it feels as powerful. That place, so deeply connected to life magic, would be treacherous for me to enter. As with the Mellafond, I sense that it may overwhelm me. I like not that magic so powerful as to daunt a goddess exists, but perhaps, as before, you may be successful where I would most likely be trapped. Such is the great strength and versatility of mortal humans."

"I will go, of course, my goddess, but...are the legends true? Is the Cradle in the lands to the south, a territory that split off in the sundering?"

"It is true."

Urun moved his mouth, like he was chewing something

that would not break down, and tried to force words out. All he emitted was a squeaking sound.

Osulin's laugh tinkled again. "Do not be so timid, my priest. I am well aware of the dangers Aesculus has put in place to keep those lands separate. In that, I can provide aid. Here is a talisman. It will ease your passage, hide you from or repel the monsters that dwell in the depths. It will aid you a little as well in the unnatural currents of the ocean, but it is not proof against all the might of the sea. With it and a skillfully crewed vessel, you should be able to accomplish the journey."

She handed him a small token, a carved stone the color of emerald, but more like smooth rock than a gem. The design on it swirled like a frozen whirlpool but he could sense motion within it. And magic. A hole had been bored through one edge and threading it was a thin strand of some kind of string, but not one he'd seen before. He could sense its power and had no doubt he could use even such a hair-thin section of it to lift great weights. No human strength could break it.

"Wear this around your neck. Do not lose it, or you may not survive the return trip. I would provide more aid than this, but I am still rationing the power I have. It would not do in any case. Though my mother and Aesculus had an agreement for the waters upon the land, too much help from my hand would draw undue attention. You would not benefit from that at all."

Urun placed the charm around his neck and tucked it into his shirt. "Thank you. I will make my way to the south and cross the ocean as I may. How will I find Life's Cradle?"

"It is not so far. The first land south of the place called Squalls Landing is the island of Visuren, though its size might tempt scholars to call it another continent. Once you make landfall, you must find the precise location. With the movement from the shifting, it could be anywhere on that massive island."

Urun bowed his head to the goddess. "I will find it. I thank you for the protective charm."

"I regret only that I cannot do more for your assignment. Please make haste. The corruption is growing and I know not how long the heart of all life magic will be able to withstand it."

"I will go immediately."

"Go with my blessing, Urun Chinowa. It is not an exaggeration to say that the world's fate may rely upon you. Farewell for the moment. I will contact you again when I am able."

"Farewell, my Goddess."

Osulin smiled at Urun and faded away into nothing right in front of him. He watched until the last tiny glow from her was gone and he ran as fast as he could back to the others.

CHAPTER
SIXTEEN

L ily and her friends spent more time in the common room than she had expected. She wasn't going to complain, though. With the trip to Drusca finished and the master safe in the city, and now with their journey to Satta Sarak finished and the successful retrieval of her uncle's keepsakes, she was more than ready to relax a little, even if she was curious to look in the box she'd gotten from the bank. Even Jia, who seemed most interested in seeing what was considered the sum of Arten Fisher's life collected into one box, didn't seem in a hurry to end the relaxing meal and the chatting over wine and ale.

After some time, though, the group finally left their table to go up to Lily's room and see what they'd come all this way to get. On the way up the stairs, Lily had wondered if Master Liluth was still in Drusca or if she had finished her mission and headed back home to the Academy. She felt a little bad still about changing all their plans and making it necessary for the master to contact the Academy for more escorts.

They piled into the room as she retrieved the box, ready to satisfy her curiosity—and that of her friends—about what the wooden container held. It wasn't heavy, and didn't look like much. Only a thin-walled wooden crate the bank provided. The lid fit over the top but did not possess a latch or lock. It could be lifted up with little effort. She began to do just that when her door slammed open.

Four sets of blades left sheaths and scabbards, glinting in the lamp light, before the door could even bounce off the wall. The reflexes of the heroes had been honed to an extreme degree through facing constant danger over the last several months. Someone would have to be a complete idiot to charge the group gathered in the room.

Urun didn't even blink at all the bared steel in front of him.

"I have to leave immediately. Osulin has given me a task and the fate of life magic in the world depends upon it."

For a moment, the room was completely silent, so much so that Lily could hear the whisper of the burning lamp wick. The spell was broken by Tere slamming his knives into their scabbards on his waist.

"For Surus's sake, Urun," Tere said. "Rushing in like that is a good way to be sliced into little bits, even if it was on accident."

The nature priest blinked at the archer. His eyes darted, finally noticing everyone else, their weapons still out and on guard. "Oh. Sorry. Osulin just appeared to me and I have to leave."

Aeden replaced his swords in his scabbards. "Urun, calm yourself, and slow down. I'm sure you have a few minutes to tell us what this is all about. Can you do that?"

"I...I can. Yes. I'll tell you all about it."

"Good. Thank you."

"As you know, I went to the forest to relax and gain some peace. Osulin appeared to me and told me that there's some kind of corruption at Visuren and that I had to go and try to stop it. It's like what happened in the Mellafond in the sense that she said it would be dangerous for her to try to do anything herself. She's more sensitive to corruption of pure life magic."

"Wait a minute," Aeden said. "Visuren? What is that?"

Urun's mouth dropped open and he stared at the Croagh. "Visuren. Life's Cradle?"

"Never heard of it."

"Oh for..." he took a breath, then started again. "Sorry. Okay, I'll give you the short version. After Surus created all other life on Dizhelim, he moved them from the Origin to what was called Life's Cradle: Visuren. Animals, people, all things that moved. From there, these creatures migrated north and out to the west to settle in different parts of the world. Of course, this was long before the sundering where the land broke up and the Aesculun Ocean rushed in between them, creating the great islands of the world."

"When Surus created all life?" Tere said. "He didn't do that. It was the Power itself that created all life, including Surus."

Urun exhaled loudly through his nose. "No. The Power created Surus and then used him to create everything else, including the other original gods and all the races on Dizhelim. Osulin told me the details of the story herself."

"Oh. I didn't know that. Why didn't you correct me when I explained all that creation stuff to Aeden all those months ago, just before you and Aila got into your first argument about Vandalism?"

"It didn't seem important at the time. It didn't affect what you were trying to explain, so I saw no need to correct you and sound like some kind of know-it-all."

"I appreciate that," Tere said. "Still, I wish I'd known I was wrong."

"Well, you do now. Can we please move on?"

Tere rolled his hand at the wrist, indicating for him to continue.

"Thank you. So, Osulin said the heart of Visuren is

corrupted and that I need to go. I'll leave in the morning to try to find passage."

"Passage?" Aeden asked.

"Yes. The name Visuren isn't just used for the Cradle itself, but the entire island on which it resides. When the one continent was split, it became separated from Promistala."

"But we can't get to the islands," Jia said. "There are monsters and tidal currents and all kinds of things meant to kill anyone who tries."

"There are," Urun said. "That's why Osulin gave me this." He pulled the talisman from his shirt and held it up for everyone to see."

"There's a lot of magic concentrated in that one little stone," Tere said. "It's hard to look at, it glows so brightly in the magical matrix."

"I would hope so. Osulin said it will keep the monsters away, for the most part, and it will help with the dangerous currents as well. The island is the closest one south of Squalls Landing."

"Closest," Aeden said. "What does that mean? Is it ten miles? A hundred?"

"I don't know, and I don't care. If I could get going faster by leaving right now, I would do so. I'll save time, though, if I take one of the riverboats down the Gwenore River before going toward Horizon by land."

"Horizon?" Lily said. "I thought you said Squalls Landing."

Urun nodded. "The island is directly south from Squalls Landing, but traveling southeast from Horizon will get me there, too. Plus, Horizon is bigger than the other city, so the chances of finding a ship's captain who's willing to take me are better."

"If you can find anyone to do it at all," Tere said.

"I'll have to find a way, even if it's taking a rowboat."

"Okay, then," Aeden said. "I think we should get some

sleep. We'll need to get up early to try to catch a riverboat. We can pick up supplies at a town along the route."

"We?" Urun said.

"Of course. Do you think we're going to let you go on your own to help a goddess in protecting the origin point of all life magic? Are you daft? If there were ever a mission the Malatirsay was meant to take part in, this is it. We'll have to settle for half the Malatirsay, but that's just how things go."

"I...didn't expect anyone else to go with me," Urun said softly.

"Boy," Tere said, slapping the priest on the shoulder. "How long will it take for you to get it through your head? Even if it wasn't as important as what Aeden just said, we're not about to let you go alone. You need to come to terms with it: we're family and we'd never let you go off into danger without trying to help you. So, do as Aeden suggests. Get some sleep, get your gear—and your mind—together, and meet us down at the common room before the sun rises. We shouldn't have any trouble finding passage down river. It's a busy stretch from here to the ocean."

"Thank you," Urun said. "I'll be happy to have you along. I feel much better about going into the unknown with my friends."

"We'll watch your back, Urun," Jia said. "Besides, going across the ocean? I mean, who ever gets to do that? It's going to be fun!"

Lily stared at her fellow former Falxen, wondering at her sanity. Important, yes. Dangerous? Definitely. Fun? The blue-haired woman had to be out of her mind. She shook her head and began to bid the others goodnight, but stopped herself. Glancing at the box, she made up her mind.

She bit her lower lip. Urun had helped her at the very beginning, when no one had any reason to be nice to her. Along with the other Falxen, she'd hunted them down to kill them, but the nature priest healed her of her injuries, ones

Tere had given her, and rightly so. She had always liked Urun, though he was strange sometimes, and she would do nearly anything for him.

But she couldn't help him now.

"I can't go with you," she blurted out.

"What do you mean you can't go with us?" Tere asked.

"I...I have to get back to Drusca. My uncle's life is on the line. I need to bring his things back and then talk him out of doing something stupid. If I take a detour, he might think something happened to me and he may go ahead and take his own life. I really want to go and help you, Urun, and your goddess, but I have to look out for my uncle."

Tere gave her a disappointed look, but it was Aeden who spoke.

"Didn't your uncle promise you that he wouldn't harm himself until you returned and the two of you had your discussion?"

"Yes, he did. But the way he's thinking lately, he may find an excuse to do it anyway."

"Is your uncle an honorable man?" Tere asked. "Honest?"

"Yes."

"Even in his mourning, do you believe you can trust him and his word?"

"Yes, but..."

"No one wants to bully you into going with us, Lily," Jia said. "If you trust that he'll stand by his word, though, we could really use your help in this. It's something even a goddess couldn't handle on her own."

"I don't want to abandon you all, but my uncle..." She put her hands to the sides of her head and squeezed. "Arrrgghhh! I don't want to choose."

Aeden raised a hand to get her attention. "I have an idea. We send a message. At the very least, Master Qydus is at the Academy. Marla may be there by now, too. One of them can message Master Liluth, if she's still in Drusca. If not, then they can send a messenger. The message can let your uncle know that you have the items but that something very important has come up that could mean the lives of your friends. That way, he knows you're planning on coming back, that you already got his things, and he can even send a return message."

"I don't know. Can I sleep on it and tell you my decision in the morning?"

"Sure," Tere said. His disappointed expression had changed to a concerned one. "We don't want to cause you any trouble, girl. It would be nice to have you along, though. These others are crap at hitting enemies from far away."

CHAPTER
SEVENTEEN

Lily didn't sleep much before it was time to meet everyone in the common room. They'd had a late night anyway and though she knew that Aeden probably had been up for two hours training already, she felt like someone had sucked every last bit of energy from her body.

She dragged herself down the stairs, carrying her pack and saddlebags. And Uncle Arten's box. Aeden was eating breakfast, as she knew he'd be, but the others weren't there yet.

Rapid footsteps behind her caused her to jolt and dance to the side to avoid a collision, but they stopped at exactly the same time a hand landed on her shoulder.

"Good morning, sunshine!" Jia said, laughing. "Actually, with that hair, maybe I should call you sun*rise*."

"Very funny. I know you can run around, even stomp and jump, without making any sound. You only did that to startle me, huh?"

"Maaaaaybe." Lily's friend smiled at her in the most adorable way.

"I'm glad you're in a good mood, but I didn't sleep much, so pardon me if I don't caper around with you."

"It's fine. We can save the capering for later. Hmmm, I guess I'll need a cape for that? Is my cloak sufficient?"

"Come on. Let's get some breakfast. Ugh. Morning people."

By the time she and Jia joined Aeden at the table, Tere and Urun appeared on the stairs. They all greeted each other and began eating. Lily appreciated that they didn't push her. No matter what she decided, they would be supportive, which made it all the harder for her to reach a conclusion.

When she couldn't take it any longer, she told them what she'd do. "I decided to take your advice. We'll send a message and I'll go with you to try and not die on some island far away."

"That's great," Jia said.

"Do you want to write the message, Aeden, or should I?"

"The message to your uncle, the message within the message, should come from you. Either you or I can write the other part of it, telling our other friends what's going on and asking Marla or Master Qydus to get a message to either Master Liluth or to send a messenger to Arten."

"Uh, I think asking for that kind of thing is probably better coming from you," she said. "I'll tell you what I want the message for my uncle to say and you can incorporate it in there, if that's okay."

"It's fine with me. Do you want to send it now or wait until we're on the boat?"

"Now, please. The sooner we can get this started the better."

Aeden took out the message tablet and pulled the stylus from its little holder in the side. After Lily told him what she wanted to say to her uncle, he started scratching out a message.

GOOD MORNING. THIS IS AEDEN AND I HAVE NEWS AND A REQUEST. FIRST, THE NEWS.

OSULIN HAS CONTACTED URUN AND CHARGED HIM WITH GOING TO TRY TO STOP CORRUPTION ON VISUREN. SHE GAVE HIM A TALISMAN THAT WILL ALLOW US TO CROSS THE OCEAN WITHOUT GETTING TOO MUCH ATTENTION FROM SEA MONSTERS AND TROUBLE FROM THE DANGEROUS CURRENTS. WE'LL ALL BE GOING WITH URUN TO HELP OUT.

THAT BRINGS US TO THE REQUEST. LILY HAS PICKED UP A BOX OF HER UNCLE'S ITEMS FROM A BANK IN SATTA SARAK. HE'S HAVING ISSUES AND SHE'S AFRAID HE MIGHT DO SOMETHING FOOLISH, SEEING AS HE HAS BEEN CLAIMING HE'S GOING TO COMMIT SUICIDE. IF MASTER LILUTH IS STILL IN DRUSCA, WOULD IT BE POSSIBLE TO CONTACT HER AND HAVE HER RELAY THE MESSAGE BELOW TO ARTEN FISHER? IF NOT, COULD A MESSENGER BE SENT? LILY IS AFRAID HER DELAY MIGHT RESULT IN PROBLEMS FOR HER UNCLE. HERE'S THE MESSAGE SHE WOULD LIKE HER UNCLE ARTEN FISHER TO BE GIVEN:

"UNCLE ARTEN. I HAVE OBTAINED WHAT YOU SENT ME TO SATTA SARAK TO GET, BUT HAVE BEEN CALLED AWAY ON AN EMERGENCY THAT COULD MEAN THE SAVING OR LOSS OF MANY LIVES. PLEASE UNDER-STAND THAT I WOULD NOT TAKE THIS DETOUR IF IT WEREN'T FOR THE EXTREME DANGER TO OTHERS IT WOULD POSE IF I DON'T HELP. I WILL BRING THE BOX OF YOUR MEMENTOS TO YOU AS SOON AS POSSIBLE. PLEASE TAKE CARE OF YOURSELF AND KNOW THAT I WILL DO MY BEST TO GET TO YOU SOON.

LILY"

MARLA, IF YOU'RE BACK AT THE ACADEMY, COULD YOU PLEASE TAKE CARE OF THIS. IF NOT, I'M HOPING I CAN IMPOSE ON MASTER QYDUS TO MAKE THIS HAPPEN. WE'LL LET YOU KNOW HOW THINGS ARE GOING, IF WE CAN. BE SAFE, EVERYONE.

Aeden read out the message as he wrote it so everyone knew what he was sending.

"That's good," Lily said. "I hope everything works out and my uncle gets the message."

"I'm sure everything will be taken care of," Tere told her. "How about we all get going? The sooner we get to the docks, the better chance we'll have of finding a boat going south."

By the time they reached the dock, a message had appeared on the message tablet. Tere left them to go and find a boat so they could read the message and answer it.

AEDEN, ET AL, THIS IS MASTER QYDUS WRITING. I SAW YOUR MESSAGE AND USED THE OTHER MESSAGE TABLET CONNECTED TO THE ONE MASTER LILUTH HAS. SHE RAN INTO SOME DELAYS AND SO IS STILL IN DRUSCA. SHE WILL PASS ON YOUR MESSAGE TO LILY'S UNCLE. I UNDERSTAND HE'S GRIEVING FOR HIS WIFE WHO PASSED ON AND WOULD LIKE TO EXPRESS MY CONDOLENCES. IF THERE IS ANYTHING ELSE I OR THE ACADEMY CAN DO TO HELP, DO NOT HESITATE TO ASK.

AS FOR YOUR UPCOMING JOURNEY, IT SEEMS YOU WILL BE MAKING HISTORY ONCE AGAIN. TO VISIT LIFE'S CRADLE AND TO DO SO WITH A TOKEN FROM OSULIN HERSELF IS THE STUFF OF LEGENDS. TAKE CARE OF YOURSELVES. I SHALL WAIT ANXIOUSLY TO HEAR THAT YOU HAVE COME THROUGH YOUR MISSION, SUCCESSFUL AND UNSCATHED.

Another message was also waiting.

AEDEN, YOU AND THE OTHERS BE VERY CAREFUL. IT'S OBVIOUS THAT YOUR TRIP IS WHAT MY VISION WAS REFERRING TO. SARIA TOLD US ALL ABOUT VISUREN AND LIFE'S CRADLE, AS WELL AS THE DANGERS OF TRAVELING ACROSS THE OCEAN. DON'T YOU GO AND GET YOURSELVES INJURED OR WORSE. YOU BETTER SEND MESSAGES OFTEN SO WE WON'T WORRY AS MUCH. I'LL LET YOU KNOW IF I HAVE ANY MORE VISIONS THAT CAN HELP YOU. I MISS YOU ALL.

—FAHTIN

"That makes me feel a lot better," Lily admitted. "My uncle will get his message and our friends know what we're about. Thank you, Aeden."

"You're welcome. All I did was write, not one of my greatest strengths, but we got the point across. I am a little worried, though. Neither Marla nor Evon answered. They have two message tablets between them and they must have found each other by now. I hope they're okay."

"I'm sure they're—"

Tere appeared suddenly as if he'd been invisible and then magically reappeared. "I got us passage on a riverboat. Get this, the boat is Brenain's Tears."

"Brenain, the heroine who stole magic from the god Migae?" Jia asked.

"Yes, yes. That's not what I'm talking about, though. The riverboat, Brenain's Tears. It's the one we booked passage on when we were here last. We were going to take it north toward the Academy, but you and your other Falxen friends decided to chase us instead. The captain remembered me and though he said he couldn't give me our money back, he did cut some off the price because of it."

"That's quite a coincidence that it's the same boat," Aeden said.

"Maybe it's a good omen," Jia chirped.

"Better than being chased by assassins, in any case," Tere deadpanned. "The boat leaves in an hour, so we should get over there and get aboard. We'll be heading south soon."

The group made it to the dock with time to spare. Tere led them over to the vessel they would be spending the next several days on and, after they watched their horses being loaded onto the vessel, they went aboard themselves.

The riverboat was a portly looking vessel, at least to Lily. She'd taken passage on riverboats before, but they had all seemed to be longer and thinner than the one before them. Its

141

shape was deceiving, though, because as she approached it to board, she realized it was just as long as others she'd seen, but swollen as if it had a belly.

Tere noticed her tilted head and he chuckled. "It takes cargo *and* passengers. The design is not common, but it does its job in not only carrying things up and down the river, but it has more rooms than most vessels. We didn't pay for separate rooms for everyone, but we do have two private rooms split between the men and women. It cost more than a communal room with everyone sleeping in bunks together, but I hate those things."

She smiled at the old archer. "You really know how to show a girl a good time."

"I do," he said. "That, and I didn't want to hear you whine about how you didn't sleep because some smelly man snored all night long right beside or above you. In a bunk above you, I mean."

She chuckled. "I knew what you meant. Thanks. I appreciate it more than you know."

As they boarded, a hefty man dressed in colors that would have made a Gypta grin stood with a thinner fellow in a subservient stance watching as the deck hands prepared to shove off.

"Ah, Captain Arstat Filz," Tere said. "These are the other passengers we spoke of."

He introduced all of them and the captain nodded politely at each of them. Lily couldn't tell if he smiled or frowned due to the bushiest beard and mustache she'd ever seen. She wasn't sure about his attitude until he spoke.

"Welcome aboard. You've got two of the private rooms. There's chow in the galley twice a day. You let me know if there's anything amiss or if you need anything. I'd ask you to please stay out of the men's way as they're working, but when we moor each night, you can move freely about the deck without having to worry about tripping them up."

Tere thanked the captain and his first mate—as he told the others the thin man was—and they found their rooms. They were cramped and smelled of mildew, but so did the entire ship, so Lily thought nothing of it. Soon enough, the Brenain's Tears jerked into motion and they were on the way.

EIGHTEEN

T he shadowy figure had listened to the meeting between Ironspike and Waterdancer, two of the high-ranking members of the Falxen Council, and the thin, pale woman who kept referring to the Dark Council. He wasn't sure what that was but it seemed important. The proper name was apparent by the way she said it, and even the two Falxen spoke about it with respect. He would have to research it further to discover more specifics.

After he left the estate where the meeting had been held, he headed to a safe house he's used before, one he didn't think any living Falxen knew of. What he'd heard still cycled through his mind. It wasn't unheard of for very wealthy clients to request a blade or two for long-term service, but what the three had spoken about was much greater than anything in the recent histories he knew about.

A force of Falxen, acting as soldiers in some army that, if he understood correctly, hardly existed at the moment. True, that was the type of work the Falxen had originally been created for, but since the time when Maser "The Blade" Toroli had been alive, the shadow was unaware of such a thing happening.

And for what? To match armies, soldier for soldier with the vaunted Hero Academy and the mysterious force of dark monsters opposing them?

Once he arrived at the safehouse, he busied himself with unwrapping and re-wrapping his arms with strips of cloth he kept with him at all times. It was a quirk, something that might allow enemies to identify him—though he'd never really made any attempt at disguising himself or covering his face—but it was soothing to him. Cathartic. And more.

The odd habit had saved his life not so long ago. When he and the eleven other Blades under his command tracked and confronted their prey, he had been severely injured. So injured, in fact, that he had not thought he would survive it. Bleeding, slashed nearly to ribbons, he had fled the battle, leaving those remaining of his brace to die.

When he had made it a fair distance from the ones who had done the damage, the blue woman in particular, he had used the cloth he kept wrapped around his arms to bind up his wounds. It was a shoddy job, but it helped him to survive long enough to find herbs to slow the bleeding, dull the pain, and allow him to hunker down rather than becoming a corpse in the desolate area in which he'd fled. Broken Reach was not the best place to be injured and stranded.

Featherblade tied off the cloth, reminiscing about that day, the first mission he'd ever failed. It took nearly three months to make his way back to Vatheca to report to the Falxen command and to explain what had happened. He couldn't go back to Satta Sarak for fear that his prey, which had split into two groups, would find him there and finish him off. He was so weak that it was more than ten days before he moved much more than a few miles from where he hid, waiting for his injuries to stabilize. With only a knife and his knowledge of edible plants and herbs, he had come back from the brink of death to regain enough strength first to hunt and get more food, and then to travel all the way back to the Falxen head-quarters.

Even after he arrived, it was still months before he was fit once again to take missions. Surprisingly, he was not chastised or punished for the decimation of both braces under his command. The half that had gone after the archer, the priest, and that small woman apparently not only had most of their members slaughtered, but two of them—Pheonixarrow and Shadeglide—had actually joined their former prey. He still wasn't clear on exactly what happened there.

During his convalescence, Featherblade researched, learned many things, and spent a great deal of time meditat-ing. He had always done such things, but with so much time available, he took to the tasks with a passion. Doing so, he found out about a surprising development.

As it turned out, the blue woman he had originally been sent to eliminate was the former leader of the group of dark monsters that was the source of much of the news being passed around. She also had turned her side and joined the strange group of people he and his Blades—all of them experi-enced and deadly in their own right—had hunted. What was it about that group and, maybe more importantly, what was their connection with the monsters and Featherblade's former employer?

It all became more and more curious.

His health was regained and, if anything, his skills were even better than before from his experiences and hardship. Now, the mystery of the dark monsters and the small group that opposed them was like a burr digging into his brain. In a place he couldn't retrieve it or soothe. With his health and those skills, he had investigated even more than books or tavern news could provide. Resorting to following and eaves-dropping on two high-level Falxen was maybe not the best move for a Blade wanting to get back into the good graces of

Falxen command, but he simply could not let the mystery go. One way or another, he would find out what was going on.

Featherblade was afraid that when he did, he might find that the Falxen, to whom he had always been loyal and believed were honorable, might be dipping their toes into a pool that turned out to be not only vile, but dishonorable as well. If, as it sounded from the spied upon conversation, Falxen would be involved in supporting monsters that had come to destroy every living person, the assassin might have to part ways with the assassin organization.

It might even come to pass that he may become an enemy of the greatest assassins on Dizhelim.

CHAPTER
NINETEEN

O nce the party was settled in on the Brenain's Tears, it was a whole lot of waiting around. Lily had almost forgotten that part and parcel of traveling by boat was boredom and the inability to go someplace else to search for more stimulating things to do. It was this, more than her previous anticipation, that made her ask her friends a simple question.

"Should we look at Uncle Arten's things now?"

Her friends, apparently not looking forward to a few days in exactly the same spot on the boat, even though it had seemed large only a few hours ago, readily agreed. She retrieved the box from the room she shared with Jia and the group found a space below deck where they wouldn't get in the crew's way.

"I'm sure he wouldn't mind us looking at it," she said, biting her lower lip.

"You know him better than we do," Aeden told her. "If it's a problem, we don't have to see whatever is in the box. You can look through it on your own."

She was sure he meant it to be helpful, but that tiny part of her still nagged that she didn't have express permission to share his secrets with others. He had told her that there was at least one thing in there that he had always planned on giving her, but still, she wasn't completely comfortable with what she was doing. Why hadn't she asked him before she left? She was fairly certain he wouldn't mind. Most of the pressure came from herself.

"It'll be fine," she said, even as she had an urge to shake her head. She took the lid off the box quickly, knowing that once she started, it would be too late for the internal arguments.

The first things she pulled out were several portraits on thin pieces of wood. Most of the people pictured were strangers to her, but one painting caught her eye as she handed it around to the others. An involuntary hitch in her voice dragged Tere's head around to look at her, his eyebrows arched in question.

"It's me with my parents. I must have been about five years old at the time. The artist got the color right. I was very pale and sickly during that time.

"Aww, you're so cute," Jia said, patting Lily's leg. "You do look a little drawn, but nothing could hide the beauty that was there for you to grow into."

Maybe it was the shock at seeing her parents, but she had to clear her throat and blink rapidly at Jia's words to keep from getting sappy and stupid. She moved on to a small stack of books. She skimmed the titles as she handed them to Tere, who would then hand it to Aeden, and onto Urun, finally to Jia. Three were history books of Drusca and the nation it belonged to, Sutania. Two were collections of hero stories.

"I remember these two well. I liked it when my uncle would tell me stories from memory. With nothing in his hands, he would act out the motions of combat and would even make faces and change his voice. Sometimes, though, he'd read stories from books, including these two."

She handed them on, waiting to see what Tere would do. He flipped through them, but didn't comment. She released a breath, but it was too early.

"Most of these are stories of Erent Caahs," Aeden said, and she immediately felt her face flush.

"Most books of hero stories are," Jia pointed out. "He is the most famous hero in the last few hundred years, at least."

"*He* is sitting right here," Tere grumped.

"Oh, and we appreciate that," Jia said in a voice she would expect one to use to talk to their cherished dog. "Yes we do."

Tere released a breath in a hiss. Not an angry one, but sort of a laugh that hadn't quite gathered enough steam. She smiled at the old archer.

"Moving on," she said. She reached to the bottom corner of the box and found a smooth stone with odd coloring. It was a dull green overall, but it had streaks and spots of red, yellow, and even some blue. She recognized it immediately and this time, there was no coming back from the wash of emotion that struck her. Her eyes welled up, though she was proud that none of it escaped as tears.

"Are you all right, girl?" Tere asked gently.

Lily sniffed and blinked away the moisture. "I'm fine." She rolled the stone in her hand, then handed it to him. "I found this and carried it around for weeks. I loved how I could see different colors if I moved it around in the light, especially when it was wet. I rubbed it constantly, because someone had told me that if I did that, the oils in my hands would make it seem like it was wet all the time. One time, when my uncle had been having a hard time of things, I gave it to him to try to cheer him up. It was the first time I'd seen him cry. He accepted it, hugged me until I couldn't breathe, and I never really thought about it again after a few days later. I never did find out why he was depressed, but I remember that he seemed to be a little better after that."

"That's very sweet," Jia said. "It must have really helped for him to have kept it all these years with his other treasures."

Lily glanced over at Urun, who was inspecting one of the books. He'd been very quiet again after they decided to go with him. She wondered if he was okay. As if he heard her thoughts, he looked up and caught her eye. He gave her a smile and it seemed genuine. He was probably just deep in thought.

The next items she brought out made her gasp audibly. Two rings, bound with a bit of ribbon. They were simple, some kind of metal alloyed with gold. To her, though, they weren't important for their value, but what they represented.

"Gods. Where did he get these? They're my parents' rings."

"Are you sure they're the same ones?" Tere asked. "That simple design is popular."

"They're my parents'." She ran her fingers over them. "I used to play with them when I was a child, twist them around their fingers and run my hands over them. I'd never forget them. I wonder how he got them. When they were killed, I was too much in shock to check for what they had with them. Had they left them at my uncle's house on accident when we left Drusca or had someone sent them to him as the closest kin? Well, aside from me, but who even knew if I still lived? I'll have to ask him about them."

"He must have really loved your parents to put their rings in his treasure box," Aeden said.

"He did. They were very close." She stared at the rings, her fingers finding the unique little bumps and scratches on them. She handed them to Tere and turned her attention to the box again.

This time, her hand came out with several letters. She unfolded them and scanned them and their unfamiliar handwriting.

"Oh. These are all from Iriam Dufour, the daughter of Nadine, the healer. She tells them where she is and what she's doing. She writes about why she left, that she couldn't stand her parents always trying to push her into the healing profession like her mother and grandmother. The way she writes, she must have been very close to Uncle Arten and Aunt Elenya. The most recent one says she's in Rustek, a town in Telna. That was a few years ago. I wonder if she knows about my aunt dying. I also wonder why he kept his box all the way over here in Satta Sarak. Were there no banks in Sutania?"

She held the letters out for Tere to take and put her hand into the box to get the final two items. When she drew them out, Jia paused in her examination of the rings to exclaim, "Oooh."

Lily raised her arms so the others could see what she held. A pair of long knives in hard scabbards shone in the meager lamplight. The pommels were polished and the quillons reflected the lamp's glow, but the lacquered scabbards held whispers of the light in their dark paint, as if they held a whole world within them.

She drew one with a soft ringing sound. The blade had the soft curve she was so, so familiar with, the keen edge splitting the light striking it, the point dangerous even stationary as it was.

"Those look just like your long knives—and Tere's," Aeden said. "But they're smaller."

It was true. The blades were nearly identical—if shorter—copies of the weapons at her waist and those Tere had on his own belt, and rightfully so.

"These were made off the wooden knives I carried around everywhere when I was a girl," she told them. "I researched the style of Erent Caahs's blades for a long time before I spent months carefully carving them out in wood. My parents and my uncle laughed about my intensity, especially when I told them that if the only steel knife they would let me wield was a carving knife, then I would make a pair of hero's knives myself. Uncle Arten always told me he was going to have a pair made exactly like my wooden knives for me, but of good steel.

"I guess he actually did it." She slid the bared blade back into the scabbard and handed the pair to Tere, who exposed the blade again. "He must have commissioned them but they weren't ready in time for our last visit. He was probably going to give them to me the next time I saw him. But the next time I saw him was last week. Only nearly twenty years too late."

Tere twisted the blade in the air, mimicking half-hearted strikes. "The balance is nice. If it weren't for them being barely a foot long, *I'd* use them. They're fine blades."

Lily's eyes went to her knives and Tere's, both with sixteen-inch blades and a unique sweeping curve that made them so beautiful—if not nearly invisible—when the older archer used them. His slashes with them were a thing of beauty. "They were a good size for a girl. Maybe just a hair bigger than they should have been, but I would have grown into them in a year or so."

Tere passed them to Aeden, who also examined them closely. "They're beautiful," the Croagh said. "'Tis a shame he wasn't able to give them to you."

"I only hope he hadn't planned on using them to kill himself when I brought them back to him."

That soured the mood of everyone present, if the dropped eyes and mouths were any indication.

"Sorry," Lily said. "It's been on my mind a lot. I need to find a way to keep him from doing what he plans. I've already lost my parents. I don't want to lose him, too."

The knives made the circuit and Jia handed them back to Lily, who put them in the box with the other things.

"So, this is it?" she said. "Is this the sum of a man's life? I can't accept that. I'll try to put my worries away in this box until we finish our job on Visuren, but after that, I will do whatever I need to in order to keep my uncle alive and—somehow—thriving. If I have to give up all the traveling and hero quests to stay with him and watch him every day to make sure he survives, then I'll do it. He would have done the same for me. He *did* do the same for me."

The others had nothing to say. Tere took her hand as they returned to the deck to get fresh air and a bit of sunshine, but Lily only saw the dark clouds threatening them from the west.

TWENTY

A few hours later, as the group sat sullenly on the deck, Aeden leaned precariously over the side of the rail like he'd drunk too much. At the same time, Tere scrunched his eyes shut and put a hand to his head. Urun jumped like he'd been goosed.

Lily and Jia lunged for Aeden, each catching an arm and hauling him back to the deck.

"Aeden," Lily said. "Are you all right?"

"Unh. I got hit by a dizzy spell. Thanks for the save. I'd rather not be swimming and trying to catch the boat."

"Was it...?" Jia started.

"Yeah," Tere growled. "Another damn magical shift. That one caused everything in my sight to swirl. If I wasn't already sitting, I might have almost fallen like Aeden."

Aeden shook his head and worked his eyes, trying to regain his equilibrium. "Where's my pack? Oh, there it is. I need to find out if that was another well or just a random shift." He dug through his pack and pulled out the message tablet.

"Have we had any random shifts since we started finding the wells?" Tere asked. "I can't recall any. It seems like every time there is another one of those magical episodes, it's because someone has found a well and released it."

"True," Urun said, "but with how many wells we've found, it can be expected that someone else might run into one on accident. After all, most of the ones we've found were when we weren't looking for them."

Jia frowned at the priest. "Are you saying that people other than those from the Academy might find a well and release the magic, causing a shift?"

The priest shrugged. "Why not? I'm not concerned as much about some random person finding a well—they'd have to defeat or bypass the guardian, after all. What worries me is someone with the knowledge and power to beat the guardian taking control of the well and trying to use the magic for their own ends."

"Gods!" Aeden said, stylus in one hand and message tablet in the others. "Why haven't I ever considered that? You're right, Urun. What if someone wanted to hoard the magic, harness it in some way, instead of releasing it for the entire world to use. Is it even possible?"

"I don't see why not," Tere answered for the priest. "Maybe it's what we should have been doing all along. If we had that much powerful magic at our disposal, the animaru couldn't stand against us."

Jia gasped. "What if the animaru find a well? They've been alive for thousands of years. Some of them are very powerful mages. Maybe they can take control of the magic."

Urun ran his hand through his hair. "Have you not been paying attention? That's already happened. When we went to save Osulin in the Mellafond, one of the animaru mages had assimilated the magic of the swamp. It corrupted him even from his normal unnatural state, but they tried to do what we're talking about. They obviously know something about the wells. Or, at least, that one did. Aeden, those other animaru were looking for the well where you found all those books, right?"

"Why didn't you bring this up before, about the Mella-fond?" Aeden asked.

"I didn't really think about it? It seemed evident. The point I'm trying to make is that even though the shifts have been wells lately, it doesn't mean it's us or our friends necessarily freeing the wells. Uh, maybe check the tablet?"

Aeden blinked, then looked down at his hands, which held the tablet and the stylus. "There are no messages. I'll ask everyone what happened." He jotted a short message and looked back up at the others.

Tere raised an eyebrow. "What did you write?"

"Oh. Sorry." Aeden read off the short message he'd sent.

Was that another shift from a well being found? Who found it and what happened?

—Aeden

A moment later, another message appeared and the Croagh read it to his friends.

We felt it, too. It wasn't us, though. Marla? Evon? Is everyone all right?

—Fahtin

Another materialized on the tablet before he'd even finished reading the first one.

This is Master Qydus. We felt the shift at the Academy as well. We have no further information on it. Marla, Evon, were you involved? Please respond.

They waited, but no further messages came over the next fifteen minutes.

"It was probably Marla and the others," Lily said. "You know how those things are, though. They're probably recuperating from whatever trials or tests or battles they had to go through to free the well. They'll send a message soon, I'm sure, unless the message tablet was damaged or lost."

"Umm," Jia said, "with Evon and the others finding Marla and heading to Iracundia like they told us, they had two tablets between them. What are the chances of both being damaged or lost?"

"Enough with the conjecture," Tere said. "Trust in them. They'll tell us when they're able. In the meantime, you should probably keep the tablet handy, Aeden, so we'll know when more messages come through."

"Are you kidding?" Aeden said. "I'm going to keep it in my hand until we've solved this mystery. I'll be eating my next meal with one hand if we don't get a message by then."

Just before eating their evening meal, Aeden sent another message.

MARLA AND EVON? WHY AREN'T YOU ANSWERING? IS EVERYTHING OKAY? IT'S BEEN SEVERAL HOURS SINCE OUR FIRST MESSAGES.

—AEDEN

The answer finally came the next morning.

SORRY, EVERYONE. THIS IS MARLA. WE WERE A BIT BUSY. YES, IT WAS US. WE FOUND THE WELL OF ANGER ON THE ISLAND OF IRACUNDIA. WE RELEASED THE MAGIC AND WE'RE ON THE WAY BACK TO THE MAINLAND. WE'LL FILL YOU ALL IN WHEN WE GET BACK TO THE ACADEMY.

This time, it only took a few minutes for a response.

IRACUNDIA? YOU TRAVELED TO THE ISLAND NO PERSON HAS EVER VISITED AND DEPARTED ALIVE? PLEASE REPORT TO MY OFFICE AS SOON AS YOU RETURN. I ASSUME MASTER YXNA HAS FOUND YOU AND ACCOMPANIED YOU, THOUGH I AM NOT SURE IF IT IS WORSE THAT SHE JOINED YOU IN YOUR MADNESS OR THAT YOU WENT OFF ALONE ON SUCH AN ERRAND. I WILL WAIT ANXIOUSLY FOR YOUR ARRIVAL.

—QYDUS OKVIUS

The message tablet was filling with text faster than Aeden could read them out to his friends.

MARLA, THIS IS FAHTIN. I HAD ANOTHER VISION SINCE YOU LEFT. SEVERAL, IN FACT, BUT THE ONE I HAD ONLY TWO DAYS AGO INCLUDED SOMETHING ABOUT YOU. I'M NOT SURE IF IT MAKES ANY SENSE, BUT I SAW A DARK CREATURE STALKING YOU. IT SPRANG, BUT YOU INJURED IT, THEN TOOK IT PRISONER.

THOUGH IT SEEMED TO BE MADE OF SHADOW, AND I COULDN'T EVEN TELL WHAT FORM IT TOOK, I DID GET A FEELING ABOUT IT, A SENSATION I RECOGNIZED. I'VE FELT IT BEFORE, AT LEAST TWICE, IN VISIONS ABOUT THE DARK COUNCIL. I'M PRETTY SURE THE CREATURE IS A PERSON. THOUGH IT MIGHT NOT MEAN ANYTHING, WATCH OUT FOR ANY ATTACKER THAT AMBUSHES YOU. IT MIGHT HAVE BEEN SENT BY THE DARK COUNCIL. IT MIGHT EVEN BE PART OF THE DARK COUNCIL.

BE SAFE.

And finally...

THANKS, FAHTIN, BUT I READ TOO SLOWLY. WHILE I WAS READING YOUR MESSAGE, OUR PRISONER JUMPED OVERBOARD AND WE LOST HIM IN THE WATER. DOES THE NAME SIRAK ISAYU SEEM FAMILIAR TO YOU?

It does, though I don't know why. I'll try to focus on it the next time I have visions about the Dark Council, but I'm afraid I'll find out he's actually one of the thirteen. I'm sorry I didn't warn you in time.

"Well," Aeden said, "at least it's good Marla found the well. Bad luck about losing their prisoner. I can't wait to hear about that. How did that Sirak Isayu even follow them across the water like that?"

No one had an answer to that and no other message came the rest of that day. The next morning, the day they were to arrive in the hamlet of Teldon, the group were sitting in a small area of the deck they'd staked out for most of the trip, enjoying the breeze and watching the light play off the river's water.

Aeden looked around at his friends and chuckled. They were a group of bored individuals. Tere had his elbows on the rail, chin in his hands, looking out at nothing. Lily, sitting next to him, leaned back against a different part of the rail, her head back, her eyes straight up into the sky, or at least, they would have been watching the sky had they been open. She reminded Aeden of a cat basking in the sunlight.

Jia and Urun sat side-by-side leaning slightly toward each other as if they were threatening to fall over onto the other but never doing so. Both of them swayed with the motion of the boat and had a languid, lazy look about them.

As for Aeden, he sat cross-legged on the deck, carving a piece of driftwood he'd found floating close to the boat. He was attempting to make some epic heroic figure, but the more he carved and refined it, the more it came to resemble someone he knew. If the shapely body wasn't enough to prove it to himself, the detailed head did so. The figure didn't have hair, but fine strands of what looked like tentacles waving as of their own accord.

He hadn't even realized he'd been carving the likeness

until he was almost completely finished with it. He examined it and sighed.

"I'm sure she's fine," Tere said, not bothering to turn his head. Him being able to see literally from the back of his head always gave Aeden a bit of a shiver.

"I know. If anyone could be, it's her. This is the longest we've been apart since we met. I miss her. It's silly. I mean, I miss the others, too, but I've spent literally every minute with Khrazhti since we fought and she joined our side."

"She a fantastic woman," Jia said. "Can you imagine if the other animaru were like her, honorable and dutiful? All we'd have to do is sit down and talk with them and this whole thing would blow over. I miss her and the humor she's exploring."

Aeden tilted his head at Jia, wondering for just a second if she was teasing him. He decided she wasn't. The former Falxen loved laughing and could be a joker, but she was one of the kindest people Aeden knew. She was being sincere.

"Thanks, Jia. I agree. Sometimes I wonder what things will be like once we've won and life goes back to normal, or at least as normal as it can be after all this." He waved his hand out to encompass everything.

"It'll be great," she said, "and it'll be tough, and there will be laughing and crying and all the other things that make us human. Just like always. We'll look back and realize that the best times and the worst times of our lives were what we're living right now. It's just how things work."

Aeden turned the little figurine in his hands and chuckled again. "You're probably right."

Jia cocked an ear and scanned the area. "Do you hear that?"

Urun, surprisingly, was the one to answer, though it was with a question. "What?"

"That buzzing, like a bee is caught in someone's pocket or something."

Aeden closed his eyes and focused on his hearing. It took

several seconds, but then he heard a little vibration over the sloshing of the water and the crew talking in the background.

"Oh," he said, realizing what it was. He reached over and grabbed his pack, which he'd brought on deck with his carving knife and work in progress. He brought out the message tablet, which glowed faintly, showing there was a new message. "Great ears, Jia."

She tilted her head back and brushed her dark blue hair over her ears. "Why thank you, Aeden. I have always thought they were rather cute." She giggled at his poleaxed look, eliciting a laugh from him in turn.

"You're too much," he said, checking the message tablet to see who had written. "Oh, it's from Marla. She must have found time to write a longer message. Listen to this:

Aeden, regarding your trip to the island of Visuren, I have some information you may welcome. The captain of the ship we took to Iracundia has a brother, one whose life's ambition is to sail to one of the islands other than the one we visited. His name is Tesnair Balstad and he mostly works out of Squalls Landing, but at times sails as far south as Hirsen. I'm not sure how you can find him, but if you locate the man, the chances of him agreeing to take you are better than most. According to Asgeir Balstad, he and his brother are the only captains that will even entertain the thought of leaving sight of the mainland. Good luck and be safe.

Oh, also, Khrazhti asked me to tell you she's fine but misses sparring with you.

"That's good news," Urun said. He smirked, adding, "That Khrazhti misses you, too. But more seriously, with that ship captain's attitude and the talisman Osulin gave us, we should be able to make it to the island and complete our mission."

"If we can find the man," Tere said. "There are a lot of

ships that travel up and down the coast. Finding a particular captain in a reasonable amount of time won't be an easy task."

Aeden nodded. "Aye, but it's something we can manage, even if not quickly. We'll reach Teldon today, disembark, and head toward Horizon. With a city with docks that big, someone will know the captain's name. I'd expect that a man who has made it known he wishes to brave the oceans would be someone others remembered, even if it's because he was a joke to them."

Lily laughed. "He's right, there. Ship captains, warriors, merchants, it doesn't matter what profession one has. If someone is odd, there are jokes that spread far and wide. If he's a little outside of the normal trajectory, it'll only make him easier to find."

CHAPTER

TWENTY-ONE

At a sharp bend in the Gwenore River, about halfway between Satta Sarak and Caes Linur on the Aesculun shore, sat the small town of Teldon. The community's sole product wasn't a product at all, but the trade conducted on the great river. The bustle that greeted the party when they disembarked from the Brenain's Tears made that clear.

Lily kept a tight grip on Nobelflame's reins, both to keep the dark red gelding from running from the crowds around them and also to keep him from harming anyone who was stupid enough to jostle the animal in any of his touchy spots. All the horses were skittish enough after being cooped up for so long.

"We'll be through it in a moment," Tere said. "It's worse around the docks. A couple of streets over and we'll have breathing room. Just keep going straight ahead."

Lily had a few choice words she would have liked to have expressed. She was also sorely tempted to mount and ride Nobleflame through the throngs. Let them get out of *her* way instead of blithely bumping into her and expecting her to get out of theirs. She sighed, knowing she wouldn't do that, of course. But she did not enjoy crowds.

Tere was right, as always, and in a short time, the crowds dissipated and the group was able to mount up.

"The road between Teldon and Horizon is good," Tere told them. "A lot of trade from the riverboats goes overland from here. It's shorter than floating all the way down to Caes Linur and following the coast up to Horizon. We'll make good time, but it's nearly fifty miles, so it'll still take us more than a day. The good news is that there are several towns and villages along the way, so if we're lucky, we'll be able to get rooms instead of having to sleep alongside the road."

As it turned out, they were lucky. A bit more than a day and a half later, they caught sight of Horizon.

"What's that I see on the horizon?" Jia asked, chuckling as she pointed toward the buildings they could see as little smudges at the extent of their vision.

"Very funny, clever, and original," Tere said. Lily got the sense that if he could, he'd be rolling his eyes. "I'm sure no one has ever spoken that joke before."

Since it was evening when they arrived, the first order of business was to find rooms, which they did in a small inn near enough to the docks that they wouldn't have to travel far to search the next day. It was also just far enough from the docks to still be a nice, if moderately priced, place to stay. As with many cities, inns and taverns butted up against the docks tended to be a little rougher than what most typical folks wanted to deal with. Cheaper, sure, but still not as "civilized." Lily was happy to spend the extra coin so she didn't have to defend herself from the drunk and unruly men she would no doubt run into at a dockside inn.

After a good meal and a good night's sleep, the party was up and ready to search for Captain Tesnair Balstad.

"Don't get your hopes up," Tere cautioned them. "Marla said the man usually sails out of Squalls Landing. We'll search as best we can, but we might have to go all the way up the coast to find him."

"We might get lucky," Jia said. "Don't most ships go up and down the coast, staying in the shallower waters and delivering cargo between the four big cities on the Aesculun Coast?"

"That's true, but technically Squalls Landing is on the Netali Ocean, I think. The point is, though, that there are almost five hundred miles of coast between Hirsen and Squalls Landing. He could be anywhere along that path. I am only trying to be realistic so you'll know what to expect."

Leaving the horses in the inn's stables, the travelers went to the closest dock on foot and asked everyone they saw if they knew the captain. A few of the deck hands gave them wry smiles, but didn't admit that they knew the man. It was as they had discussed. Tesnair Balstad had a reputation. Whether that would help them to find him or not remained to be seen.

"Old Tesnair?" one man they talked to said. He wore boots, unlike most of the bare-footed deck hands, and his clothing was better than the rough pants seen on most of the workers. "Aye, I know him. Ain't seen him in months, but if he's sticking to his schedule, he should be about sometime soon. Maybe even today, if the gods grant you some luck." He chuckled.

"Thank you," Aeden said. "Would you know how we could locate him? Does he frequent an inn or tavern or is there another way we can be sure to catch up to him?"

"I don't know about all that. Easiest way, I'm thinking, is to watch for his ship. The Eurus is his baby. If you loiter around the docks, you're bound to see it eventually. He'll probably stay in port for a day or so, but if you don't find him, he'll be gone again up north for some time. Can't make money sitting at the dock, eh?"

That was good news, and Jia definitely had the look of gloating about her. To be sure, they continued asking others and found two other men who said similar things.

"It seems like the ship captains all know each other," Lily said. "That's lucky for us. If he's really going to be here in the next day or two, that would be the best thing we could hope for. If he'll agree to take us."

"He will," Urun said. "He has to. Osulin has charged me with getting there. We'll convince him, one way or another."

The party did as the man they talked to suggested and wandered around the docks, watching carefully as each ship came in and moored. Few of the vessels had their names painted on them, so one of the group asked any seamen nearby which ship they were looking at. Only once did they have to ask several people. Apparently, the shipping industry was small, or at least closeknit enough for even the lowly dock workers to know the ships by sight.

All of that day they stayed, waiting anxiously for the Eurus to come to port. They ended up going back to their inn two hours after dark, disappointed they hadn't seen the ship and nervous that it might come in during the night and leave before they got back to find it.

"We'll need to get to the dock before sunrise," Tere told them, "just in case the Eurus gets here during the night and leaves early. We don't all have to go, though. One or two of us is sufficient."

"I'll go," Lily said.

"I will, too," Urun said. "I'm the one Osulin charged with this task. No use in all of you doing any more work than you have to. I appreciate you joining me at all."

"I'll accompany you two," Aeden told them. "What else am I going to do here, sit around and drink ale?"

Jia raised her hand and opened her mouth, but Tere didn't let her get a word out.

The archer grumbled. "Fine, we'll all go. Just because we don't have to doesn't mean we don't intend to."

As he said, they all gathered in the morning and were back in place before the sun came up. The dock was busy, the workers loading the ships finishing up their night's loads and the crews readying some of the ships to depart. The group made a quick scan of the area and still didn't find the ship they were looking for.

Tere had chanced upon an employee of the dock master the day before and he found the man in his office.

"Has the Eurus come into port?"

"No, sir. Not yet. Not unless old Tesnair is trying to sneak in and out again."

Tere's face went stony and Lily thought he might be preparing to attack someone.

The man laughed. "I'm joking, of course. Tesnair is a strange one, but he's honest. If he's got cargo to load or unload, he'll check in, as required."

Tere's exhalation mirrored Lily's relief. Tere thanked the man and left his office.

"It might not be a bad idea for one of us to stay around here to try to catch the captain as he checks in," Tere said. Aeden volunteered, so the group left the Croagh sitting on a bench near a seafood stall and continued their search.

Finally, in the early afternoon, the fifth ship arrived that day. As it glided toward the dock, Lily had a good feeling that it was the one they were looking for. It wasn't a massive ship, but as it came closer, she realized that it was quite a bit larger than the riverboat they had been on. With three masts, the crew was busy stowing the sails, impressing Lily with their efficiency.

"Pardon me," she said to the nearest dock worker. "Do you know the name of that ship?"

The man squinted at the ship and tilted his head. "Aye. That be the Eurus, Tesnair Balstad's vessel."

"Thank you." She turned to the others, her heart beating faster. It was a testament to how boring her days had been lately that she was excited about watching a ship pull in to dock.

The crew expertly brought the Eurus to its slip and tied her down. When a plank was lowered onto the dock and the crew started to disembark, the group moved closer, waiting to see if someone who looked like a captain would come down the plank. No one did.

"Well," Jia said, "either the captain dresses like the rest of the crew, bare feet and all, or he's still on board."

Surprisingly, it was Urun who took the initiative.

"Ho, the Eurus!" he shouted from the edge of the dock.

"Ho, the dock!" a voice answered.

"Are you captain Tesnair Balstad?"

"If'n you brought me money, women, or spirits, then I be he. If he owes you money, I've never heard of him."

As he said the last words, a man appeared near the end of the plank. He was not barefoot and he did not wear the rough, simple clothes of the crew. Instead, he had boots—which looked a bit worse for wear—rugged trousers, a shirt with toggles on the front, and a jacket that extended down past his waist.

He was a hefty man with longish black hair struck through with a little grey. His sun- and wind-weathered face looked lumpy and he was in no way attractive, but he did have kind eyes that twinkled in amusement, probably from his earlier joke.

Urun seemed to have run out of things to say, so Tere took over.

"May we come aboard? We haven't brought women or spirits—not for your use, anyway—but we could mean money to you."

"In that case, come on aboard," the captain said.

He watched them as they made their way up the plank. It was long and flexed more than Lily would have liked, but from the man's satisfied look, they didn't do a bad job in navigating it. Soon they stood before him on the deck.

Interestingly, while the captain was observing them

coming aboard, he shifted his head occasionally to stare out to the south or east. His eyes didn't really focus on anything, but it was clear he was looking out over the water, almost like something dear to him was out in the waves somewhere.

"Thank you for seeing us," Urun said, taking control of the conversation. "We have a proposition for you. We're in a hurry, so I'll get right to the point. Word is, you are the only captain willing to brave the ocean and visit an island other than Iracundia. We would like to charter your ship to take us to Visuren. It's—"

"I know where it be," he snapped. As he glared at the priest, his right eye twitched. "Did Ichod put you up to this? Are you to have your sport by poking at old Tesnair, making fun of his dreams? Off with you. Tell that disappointment to his parents and all the world that I'll be having the last laugh. He'll see. Just because he's a coward doesn't give him the right to insult me. I'll—"

"Whoa, there," Tere said. "Hold on, Captain. First off, we don't know who you're talking about. Second, our friends have just traveled with your brother Asgeir. They went to Iracundia."

"What? Asgeir took folk to Iracundia? Did he set foot on the island?" His eye twitched faster and he pulled on his hair with both hands. "No, no. He wouldn't have done so. If so, you'd be telling me he was dead."

"*He* didn't set foot on the island," Lily said, "but our friends did. They told us that Asgeir's brother is the only ship captain who might be willing to take the charter to Visuren."

"'Tis true," he said. "No one else has the stones to go out there." He looked longingly out at the ocean again. "Still, it's death to do so. True, I have a dream...but, no. It's too dangerous."

Urun stepped closer to the man. "Sir, my name is Urun Chinowa. I'm the priest of the goddess Osulin. She has charged me with going to Visuren on a very important task.

She gave me this." He pulled the token from his robes and held it up for the captain to see. "It is proof against the sea monsters and will help with the dangerous currents. My goddess would not send me into extreme danger. We can trust that it will allow us to reach the island."

Tesnair's eyes glazed over as he stared at the talisman in Urun's hand. Then his eye twitched again, though not as rapidly as before.

"Truly?" the captain said. "You are the priest of the nature goddess? Is it true she alone among the gods did not abandon us?"

"It is. I saw her not a week ago, spoke with her face-to-face."

Tesnair licked his lips and blinked rapidly. "Proof!" He yelled it so loudly and abruptly that Urun jumped. "Have you proof of what you say? Can you prove you are from the goddess?"

Urun was still holding up the token, confusion written all over him. Lily decided to help him understand.

"Do you have any injuries or illness, Captain Balstad?"

The captain's head whipped around to consider Lily. He tilted his head to look up at her face, eyebrows raised. "Injuries?"

"Yes, do you have some issue with your health? As the priest to Osulin, Urun can heal. Would that prove to you that he is what he says?"

The captain's mouth formed an O. "Aye, now that you mention it, I have some pain in my foot. I've got a small cut there that seems to want to be infected. I've lanced it three times, but it still gives me problems."

"May I see it?" Urun asked.

"Sure, sure." The captain leaned against the rail and pulled his right boot off. A wave of stench washed over those standing around him. His big toe was about as close to green as was possible, with some kind of fluid dribbling out where it appeared a small cut was.

"Osulin's emerald hair!" Urun said. "Captain Balstad, that infection is gangrenous. Any surgeon would remove it to keep you from dying."

"Ah, it's not so bad. Pains me a bit, but I think if I can drain it enough, it'll be fine."

Urun glanced at the others and when he met Lily's eyes, he shook his head. She motioned toward the captain's foot.

"Here," the priest said. "Let me help you." He bent near the foot, though he had to turn his head because of the odor. He chanted something under his breath in shallow gasps and waved his hand toward the offending toe.

As Lily watched, the enlarged toe diminished in size while the color returned to that of the rest of his toes. The liquid that had been coming out stopped and within seconds, the foot looked normal. Thankfully, the smell also dissipated.

"I'll be," the captain said. "That's a neat trick, no doubt. Either you're one of them folks from that Hero Academy or what you say about the goddess is true. Well, then, if you have a way to get through the waters to Visuren without being eaten by monsters or smashed by currents and rocks, then I'm your captain."

Urun sighed in relief as he straightened to stand again. "That's wonderful. When can we leave?"

"As soon as I offload my cargo. No use shoving off in the dark, though, so how about tomorrow morning, first thing?"

"That would be perfect," Urun said. "Thank you so much, Captain. We'll be here before sunrise." He smiled at his friends.

Everyone was silent as they all looked at each other. Lily wasn't sure what else needed to be said. They probably needed to go back to the inn and prepare.

Finally, it was Jia who spoke. "Uh, you can probably put your boot back on, Captain Balstad."

CHAPTER

TWENTY-TWO

T he party was up and traveling to the dock while it was still dark the next morning.

"Two days in a row," Lily said. "I sure hope we're not going to make a habit of getting up before sunrise every day. We're not Aeden."

The Croagh laughed. He, of course, wasn't put out a bit by getting up so early. Lily, on the other hand, was. If the gods wanted people, to get up so early, they would have made the sunrise earlier. Waking up when it was still dark was unnatural. She absently patted Nobleflame's neck. At least the streets were empty enough that they could ride rather than walk their horses.

The Eurus was a hive of activity, as was much of the dock. Sailors, it seemed didn't have a problem with waking up early.

The captain spotted Lily and the others while he was pointing out something to one of his crew. His eyes widened, then that twitch took over on his right eye.

"What are you doing?" he shouted at them.

"We're here to board, like we discussed yesterday," Lily said.

"Yes, yes, I know that. Why do you have horses?"

"It's faster than walking everywhere."

He gave her a flat look that told her he thought she was being difficult. "I know why people use horses. What I mean is why do you have them here and now? You can't take them on my ship. They don't do well in the ocean."

Lily hadn't even considered that. Apparently, neither had Tere or any of the others.

"We've taken these horses on boats before," Tere said.

"Not on the ocean, you haven't. There aren't many captains who will transport them, even if their ships are set up for them. The water is rougher than rivers. You'll have to leave them."

Lily looked to Tere, who shrugged. "It's his ship," he said.

"There's a good stable nearby," the captain told her. "Frip's Boarding. It's two blocks to the south and over one toward the west. Tell Sasel Frip I sent you and maybe he'll give you a good deal. He's an honest one. Pay him for several days in advance and even if it takes you longer to get back, he won't sell your horses."

Aeden let out a breath. "I don't think we have a choice here."

"Agreed," Tere said. "I'm concerned about the horses, of course, but it also means that we won't be able to travel as fast when we get to Visuren. I think it's a big place, though to be honest the maps that exist vary widely as to its size and shape. I think all of them are just fancy, created by scholars piecing together information from old fragments of records."

"Fine," Lily said. She turned back to the captain and raised her voice. "We'll go and take care of that. Don't leave without us."

"Not a chance of that," Captain Balstad said. "You've chartered the Eurus for the trip. It goes nowhere without you."

"That's good at least," Urun said softly enough that the captain couldn't have heard him. "Let's take care of the horses and board so we can get started."

Sasel Frip was a small, energetic man who seemed excited to meet the party's horses. He scrambled around, greeting each of the equines—though he hadn't properly greeted the humans yet—and set a few hands to leading them to a row of large stalls that were obviously well-maintained.

Lily stroked Nobleflame's cheek and talked soothingly to him. "I'm so sorry we have to leave you here for a little while. It seems like a good place. Try to enjoy your stay. We'll be back as soon as we can." The gelding nuzzled her and snorted, one black eye looking into hers.

It hardly took any time at all to settle accounts with the stable owner and the group was back on the street, heading back to the Eurus.

"He seemed like a nice guy," Jia said. "He obviously cares about horses. It was like dealing with us was a necessary chore, but the chance to meet the horses was like a treat to him."

"It's good," Aeden said. "Knowing he'll take care of them relieves at least one of my worries. I'd not like for Snowmane to be neglected or mistreated."

They found the captain and his first mate—Fior Tassen—standing at the top of the plank, waiting for them. He waved them aboard when he spotted them and barked out orders to his crew to prepare for departure.

"Come," he said once they were all gathered on the deck. "I'll show you where you can stow your things." The first mate took over in directing the sailors, though it seemed to Lily that they knew well enough what they were doing already.

As he led them to a couple of cabins, he continued speaking. "Sorry about the horses. I should have mentioned it, but it's such a familiar thing, I didn't think of it. Probably best in any case because I don't have horses for the men who will be joining you."

"Wait," Urun interrupted. "What do you mean?"

"Arr, sometimes my mind doesn't seem to be in place. There's a condition to taking you to Visuren."

"A condition," Tere said. It wasn't a question.

"Aye. You have to understand that I'm risking my ship, my crew, my very life to take you to where you want to go."

"We're paying you well enough."

"You are, you are. It's a small thing, though. Nothing to get too heated up over. I just want you to take a few of my men with you. This is historic. We're to be the first to set foot on an island in thousands of years. Well, other than Iracundia, which I just missed, it seems. I want some of my men with you and I want a cut in any treasure you might find."

"Captain," Urun said. "We are not going to the island to find treasure. We're going on urgent business for Osulin."

"I know. I'm not asking you to change your plans, but if you do run into treasure—historical or magical artifacts or the like—I want a share. If you don't, it's no skin off my nose. You can even use the men as porters. They'll do what you say."

Lily stepped right in front of the man, just a few inches from him. He was of average height, but she was taller. She'd been told she loomed at times, and she tried to do that now. "Captain Balstad, you do realize that what we're doing is very dangerous. I don't just mean traveling over the ocean. There is magic on that island, and probably monsters. We are...well-suited for surviving such things. Most people aren't. There is a very good possibility that we won't be able to protect your men adequately. It'll be hard enough to protect ourselves. They could all die."

"The men know what we're about. I met with all of them last night and told them what we're doing. Two of my crew decided to stay in Horizon and wait for the Eurus's return. Those who will go with you will be volunteers. They're not your responsibility. I've ordered them to act according to your commands and not to get under foot."

Lily met Urun's eyes, then Aeden's, and finally Tere's. As with the horses, it didn't seem that they had a choice.

"We'll want to talk to the men who will go, to make sure they understand how dangerous it is," Tere said.

"I told them as much. I'd go myself, but I'm not as young as I used to be and more'n likely, I'd slow you down. Besides, braving death by sailing where no one has sailed for millennia is enough excitement for me for one trip."

Lily tilted her head at the captain, not sure if he was showing a disrespect for his crewmen's lives or if that was just the way of the sailors. She'd have some hard questions for them to make sure.

"Fine," Urun said. "Are there any other conditions you were planning on bringing up? If so, tell us now. After this moment, there will be no other changes."

If the captain took offense, he didn't show it. "No, nothing else. From here on, it's smooth sailing, if you'll pardon the expression."

They headed directly toward the sun that barely hung above the horizon. Lily had been on boats in the Kanton Sea, between Munsahtiz and Sutania and the Great Enclave, so she had experienced the movements of the waves. She figured the trip would be similar to those crossings. She soon learned she was wrong.

From the start, Lily recognized that what the captain had told them was true. Sailing on the open ocean was not like being on a riverboat at all, not even like being in the inland sea she'd traveled. The surges as the wind shifted and the crew reoriented the sails seemed to electrify the air around her and the sense of speed from it was surprisingly energetic.

Speed wasn't the only difference, though. Lily had expected it to be a little rougher than a river near land. After all, that's where all the waves broke, right? She fully expected that once they got out away from the shore and into open water, they would glide along smoothly.

It didn't really work out like that.

At times, waves slammed into the hull so forcefully, the ship shuddered with a boom. The archer, always proud of her balance and ability to keep her feet, found herself an inch or two off the deck at times and her heart galloping as she imagined herself being thrown off the deck completely. That fear was only the start.

The rolling and pitching did unfortunate things to her stomach as well. She spent a good amount of time trying to lie as still as possible in the dark corner she'd retreated to when she started to feel nauseous.

Her friends didn't do much better. Aeden and Jia didn't seem to be affected quite as much as Lily, but they had a greenish tint to their faces in the first few hours. Urun, surprisingly, didn't show any signs of overt nausea, though he did become quiet and stoic again. Tere, of course, was having no problem with the movement of the huge chunk of wood beneath his feet. He stood on the foredeck, hand on the rail, chin high as the salt spray pushed his long hair back from his head.

After a time—and a few purgings of Lily's stomach—the rough sea became more stable and she was able to move around more easily.

"You all right, girl?" Tere asked with an infuriatingly smug smirk on his face.

"Never better," she spat. "Was all that the currents Aesculun put in place to keep people from going out into the ocean?"

"No. That was just normal chop. We've barely cleared where the ships normally sail up and down the coast."

"Gods," she said.

"Don't worry. You'll get used to it. Here, chew on this root. It should help. I was going to give you some earlier, but it didn't look like you would have been able to keep it down."

She accepted the tan root from him. It was twisted and

wrinkled like it had been sitting in the sun. The taste was a little bitter, with a sharp tang, but not unpleasant. "Thanks. I guess we should start talking to the crew members who volunteered to go with us onto the island?"

"Yeah. Soon. Let me give some of the root to the others and we'll get our sea legs under us. We've got hours yet until we'll even be able to see Visuren. No need to rush."

Lily blinked at Tere. Hours yet? She hadn't asked before about how long it would take to get to Visuren. What if they had to be stuck bobbing in the ocean for days? Her understanding was that the island was close to land. Not quite as close as Iracundia, which could be seen from Bandit's Roost on a clear day, but still, it was supposed to be close.

Tere must have noticed her expression. "We should get there today, possibly in the evening. Actually, Captain Balstad said he wanted to talk to all of us once we were under way. We should probably do that before speaking with his men. We can ask him any questions we have. I think he has some of his own, like what we need to do to activate the protection from Osulin's talisman.

"He can ask," Urun said, joining them. "I won't have any answers, though. My goddess didn't give me any specific instructions."

"Then that's what we'll tell him," Tere said. "Let me go and see if he's available now and we can have our chat. Is that okay for everyone?" Lily nodded and grunts of affirmation came from Jia and Aeden. "Good. I'll be back in a few minutes. Chew your root, have a little water, and hold tight. We've got some conversations ahead of us. Hopefully the weather and the waves will let us do it in peace."

CHAPTER
TWENTY-THREE

T ere led everyone else to the captain, who was standing at the wheel, directing the ship.

"It's good to see you all up and about," the captain said as a greeting. "It looked like a few of you had some issues with sea sickness. You're feeling better now, I trust."

"We are," Lily told him. "Thank you. Tere said you wanted to speak with us before we talk to your crew members who will go going onto the island with us?"

"True. Let's go to my cabin to speak." The captain turned to his first mate, a wiry man of average size, barefoot and bare-chested. He moved with a grace Lily could respect, swaying with the deck without really paying attention to it. "Fior, take the wheel. You know the heading. If anything is amiss, anything at all, you send one of the men to me immediately."

"Aye, Captain."

Tesnair turned to leave, but stopped and faced the wheel again. "Have I introduced you to my first mate? I know I mentioned his name. This is Fior Tassen. Been with me many a year, he has, and I couldn't find a finer first mate if even I tried." The captain introduced each of the visitors, impressing Lily with his memory for names.

After the greetings, the captain motioned for them to follow him to his cabin. Once there, he sat in a chair attached to the deck and the others sat on benches built into the walls.

"Now, I don't want to take too long. We'll be leaving familiar waters soon and I want to be at the wheel when we journey out into the ocean proper. No telling what'll try to get us there."

"The talisman will protect us from most things," Urun said.

"That's what I wanted to talk about. Mostly, I'd like to know how it works. Do you have to invoke the magic? Do you need to be on the bow at all times, holding the thing up for its magic to cut us a path through the danger? If so, how long can you do that for before you need to take a rest? I'd not like to be sunk because you had to relieve yourself or stop to eat."

"I...don't know," Urun admitted. "My understanding is that its presence will shield the ship from being discovered, but the goddess didn't give me any specific instructions. I am confident that if I needed to do something, even holding it up like a beacon, she would have mentioned it to me."

"You're not inspiring a lot of confidence, priest."

"I'm sorry, but that's the truth of things. Would you prefer I lie to you?"

The captain put his hands up. "No. I mean no offense. I've known of ships that got too far out from the coast and all that was left was driftwood. I'd not like that to happen to the Eurus and her crew because we misunderstood what we should be doing."

"We understand your concern, Captain Balstad," Aeden said. "We'll stay on deck as much as possible after we're finished speaking with the men who will come with us. If any danger appears, Urun will be able to respond as best he can."

"Aye," the captain said. "I'd appreciate it. I'm sorry if I

seem to be nervous, but this thing we do, no one has done it since Aesculus flooded the world thousands of years ago. There are reasons for that."

"I'm confident Osulin would not have left it to chance if there was danger involved," Urun said. "We'll be fine."

"Alright, then. I'll leave it at that. Are there any questions for me before I have the first man brought to you?"

Urun nodded. "Yes, actually. I was wondering what the trip entailed. When will we get there and what can we expect?"

"Expect? Up until you told me about the talisman, I'd say that you should expect to be eaten by sea monsters and that the ship would be torn to kindling from dangerous currents and rocks. Aside from that, I have no idea what to expect. Neither I nor anyone else I know of has ever gone this way."

"Fair enough. Do we have any idea how long it will take?"

"Not much. There are rumors, legends really, that say the island is only fifty or sixty miles away from the coast near Horizon. If that's true, we'll be there late this afternoon. We'll probably get there before dark, but I'd suggest passing the night on the ship at anchor and then setting foot on solid ground in the morning so you have as much daylight as possible. The legends also say that island is large. Very large. I'm not so sure about the way of scholars and mapmakers, but I get the sense it's so big, it would be considered another continent, though it's not nearly the size of Promistala."

Urun seemed to be satisfied with the answers, but Lily was still curious. "Is there any other information that might be useful, Captain?"

"Sorry, lass, no. We'll be grabbing more information in the first few minutes than all of Dizhelim has in these last several millennia. That's a good thing and a bad one. Good because we'll be heroes when we get back and can tell folk about it. Bad because we have no idea what we'll be facing, or if we'll get back at all. What *you* will be facing, I mean. I'll be sitting offshore, with any luck in shallows that will keep us from being eaten by monsters, while you are all braving the dangers to explore the new land."

"We won't be exploring," Urun said. "We have a specific job to do. We won't spend any extra time surveying."

"Aye. You've made that clear. Still, as you go toward where you'll complete your mission, you'll see new things and discover what at least a part of the island is about. That's what I mean by exploring. Finding new things as you work on your mission."

That seemed to mollify the priest.

"Okay," Tere said. "I think that's all the questions. We'd like to see the first man now. We'll talk to them one at a time, if you don't mind."

The captain stood from his seat. "It's no bother to me. The others can rotate through to cover for the men to talk to you. They won't be so busy until something happens or we get to our location. I'll send the first one down." With that, he left the party in the cabin and headed back up on deck.

A few minutes later, a sailor knocked on the cabin door and poked his head in when Tere told him to come in.

The crewman swaggered into the room as if he owned the place. When he sat down at the spot on the bench Tere gestured to, he seemed to be more reserved and respectful. Lily thought that maybe his strut hadn't been so much a prideful walk as simply the walk of a sailor used to being on a ship. She'd noticed the way the men on the ocean-going vessels moved, in a sort of sinuous sway.

"Your name?" Tere asked the man. Tere looked to have taken charge of the interviews. That was just as well for Lily.

"Grobel Saltaran, sir."

Tere cocked an eyebrow at him. "No sir necessary, Grobel. I'm Tere Chizzit and these are Lily Fisher, Aeden Tannoch, Jia Toun, and Urun Chinowa. You can call us by our first names."

"Pardon me, Tere, but I've heard a rumor that you used to ago by another name?"

"Is that a question?"

"Uh, it should have been. Did you used to go by another name?"

Tere sighed. "I did. What have you heard?"

The man leaned forward on the bench, his face getting a conspiratorial cast. "It's true? You're Erent Caahs?"

"Gods. Yes, Grobel, that's the name I was born with, but—"

"Erent Caahs," the man said right over what Tere was saying. "I remember hearing your stories when I was younger. A true hero. It's an honor, sir."

Tere put his hands on his lap. "I appreciate that, Grobel, but let's just keep it at Tere. I don't want to make a big deal of it, okay?"

"Yessir. I mean, yes. Tere." The man swept his unruly brown hair out of his face. "I can keep a secret, though I think it's already made the rounds on the ship. The lads do love to gossip. Just like old women. Uh, pardon me." He ducked his head toward Lily, then Jia, and Lily had to laugh. At least he'd be entertaining.

"Now that that's out of the way," Tere continued. "You do realize how dangerous it will be to go onto the island with us, don't you Grobel?"

"I know it's dangerous even *sailing* to the island. The captain said no one's set foot on that land in thousands of years, that it's probably full of monsters and magic and that we probably won't survive."

"Yet you still want to go?"

"What's life without action and adventure?" He chuckled. "Look who I'm asking. Psht. I understand I might not live through to tell anyone about the island, but for the chance to see what no man has seen since long before the War of Magic? I joined up as a sailor when I was thirteen years old because I wanted excitement and adventure. I signed with Captain Balstad because of all the other captains out there, I figured he would give me a chance to do what no one else had done, to cross over the ocean and see things no one else had. I won't let a little thing like danger to my life affect my chance to finally live out my dream. If something kills me on my first step on the beach of the island, I'll judge it a fair price."

"Uh...okay." Tere looked to the others, seeming at a loss for what to say.

"Thank you, Grobel," Lily said. "We wanted to make sure you understood it was dangerous. Of course, we'll do our best to bring everyone back safely, but as you said, no one knows what we'll find there."

"I understand. Don't you worry about me. About us. The other lads that volunteered, they're all hard workers. We'll do right by you, you can count on it. We can fight a bit, too, but our strong points are tavern brawls, not magical monsters. You just let us know what we need to do and we'll hop right to it."

"Thank you," Tere said. "Please send in the next man. We'll see you when it's time for us to go and seek the new things you speak of."

"Aye-aye. I'll fetch Denos for you."

The man hopped to his feet and went out the door, leaving Lily and her friends looking at each other with the same expression of disbelief on their faces.

TWENTY-FOUR

The next sailor to enter the room was Denos Chal, a thin, wiry man of average height. Lily thought he was probably about her age, whereas Grobel was more than a decade older. Denos had brown eyes, like Grobel, but his hair was black to the other man's brown.

"I'm Denos Chal," the man said in a voice that lacked any enthusiasm. In fact, it lacked any emotion whatsoever.

Tere invited Denos to sit and introduced everyone.

"Denos, we wanted to speak with you to make sure you were aware of the danger of joining us on the island."

"I know. I'll most likely die, but then again, we'll probably all die on the way over there, so it won't matter much."

"Maybe the captain didn't tell you, but Urun here has a talisman from the goddess Osulin that will keep the sea monsters from attacking us and may help with the currents, too."

"He told us," Denos said sadly. "It doesn't much matter. One way or another, we'll die. If we make it to the island alive, then I'll have another chance to be killed when I go with you."

"Wait a minute," Aeden said. "Are you saying that you want to die?"

Denos showed the first bit of emotion so far on his thin, sharp face. "Want to die? Of course not? What do you think, I'm crazy? Who would want to die?"

Aeden looked over at Lily and Tere, confusion on his face.

Tere addressed the man's concerns. "Uh, okay. So, you understand the danger of going with us and you still want to come along? It'll be rough travel and hard work with danger all around us."

"I know."

"And you want to go?"

"I do."

"Right. Well, that's about it, then. Do you have any questions for us?"

"If something is eating me and I'm taking too long to die, will you put one of those arrows in my head so I don't have to feel the pain."

"Umm, yes?"

"Thank you."

They excused the man, asking him to send the next crew member in. As soon as he cleared the doorway, Aeden turned his head toward Lily and crossed his eyes while lolling his tongue out of the side of his mouth. She couldn't help but to laugh, but she wasn't alone. Jia barked so loudly, Denos had to have heard her.

"Goddess send that the next one is at least relatively sane," Urun said.

The next one was a man a bit younger and a bit shorter than Denos, though his build was more average, fit but not muscular. He was one of the few blond crewmen Lily had seen. This time, when the man walked in, she recognized his walk as a swagger and not a flowing movement due to making a living on the water.

"Mirkus Rigas," he stated proudly, flashing his smile at everyone in the room. "No doubt, I'll be the one you'll be relying on most during this little trip. Anything you need, just let me know. I'm the man who can get it done for you."

"Thank you, Mirkus," Tere said. "Please sit down. We are mainly talking to each of the men who volunteered to go onto the island with us to make sure you all know the danger involved, and to answer questions. Do you understand that there are unknown dangers on Visuren, ones that we might be hard pressed to survive?"

"Of course. The captain mentioned it. Thousands of years with no people, lots of magic, most likely monsters and wild beasts. Nothing I haven't faced many times before."

"You've faced monsters, magic, and places where no one has set foot for thousands of years?" Jia asked.

"Psht," he said as he waved the question away. "I was made for trips like this. I'm indispensable to the captain, or I'd be out making my name as an adventurer. I just can't bring myself to leave him. He'd be lost without me. Why, just last week, we found an ancient cave full of monsters and treasures. There I was—"

"I'm glad you understand the danger," Tere said. "And that you're...accustomed to facing such things. Are there any questions you have for us?"

"No, I'm good." Mirkus tilted his head for a moment. "Actually, maybe I have a question. When we find grand treasures or some ancient civilization and unknown monster, can we name it after me and will my name be spread around as the key member of the group I am?"

Tere traded an incredulous look with Lily, and she fielded the question as diplomatically as she could. "If such a situation arises, we will certainly discuss options if you wish. Our purpose of the trip is not to explore, however, but to perform the mission the goddess Osulin gave us."

"Oh, old Ossie," he said. "Tell her hello from me the next time you talk to her. She's very fond of me. Too fond, really." He waggled his eyebrows.

Lily rushed through what she said next. "Okay, Mirkus, thank you for speaking with us, please ask the next crewman to come in." She noticed as she did that Jia had hold of Urun's arm and was pulling him back into his seat. Lily flashed an apologetic look at the priest as Jia settled him down, allowing Mirkus to parade out of the room before Urun could attack the man.

The next crewman stepped into the room and stood with his shoulders hunched and his hands clasped in front of him. His heavily muscled form seemed to fill the cabin by himself. He was well over six feet tall, his head brushing the ceiling. Watching him go through the doorway looked to Lily like a hatchling emerging from a tiny hole in an eggshell, stretching and squeezing to get his massive frame through.

"Please sit down," Tere said. He introduced everyone and asked for the man's name.

"I'm Jun Freemud," he said in a quiet, tentative voice. He rubbed one hand across his scalp, where his hair was cut close to the skin.

"Well met, Jun. We wanted to make sure that you are aware of the danger in the task you volunteered for."

"Volunteered?"

"Yes. You did volunteer to go with us on the island, right?"

"Volunteer," he said, nodding.

"Do you know that it will be dangerous on the island? That there might be magic and monsters that will try to kill us."

"Magic monsters."

"Yes," Tere said. "Magic *and* monsters. We'll try to fight anything that attacks us, but we're not sure how well we'll be able to protect you and the other crewmen."

"Fight monsters." Jun pounded a fist into his chest.

Tere gave Lily an uncertain look. She caught its meaning. Luckily, Aeden had, too.

The Croagh leaned forward toward the big man. "Jun, is it

okay with you that monsters might try to kill us? You don't have to go to the island. You can stay on the ship if you want."

A look of confusion, then concentration, and finally resolve flashed on the man's face. "Jun go on island with fancy people. If monsters come, fight. Jun work hard. See island no man has seen."

"Sure. If that's what you want, then we'll be glad to have you."

"I want."

"Good enough," Tere said. "Do you have any questions about it for us? Even if you don't right now, you can always ask us later if you think of one."

"No. Maybe later."

"Thank you, Jun. We appreciate your help."

The man grinned at them. Tere dismissed him and asked him to tell the next man to come in.

If Denos's attitude and demeanor was lacking, the next man's belonged on a corpse. He was of average build for a sailor, which was to say that he was fit but not particularly muscular. His black hair was long and separated into many braids with beads tied up in them. What was striking about him, though, were his eyes. Lily guessed they could be considered brown, but they were more a rust color, the closest to red that she'd ever seen on a person.

The man stepped in and stopped, looking straight ahead of him, apparently at nothing. He didn't say a word.

After dealing with the other men they'd seen, Tere didn't seem fazed by this one. "I'm Tere Chizzit and these are Lily Fisher, Aeden Tannoch, Jia Toun, and Urun Chinowa." As he had with the others, he pointed each of them out as he said their names. What is your name?"

"Vorun."

Tere waited for a few seconds, but the man didn't say anything else. "Vorun? Do you have a last name?"

"No."

That was strange, though some of the tribes of the Sittingham Desert didn't use surnames. With his hairstyle and those strange eyes, Lily thought he might be from one of the desert tribes in the northwest of the massive desert.

Tere explained about the mission and the danger and then asked the question as he'd already done several times before. "Do you recognize the danger that you might be facing by volunteering?"

"Yes."

"Do you still want to come with us onto the island?"

"Yes."

"Okay, good. Are there any questions you have for us?"

"No."

The way Vorun was staring straight ahead, right at Tere's white eyes, seemed unusual to Lily, but she wasn't going to say anything. If he wasn't uncomfortable looking into those eyes, then all the more power to him.

"Well, if you do have any later on, you can always ask. If there's nothing else you want to talk about, I'll ask you to tell the last man to come in and you can go back to whatever you were doing."

The laconic man nodded fractionally, turned from where he'd been standing the entire time, and left. The expression on his face—or the lack of one—never changed.

As they waited for the last man to come in, Lily pondered the strange, quiet man who had just left. Was he shy, or was he simply one of those people who didn't talk much? His lack of emotion was a little strange, but she didn't think it was necessarily a bad thing. Just because he was quiet didn't mean he was a criminal or anything.

"That Vorun is definitely a strange one," the man who entered the room said. He smiled as he sat down on the bench next to Lily, seeming at ease. "Brek Zexus, at your service.

Luckily, I have no issues with speaking like our dear friend Vorun does. He's a solid sailor, mind you, but you have to wonder what he's hiding. I don't think I've ever heard more than three words out of his mouth at a time."

Brek's smile didn't slip a bit as Tere cleared his throat to get the man's attention. He introduced himself and said the same things as he had with the others. To the question regarding whether he knew about the danger, Brek gestured with his hands and answered.

"Sure, sure. The captain told us it was dangerous. He also told us we'd get a bonus for every bit of information we brought back and for anything we carried out as the ship's share. I figure it's worth it to face a little risk to get some money out of him. I swear I've heard a coin groan being held by that man. I'd not like to be the one who had to try to pry money from his grasp, if you know what I mean."

"Are there any questions you have for us?" Tere asked.

"Nah. If any pop into my head, I'll just ask then. I'm ready to go where no one has ever gone before and to maybe make some money doing it."

"Okay, good, then I guess we're done," Tere said. "We wanted to make sure you know what you're getting into."

"Oh, I do, like I said. Don't you worry. I'm handy enough in a fight and I work hard. I know we're supposed to help carry whatever needs carrying, but if you have anything else that might take a little more intelligence, you let me know. I'm not as big as some of the others, but I'm smarter. Try me out and see."

"We'll keep that in mind," Aeden said. "Thank you, Brek."

"You're welcome. I suppose I'll get back to work now. You let me know if there's anything special I can do. I'm your man."

He bounced from his seat and scurried out the door.

Tere turned from watching him leave to Lily, shaking his

head. "Quite a group the captain has saddled us with. Gods help us."

"I'm sure it'll be fine," Jia said, a smile on her face.

"I sure hope so. I guess we're stuck, though. Let's check on where we are. We're living history by crossing the ocean, so we might as well see it. Shall we go back on deck?"

TWENTY-FIVE

"Quiet, you fools."

These were not words that Lily would have expected to hear as she came up onto deck, nor ones she would have desired. Taking a look around, she saw the captain and his first mate in their normal positions near the wheel. The three crew members nearby had all stopped in their tracks, as if the captain's prohibition to make noise included footsteps on the deck. For all she knew, it could have meant just that.

Captain Balstad spotted Lily and the others and motioned them to him, following the gesture with a finger over his lips.

Lily strode across the deck, her boots thumping lightly on the planks, but not at a cringe-worthy volume. She could hear Aeden's and Urun's footsteps behind her, but that was it. Jia and Tere rarely made any sound when they walked. How the aging archer managed that with the boots he wore—nearly identical to hers—she couldn't figure out.

The captain leaned in close as they gathered around him. He pointed out in front of the ship, to the left—she should probably call it port—and admonished them. "Keep your voices down. We can speak, but do so in a whisper. I'm not sure how sensitive its hearing is."

It? Lily followed the man's finger. At first she didn't see anything, but after a few seconds, a disruption in the water drew her attention. It started as a ripple, but then a shape cut through the liquid and emerged into the air. Even watching it, though, she couldn't tell what it was. Some kind of driftwood?

The ocean was unbroken by waves like she'd seen them on the coast. There was no white as they broke, just the entire body of water rolling. She watched a new wave as it raced out from where whatever she'd seen had broken the water. As it hit the bow of the ship, the deck rocked upward and then settled back down.

"Is that...?" Aeden said, his eyes on where the wave had been generated.

"Watch," the captain said.

Lily had no doubt that every eye on board was watching where she was. Half a minute later, more ripples, larger than before, preceded another break in the water. This time, the shape that emerged was recognizable. It looked like a ribbed fin. Not like a shark or a dolphin, but one that looked like one of those folding fans. Like she'd seen in pictures of dragons, the fin some of them had along their backs.

The thing cut through the water, rising up several feet above the surface and then knifing back down into the ocean. As it did, another wave, bigger than the first one, made the ship bob again.

"How big is that thing that it'll make a wave like that?" Tere asked.

"I don't know," Captain Balstad answered. "Bigger than the Eurus, that's for sure. A lot bigger."

Urun shifted his wide eyes to the captain. "Have you seen any more of it than that...that...?"

"Fin," Tere finished. "It's a dorsal fin. The dreigan I've met have fins like that, and some more common lizards do.

Dragons are said to have them, too. I've seen drawings of what the beasts were supposed to look like. That thing must be some kind of water dragon."

The captain nodded, his eyes still pinned to where the thing had been. "No one knows what different kinds of monsters Aesculus put in the oceans to guard them. We've always just called them sea monsters."

"Do you think it—oh!" Lily nearly shouted that last part as the ship grew closer to where the monster was and even more of its fin left the surface. There had to be twenty feet of fin protruding from the water, though it was hard to judge size because they were still some distance away.

"It's still a quarter mile away," Captain Balstad said. "I'm hoping it finishes whatever it's doing and moves on before we get there. In fact, I'm going to go off-course slightly to help out."

He turned the wheel and the ship listed to the starboard side. If anything, the monster was moving slowly in the other direction, though it seemed to be going under, turning around, and surfacing in nearly the same place each time.

"What's it doing?" Jia asked.

"Hunting," Tere said. "Not us, not yet, but I've seen water animals do similar things. I don't think sea dragons breathe air, so I'm not sure why it's surfacing like a whale does. It's not breathing, only allowing its fin to leave the water. Urun?"

The priest, intent on watching the water, jumped. "Me?"

"Yes. If there's something that you sense you need to do, like with the talisman, now might be a good time to do it."

"I've told you," the priest said, "I don't know if I need to take an action. I can't feel anything from the token Osulin gave me. We'll have to wait and see what happens."

They did just that, watching the thing surface a few more times. On the last time, they were close enough to see a huge, cylindrical shadow under the water. The captain had been right: it was at least twice the size of the Eurus. Nothing but its fin ever broke the water, but that was enough to leave Lily shaking in anticipation, and probably not a small amount of fear.

Then they were past it, the monster still hovering in the same area. All present let out loud breaths.

"I wonder what it was hunting for," Jia said. "Wouldn't it be fantastic to be able to go underwater and see not only the thing's whole body, but whatever it was fixated on? It might be a complete underwater city. Do you think those exist?"

Lily could only shake her head and laugh at her friend. "Only you would be excited about something like that."

"Me?" Jia asked. "No, not at all. I know at least one person who would be more excited about seeing a monster and maybe an underwater city."

"Evon." Lily, Aeden, and Jia said it at the same time.

Jia laughed. "We'll have to make sure to tell him about it. Maybe draw him a picture. He's going to be so jealous. I bet they didn't see any monsters like this when they went to Iracundia."

"I guarantee you they did not," the captain said. "There are no records of anyone seeing such a beast. I would know. I've looked my whole life. I believe it's because anyone who came close enough to see them before now drew the creature to them and they were destroyed. As far as I'm concerned, Urun, your talisman has just been proven to work." The ship captain beamed and Lily could see from his excitement that he'd truly been waiting his whole life for such an occasion. "In any case, we'll make a course correction and see what the fates hold for us between here and Visuren. This'll not be the last surprising thing we see."

As if his words were prophetic, the entire ship shuddered a few minutes later like they had struck something large and solid.

"Did we hit another monster?" Aeden asked.

"No," the captain answered. "That's not what it feels like

to strike something. It felt more like..." the man rushed to the rail and looked down at the water. "Aesculus's watery gizzard. We're moving sideways."

The rest of them joined him at the edge and found what he said was true. Where there was typically a trough through the water and a wake, there were waves like those that would normally be seen at the prow as it cut through the water.

"Are these one of the dangerous currents we've heard so much about?" Urun asked.

The captain shook his head, not bothering to turn from watching the strange sight. "It doesn't seem dangerous...yet. It will only become so if it runs us into something, but there's nothing as far as the eye can see. No doubt it's one of Aesculus's unnatural currents, but until we see something that will put a hole in the ship, it's only an irritation. We'll wait it out for a few minutes before trying to hoist all the sails to escape it."

As it turned out, whatever current they were in grew weaker and eventually stopped pushing them sideways. The rudder responded normally again and they continued on their way, readjusting their course to compensate for their new location.

In the hours that followed, they spotted monsters three more times. Twice, it seemed to be the same type as the first they'd seen, but one time, the massive shape that seemed a land mass unto itself lazily passed by them with infrequent flaps of gigantic flippers. None of the beasts reacted as if they'd noticed them and they were able to keep to their course. They didn't run into any other currents, though whether that was Osulin's help or pure luck wasn't clear.

"Land!" one of the sailors finally called out from a little wooden platform near the top of the mast. "Land, Captain."

The group of travelers crowded the prow to look, but they couldn't see anything but water for as far as the horizon.

Captain Balstad chuckled. "Don't get in a hurry to see

anything. It'll be some time yet before you can spot what old Grobel picked out. Unless there are mountains on the shore, you'll not see anything for quite a while. Don't you worry. He'll keep us abreast of what he can see from up there. The important thing is we're close. We're almost to a land no one has seen in thousands of years."

Lily focused her eyes on the horizon ahead of them, trying to pick out anything that looked different than the rest of the blue-grey water that made up the entirety of the world in front of the ship. After a few minutes of silence, she blinked and looked around to find that her friends were all doing the same thing. A small smile formed on her mouth and she turned back to scrutinizing the ocean.

Several times over the next hour, she thought she spotted something right at the line where the ocean seemed to curve and drop into nothing. She could more readily understand now how some people—ignorant as they were —could imagine ships actually going off the edge of Dizhelim and falling forever in the void of space. She wasn't able to resolve the shapes or shadows she thought she saw, but one after another they disappeared as quickly as they'd come, some type of manifestation of wishful thinking, no doubt.

What she thought might be an hour after the original sighting, she finally saw a smudge far ahead of them, and this one did not disappear as they continued on. After several minutes of the sustained existence of the unidentified object, she was sure she was seeing something real, though she didn't quite know what.

"This one isn't disappearing," she said, more to herself than to anyone else.

"What one?" Urun asked in response.

Lily blinked a few times and turned her head toward the priest. "Sorry, that wasn't supposed to be out loud. It's just that I thought I saw things earlier. The one out there now isn't going away. I think it's Visuren, though I guess it could be some other huge monster."

"I don't see anything," he said.

"There!" This time it was Jia. "I see what you're talking about. That smudge, right? Is that brown or green? I can't tell."

"A little of both," Tere told her. "That's no monster. It's land. I'm assuming it's the island we're looking for."

Aeden breathed in sharply and Lily knew that he'd seen it as well. Poor Urun, though, didn't seem to have eyes as sharp as the rest of them.

"Give it a couple of minutes, Urun." She pointed out straight ahead. "You'll see it as we get a little closer."

The priest finally did see it and all of them locked their eyes on what resolved itself into a hazy image of a long brown strip with green shooting upward. The closer they got, the more they realized just how big was the thing they were looking at. Long before they could pick out details, the massive shape filled the entire horizon, a beach bordered by a thick forest.

When they finally drew close enough to see everything clearly, they found a nice natural bay with a sandy beach. At the edge of the sand, gentle cliffs rose up into a massive bunch of trees and plants that seemed to dominate everything on the island.

"That's going to be tough to get through, I think," Tere said. "No easy stroll across the island, not unless that jungle thins out into plains or some other clear space."

"Jungle?" Jia said.

"Yeah. It's not just a forest. Can you see all the vines and creepers everywhere? There's ivy everywhere, too. I think we're probably going to spend a lot of the time wet here, whether from rain or from the humidity."

Lily hadn't realized it before, but he was right. The humidity didn't seem as bad on the ship, with the breeze constantly blowing on them, but inside the confines of vegeta-

tion that thick, it would be worse. She inspected the vegetation and could see how lush it was. Tere was probably right.
They'd get rained on and even when water wasn't falling from
the sky on them, the moisture in the air would cling to them. It
was evening, and the temperature was still warm.

The captain commanded the crew to take down the sails.
They glided for a time and when they were a few hundred
yards out from the beach, they dropped two massive anchors.

"It appears we are here," he said. Cocking his head and
scanning the sky behind the ship, he continued. "It'll be dark
in little more than an hour. I would suggest that you sleep on
the ship tonight and then make landfall in the morning so you
have a full day's light to travel, as I mentioned earlier. No
telling what you'll find there in the dark and no use risking it
until you're more familiar with the landscape."

"That's wise," Tere said, "and I agree. Sleep on the ship,
have a good meal, and start fresh in the morning. Any
disagreement?" He looked right at Urun as he said it, no doubt
expecting—as Lily did—that the priest would complain about
losing the time to travel. Surprisingly, he shook his head.

"Good, then," the captain said. "We'll eat dinner and I'll
open a couple of casks of ale. We've made history today, and
you'll make more tomorrow. A small celebration would not go
amiss."

TWENTY-SIX

That night, the captain had the cook make up a fancier meal than the crew normally had, selling the idea as a grand feast of sorts. Because the galley couldn't fit more than half a dozen people at a time, the food was brought out on the deck so everyone could eat under the stars.

Lily sat on one of the barrels the crew had brought out as impromptu seats. She ate her dinner while watching the crew interact with each other, and with her friends. The entire thing had the feeling of a feast, she'd give the captain that. Crew members slapped the backs of those who would be joining the group to set foot on the island the next day, treating them like they were already famous.

Tere wandered over and sat on a barrel near Lily. "They seem to be having fun. It's good for them, to feel like heroes for at least a brief time."

"It's a little silly, when you think about it," she said. "Going into danger, seeing things no one has ever seen before...it's what we do every day. Are we so much different than them?"

He barked a laugh. "You have to ask? Most people go their entire lives without catching glimpse of momentous things like these. Not only has no one been here in thousands of years, but we're on a quest from a goddess, to help protect something that could mean the difference in thousands of lives. That's not how normal people live."

She chuckled. "I guess you're right. I've spent so much of my life trying to be a hero, it seems like a normal life to me."

"It gets that way. When I was running around, trying to help everyone I could find who needed it, that was just the way my life was. I didn't think a lot about how different my life was from the average person's. Not until later. Most people live their lives, have their families and other loved ones, and do what they can to make a difference. Most are happy with that."

"But not us."

"But not us," he agreed. "Whether it's because we have the circumstances or the drive or something else, we're in a position to do more, to help many other people. And so, we do. But these men—" he gestured at the sailors around them "—this is something really special for them, a chance to be a kind of hero and explorer. To help make a difference in the world, where in their normal lives, that's not something that happens."

"I see your point. I'm happy for them. I hope we all make it back here safe and sound."

As they watched the members of the party that would make landfall the next day, the blond head of Mirkus Rigas fluttered around as if he fed off the energy from the others. He swaggered and he joked and he sang, obviously seeing himself as the life of the event. He stopped and swung his head toward Lily, then raised his eyebrows at her and lifted his chin as if in question.

The archer rolled her eyes and looked to Tere next to her. "Gods help us with the group we're stuck with. They may survive the island only to have one of us kill them anyway."

Lily had never been one for large social gatherings, and to

her, large was more than three or four people. At Batido, she didn't mind sitting around the common room with all her friends, even when things got loud. It was different with them, somehow, probably because of her deep affection for them. But a group of sailors, even with her friends mixed in? She finished eating and went to turn in early. There would be plenty of excitement the next day, and she for one was going to be well-rested to meet it.

THE GROUP GATHERED on deck just after sunrise to begin ferrying over to the island. Lily, Tere, Aeden, and Jia went first, with the two crew members who were tasked with rowing them ashore. They jumped onto the sandy beach, the first people to do so in countless millennia. Lily watched as the boat went back to the ship, another batch of people boarded, and it came back toward them. Eventually, all of their party was there.

Lily, Tere, Aeden, Jia, Urun, Grobel Saltaran, Denos Chal, Mirkus Rigas, Jun Freemud, Vorun, and Brek Zexus all stood with the ocean at their backs, looking toward the massive wall of vegetation they would enter. Each had their pack, as well as other goods tied up into bundles to be carried by the crew members.

"Well," Aeden said, "we're here. Even that has defied everything known to be possible by sane people. Shall we get going?"

All eyes turned to Urun.

The priest noticed everyone's gazes after a few seconds and he gulped.

"Urun," Aeden said. "It's your mission. Where do we need to go?"

The priest put a finger down the neck of his robes pulled them away from his skin a few inches. "Uh, yeah, about that..."

"You do know where we're supposed to go, right?" Jia said, her eyes narrowing at him.

"Actually...I have no idea. Osulin only told me that we needed to get to Life's Cradle and that something was corrupting it and we needed to try to stop it. I didn't realize this place would be so big."

Lily put a hand over her eyes and shook her head. "So, you're saying that we're here on this huge island—which, by the way, looks to be covered completely by thick jungle—and we don't have a clue as to which way we're supposed to go?"

"Umm, yes?"

"We can search the whole island," Tere said. Urun perked up at that. "But it'll probably take us years to do so. I don't think Osulin expected us to take that long to do what she asked."

Lily could't help but form a wry smile. "Too bad we don't have an expert tracker who can actually see magic. Maybe that person could help us to find the source of all life."

Tere gave her a flat look. "This entire place is filled with magic. What kind of path am I supposed to pick out?"

"Maybe you can sense where the biggest source of magic is and we can head toward that," Aeden said. "I would expect such a place as Life's Cradle to be the most powerful concentration of magic."

Tere lifted a finger to make a point, the stopped with his mouth open. He lowered his finger again. "I could try. No guarantees, though. With all the ambient magic around, things in the matrix sort of blur together if I look at it as a whole. I can distinguish things better if I focus on close-up details, but I can't be sure I won't have us running off in the wrong direction."

"It's the best we've got," Lily told him. "We appreciate any help you can provide. It's either that or just pick a random direction and hope we come across the Cradle in the next year or two."

The man who had been called Erent Caahs frowned at her and turned his attention to the jungle ahead of him. Lily wasn't sure if he was scanning it to see if there were any likely spots to break into the vegetation or if he was using his magical sight to try to detect magic that would lead them to where they needed to go.

She started to feel bad about putting him on the spot like that. If he thought he could direct them to where Life's Cradle was, then he would likely have volunteered. Was she setting him up for failure? She'd only meant to prod him into leading them, not embarrass him.

While she pondered, he apparently found a location to enter. He turned to the rest of them. "We might as well get going. There's only so much daylight, and we're wasting some of it standing around." Without checking to see if anyone would follow, he pushed his way through large leaves and vines that Lily could not have identified if her life depended on it. She hurried to be the next one in his footsteps. It was the least she could do.

From the start, it was a slog. As expected, the heat and humidity inside the jungle was even more oppressive than outside it. The air was close and dank, giving Lily the sensation she was trying to breathe water. Though it hadn't rained —not that they'd seen—water was still on every leaf, fat dewdrops that would roll off and onto them with every step. Within the first ten minutes, they were soaked to the skin. Their damp clothes made the heat even worse because no matter how much perspiration their bodies added to the moisture, it wouldn't evaporate to cool them.

Sounds were everywhere. Creatures were moving through the plants and in the trees above them. Lily caught glimpses of brightly colored birds, somehow still able to blend in with the dark green canopy because of the presence of flowers of such vivid colors, she wasn't sure she'd ever seen the pure tones so brightly.

A commotion directly in front of them ended up being a small rodent-like animal zipping through the low-lying bushes like it was running from something. A few seconds later, a larger animal, some type of cat Lily thought, caught up to the smaller one and took it down with a well-placed bite to the neck. Just as Lily was watching with eyes wide, a massive shape dropped from above, looking like bundles of green rope. When the shape landed on the cat creature, it immediately squirmed and wriggled to surround the hapless hunter with a few coils of what Lily realized was a massive snake. It squeezed the cat so quickly it was only able to emit a wheezing squeak before all the air was forced out of it. The cracking of bones within the snake's coils were much too loud, almost echoing in the silent jungle.

"That thing has to be close to fifteen feet long," Aeden said, "and as thick as a leg."

"Yeah," Tere said. "You might want to keep your eyes on the canopy above. One of those things falling on you would make for a very bad day."

A blond head of hair wagged, a gaze moving from the snake eating the cat thing to one of the sailors and blue eyes flashed. Lily was already expecting it when Mirkus Rigas lifted his hand up as if to shield his voice, and then spoke in a loud tone, "Don't worry about those little things. The snakes down in the Blackpool Swamp, now those things are monsters. In four days of hiking through the jungle I killed three of them. Of course, that's only because I let some of the other fellas have a crack at them. I still had to finish one that a group of four couldn't handle."

Lily shook her head and followed Tere as he pushed farther into the jungle.

CHAPTER
TWENTY-SEVEN

More than half the day, the group bashed their way through the vegetation. Thankfully, Aeden had taken up a position alongside Tere and used his swords to cut some of the more stubborn vines and other plants.

Lily had been in crowded terrain before, but never with plants like the ones she was seeing now. At least they didn't have to deal with tanglevine. Those plants seriously made her consider burning an entire forest just so she could walk through it. The insidious way the bush's thin, twisted branches and the barbs that grew from them tangled themselves together made the going worse the harder someone tried to push through them. She'd faced them when she had to hunt down a target outside of Kruzekstan as a Falxen. The insufferable man had hunkered down in a miles-wide patch of the stuff. She was confident no one had ever found his body in that mess. At least the big leaves and the vines they were pushing through now were a bit easier to navigate.

As they traveled, they didn't talk much. Not that she felt like it anyway, but it was odd for her friends. Especially Jia. The sailors would speak to each other occasionally, but their words were muted. Even the two most loquacious of the crewmen, Mirkus and Brek, didn't say a lot, almost as if the jungle was stifling them.

Three hours had passed, judging by the sun, without the party seeing more than the constant battles between predators and prey of different sizes. None of them were large or powerful enough to try attacking them, but it was clear the law of "kill or be killed" ruled the jungle. Lily decided she was tired of the lack of conversation, and brought up the topic she'd been pondering.

"Other than these infernal plants, it's not as bad as I would have thought. I haven't seen much but small animals all morning."

The huge man, Jun, made some sort of gesture from his head to the sky, and Denos Chal sucked in air noisily.

"You really shouldn't say things like that," Denos said, bobbing his thin head like a fisher bird. "It's certain we'll run into dangers and be killed, but there's no use in inviting them."

Great. At least two of the sailors were superstitious. Lily would have to remember not to step on their toes in what she said or did.

As she averted her gaze from the men, she noticed something that made her stop.

"Hey," she said. "Has anyone else noticed rocks that look way too straight and square to be natural?"

"What?" Urun said.

"Like this one here. It looks like cut stone, though it's deteriorated quite a bit."

"There are several pieces of evidence that there was some kind of structure or city here," Tere said.

"City?" This time it was Grobel who spoke, the apparent leader of the crewman said. "Do you think there are trinkets or treasures we can bring back to the captain?"

"And that's why I didn't mention it," Tere said.

"Sorry," Lily replied, but she continued to watch for more of whatever evidence Tere had been talking about. When they took a break for lunch, she decided to look around while eating some dried meat, fruit, and a hunk of bread. Now that she had time to really inspect some of the stone poking up between the plants, she could see a pattern to them.

"You're right," Jia said from right next to her, causing Lily to jump. "That definitely looks like a wall or some part of a building.

Lily glared at the shorter woman. "It's eerie the way you move around without making a sound or leaving a trail, you know."

Jia dropped her eyes to the ground. "Sorry."

Lily hissed. "You make a good point, though. I bet there's a lot more under all these plants. If we cleared it, do you think we'd find something buried but still intact? How old would it have to be?"

"Older than possible, unless magic was involved. I mean, how many thousands of years will something last in an environment like this?"

Lily tapped her temple. "Maybe it wasn't always like this. For all we know, it could have been a desert here."

"The place where Life's Cradle is? I doubt it. Maybe it wasn't always a jungle, but I doubt it was barren. I wonder if some people stayed here when everyone else fled and then when the oceans surrounded everything, they were trapped here. They could have built cities and things, right?"

"Maybe. Better not to think about it, though. Tere's right. We need to focus on our mission. Once that's done, maybe we can look around a little bit. It doesn't seem to be all that dangerous. Not like I thought it would be."

A roar echoed across the forest and Lily wondered when she would learn to keep her big mouth shut.

~

Sɪʀᴀᴋ Iꜱᴀʏᴜ ᴅʀᴏᴘᴘᴇᴅ himself heavily into the chair at his desk in his home in Campastra. After a harrowing swim to the shore near Hirsen—making sure he wasn't spotted or tracked by the ones who had captured him—he had made his way slowly back to his tribe, all the while thinking about what he would tell others about his absence.

The tribe itself was easy enough to explain things to. "My hunting party went after an Academy person who had the nerve to enter Campastra." That wasn't anything new. He'd told them the same thing when he gathered his warriors to go after Marla Shrike, though he kept silent about chasing her into another tribe's territory. "She led me into a trap with a large group of her other Academy friends and though we battled fiercely, they overwhelmed us with magic. The others were all killed and I was taken prisoner. I was able to escape them near Hirsen and now I'm back home. I will miss those who sacrificed themselves trying to defeat the mages from that school."

It was good enough for an explanation. Arunai hated anyone associated with the so-called Hero Academy more than anything else in the world. Most of them were also deathly afraid of the power and skill of those from the Academy. He would lose no face as a warrior for being bested by a superior number of Academy people. Everyone knew they dabbled in dark magic and could sear the soul of a strong warrior.

That left another group to whom he would have to explain, but this time, there would be no half-truths. Well, not many. Sirak might embellish a bit the precise things that happened, but he would tell them what he'd experienced, what he'd seen. After all, he had learned valuable information, besides also exploring a place no one had set foot on for possibly thousands of years.

Sirak closed and locked his door, then went to a secret compartment in the wall. From it he removed what was probably his most priceless possession: his meeting stone. As he placed the little stand for the stone on his desk, he wondered if any of the Dark Council members had ever lost their meeting stones. Someone had to have done so. How could a group of people have gone three thousand years without someone damaging, losing, or misplacing at least one of the stones?

He breathed out a nervous breath. He himself might have lost his, if he had decided to take it with him. If he had not decided it was too dangerous to carry with him, those who captured him would have found it and may have been able to find the rest of the Council with it. Whatever anyone said about the Academy, they were the world's experts on magic. A flush of heat suffused him at the thought that he could have been responsible for ending the millennia-long Council with one stupid action.

But he had not taken it, so it wasn't found and he could now use it to call a meeting. And he did need to call a meeting. The information they had received from their spies before barely scratched the surface of what he knew now. While he wasn't proud of and didn't like that he had been captured, the situation did allow him to gain valuable insight.

With a word of command, he set the meeting stone to request a meeting. The function he used would communicate his desire to the Vituma and she would set up the meeting for the rest of the Council. She may communicate directly with him beforehand to make sure his reason was sufficient for actually calling the group together.

He waited patiently for Alloria Yurgen to speak with him through the stone. He was surprised ten minutes later when his meeting stone flashed that he was being called for a meeting. Apparently the Vituma trusted his judgment enough to call the meeting without double-checking with him and his reasoning first. The glow of pride that infused him made him feel a little better about having to admit to the Council as a whole that he'd been bested and captured, even though he did eventually escape.

Sirak sat straight in his chair and took several breaths, then activated the flashing gemstone. His room and his home swirled and evaporated around him, bringing the familiar light-headed feeling. He closed his eyes and rode through it, opening them again when the sensation settled.

He was in another room, one that he recognized well. The meeting room in Alloria's home, the one they used for the virtual magical meetings of the Dark Council. The familiar long table with the seats around it, the maps and tapestries arrayed on the walls, and of course, the figures seated in the chairs. Twelve besides him, all but one with an ethereal quality, as if he could pass his hand through them.

He could, of course, since not only they, but he as well, were not there physically but through the magic of the meeting stones. The one solid figure was Alloria herself, since she was present in truth, at the head of the table.

"It has been some time since you contacted us," she said, her long, pale fingers steepled in front of her. "I was beginning to think something was amiss."

"Apologies, Vituma. I did not take the meeting stone with me when I left my home after the last time I updated the Council. I had cornered Marla Shrike in the lands of the Den-Uto tribe. I demanded her from the chief, but before we could press our claim for her, she dashed off on her horse. My warriors and I followed but could not travel as quickly. Before I could catch her, she met up with other of her friends and made their way to Hirsen.

"I found that she had hired a ship captain to bring her to the island called Iracundia."

"Iracundia?" Amatia, the cocoa-skinned seeress said. "I had visions of an island, but they were disjointed and unintelligible."

Sirak nodded and continued. "I found another ship whose

captain I was able to convince to take me there as well. He made it clear that even if I killed him, he would not set foot on the island. That was no matter to me.

"We followed her and four others, including the blue woman, Marla's blond-haired friend, and one of the masters of the Academy. The place is inhospitable and the monsters there are powerful. We were able to catch Marla and engaged them in battle, but during our fight, the ground collapsed from beneath us and when it was all over, two of my warriors and I were taken prisoner. Even those two lost their lives when we were attacked by some of the island's monsters."

"You were captured?" Thritur Nyhus said, shaking his massive head. "By a woman?"

Alloria raised her hand. "Please, Thritur, save your comments until Sirak has finished getting to the point of his tale."

The warrior grunted.

Sirak carried on. "What I have told you is simply background information. The important part of my tale is this: accompanying the Academy people, I witnessed firsthand what they were doing. We found a labyrinth that presented us with challenges. At the end was a hole surrounded by a low stone wall. It looked like a village well and within it was power. Magical power."

Evindia Elkien leaned forward, her blonde hair hanging down to touch the table. "Magical power? What do you mean?"

"I mean that within the well was concentrated magic that, when they placed a gemstone they obtained from defeating the guardian into a place on the wall, exploded into the air. When it did, I saw the effects on the magic users in the group. It staggered them for a moment, overwhelmed them."

"Like the other such occasions lately," Alloria said.

"Yes. We learned that they were looking for concentrations of power, but now we know that they are searching for more of these wells. From what they discussed, the wells contain nearly all of a certain kind of magic in the world. With each one that is released, more magic becomes available."

"But if we were to get to these wells before them, we might be able to keep the magic to ourselves, for our own use," Isbal Deyne said, an evil glint in her eyes. Set into the grandmotherly face, the look threatened to give Sirak chills. Thinking of the woman with magic was a frightful notion.

"Those were my thoughts, yes," Sirak agreed.

"This *is* valuable information, Sirak."

Cara Moore raised a hand to wave. "If you were their prisoner and you saw all this, how are you back home now?"

"I waited for my time and when the ship came close to Hirsen, I jumped overboard, swam to the shore, and traveled back home," Sirak said. "I was not going to let them take me to the Academy. Who knows what those monsters would do to me or what magic they would use to get information from me."

Ren Kenata nodded at Sirak in respect. Sirak wasn't sure if it was for his escape or that he had battled the Academy people, but he returned the nod. He, as a warrior, had nothing to be embarrassed about.

"We're glad you made it back, and that you had the foresight not to bring the meeting stone with you," Alloria said. "It would have been disastrous for the Academy to have obtained one of our stones. As for these wells, your information will help us, I believe. Amatia? Will knowing what we're dealing with aid you in finding appropriate visions?"

"I believe so, Vituma, yes."

"Excellent. You may relate to me the specifics of your journey, your capture, and your escape at another time Sirak. For now, well done. We have work to do. We will meet in three days. In the meantime, everyone gather as much information from your spies and contacts as possible. We may have a new objective."

CHAPTER
TWENTY-EIGHT

Tere Chizzit stood several feet from the next person in the group, which happened to be Lily. The old archer cocked his head in a way that screamed confusion—or at least uncertainty—to Lily, though she'd not seen much of either in the man since she'd known him. It didn't give her a good feeling.

She slipped up beside him and offered him a waterskin as an excuse, as she whispered, "What is it?"

He nodded, took the skin, and drank. After handing it back to her, he ran a hand over his face. "I don't get it."

"Get what?"

Tere looked back toward the others, all strung out in a line of unhappy faces, then answered in a low voice. "I've told you all that there's a lot of magical interference here, that it's tough for me to pick out a trail. Actually, that's not true. It's impossible to pick out a trail. Have you ever tried to follow footprints in the middle of soft dirt where there were literally hundreds of other prints and trail signs?"

"No, but I've seen scenarios like that."

"Well, this is worse. The magical matrix is so crowded

with tracks, I'd be doing well if I could find my own, the one trail in the world I am completely familiar with."

Lily cast a glance back at the others, too, seeing that they took her lead and were taking sips of water or pulling snacks from the packs. "But I thought you were trying to detect the most powerful magical signature and we were heading toward that? You don't have to follow any specific tracks because we don't know of any creature or person who would lead us to Life's Cradle."

"That's the thing," he said. "I think I am following the biggest source of magic."

"You think?"

"Yeah. Listen, it's not like there's a big, glowing beacon for me to chase. This place is so saturated with magic, it's a subtle thing. Even that isn't what's got me irritated, though."

Here we go, Lily thought. When Tere used words like *irritate*, they were getting close to the core of what he was feeling. She had to stomp down on an urge to smile. "What's got you bothered, then?"

He snapped his white eyes to hers, probably hearing the humor in it. He watched her for several seconds, then shook his head. "I've been dutifully following what I think is the strongest magic, but the way we've been going conflicts with my normal sense of direction. There are a very few times in my life where my sense of direction played me false, but it's happened. In this case, though, I'm leaning toward it instead of my magical sight."

"Meaning that your sense of direction is telling you to go another way?"

"No, not really. It's not trying to lead me anywhere, but it's telling me we're not doing a good job in going straight to anyplace in particular. I can't tell with this blasted canopy because I can't see the sun, but at the least, I think we're zigzagging, wasting a lot of time and effort. I don't know what to do."

She stroked the side of his face. "Do your best. We know it's not a perfect situation, but we don't really have much else. Anything seems better than randomly wandering a place this large. At least the roar we heard earlier didn't end up being anything we encountered. It's obvious there are predators here, but so far we haven't seen anything we can't take on as a group. Keep leading us and we'll follow. Eventually we'll figure it out."

He grunted, then decided to speak what was really bothering him. "I don't like to feel like I'm letting everyone down."

"You've been honest about your magical sight not being that reliable here. No one will think any less of you if we end up lost."

"So you say. You can't convince me that it's not my fault, though." He sighed. "We'll keep on. There's not much else we can do at this point. Thanks for the pep talk."

She flashed him a wide smile. "It's what I'm here for." Her smile slipped a little as she said the next bit. "You want me to go and talk to Urun, see if maybe he can try to get in contact with Osulin?"

"Sure, give it a try. I'm not too proud to admit I'm unsure about where we're going. I told everyone that before you all asked me to do it."

"Okay, I will." She turned and headed back toward where Urun and Jia were sitting between Aeden and the crewmen. When she got to the priest, she pulled him aside, gripping his arm.

"Lily?" he squawked.

She hiss-whispered at him. "Urun, are you sure you can't get in contact with Osulin or that you don't feel anything that tells you where we should be going? Tere's having trouble with all the magical interference. He says it's conflicting with his natural sense of direction and he's doubting we'll be able to find whatever it is we're looking for."

"We're looking for Life's Cradle."

She glared at him, her mouth turning down. "You know what I mean. Can you do something or not? It's not fair that we're putting all this on him. He's already told us his magical sight isn't working to find the way to go."

"No," he said. "I still can't feel anything guiding me and Osulin hasn't been answering my prayers for her attention. I don't know why."

"Damn. Well—"

"I could find our way, sure," a voice said within the group of crewmen passing them. "Why, back when I was exploring the Aerie Mountains, I homed in on the treasure the big shots were there to find. Led them right to it. I've got a sense, an uncanny knack for finding things."

Lily dropped her head and rubbed her face with her palm, allowing a low growl to escape. "Mirkus!"

The voice quieted and the man's blond head swung toward her. His eyes scanned her up and down and a big smile jumped onto his face. "Lily! Have you come back to keep me company?" He elbowed the man next to him, Denos, as he winked. "Told you she'd come around," he said in a voice loud enough for not only Lily, but probably everyone else out in front of them to hear.

"So, I heard you bragging about how you could find the way for us."

A look of uncertainty crossed his face, but he smoothed it away with his normal haughty expression. "Oh, I wouldn't dream of trying to take the job away from Tere."

"That's not what I asked you," she said. "Can you do it?"

"Do...it?"

Lily huffed. "What exactly is it that you think you can find, Mirkus?"

"Treasure? Ancient ruins where we can find lost artifacts that will not only make us famous but also make us rich?"

"Noooo," she said, drawing the word out. "Life's Cradle and the corruption that has afflicted it. Can you find it?"

His eyes darted toward his companions and then back to her. "Uh, sure. Yeah, I can find it. No problem. Give me a chance and I'll prove it to you."

"Great," she said with fake happiness. "That will be wonderful. We'll give you the job, let you lead us to the Cradle and to whatever is corrupting it."

"Uh, okay."

"How long do you think it'll take to find it?" She could almost smell smoke from the ideas zipping around in his head.

"Three days, maybe four."

"Good. Let me go and tell Tere and you can switch places with him." She started walking back toward the archer, but stopped and turned back around to Mirkus. "Oh, and if you don't find it in four days, you're out of the party. We'll give you a waterskin and three day's rations and you'll be responsible for getting yourself back to the Eurus. Four days. No extensions, no second tries. You don't need them, though. You're confident, right?"

"Uh, wait. I really don't want to hurt Tere's feelings or anything. Why don't we let him do the job? I didn't mean to insult him or anything."

She leaned closer and cocked her head, with her left ear closer to him. "Wait, are you saying you can't find it in four days, let alone three? It would really help us out. The magic here is affecting Tere's magical sight. You're not saying that you can find it but that you don't want to help us, are you?"

"No, no. Of course not. It's just..." He looked at his shipmates and finally his shoulders slumped. "I'm not completely sure I can find it in four days. When I have pressure like a clock ticking on me, sometimes my abilities don't work like normal."

Lily straightened up. "Ah, I thought so. Maybe this will help you learn to keep your mouth shut. Why don't you bring up the rear of the group? I don't want to hear your voice anymore."

He turned sullenly and carried his large pack back behind the others while Lily shook her head.

Urun gave her a smirk. "Thanks for that. He was getting on my nerves, too."

The day continued as it had been, with Tere leading the group through unending vines and bushes and trees. At one point, less than an hour after they had stopped and had their chat, resulting in Mirkus being banished to the back of the line, a strange looking tree caught Lily's eye. She was once again in place near Tere, who noticed her head cocked as she tried to make out what she was seeing.

"Tower," Tere said.

Lily shook her head and blinked. Was he talking to her? "What?"

"Tower. What you're looking at. It was a tower at one time."

She narrowed her eyes and scrutinized the shape. It made sense. She thought it was a dead tree, its branches fallen off and its trunk covered in moss and vines. As she looked, she noticed bits of what could be stone peaking through. They were dark with plants and mildew stains, but it could be...

"It's still standing after all this time?" she asked. "How old must it be?"

"I don't know, but I can see magic radiating out of it, so it could very well be from when all land on Dizhelim was part of the one continent."

Aeden came up, having heard their discussion. "Is that possible, for a structure to remain intact enough to stand like that after millennia? Did the original inhabitants of the one continent have that kind of building technology and magic?"

Tere eyed the rest of the party gathering up near him, checking out the shape they were talking about. "No one knows. The time period from when people and animals were created until they were moved over to Life's Cradle was pretty short, but between then and when the land split and the gaps were flooded? No one really knows. At least, as far as I've heard or read about it. Urun?"

The priest shrugged. "I don't know. There had to be some time during which Aesculus finally took offense to Mellaine's popularity and split things up. There may have been time to build great cities and monuments. Osulin hasn't told me, but I'll be sure to ask her when I can. It's conceivable that here, the place where essentially all life was brought to grow and progress, there would be complex structures, even magical ones."

"Wow," Jia said. "That ugly, leaning hunk of rock could be thousands and thousands of years old. Too bad we don't have time to check it out."

"You're right," Tere said. "We don't. Focus. We need to find Life's Cradle and whatever is affecting it. Maybe when we're done, we can explore a little." At that, Grobel's eyes went wide. "I said maybe. Don't count on it. It's enough that we're trying to tackle something even a goddess couldn't handle. Now come on. We're not there yet."

TWENTY-NINE

During one of the rest breaks, Lily wandered among the others, her legs not quite ready for her to sit down and rest. When she went near where the sailors were congregated, she had to look twice. Denos Chal sat like he'd passed out, leaning against a rock on one side and his huge pack on the other. The thin, wiry man's face was pale and drawn.

Grobel was nearby, as was Mirkus, both of them positioning themselves near Denos like they were trying to block her view.

"Why does he look that way? Is he all right?"

Mirkus, fresh off being told earlier by her to keep his mouth shut, looked to Grobel. The older man answered her. "He's not feeling well. It's no problem. He'll pull his weight."

"Is he sick?" Lily asked. "Did he eat something that didn't agree with him?"

Grobel looked toward Denos with concern. "We don't really know. Brek and Jun said they didn't feel quite right, either. I don't know if it's the heat or something in the air or maybe one of the bugs that keep biting us have some kind of venom? We'll sort it out, don't you worry. We won't hold you up."

"I'm not worried about you holding us up. I'm concerned about Denos. We can help carry some of the packs, if you aren't feeling well."

"No, ma'am. No need for that. We'll figure it out. Thank you for your concern, but we'll be fine. Sailors are tough folk. Takes more than a bout of turned stomach to slow us down."

She eyed the man suspiciously. "Okay, but you let us know if it gets worse or if anyone else feels sick. We want to finish this mission with everyone intact."

"Yes, ma'am. We appreciate it, we sure do."

She left them and went back toward the front of the group as Tere was calling an end to the break and getting ready to move on again. She decided to keep an eye on the crewmen. She didn't want them to push themselves into injury by lugging heavy packs while they were ill.

"Urun," she said once they began walking again, "could you maybe check on the captain's men? Denos is sick and Grobel said two of the others were feeling out of sorts, too."

"I'll delve them with my magic and see if I can find anything amiss."

"Thanks. How do you feel? Anything strange going on with you?"

The priest paused, his eyes going unfocused as he did a mental diagnostic. "No. I do feel an urge to lose myself in the jungle, to join the eternal struggle between predator and prey. It's weird, but they're just random thoughts. What about you?"

Lily did her own mental inventory. "Now that you mention it, I have an urge to go out hunting, but that's it. Do you think maybe the magic of this place is affecting them? Us?"

"It's possible. I'll check them out on our next break and maybe I'll try to detect anything in the rest of us as well. It wouldn't be unheard of that the ambient magic is having some effect on all of us."

Lily went back up to the front of the group, whispering to Tere about what she'd seen.

"What do you think it is?" he asked. "Something in the food, maybe? Is it only the sailors or are any of us showing symptoms as well? I feel fine, if a bit frustrated."

"Urun is checking on it. I haven't heard complaints other than from the sailors. I'll ask everyone at the next break, at the latest."

"Just what we need, for there to be some kind of illness or poisonous bug or something that afflicts us without us even knowing how. I'll focus on trying to get us where we need to go and you keep up with your investigation. Thanks for watching out for all of us, Lily. Good job."

She slowed down so she could talk to Aeden but found her mouth curving into a smile. What the archer, her hero, had said was a little thing, but praise from him was always something special, and not just because he was sparing with compliments. She had idolized the man her entire life and it was a wonderful surprise to finally get to know him and confirm that her expectations had not been incorrect. He was just as much a hero as she had always thought, more so for his flaws and his humanity.

People often forgot that heroes of stories not only were human, but had problems like other people—some of them nearly insurmountable. It was like her uncle had always told her: heroes were not heroes just because they could defeat the villains but also because they could do so while not being distracted or beaten down by the bad things in life. She would have to remind her uncle of that when she returned to him.

The rest of the day passed slowly and Tere, after Lily reported to him that Denos was having a hard time keeping up even with the other sailors taking turns helping with his load, called a halt more than an hour before sunset.

"This seems like a good place to stop, anyway," he said.

The place was as close to a clearing as they'd seen in the jungle, but that meant it had a few feet that were not covered in vines, prickle bushes, or strange plants that may or may not have been mutated somehow. There were also several bushes with large leaves that were easy to remove to clear a space for a fire.

They hadn't started one the night before, but decided to try to keep one going this night. It would be difficult with the damp vegetation, the wet air, and the occasional rain, but they'd found a fallen tree and several large branches that looked ideal for burning.

Urun reported that Denos's condition didn't seem to have gotten worse, but that he was simply fatigued by pushing through the day. The other two crewmen still didn't feel well, but they all seemed fine, as far as the priest could tell from his delving. None of Lily's friends had shown any ill effects.

The party took advantage of stopping sooner than normal and ate dinner early. They all went to sleep quickly, all except Jun, who had first watch. Lily didn't have to take a turn at watch that night, one of the good things that came from traveling with so many people.

In the morning, they headed off again, the three sailors who had felt ill the day before saying they felt almost normal. Denos bobbed his head at Tere, Lily, Urun, and Aeden when they asked if he felt better.

"I do. Thank you for asking. I don't know what it was, some kind of stomach malady. I'm a little weaker than I should be, but I feel just fine, ready to carry my load."

When Tere suggested they split up the items in the pack he carried and distribute it to several others, including himself and his friends, Denos took it almost like an insult.

"No, sir. Please, don't take away my load. I'll not be the one who doesn't carry my own weight. I feel fine. I'll keep up, don't you worry, sir."

Tere gave Lily an exasperated look, but acquiesced. "Okay, Denos, but if I find out you're hurting or getting weaker because you're not getting a rest, I'll carry your damn pack myself. I might even ask one of my friends to carry you."

The look of horror on the sailor's face had Lily turning her head and holding in her laughter. Denos definitely didn't want to be the one who suffered such indignity. If there was one thing Lily had learned about the men, it was that they rode each other hard and they would never let the sailor live it down if he had his load taken away *and* if he was carried like a baby. Or a princess.

It wasn't more than an hour and a half into their travels for the day before Lily heard Tere spitting and cursing like a cat that had gotten its tail stuck in a door. She closed the distance between them in a few seconds and could hear him clearly.

"Surus's hairy ass crack! Son of a she-wolf's flea-bitten carcass. Gods damned—"

"Tere!" she said, getting his attention. "What's wrong?"

For an answer, he didn't continue his tirade, only pointed up ahead and to the left.

There, standing out as if in defiance of the entire jungle and all of the party's intentions, stood a familiar vine and lichen covered stone tower.

THIRTY

"I'm sorry everybody," Tere said. "It's obvious that the interference to my magical sight has left me unable to find our way to Life's Cradle, unable even to keep from going in circles, apparently."

"We didn't go in circles," Lily pointed out. "We got to the same tower, but not the same place. It's not like we ran into our trail from before. It's fine. You warned us when we started. We appreciate you trying."

"Sure," Tere grumbled. "So what now? Urun? Anything from Osulin that can help us, or any epiphany about how to find where we're going?"

Urun shook his head silently, seeming as embarrassed as if he was the one who had led the party back to near where they had been before.

"Anyone else have any bright ideas?" Tere asked.

Lily watched Mirkus out of the corner of her eye. She expected it would be too much for him to keep silent, not with the ideal opportunity to be the center of everyone's attention. The man fidgeted, but kept his mouth shut.

Surprisingly, it was Aeden who spoke up.

"I have something I can try," the Croagh said, "but there are no guarantees it'll work."

"Something is better than nothing," Tere told him, "even if it ends up running us in circles."

"The thing is, I'm going to need a little bit of time. At least fifteen or twenty minutes so I can work something out. I think I might be able to enhance one of my spells to point the direction we're supposed to go."

"Ooh," Jia said. "How does that work?"

Aeden ran his fingers through his hair. "I've been studying Tsosin Ruus's book and learning about different ways the magic might work. I have a spell. It's from the eleventh quatrain of the Song and it's called Home of Magic, Knowledge of Power. It's probably the least used spell in the whole Raibrech. It allows me to center myself, to increase my focus. They hardly even taught it in training when we were boys. All the warriors figure it's pretty useless.

"Anyway, I think I've worked out how to cast that spell to help put my mind in a condition so I can not only think better, but I can cast magic more strongly. If, under the influence of that spell, I can work out the enhanced version of another of the Raibrech spells, I might be able to call magic that will help us find what we're looking for."

"That sounds promising," Urun said. "Let's try it, Aeden, if you think it'll work."

"I'm not sure if it will or not, but it's something to try. It couldn't hurt, as long as no one minds me taking a little time to try to home in on where we're going."

"Do you need anything?" Tere asked. "A clearing, a place to sit, food, anything?"

Aeden chuckled. "No. Maybe a little privacy. I'll go ahead a short distance while you all take a break here. Keep an eye out for predators for me, but otherwise, the fewer distractions I have, the better."

He scanned the party as if waiting for some objection. When none arose, he walked ahead as he had said he would.

"I'll go up ahead between him and the rest of us," Lily said. "Just enough so I can keep an eye on him in case something does come trying to eat him. It wouldn't be good luck for us if the Malatirsay got eaten while trying to work on magic to tell us where we need to go."

Lily took up a position just close enough to see where Aeden was settling into a small space, but not so close as to make him feel like he was being watched. The rest of the party settled in to wait, chatting quietly.

Instead of sitting down, the Croagh went right into one of his dance-like sets of movements. At first, Lily thought that he might be going through the exercises he performed every morning, but then she realized that his actions didn't have that martial feel to it. In even the most obscure of his forms, she was usually able to pick out the stylized strikes, blocks, and evasions as being fighting moves. What he did now wasn't that.

It was definitely the type of actions he performed when casting a spell. Collecting whatever magical energy the Song provided for him to get his desired result.

For a change, he wasn't moving his lower body. In fact, he was in a relaxed stance, unlike even some of the spells he cast where he seemed rooted to the ground, almost like he was planted in the soil. His hands swept out to either side in wide, circling motions, fingers splayed out like he was catching something.

Whatever he was gathering, the motions looked like he was taking it and pushing it into his head. Once that was done, he rotated his wrists and swept his hands out, tracing the path they'd taken before, but in reverse. Again, he pushed his palms toward his head, but this time it was from underneath instead of from above.

Lily could hear his breaths, hissing softly as he breathed in through his nose and out through his mouth, the rhythm almost hypnotic. After repeating his motions twice each, he intoned words of power she couldn't hear clearly enough to recognize.

After speaking the last word, Aeden relaxed so completely that his body slumped slightly. He resumed normal breathing and shook out his limbs, rolling his head on his neck to loosen up. He glanced toward her and she raised a hand in greeting. He returned the gesture with two fingers and a faint smile. Of course he'd known she was there. The man had the senses of an animal.

Aeden only relaxed for a few breaths before dropping to sit cross-legged on the ground. His breathing changed again in a blink, going to the slow, controlled cadence that she knew indicated he was delving deep into his mind. Meditating.

For several minutes, he sat unmoving, breathing so slowly she had to stare at him to notice his chest and abdomen moving with the process. She could no longer hear his breaths, they were coming so slowly and softly.

So suddenly it caused Lily to jump, Aeden's eyes snapped open and he got to his feet. Lily looked over her shoulder to see if anyone had noticed her being startled, but the others were all busy resting, chatting, or eating snacks. She swung her head back to watch what Aeden would do next.

This time, he positioned his feet as if he expected to need to move quickly, the weight more on the balls of his feet than distributed evenly over the whole surface. He reached out, swiping slowly at the air. Lily narrowed her eyes, looking to see if a swarm of bugs had latched onto him and were pestering the man, but she couldn't see anything. Still, the way he swiped with one arm, then the other, it did look a lot like he was chasing flies, but much more slowly than would ever work for insects.

Strangely, with each wide, swooping swipe, he pulled his hand back in and patted his stomach with it. Lily cocked her head and wondered what had gotten into him. He continued for several repetitions until she realized—tipped off by a soft chanting or singing of words—that he was actually casting a spell again. Using the motions only he knew how to synchronize combined with what was undoubtedly the Song of Prophecy to bring magic into being.

Twice, he stopped in the middle of what he was doing, letting out a breath that was close to a sigh. He merely shook his head, set himself in his stance again, and repeated the spell. When Aeden finished his motions for the third time, there was nothing so subtle as his body relaxing to indicate that he completed his spell. Instead, there was an explosion of colored light which gathered around him and shot off to his right. If his body was facing north—and she had no idea if that was the case—then the light blasted out to the northeast, zipping through the vegetation as if it wasn't there, and finally disappeared when the very real plants came between her sight and where the light was going.

Lily was so intense in following the light, she really did jump when Aeden put his hand on her shoulder.

"Gah!" she whisper-shouted. "Gods, Aeden, you scared the warmth out of me."

He snorted. "Sorry, Lily. You were so focused on the light, I wanted to make sure you knew I was here. I figured if I tried to walk by you, you'd slash at me with your knives, not recognizing me before attacking. It was a judgment call."

She blew out a breath. "You're probably right. What was that thing you did?"

"It's called Pieces of Evil. I learned a while ago that I could use it to point me to where the closest animaru were. The first spell I cast, Home of Magic, Knowledge of Power, helped my mind to be more open to figuring out the magic for the second spell. Once I cast that, I figured a few things out with Pieces of Evil. It still took a little experimentation until it felt right, but now I think I can make it find the magic of the wells. At least, if we're close enough. I don't think I'll be able to use it at the Academy, for example, and find the next well for us. That would be too easy. Life is rarely that accommodating."

"Oh, sure," she said. "We wouldn't want things to be easy, right?"

He gave her a smile. "Exactly. For now, though, I think we might be close enough for it to lead us to Life's Cradle."

"Wait. Are you saying that the Cradle is a Well of Power?"

"Not for a certainty. I just figure that with all the things we've dealt with lately, they each ended up having a well involved. It seems like there might be hundreds of them. Either that, or magic is paving the way for us to find them. I tried focusing my mind on Life's Cradle, but I couldn't imagine what it looked like. It was only when I pictured a well that the light came. It could be coincidence or it could be that the Cradle is a well or has a well somewhere near it. That would fit in with the corruption Osulin told Urun about, like with the Mellafond. In any case, we have a direction to head toward, for better or worse. Shall we tell the others?"

She swept an arm out, gesturing he could go on ahead of her. He nodded and took the invitation, heading toward Tere, who had stood to face them.

"What was that all about?" the archer asked. "I saw a burst of magic flying off toward that way." He pointed in the direction Lily had seen Aeden's light go.

"I think we may have just found a direction to go," Aeden told him. "Hopefully, it'll be the right one."

THIRTY-ONE

Aeden stopped every few hours to cast his spell again. The light continued to point toward the same direction, which turned out to be southeast, not northeast. It took chancing upon a few clear areas in the canopy for them to figure that out. Each time the Croagh cast Pieces of Evil, Lily watched him for signs he was taxing himself. She'd seen him grow too fatigued to stand by casting magic in combat and wanted to make sure he wasn't pushing himself too hard to direct the group. If an inevitable confrontation with something hostile came, they would want him to be capable of joining them in combat.

She couldn't see any overt effects of fatigue, so she decided to ask him straight out.

"Aeden, is casting that spell over and over again tiring you out? We can take more rests if it'll help."

He shook his head. "No need. That spell doesn't take much out of me. In fact, for an enhanced spell, it barely takes any power at all. I don't know if it's because I figured out how to use it while under the influence of the other spell so I am doing it more efficiently, or if it simply doesn't take much qozhel. Either way, I'm fine. I can cast that spell all day long and not get tired. Tramping through the vegetation tires me out faster than that."

"Okay. We all appreciate you doing this for us, so if there's anything you need, let me know."

"I will. Like I said, though, it's fine. I'm glad we're heading in a particular direction to a specific location. There are enough unknowns without not knowing where we're going."

She had to agree with him there, but she'd been paying close attention to their surroundings as they traveled, and she didn't like the changes she was seeing. It wasn't just the appearance of the jungle and its plants, but everything else.

It was a gradual difference, but she had noted that the plants were progressively looking more wild, as well as thicker, if that were even possible. There were more sounds of quick movements and attacks around them, with the flashes of the creatures they spotted becoming bigger and more ominous looking. Very few had showed themselves thus far, but the farther into the jungle they got, the more Lily had the feeling that the animals cared less and less that the humans were something strange and dangerous and more that they were curious what the people tasted like.

She hadn't brought her observations up to the others yet, but they had to have noticed too, hadn't they?

She'd observed things about the others, too. Attitudes and actions that didn't quite seem to be right compared to how they were before they'd entered the jungle. She didn't like any of it, though if she were honest with herself, she wasn't quite sure why. It wasn't so much that things were wrong, just different than normal. Maybe she was tired and not thinking clearly.

At midday, as they were plodding along like they had been for the entire interminable day so far, a crash and a shriek sent everyone into immediate readiness. The plants near them exploded with motion and one of the elusive green-tinged cat creatures they'd only got glimpses of shot through the foliage so close that Jia could have probably reached out and touched it. The former assassin's eyes held an excitement and joy that made Lily expect the shorter woman to try.

Even Jia must have been thinking twice as the reason for the cat's flight and its previous scream made an appearance. A...*thing* was chasing it. Not only chasing, but gaining on the feline. Looking at the pair of them, Lily knew for a certainty if either one was chasing her, there was no way she could outrun the predator.

But neither creature seemed concerned with the humans. The monstrosity chasing the cat looked to be wanting to eat it and the cat's only thought appeared to be escaping.

As they raced by the party, Lily blinked, still not quite believing what she was seeing. The predator ran on four legs, like the cat, but it had two other appendages up in the front of its body. The whole thing was reminiscent of the myths of centaurs, the creatures with the body of a horse and the torso of a human. This monster, though, was in no way part human. The front part—or maybe the top part?—vaguely resembled a human torso with arms on the sides and a neck and head above the shoulders, though on this creature the shoulders were not very pronounced at all, like a very skinny man or an adolescent human.

Occasionally, the creature would put its arms down to gain a little speed or to make a sharp turn, otherwise, they reached out for the cat, its three fingers on each hand clawing at the air with the sharp nails like spikes that grew from the ends of its digits.

The body, too, wasn't quite centaur-like in that it was bulkier, with legs that were thicker and more robust looking. In fact, they even resembled the cat's own legs. All in all, whatever it was, it was built for speed and, Lily assumed, for killing what she thought would have been an apex predator.

The pair disappeared into the jungle, still crashing and continuing their chase. Lily took the opportunity to look to her companions and was shocked to see Tere with an evil grin on his face, as if he were a spectator watching gladiators clash in a fight to the death. Fortunately, he didn't notice her gazing at him because with the way her heart jumped—as well as her physical body—she knew her expression must have been something close to disgust.

Shifting her eyes to the others, she saw expressions that were likewise too interested in the life and death struggle that had just rushed by them. As the cat's scream of pain sounded and then cut off abruptly, the excitement dancing in Aeden's, Jia's, and even Urun's eyes made her stomach turn. The sailors seemed energized by the chase—and its unfortunate end—as well.

For nearly a minute, everyone looked at everyone else, furtive glances that reminded Lily of people who had just been caught vigorously scratching their crotches. Then Aeden cleared his throat and spoke.

"We should probably get moving. That thing, whatever it was, may still be hungry after it eats the cat. I don't fancy trying to outrun it. I'd rather not fight it, either, I think. It looked strong and it's wickedly fast."

That broke everyone's reverie and they all went into motion at once, Lily included. She was glad of the movement. They would probably talk more about what they'd seen later, but it seemed too close for them to do so now. At least, that's what she thought.

"That cat was stalking us," Tere said nonchalantly. "I thought I detected it before all the action, but it seems that the other monster attacked before it could pounce on us."

"Were you going to warn us?" Lily snapped, and immediately regretted the venom she imbued her words with.

"I was about to. I still wasn't completely sure. Looking back, though, the only way that cat was as close as it was when it was attacked was if it was stalking us. I told you my senses, especially my magical senses, are affected by this place. I don't want to send off warnings when I'm not sure, but I also have to balance that with trying to warn everyone in time if there's real danger nearby. I can only make judgment calls. I may end up being wrong, either too paranoid or not enough." He shrugged as if his explanation was good enough.

It might have been, had Lily not seen how he reacted to a monster chasing down and killing another monster. She hoped she could get that expression he wore out of her memory. It was like...ecstasy.

They didn't have any other close calls the rest of the day and by the time they set up camp, it almost seemed like a distant memory. Lily had been thinking about it the entire time they walked and the others weren't very talkative, either. She wondered if it weighed heavy on their minds as well.

"Have you ever seen or heard of something like that four-legged and two-armed thing we saw earlier?" Aeden asked as they sat around eating a stew Tere had made over the fire they built. "I can't remember ever hearing about anything like that other than a centaur. And I'm pretty sure that wasn't a centaur, not unless the myths got it very wrong. The front part of that thing was definitely *not* human. Not even close."

"I've never seen a picture or reference to them," Tere said. "Never even heard an oral tale of such a creature. For that matter, it's the same with those cats, though maybe they're the same as we have on Promistala but with different coloring."

"It was kind of scary having two monsters fighting for their lives so near to us," Lily said. "Either could have turned on us at any second."

"Scary?" Jia scoffed at the idea. "More like exciting. Two creatures, locked in combat, each one needing to kill or be killed. Life doesn't get any simpler or real than that. Or more exciting."

Lily wasn't sure how to answer that. As she looked around at the others, she realized even if she could come up with an answer, it would probably start an argument. The fervor in the eyes she looked into was a frightening thing. She'd seen the look before. In people whose emotions whipped them into mob violence.

She decided it was best to leave things as they were, turning her attention instead to the sailors. Several of them at any given time seemed to be suffering some strange sickness. Weakness, sometimes nausea, even disorientation. The symptoms would last for a time, up to a day, and then disappear as suddenly as they had arrived. As she scanned the group, she could tell which were afflicted because the exhilaration displayed in their eyes was absent compared to the others, as if the sickness precluded the strange phenomenon of being fixated on the predator and prey interaction they had witnessed.

She was as uncomfortable as she'd ever been in her life, and that was saying something with the life she'd had. Whatever was happening—to her friends and to the sailors—it was something she'd never experienced before. She wanted to talk to someone...to Tere. She wouldn't, though. He was as caught up in the feeling as the others.

For the time being, she had to wonder why she was the only one unaffected, and she had to pay close attention. If she could discover the reason for the change, maybe she could help her friends regain their normal composure. She had to do it before it affected her or the sour feeling in her gut told her that all would be lost.

Then again, what if she was truly the one affected by whatever foul power this was and her friends were too polite to tell her she had lost her mind.

CHAPTER
THIRTY-TWO

Lily got up the next morning more than an hour before the normal dawntime waking the party had adopted. She spotted Urun sitting on a rock someone had stripped of the vines and other plants every surface seemed to be covered with. The priest raised an eyebrow in question as she picked her way between slumbering people to join him.

"Good morning," she said.

"Not yet it's not. To me, if it's dark, it's still night."

She chuckled but didn't disagree. She was definitely in the camp of people who felt that waking up before the sun was too early.

"I wanted to talk to you and this seemed like the best time. I've been watching the men, trying to figure out this mysterious sickness that's been afflicting them."

"It is puzzling," he said. "I can't detect any illness in them, but I've seen them in distress. I don't know what it is."

"I've been thinking about it. Do you think it's the magic of this place affecting them? I don't know if it could be magic of the island itself or maybe the magic if there's a well, like Aeden thinks."

"Magic could definitely be affecting them. Even the Academy doesn't know everything about all types of magic."

"If it is that, then why isn't it affecting the rest of us?" She wasn't quite ready to broach the subject of something affecting her friends, not until she came up with a theory.

Urun scratched his head. "I don't know. My specialty is nature magic. I can use it to heal, but I'm not an expert on how all things can affect people. My delving may not be as complex as something they can do in the Medica at the Academy."

"Hmmm. Besides the weakness, nausea, sometimes vomiting or diarrhea, I've noticed something else in some of the men."

"You've been watching them closely. What else did you see?"

"Some of them—most of them—are scared and paranoid beyond what I would consider normal. Something is unnerving them, though they try to hide it."

A feral look entered into Urun's eyes. If Lily hadn't been looking right into them and the fire hadn't been lighting his face, she wouldn't have noticed it.

"They're probably just weak," he snapped. "Nature is not soft and only the strong survive." As soon as he finished speaking, he blinked several times and shook his head. "I...I don't know why I said that. It just kind of came out. Maybe I'm tired from my watch duty." He forced a smile, but it didn't fool Lily.

"Well, I'll keep watching them. I might try to talk to some of them today as we walk. I don't like the feel of it all. It seems like something is amiss."

"Let me know if you come up with anything I can do to help," Urun said. "We definitely don't need people falling apart in the middle of the mission."

"Yeah," she agreed. "Much better if we all fall apart at the end of the mission." She winked at him and went back to her bedroll to start rolling it up in preparation for her day.

From the start of the day, when the rest of the party woke

and packed up their bedrolls and ate their cold breakfast, Lily sensed that something was off. More off, anyway, than it had already seemed. Like many things since she'd come to the island, it didn't make any sense and she couldn't quite explain the feeling. All she knew was that whatever was affecting her friends, it had reached some kind of new level.

"Maybe we should explore a little bit while we travel," Aeden said to anyone who was listening as they sat eating. "We can't be so sure that my spell is leading us to exactly where we need to go. What if there's more we're missing. Treasure, battle, new monsters no one has ever seen, they might all be waiting for us somewhere in this jungle."

Lily waited for Urun to disagree, but the priest, sitting across from her, nodded with a faraway look in his eye. After a solid minute of no one responding, she spoke up.

"We can't do that, Aeden. We are on a mission for a goddess. It's important, especially if it involves another well like you believe. How can you want to go off exploring while the corruption continues to spread? What if, while we dally, whatever lies in the heart of Life's Cradle dies or turns deadly and evil?"

The Croagh blinked at her, like he didn't understand what she was saying. Then he shook his head and gave her a lopsided smile.

"You're right. To be honest, it even surprised me, coming out of my mouth like that. I must not be all the way awake yet."

She found that excuse suspect. Of all the people she knew, Aeden was the closest to being a true morning person. Now that she thought of it, he hadn't gotten up early to train after the first night they spent on the island. She hadn't known him for very long, but she rarely saw him skip his morning exercises, no matter their traveling situation.

The others remained silent during their exchange, watching both of them and keeping their thoughts to themselves. When everyone had eaten but no one had called a start to their day's hike, Lily realized that again, it would be up to her. Even looking pointedly at Tere for several minutes didn't spur the archer to take command.

"Aeden," she said, "do you want to cast your spell so we can confirm the direction and then get started?"

"Oh, right. Yes, we should get going, huh?" He cast his spell smoothly and quickly, what with all the practice he'd been having. Once it established the direction, another day of slogging through the increasingly thick jungle began.

In hardly any time at all, the anticipation of a significant event suddenly ended.

One moment, the party was walking along, pushing through the vegetation among the many sounds of the jungle. Then, as if Lily had suddenly lost her hearing, the world went silent. Not the crunching, breathing, and soft cursing of a few of the party members fed up with tramping through the tangled jungle, but something more important. All the sounds of birdsong, small rodents chirping and chittering at each other, even the little sounds of movement within the brush that had no visible source ended abruptly.

Only one thing Lily knew of would cause all life in an area to stop their activities and cease to make any sounds.

A predator.

By reflex, she swung the bow off her back and nocked an arrow. Tere beat her by half a breath as he scanned the surroundings with his own bow ready to shoot. It was no surprise that Aeden reacted as quickly as she. Jia and Urun brought their own weapons, knives and a staff, respectively, to a guard position. All of them moved so quickly and fluidly, two of the sailors startled, one falling over when his little jump caused the heavy pack he was carrying to upset.

Another of the sailors, Mirkus, of course, opened his mouth and emitted the start of a word, but Tere shushed him so vehemently, the talkative man put his hand over his mouth, eyes wide. He didn't make another sound, though, nor did any of the other sailors.

Tere loosed an arrow off to his left. Lily wondered what he was doing until, a fraction of a second later, something screeched within the foliage. As if a signal, the vegetation exploded with motion, more than a dozen large shapes leaping out toward where the party was waiting. One of those shapes had an arrow jutting out of its hindquarters.

The creatures resembled wolves in size and shape, though they had very short hair that laid close to their skin. In colors of browns, greens, and greys, they weren't just wolves of a different color, but had other dissimilarities. Their heads seemed bigger in relation to their bodies and they had a sleeker look, though they still had canine features such as their black noses and the tufted ears located on the upper sides of their heads.

Like wolves or other of their canine relatives, they ran fast, growling low in their throats as they charged their two-legged prey.

"Kill them all," Aeden shouted as he rushed out to meet a trio ahead of him. Several others went around him and headed straight for the sailors, who were dropping packs and fumbling for weapons as quickly as they could.

"No," Lily yelled. "Protect the sailors. Stay together."

It wasn't her place to shout out commands, but Aeden seemed to be under the spell of blood lust, something she'd never seen, or even heard of, him doing. He was always so meticulous and controlled when he engaged in combat, it struck Lily as frightfully unusual that he went after the animals in such a way.

Thankfully, the others did as she said, or at least didn't go rushing off to engage with the beasts before they reached the humans.

Tere let fly arrows with the same mechanical precision he always did. Lily, too, fired off several shafts per second, focusing on her right side while Tere was peppering the left side. She nearly released an arrow at a running wolf thing until a flicker of shadow caused her to re-aim her shot to another enemy. As she expected, Jia flickered into view, slashing the monster Lily had originally targeted four or five times before rolling off into the vegetation and out of sight. The unfortunate creature she had attacked dropped to the ground and slid, not getting back up. Its tan and grey fur showed clearly that the woman had cut it deeply, including a gash in the throat that spilled blood down the front of its chest.

Urun uncharacteristically cast magic at two of the creatures, slamming them off their feet with a wave of force. It was a spell Lily hadn't ever seen him use and she wondered why he wasn't casting protective shields over himself and the sailors. In rapid succession, he brought forth another bit of magic that made the vines near two more monsters reach up and grab them until, finally slowed down enough, they lost all momentum and were reduced to squirming to escape.

The next spell was a true surprise, one he had apparently learned when fighting the well guardian in the Mellafond. A sickly green light poured from his hands and sunk into the two captive creatures. Before Lily's eyes, they began to wither and become feeble, as if they had aged many years in only a few seconds. In a handful of breaths, they both collapsed to the ground, dead.

Realizing she'd been staring at what Urun was doing, her mouth hanging open, she picked out a new target and shot two arrows, barely a blink separating them. One threw the creature off its stride when it sunk into its shoulder and the second took advantage of the shift in body position, finding the spot between two ribs to lance the creature's heart.

Especially with the two archers, the battle seemed to be suspiciously easy, but Lily tried not to think about it. She continued to whittle down the numbers, as did her friends, and soon there was not a canine left standing. Or running. From what she could tell, none of them even got close enough to hurt anyone.

"Anyone injured?" Tere asked, as if reading Lily's mind.

Several answers came at the same time, all saying the same thing: no human had sustained injury, not even a minor one. At least, no one had been damaged physically. Meeting eyes with Aeden, Urun, Grobel, and Denos, Lily saw a disturbing fervor there, like they were pumped up and excited.

Bloodlust.

"Does everyone *feel* all right?" she asked, stressing the word. To this question, no answers came, but after some self-reflection, the light in the others' eyes dimmed a bit. She continued. "Are we ready to move on? Maybe we can go another mile or two and then take a rest." To this, she got a few grunts she took as affirmation. She chivvied Aeden to lead them along their path, leaving the animal carcasses to the jungle.

CHAPTER
THIRTY-THREE

I t was as if the party had crossed an invisible threshold into a land of pandemonium. After the somewhat unchallenging attack of the short-haired wolf creatures, they were soon attacked by a number of other animals.

By midday, the sailors were exhausted and Lily was frustrated at being constantly on edge. Her friends shifted their moods between their own anger and tension and excitement to finally be doing something other than pressing through the jungle.

First it was half a dozen of the green-tinged cat creatures they'd seen being chased by the monstrosity a couple of days previously. Then there were thirteen of what seemed to be flightless birds of prey, similar to ostriches in size but with razor sharp claws, sharp beaks, and surprisingly tough skin. From there, the party encountered gigantic lizard creatures, complete with venom dripping from their wicked fangs, and finally a handful of some kind of squat furred animal that reminded Lily of a badger with its sharp claws and teeth, but larger than the wolves they started the day off fighting.

By the time Aeden called a halt to the day's travel—mainly because the sailors were stumbling along as if a stiff breeze would knock them over—no one wanted to continue. They made camp hastily and collected plenty of wood to feed the fire they started.

"I don't know how well it'll do to scare the creatures off tonight," Tere said, adding more wood to the blaze. "We didn't have problems with them attacking the camp at night before, but it seems like all that changed today."

"Do you think it was a time thing?" Jia asked. "We've been in the jungle long enough so that the monsters here are more comfortable with us and now will attack us? Or is it that we reached a location, some kind of dividing line that we crossed over into the land of constant battle?"

Aeden leaned back against a vine covered boulder. "That's a good question. I don't know how we'd get an answer, though, not unless we backtrack and suddenly don't get attacked anymore."

"The character of the jungle is shifting," Urun said without looking up. The priest seemed more tired than the rest of Lily's friends, his head hanging and his eyes fixed on the ground in front of him. "I can feel it changing, but I don't know what it's changing from or to. I think it's obvious that it's getting more dangerous. Does that mean we're heading in the right direction or are we going the wrong way, right into some kind of zone where we'll find nothing but fighting and death, without ever finding the Cradle?"

"That's kind of depressing, Urun," Lily said. "I noticed how much the jungle was changing just by the way the plants are. There are new ones, and even the ones we've been seeing since we first set foot on the island are growing more thickly. I have no idea if we're going the right way, either, but at least we're going somewhere. Without a destination, we'll wander the jungle until we die of old age or we run into things that are tougher than what we've seen. Those last few battles weren't easy."

"True," Tere said. He glanced over at the sailors, all of

them sitting or even lying limply like they had no energy. Lily wasn't sure if it was just fatigue or if it was in some part due to the sickness most of them faced over the last several days. "Grobel."

The de facto leader of the crewmen lifted his head to look at Tere. "Yes, sir?"

"How are your men holding up?"

"We'll be fine, sir. Just tired, is all."

"Listen, we can probably expect to run into more monsters, either the same types we had to fight today or some new ones. I know several of you have some skill with your weapons. You can fight if you want, but I think it's a better idea to stay together and let us handle it. If you do want to fight, do it behind the lines we set up. We can let one or two monsters through so you can take them out, if you want. Again, though, I think saving your energy for the hike in between battles is a better idea. Under no circumstances are any of you to come up to the battle line where we meet the rush of the attack. Is that clear?"

"It is, sir. I'll talk it over with the boys and let you know what we decide. My opinion is that we should let you all do what you do best while we save our strength for carrying the supplies." Grobel swung his head to glance around at the other sailors, but none of them so much as lifted his head to speak. They really did look exhausted.

"I'll take first watch tonight," Lily said. "I suggest we split the other two watches between Tere, Jia, Aeden, or Urun. Let the men rest up. It was a rough day."

Grobel nodded his thanks to Lily and Tere grunted his agreement.

"I'll take middle watch," Aeden offered.

"I can get last watch for tonight," Jia said. "Maybe I can catch a glimpse of a slice of sunrise through all these trees in the morning."

There was little discussion after that. Everyone was so

257

tired, they found a spot to lie down in and one by one, they all drifted to sleep, leaving Lily to watch the area as the jungle became darker outside the small bubble of the firelight.

The group had gathered plenty of wood, so though the night wasn't chilly, Lily continued to feed the fire. It was a small comfort, but it was still *a* comfort. She settled in for a long watch, mostly with her back to the fire to prevent ruining her night vision.

The jungle was eerily quiet, as if it was holding its breath, waiting for something significant to happen. Small movements of her friends and the sailors; the deep, even breaths of sleeping people; and a mumble or groan now and then were all there was to keep the crackle of the fire company.

Three hours into her watch, nearly time for Aeden to take over, the big sailor Jun mumbled to himself incoherently. Over the course of several minutes, it built into a full-fledged argument with himself. It was strange enough that Lily scanned the area, then took a chance in looking toward the fire to see what was bothering the man. Was he having a fever dream or was it simply a nightmare?

So suddenly she drew an arrow and had it nocked before thinking, Jun screamed, jumped to his feet, and took off running.

As the rest of the camp was startled awake by the noise, Lily took off running after the man, wondering what in Surus's name he was doing.

"Jun took off," she shouted to her waking friends. "I'm going after him."

For a man as big as Jun, he moved with surprising grace through the crowded jungle, especially considering that there was very little light. A small amount from the stars and the nearly full moon filtered through the canopy, but Lily could barely keep up.

It took her several minutes—and more than one risky maneuver to try to cut the man off in the dark, dangerous terrain—but she finally got close enough to kick his trailing leg hard, throwing him off balance. He shot toward the ground, crumpled into a ball, bounced, and then slid for an impressively long time in the damp foliage before stopping. Lily felt bad about doing it, but it was either that or shoot him somewhere non-vital with an arrow.

Her own rapid deceleration nearly caused her to collide with a tree as she slipped and almost went down. Twisting in a way that would have made an acrobat proud, she narrowly avoided the tree and snatched at a thick, low branch as she passed under it at speed. The resulting jerk shot pain through her shoulder, but it stopped her without any serious injury.

Jun, for his part, had curled up on the ground where he had slid to a stop. He was whimpering and muttering something unintelligible.

"Jun," she said. "Jun Freemud." She nudged his back with her foot to get his attention. When his breathing hitched, Lily hopped back and brought her bow up to deter an attack.

The big man swung his face toward her, wet with tears and with anguish twisting it. "Mistress Lily?"

"Yes, it's me. Are you...all right?"

"They're coming for us, whispering to me that they will kill us all. I tried to be brave, Mistress Lily. I really did. But the magic monsters are coming." Jun put his head in his hands and squeezed his face so hard, Lily thought he might actually hurt himself.

"Jun!"

He peeked through his fingers at her.

"You have to calm down. We're all scared sometimes. This place isn't like anywhere you've ever been. It's natural to feel a little afraid. We're all afraid. That we won't find what we're looking for, that we won't be able to do what we have to do, that we'll be attacked by monsters. What we are doing is important, though. We have to do our best and help each other. My friends and I will do our best to keep everyone safe, but you can't go running off like that. If there were monsters around, they would take the chance to attack just the two of us out here alone. We have to all stick together and we'll be safer."

The sailor nodded in understanding. "If we all stay together, it will be harder for them to kill us."

"That's right. And when we're all together, you and the other sailors can either take turns helping to fight or you can stay close together behind us so we can fight the monsters without worrying about any of you running off and letting them get you."

"Running away is not good," he said.

"Right again. If you run, then we won't all be together and it'll be easier for the monsters to get us. So, will you come back with me to the others now?" She held out her hand toward him. He stared at it for a moment before wiping his right hand on his pants and engulfing the one she proffered with it.

"I'll stay with my friends so we can be safe together."

"That's the spirit. Come on. I'm sure they're worrying about us. The sooner we're all back together, the better."

When Lily and Jun got back to camp, everyone else was awake and waiting impatiently, not the least so the other sailors. Though Jun slinked in with his head down, Grobel cleared his throat and, when the larger man met his eyes, the older sailor nodded firmly and gave Jun a slight smile.

Chenos approached Jun and reached up to pat his back. "I lost some silver betting you were dead, but I'm happy about it."

Jun didn't seem to hold it against the man, though, gracing him with a grin. Lily could only shake her head as the other sailors surrounded the largest of them to console, welcome back, or just stand alongside him. Mirkus and Brek, as vocal as ever, spoke over each other to Jun, who didn't seem to mind the confusion. The only one of them who didn't show any kind of affection toward Jun was the enigmatic Vorun, who stood in the midst of them, his normal neutral look on his face.

Meanwhile, Lily headed over to her friends, where they were gathered in their own little huddle a few paces away.

"Well?" Tere asked.

"Some kind of nightmare and a general feeling of panic from the things in the forest and what's been going on," Lily said. "He's sure that 'magic monsters' are after us and are going to kill all of us. I explained that we need to stay together and that it's normal to be scared. I think he knows not to run away from the group now, that it'll make it easier for the monsters to kill us."

"Yeah," Aeden said. "We've been talking about that since you went off chasing him. We're not sure what we're going to be facing or if we'll be able to protect Tesnair's men."

"What, then?" she asked. "We're *not* going to protect them?"

"Calm down, girl," Tere growled. "We're thinking that maybe we should give them a choice to go back to the ship instead of going on with us."

"That's—"

"Not forcing them," Jia interrupted. "*Asking* them if they'd rather do that. Things are only getting more dangerous as we keep going forward."

Lily sighed. That seemed reasonable. "There's no harm in discussing it with them, I guess, but I doubt they'd survive trying to get back to the ship by themselves."

Tere glanced over at the sailors. "That's what we decided, too. We'll give them a few minutes and then we can talk to them and see what they think."

A quarter of an hour later, Lily found herself speaking for her friends to the group of sailors, somehow having been convinced that the crewmen all seemed to think highly of Lily. Tere made a point of telling her it wasn't because of her striking lack of clothing, which of course was his way of saying that it surely was. She laughed at his teasing, but still didn't feel like the right one to be leading the discussion.

After she explained that things were getting more dangerous as they continued further into the jungle, she asked them plainly. "We would not want to force you to go into more danger. Though we appreciate your help, we are willing to carry our own supplies if you wanted to go back to the ship to wait for us to return. There's no embarrassment or dishonor in going back. Would you like to return to the Eurus?"

The men traded looks, but few words were traded. As always, it was Grobel who answered her.

"Though we appreciate you saying there is no dishonor in not completing our task, we would not feel right in abandoning you to carrying all that we have brought. We all, each one of us, decided we would face the danger and go with you and we'll not turn back."

Urun took a step forward. "None of us had any idea what we would face. Things are getting very dangerous. We've been able to protect you so far, but it's getting harder. If we get overwhelmed by strong monsters, we will have to defend ourselves first, possibly allowing some to get around us to attack you. You have to be reasonable and protect yourselves first. There is no shame in turning back when faced with dangers far above you."

"Again, sir, we appreciate your concern. We're not being stubborn. There is danger, we know. The thing is, if we turn back now, you all will go ahead while we backtrack to return to the ship. We're not scouts or trackers—" he gestured at Mirkus to keep silent even as the man was opening his mouth to declare otherwise "—and the simple fact is, we may get lost going back. More important, though, if we meet even one small group of the creatures we saw coming to this point, we'll be slaughtered to a man. We've talked about the possibility before, and most of us agree that we couldn't make it back to the ship alive, not without the luck of the gods. Forward, we might die, but going back? We'll surely die. We would like to continue, whatever happens because of it."

Urun looked frustrated, but Lily responded before he got a chance to. "Thank you for your honesty, Grobel, and the rest of you. We will not force you to leave. If it's your decision to continue with us, we will do our best to protect and aid you, as always. We only pray that it's enough."

It must have been the right thing to say because not only the crewmen's leader, but most of the rest of them let out breaths of relief. They must have really thought they were going to be abandoned.

"Well," Tere said. "That's settled. How about we sleep the rest of the night, except for Aeden and Jia, who will be taking turns at watch. When the sun comes up, we'll need to get moving again."

CHAPTER

THIRTY-FOUR

I t was a tired and somewhat disheartened group that began their trek in the morning. Conversation was at a minimum and heads swiveled to look for hidden enemies along the way, but nothing attacked and the background noise of the small animals in the jungle was present in all its chitterings, whistles, and other calls.

Lily could feel the tension from the others even as she sensed it in herself. It was a string pulled so tightly that at any moment it might snap with a twang, the ends cutting through its surroundings like a whip.

For hours they trudged on, until Aeden led them up a gentle incline within the trees where they finally crested the small rise. Looking down, it was only a few dozen feet in to the base ground, but the area in front of them was so far removed from what they had already seen, each member of the party could only stop and stare out at what lay before them.

It was a maelstrom. That was the only word Lily could think of that did justice to the landscape ahead of them. She'd seen sketches and paintings of a powerful sea storm and the twirling clouds and wind-born debris that made up the phenomenon. The jungle in front of them looked like that, like the entire thing was one swirling mass, but instead of clouds and water, it was all made up of green and brown and a few brighter colors. The hues of living things, of plants, but not such as she'd ever seen before.

It looked like it was almost...

"Sentient," Urun said. "It feels like the plants down there —all the life down there, really—is one large sentient organism. I can almost sense an intelligence, but I can't quite pinpoint what it is or where exactly it's at. I never thought I would be afraid of any natural thing, not true fear. That, down there, it makes me afraid."

Jia worked her mouth, but it took her a few tries until she actually produced words. "We don't have to go down there, Urun. We can turn back, or maybe find another way."

The priest looked at her with eyes wide. "What? No. That's not what I meant. It does scare me, true, but Osulin, my goddess, charged me with finding Life's Cradle and eliminating the corruption from it. That mess down there, it has to be the Cradle, or at least what used to be the Cradle. Regardless of what else happens or who will join me—even if no one will—I am going down into that chaotic nightmare of tainted vegetation to try my best to complete the quest I've been given. I don't expect anyone else to come with me, if they don't want to."

Lily was the first to speak. "I'm going with you. From when I first met you, you showed me kindness and compassion, even though I was technically still your enemy. You're not going down there without my bow covering you to the best of my ability."

Urun nodded to her, his eyes cloudy with emotion. "Thank you, Lily."

Three other voices spoke at the same time, indicating that Aeden, Jia, and Tere were also going with them.

"We already talked about this last night," Grobel said. "My men and I are with you till the end. There's no turning back for us, not unless you all do so."

The silence stretched on for nearly a minute, only the faint sounds of small jungle animals and the rustling of the vegetation in the wind breaking it. Tere finally ended it. "It looks like there's nothing to do but to head down then."

AMATIA HAD BEEN on the Dark Council for fourteen years, though she was barely past thirty years of age. She was the youngest member of the Council. Added to her...differences from the others, it made for a solitary existence. Her mother, occupying the seat on the Council before her, had been murdered by a rival and Amatia had never been very close to her father. Nor did she have any real friends, again because she was unlike anyone else she'd ever met except for her mother.

From when she was very young, it was clear she had the *gift* her mother and many of the other women in her family possessed, that of being able to see things no one else could. The future, possibilities in the present, even visions of the past that could be used for her own purposes were hers to command, though it was a tenuous control. Those who knew of it, even her father and members of the extended family, shunned her, uncomfortable with a power they did not understand.

When her mother died so suddenly, she didn't know what she would do. She was still a girl and seriously contemplated taking her own life. That changed when Alloria Yurgen showed up at her house two days after her mother's death. The body had not even been prepared for burial and the sending-off ceremony for her spirit had not yet been held.

The tall, thin woman with the pale complexion and hair

that was unnaturally colored—silver-white that shone almost like it was metal in the sun—took her to a secluded place outside of town and explained to her the position her mother had held. When she offered, almost pressed upon Amatia, the position, the girl accepted, mainly because she wasn't yet thinking straight due to her mother's sudden death.

There were days when she wondered if it wouldn't have been better to go ahead with her plans for suicide.

It took nearly two years for her to settle into her position on the Dark Council and to realize that the others weren't giving her suspicious looks all the time and wondering why such an inexperienced nobody had been included in their number. Once she stopped reading intent into every little smirk, smile, or grimace, she understood that some of the others seemed to feel out of their element as well. Some didn't, but there were at least a few who did, and that made all the difference to her.

A few key times, she provided necessary information she had gleaned from her abilities that helped the Council to make a success of something that was headed for failure. Finally, she felt as if she was contributing and showing that she was a valuable part of the group.

Still, for the most part, Amatia kept to herself. Her talents were not easily controlled. In fact, they were often downright unpredictable. It was frustrating, but she had no choice in the matter. She did the best she could.

That frustration was at a high point of late. They were in the end times, the period about which the Dark Prophet had not only prophesied, but for which he had created the Dark Council. At such a crucial juncture in the timeline, Amatia needed to shine, her talents working for her and not against her.

The problem was, that was not what was happening.

In her time of greatest need, her powers seemed to be furthest from her. Meditation, herbal aids, even rituals that she had always scoffed at only scratched the skin of what she had tried to get her visions to come to her, and come reliably.

All to no avail.

Amatia had gotten more and more distressed in the last several months. The Council's activities had increased dramatically with the things that were happening in the world. Primarily, it was the Hero Academy and, more specifically, Marla Shrike and the unknown Crow that turned out to be her twin brother. Those two—and their friends—seemed to be tugging a rope firmly fastened on the nose ring of the world. All the while, Amatia had felt the eyes of the Vituma and the rest of the Council upon her.

It was enough for her to question her value to anyone, even more than she normally did. She believed she had them all fooled, that she was calm and cool and in control. Under it all, though, she was shivering in fear constantly.

But then, when everything seemed to be wrong, she had a breakthrough, a flood of vision magic that would show the others her true value.

"Amatia?" Alloria Yurgen said. The Vituma was sitting in her customary place at the table within her home. Amatia, and most of the others now, sat at the table as little more than ghosts, images of them cast by the meeting stones.

"Yes, Vituma?" The seeress had gotten so deep in thought, she must have been sitting and staring into empty space. How many times had someone talked to her while she was deep in thought?

"I asked if you were ready to get started? We're missing only Gareth Bryce and—oh." The handsome Council member appeared in the chair that had been empty a second before. Cara Moore, materialized in her own seat. "Very good. We are all here. I called you all here for an important development. Thank you for coming. The meeting should be short. Amatia?"

The seeress took a deep breath, sat up straighter, and shifted her eyes around the room to meet each of the others in turn. "I have had visions that I believe to be important. In them, I have learned where one of the Wells of Power lies. One the Academy folk do not know of yet. If we act quickly, we can get to it first and perhaps take the magic for ourselves instead of them releasing it into the world."

CHAPTER

THIRTY-FIVE

T he tangled vegetation the party plunged into was deceptive in its depth and contour. For most of the day, they continued to head downward on the surprisingly steep slope, made all the more precarious by the damp, slick plant matter coating the ground.

"Are we heading into a valley or a crater?" Lily asked after they'd reached the early afternoon. "It didn't look this steep from where we started." As she said it, an idea occurred to her and she cast her eyes over her shoulder. The trees, vines, and bushes were too thick for her to see up the incline more than a few feet, but the angle of what she could see shocked her with how much like a wall it looked. A big, green wall.

"We might be heading straight into Abyssum itself, for all we know," Tere grumbled.

"This place," Urun said, "has awareness."

Tere stopped and turned toward the priest. Lily realized she had done exactly the same thing at the same time.

"Are you telling us there's something in here that you can sense or hear our thinking?" the old archer asked.

"No. That's wrong on two counts. First, it's not quite thinking; it's awareness, sensation. Second, I'm not talking

271

about something *in* the jungle. I'm talking about the jungle itself. It is sentient, though to what extent I can't determine."

Jia seemed to pop into being where she clearly wasn't present a second before. "Is it hostile?"

Urun shook his head. "I don't know, but I don't think so. There is something akin to irritation, but I can't decide if it's the jungle or something else. All of these sensations are new to me. It will take time to decipher them."

Lily traded looks with Tere, but no one commented on the priest's words. When they continued their press through the jungle, Lily thought about it, though. If Urun sensed some sort of intelligence, did that mean they had found Life's Cradle? Could it be the guardian of the well, or the well itself?

Lacking any real clearings in the jungle, the party halted their progress early that day—more than two hours before the light faded—so they could cut and clear a small area to camp in. It was hard work, but everyone working together allowed them to accomplish it even in their fatigued state. Once they were done, all of them settled into a brief rest before engaging in another flurry of activity to build fires and prepare dinner.

Lily checked on the sailors, noting that two of them—Denos and Brek—hadn't helped out with clearing out the vegetation.

"Both of them are not doing well," Grobel told her. "That intermittent sickness has grabbed hold of them again and they're weak, unable to eat food without vomiting it up again."

"I'll ask Urun to look at them," Lily said.

"He did so, an hour ago. He told me that he can find nothing wrong with them with his magic. It is as before. He has not been able to detect or aid in the illness my men and I have been suffering during the journey."

"I'm sorry. Make sure they drink plenty of water and have them eat something as soon as they are able. Is there anything else they need? Tere knows a lot about herbs and might be able to give them something to help them be more comfortable."

"He has given us such things, for stomach upset, vomiting, headache, and dizziness. They don't have a great effect, though they may help a little. We have been using them."

Lily frowned at the ground. "I wish we could do more."

"We appreciate your concern. They will recover. All of us have had the same at least once over the past few days."

"Oh," she said, remembering something. "Denos was supposed to have a watch tonight. I can cover it for—"

"That is not necessary, thank you," Grobel told her. "Jun there has volunteered to take the watch for Denos." He pointed to the giant man standing a few feet away, acting like he was inspecting some of the cut vines littering the ground.

Lily smiled at the man, who glanced up in time to catch it. He whipped his head around to look at something else, his face flushing. She liked the quiet man. He seemed to have a good heart. "Okay. Let me know if there's anything else we can do. You and your men get some rest. Maybe there's not too much farther we'll have to go to find what we're looking for."

She swept her red hair from her face and spent the next two hours checking on the others and making sure there were no issues with any of the party members. In the middle of her ministrations, she stopped and wondered at what she was doing. Who had made her the leader or the administrator of the expedition? No one had explicitly asked her to do it, but the sailors were vacillating back and forth between health and illness and her friends—well, there was still something a bit off about how they were acting.

It wasn't anything overt, not even something that set off warning bells within her admittedly paranoid mind. It was the little things they said and did. She honestly felt sometimes as if she might be going mad, imagining things and becoming suspicious of everyone.

At other times, she felt as if it was all justified.

Just before bed, she was chatting with Jia, the one she'd known longest in the group. They had traveled together as Falxen and even though she didn't really strike up a real friendship with the dark-haired woman, their shared past as assassins had always made Lily feel like they were kindred spirits.

In her conversation with Jia, the former assassin stated plainly, "I hope we get attacked, or at least that we get to witness another fight for survival between predator and prey, like before. Nothing makes you feel alive like the fight for survival, right?"

She was smiling when she said it and Lily responded with as genuine a smile as she could while nodding, not trusting her voice to speak. What was it with the predator and prey thing? It almost felt like she was missing part of a joke, the punchline making no sense to her.

One thing was certain: they couldn't finish this mission of Osulin's soon enough and get off the crazy island they found themselves on. If she thought she could convince the others, she might even try to talk them into abandoning the quest and leaving immediately. Urun would never go for it, though. Unfortunately.

With these thoughts swirling in her mind, Lily laid down to try to get some sleep. Between the thoughts and the jungle environment, which seemed more and more hostile to her all the time even if they hadn't seen any monsters in the last day, she dozed at most. It would have to do, she thought, as she lay there, eyes closed, and working through some simple mental exercises to relax her body and mind.

A strange sound grabbed hold of her ears as if it were a physical thing. She must have been dozing, maybe even fully asleep, because try as she might to replay the sound in her mind, she couldn't. It was enough to wake her up, but she hadn't been paying attention to it when the noise struck her.

It came again, a mix between a scrape and an *urk* sound.

Knowing better than to jump to her feet until she figured out if there was an animal or monster in the camp, she opened her eyes and turned her head slowly toward where Urun had been sitting for first watch when she went to sleep. Her eyes went wide to take in more of the sparse light when she noticed that the moss-covered log was empty.

Panic be damned, she snatched up her bow and a handful of arrows and rolled to her feet. She'd gone to sleep fully clothed and equipped—as normal when traveling—and her long knives were belted to her waist. With all her weapons accounted for, she crossed the distance to where the sentry should be sitting in a handful of steps.

In the low light of the fire, which had almost gone out, she saw a large shape sprawled on the ground. She recognized it when she was within a few feet of it.

It was Jun Freemud, and he was bleeding from a dozen different slashes, the most pronounced of which had torn his throat out. He didn't move, nor would he ever again.

"Wake!" she yelled. "Attackers. Wake up."

CHAPTER
THIRTY-SIX

L ily's friends leaped into action in the manner she had come to expect from them. Within a few minutes, the fire was large enough to flood the little space they made with light; Tere, Jia, and Aeden were scouting around the camp searching for monsters; and Urun knelt next to Lily to examine the corpse of Jun Freemud.

"It looks like he was mauled by a beast with sharp claws," the priest said. "How did a creature attack and silence him quickly enough that there was no sound?"

"There was a sound," she said. "I heard something, but I think it was mostly the noise of his skin being torn by whatever monster did this."

"The question still remains. How did it happen within our camp?"

"I don't know, but we're going to need to double up on the sentries from now on. Unless there's more than one, the attacker won't be able to silence both at the same time."

Tere appeared within the firelight, for all the world looking like he was stomping, though he didn't make any noise.

"Nothing. No tracks outside of camp other than the ones we ourselves made. Inside the camp, there's too much background magic for me to pick out anything in particular, but I didn't find any sign of anything other than us. It's almost like he did it himself."

Lily gave him a scowl. She could understand Tere being angry over the whole thing, but that was patently ridiculous.

"I'm exaggerating," he said, putting both hands up to ward off her sour look. "I don't understand it."

"We were just talking about that," Urun said. "Whatever got him is some kind of apex predator. It's obviously smart enough to wait until we were all asleep to attack, and we can't detect any trace of it. That's not good news."

Grobel's appearance stopped their conversation. No one seemed to want to talk about their trouble in finding the attacker in front of the crew. Lily knew she didn't.

The elder sailor's face was drawn as he looked over Jun's torn body. He shook his head sadly.

"Jun wasn't the smartest of men, but he was one of the kindest, gentlest people I ever met. He worked hard and he cared about people. He didn't deserve this."

Denos stepped up beside Grobel. "He took the shift from me because I was sick. It should have been me there lying on the ground, not him. Gods, I wish it were. I've never had a better friend than that big lump." He choked on the last two words and turned away from the body.

The other sailors were gathered nearby, all of them with sullen expressions. All of them but Vorun, that is. The expressionless man wore the same face he always did, neither happy nor sad. He did bow his head like the others, though, so Lily figured he was simply cursed with not being expressive.

"I guess Jun found the monster he was scared of the other night. Or, it found him." Surprisingly, it was Mirkus who said it, probably the first thing Lily had ever heard the sailor say that wasn't about himself.

"Maybe he's the lucky one," Denos said. "It seemed real quick. The rest of us will probably suffer."

"Okay," Tere said, breaking the mood. "Let's not make too many assumptions. It's probably a wild beast, some kind of predator that stalks and kills quietly. Don't go making up monsters. We'll get to the bottom of it. In the meantime, we need to double up on the people on watch at any given time. We need to try to be more careful now that we know something is here that can hurt us."

"Begging your pardon," Grobel said, "but we've known that from the beginning. We've seen a little of what's here. This island is dangerous. We all knew that before we set foot in the trees."

"Are you saying that you changed your mind?" Lily asked. "Do you want to go back to the ship?"

Grobel turned his head slowly toward her. "We would go back to the ship if all of you went back, too, or at least two or three of you. I don't reckon we'd make it back to the Eurus alive if we tried to go on our own. Are you saying that you'll give up your quest and go back with us?"

"No." Urun answered before Lily could. "We still have our charge from Osulin." He met Lily's eyes, then Tere's, Jia's, and finally Aeden's. There was a question in his own.

"We have to go on," Tere said. "We can't let Urun go by himself."

"Then there's your answer," Grobel said. "We go where you go. Some of us may survive if we stick close to you. We don't see any chance if we try to turn around without you."

"Very well," Tere said. "I'll take the watch. Grobel, have one of your men watch with me, and assign one for the watch after that. We'll bury Jun in the morning."

"I'll take the next watch," Aeden volunteered.

Tere nodded. "I'll wake you in three hours. The rest of you should get some rest. We not only have a mission, but now we have another task: we need to find what it is that killed our friend."

That seemed to rouse the sailors a little. They stood up

straighter and a couple of them nodded. Lily figured it was the best they could do for now.

After a virtually sleepless night, Lily dragged herself from her bedroll in the morning and prepared for the day's travel. After they had buried Jun, she watched the others as they got ready to leave as well.

It was interesting to her to observe how each of the others responded to what had happened the night before. It was expected that the sailors would be quiet and sullen, since it was their longtime friend that had died the night before. Lily's friends, on the other hand, mostly set to the work of breaking camp as if it were any other day.

Tere scanned the area more than was typical, his head swinging from side to side with such rapidity it almost made her dizzy. Aeden cast his glance often to the sailors, concern in his eyes. In his life, he had known loss and it apparently made him more sympathetic to others dealing with their own grief. Jia didn't seem to be affected, but it was hard to tell with the former Falxen. She didn't joke as much and she suppressed her normal smile, but Lily thought that was probably more not to offend the sailors than because what had happened had shocked her. She had been a high-level career assassin, after all. Death was nothing new to her.

Urun seemed in his own world. When he looked toward where they were heading, his forehead crinkled and he muttered to himself unintelligibly. The priest was carrying more weight than the rest of them combined, Lily thought. It was his mission and she knew him well enough to know that he blamed himself for the death of the innocent Jun.

Lily's feelings on what had happened were complex. While she did think it was a tragedy that someone as kindhearted as Jun had lost his life, she also knew that when it was boiled down to its most basic component, life was simply about surviving. All the other things were dressings and distractions. Each day was a struggle to maintain life, and each day, someone somewhere would lose that contest. Yesterday had been Jun's day to lose. She felt bad to think of it that way, but her life up to that point had only confirmed what she believed.

"You okay?" Tere asked from right next to her, and she realized she'd been standing in place lost in thought.

"Uh, yeah, I guess. I don't like it that one of our group got killed like that. I'm no stranger to death and loss, but of all of them, he's the one I would have hoped survived all this."

"I know. I feel the same. That man had a gentle soul. I wish he never would have come with us, even though he could carry three times as much as the others."

Lily hummed a noncommittal response. She turned to look into Tere's white eyes. "I don't like the feeling I'm getting about this place. It's not just that it's dangerous. There's something else going on. Are we going to find what Urun is looking for? Are any of us going to survive it?"

"The strong will," Tere said simply.

Lily worked her mouth, trying to come up with something to say to that. It might be true, but it didn't sound like something he would say. Tere grumbled a lot and tried to make others think he was harsh and uncaring, but he was anything but. Even after everything life had done to him, he still cared deeply about people. He was a true hero at heart. Knowing that made what he'd said even harder to take. She must have misunderstood his terse statement.

She was about to ask what he meant when shouting ahead of them threw every other thought out of her mind. Tere pivoted and took off running, Lily on his heels. Both of them pulled arrows from their quivers and nocked them on their bowstrings as they ran.

Running was difficult in the jungle, even when those ahead of them had cut down vines and cleared something of a path. Despite that, Tere ran at nearly full speed, ducking, jumping, and skipping over obstacles as if he'd practiced going through that particular patch of ground a hundred times before. It was all Lily could do to keep him in sight, let alone trying to keep up with him. Just when she thought she had been closing the gap between the aging hero and herself, something as simple as running through a patch of thicker vegetation proved her wrong.

"Get into a group and stay behind us," Aeden shouted, obviously instructing the sailors in the way that would keep them safest. Sounds of crashing through the jungle met Lily's ears as she tried to squeeze a little more speed from her legs.

Finally, she cleared a tangled section of vines, trees, and what they'd started calling razor bush. As she ran by one of the large plants with jagged leaves, a slight tugging on the skin of her leg and a familiar pain, like a thin, sharp blade had slashed it, made her curse inwardly. Looking down, she noticed blood dribble out of the fine incision and she slowed almost to a stop to get through the mess. What she saw when she reached the others actually made her forget her wound and the nocked arrow on her bow for a moment.

What looked like a formation of huge snakes, their bodies upright, balanced on their tails, confronted the humans. The reptiles moved synchronously with each other, as if they were controlled by one entity or they had been trained and drilled like a military unit.

Lily could only watch for a moment before three of the snakes in the front rank struck out with lightning-fast movements, all attacking Aeden.

THIRTY-SEVEN

The snakes were colored in shades of greens and browns, in a seemingly random pattern, but one that made it difficult to track their movements in amongst the plants of the jungle. Large pieces of them—even their whole bodies at some times—looked like they disappeared completely. An ache started building in Lily's head after watching them for a handful of seconds.

When they struck out at Aeden, her heart stopped. They were so fast! That, coupled with their natural camouflage, made her certain the Croagh would be struck by at least one of them. There was no telling if the monsters were venomous, but judging from how violent and deadly the jungle seemed to be in general, she was betting they were. She prayed that Urun could get to him in time to heal him and cleanse him of the poison he would inevitably be injected with.

Her mouth dropped open as Aeden twisted and bent his body in exactly the right way, somehow evading all three of the huge serpents. Not only that, but as he slithered around their attacks, he lashed out with both of his swords and cut deeply into one of the snakes, though it didn't look nearly deep enough to cause the monster serious harm.

The entire time, Aeden wore a manic grin that made Lily feel more than a little uncomfortable.

Dual twangs of a bowstring near her snapped her attention to the situation at hand and she noted that two arrows appeared in one of the snakes, both of them in one eye. Tere hadn't paused like she had, and she tried to mitigate her guilty feelings by launching three more shafts in rapid succession, choosing to attack other snakes in the second line and leaving the ones Aeden was fighting to him and Tere.

Jia appeared beside one of the beasts Lily had shot with two arrows. One had gone into its eye, but the angle didn't look right to have reached its brain. The other went into its mouth, skewering the tongue it flicked out to taste the air. Neither was lethal, but Jia's dagger rammed into the other eye up to its hilt did the trick. It jerked and twitched like the one Tere had struck, both of them going through convulsions that indicated they didn't have much longer to live, if they were in fact still alive.

As Aeden went on the attack against the other two that had come at him, Jia disappeared again to hunt her next victim. Urun, for a change, wasn't holed up behind a shield but was using his staff to focus magic on another of the snakes that had been trying to slither over to the easy targets of the gathered sailors. As the beam of magic struck the reptile, it wavered and then seemed to crinkle, it's skin appearing to be moulting. After several seconds, it slowed and then flopped to the ground, much flatter and more ragged than it had been.

Lily shook her head to clear it. It wasn't like her to stand and watch during a battle, but it was so strange. Everything from the monsters they were fighting to how each of her friends were attacking seemed somehow unreal. She could analyze things later, though. For the time being, she needed to help whittle down the monsters that were organized into what was too much like a human military formation for her liking.

The remaining serpents suddenly split up, moving quickly in several different directions. Most went straight at Lily's friends, especially Aeden, Urun, and Jia, though how the monsters knew where Jia was, she had no idea. She became visible as two of them came at her from either side and she had to defend herself. It was like some officer had barked an order and the soldier snakes instantly obeyed. A few even headed toward Lily and Tere. They all seemed to know exactly where they were going, not hesitating in the least.

But that wasn't what caught her eye. In the midst of the chaos, three of the snakes made a beeline for the group of sailors. Grobel and Brek stood in front of them, battered swords in their hands. Lily could see Brek's hand—and the sword in it—shaking in fear, but he didn't retreat. Denos was behind them, lacking a weapon, with Vorun standing next to him with the same blank look on his face as always. Mirkus was huddled behind even the two unarmed men, cowering and trying not to be seen. So much for all his vaunted exploits.

Lily got the feeling that the shuffle among the snakes was for the sole purpose of getting through the lines and attacking the sailors, who were obviously the weakest members of the party. The thought of it kindled a heat in her middle and she gritted her teeth, fighting the urge to sling curses at the snakes and instead focusing on getting arrows to her bowstring.

The first two were normal arrows. She aimed for the snake's eyes, but the angle was all wrong with them charging away from and askew of her line of sight. She punctured one of the monsters, but it was not a lethal injury by any means.

She'd have to do better.

Taking out one of her fire arrows, slipping it onto the string, drawing it to her cheek, and firing all in the blink of an eye, she paused for a fraction of a second to watch the shaft fly before grabbing for the next arrow in her quiver.

Midway between her bow and the snake, the alchemical compound Marla had created sputtered to life. By the time the arrow reached the snake's head, it was burning brightly. On impact, it exploded with a great gout of flame, blowing a hole in the side of the monster's head and causing a concussive force that pushed the snake next to the doomed serpent away from its path.

As it tried to right itself, Lily launched two more arrows. The first struck the reptile's head, not punching all the way through, but twisting it. The second plunged perfectly into the snake's left eye, which was visible because of the monster's head turning. Two inches of the point emerged from the other side of the creature's skull and its body immediately got rubbery and went down.

Lily spat on the ground. "Try to be clever and attack the sailors, will you?" she shouted at the two reptile corpses that were only a few feet from the men. Grobel waved his sword in a salute of thanks and she briefly waved back.

Between hers and Tere's bows and the skill of her friends, the jungle floor soon had a tangle of snake corpses resting on it. Aeden and Urun cast their magic and healed the wounds the others got. It was mostly bruises from being slammed while dodging the snakes. Luckily, no one had been bitten. The answer as to whether the monsters were venomous would have to wait. Honestly, Lily hoped they didn't see any more of the creatures. She'd be just fine never finding out if they had venom.

"Did you see that?" she asked Tere as they walked to where the others were. "It was like that was a practiced sequence. Were they that intelligent?"

Tere shrugged. "No telling. It was strange, though. They were either a lot smarter and better trained that we thought or someone or something was commanding them, or controlling them. It could have been one of them or it could be something else close by. Either way, I don't like it. If I was forced to fight another party to the death, it would be a toss-up whether I'd go immediately for the strongest foe or focus on the weakest.

Taking out a number of the weakest would probably be most logical. Pretty smart for a handful of scaly worms."

She wasn't in the mood to even respond to the joke. "I don't like it. It's one thing to be attacked at every turn. We do that all the time. Organized monsters targeting the sailors, though, that's not something I will tolerate."

"I get it," Tere said. "But what can we do?"

"I don't know. Maybe a couple of us can escort them back to the ship while the rest go on and then the escorts can catch up. It's not ideal, but I don't think it's fair to put the men at risk like that. They're not warriors."

Their conversation was cut short as they reached the others.

"Is everyone okay?" Lily asked, running a critical eye over everyone, especially the sailors. Mirkus had stood up from his cowering pose, but her mouth turned downward as she saw him. "Anyone seriously hurt?"

"None of us are," Grobel said. "Thanks to you. Your quick response saved our lives back there. Thank you."

Lily nodded at him.

"The rest of us had a few scrapes and bruises, but we're all sorted out now," Aeden said. "Did any of them get to you and Tere?"

"No. We're good. Listen, I had an idea. Maybe it would be good for one or two of us to escort the men back to the ship. If the monsters continue to target them, we'll be hard pressed to keep them safe. I think we're past where it's advantageous to have them carrying our gear. We've used up a lot of the stores we were carrying."

All of Lily's other friends besides Tere looked to be ready to argue, Aeden and Jia opening their mouths with their brows furrowed and Urun raising a finger as if he were about to make a point. Grobel got his words out first.

"We won't leave. If the group splits up like that, it could put everyone in danger. One or two of you may not be able to protect us on the way back, and it'll weaken the group that's left over to continue on. We won't put you at risk to babysit us. As before, we know the risks and we choose to continue."

Mirkus didn't look like he was so sure, and Lily thought he was going to contradict Grobel, but the other four sailors all leveled their gazes at him and, for the first time she'd seen, he backed down. Maybe it was too soon after embarrassing himself during the battle.

"You have to know that it's only going to get more dangerous," she said to the leader of the crew.

"We do, but we agreed to the mission and we won't be abandoning it. Besides, the captain would probably wrap us in chains and throw us overboard if we came back without at least trying to find some treasure."

She didn't like their answer any more than she liked what was going on with the monsters, but she couldn't force them to change their minds. A lump of guilt deep in her belly made her feel nauseous. She could do her best to try to protect them, but they'd eventually run into monsters strong enough that she'd have to focus on keeping herself alive at their expense. Just because she believed life was a simple contest involving staying alive or dying, it didn't mean she liked it when others died, even if she lived.

"We might as well get going then," she said sadly. "The sooner we can get to wherever we're going and do whatever it is we're supposed to do, the sooner we can all go back to the ship."

CHAPTER
THIRTY-EIGHT

A s they set off, Lily stayed close to the sailors in case they were attacked again. She had taken up responsibility for them, for some reason. She had always had a soft spot for those at an unfair advantage.

During their travel, she caught several glances and disappointed expressions on some of the men's faces, all pointed at Mirkus Regas. It wasn't that he had been scared, she realized, but that all his boasting about his past and how he was a brave and capable adventurer, able to meet any challenge without flinching, was finally proven without a doubt to be a load of horseshit.

She couldn't help but to feel a little bad for the man, though he really did deserve some kind of ostracism for constantly running his mouth about his supposed perfect qualities. No one forced him to act like he was a god walking among mortals, so if he couldn't do something as simple as stand up to face the danger of attacking monsters, she wasn't about to support him, either. Maybe it would cause the man to think about his choices and his actions and become a bit less arrogant.

It was doubtful, but it could happen.

The party was attacked twice more before they stopped for the night. The first was a group of four of the large cat-type monsters. They were tough and fast and dangerous, but being outnumbered so each one could be attacked by two people at once kept the ambush from being too treacherous. The cats didn't even get a chance to try for the sailors, attacking the front group and never getting beyond them.

The second attack was not quite so easy to repel. Creatures made up of dirt and rock flowed up from the jungle floor into eight distinct units and attacked with the ferocity of a sandstorm. Their several limbs—the number was not consistent between the different individuals—struck with blunt force that shattered tree trunks when their target dodged the attack. It was a good thing they were not lightning-fast or the party would have been in trouble.

Another problem with the monsters was that they were made of dirt, stone, and a few things that apparently got caught up in their gathering, like sticks and leaves. Cuts with sword and knife didn't do much damage, nor did arrows piercing them.

"I don't think they have vital organs," Tere said, after his fifth arrow thudded into what might be considered one of the thing's heads. In fact, only a few of them were humanoid at all like the one he was attacking, so even if they did have internal organs, there was no telling exactly where they were. "We're going to have to find a better way to kill them."

Urun had some success in draining energy from the monsters, causing parts of them to slough off and making them smaller. Aeden, too, could do some damage with one of his spells, the one that exploded outward from him like a hurricane.

By far, though, it was Lily who turned the tide of the battle. Using a few of her precious fire arrows, she carefully used them when two or three of the monsters were close together and not near her friends. That was the trick, and the battle lasted much longer than it should have simply because she didn't want her allies to be caught in the crossfire, or to waste the arrows.

When she was able to pick her shot and take it, the fire arrow flew as it always did, catching fire in midair and exploding when it had already embedded itself into her target. What made it spectacular was that the creatures were so dense, the exploding arrow was more powerful, working against the pressure of the thick bodies of the dirt monsters. When one went off, it not only blew the creature apart, but tore through others within a half dozen feet or so.

Actually, the impact could be felt a couple dozen feet away, but the damage radius was six or seven feet, inside of which any of the other monsters would be obliterated as well. It took her three arrows carefully launched to decimate the group, leaving two that were injured to fall before the combined attacks of her friends.

"It looks like what we talked about is true," Aeden said after the battle. "We reached a turning point with the snakes. It's only going to get worse from here."

"It's less than an hour until dark," Tere said, nodding his agreement. "I say we take advantage of the flattened vegetation here—courtesy of those dirt monsters and our heroic archer with the exploding arrows here—to make camp right here."

No one had any objections. They had already become accustomed to the new, hyper-aware manner in which they needed to conduct themselves, so they all slept a little closer to each other and the watches were doubled up, with a sailor and one of Lily's group on watch at all times.

Surprisingly, they were not attacked during the night. It almost seemed that it wasn't time that dictated when they would be attacked, but their progress toward wherever they were going.

Lily explained her thoughts to the others. "It's almost like each group of monsters has their own territory, and they stay in it and wait for someone to come to them. That's good news for when we stop, but them being territorial concerns me a bit."

"It all concerns me," Jia said. "The battles are good, though. Exciting survival-of-the-stongest type stuff."

Lily shook her head at the former Falxen. Had Jia always had that attitude? She didn't remember the woman being so bloodthirsty before.

The party members weren't in the best of shape. All of them had bags under their eyes and had lost the spring in their step they'd started this quest with. Lily felt the same. With Jun's death, getting less sleep than normal, and being on the edge of being attacked at all times, every hour they remained in the jungle continued to sap everyone's energy.

Mirkus was taking it hard that the others had run out of tolerance for him and his boasting. He spent the morning's travel at the back of the group with his head mostly bent toward the ground. Vorun still maintained the last position— one he had settled into early in their journey—a good fifteen feet or more from Mirkus, who was maybe ten feet behind the bulk of the sailors as they marched along.

Lily argued with herself about allowing the man to feel sorry for himself. He deserved to be ignored for a little while, but she got a twinge of pain every time she saw him pouting at the back of the line. She decided to let him suffer for a few hours more and then she'd talk to him when they stopped for lunch. Things were hard enough without being deprived of the only friends the man had.

She heard a sort of rattling whoosh and her eyes caught a flicker of motion ahead and to her left. She looked just in time to throw herself onto her chest on the jungle floor as some kind of eagle swooped past where she had been.

"Attack!" she yelled. "Birds."

Aeden and Jia had dodged attacks from similar flyers, but

Urun didn't move out of the way fast enough. The bird that attacked him wasn't large enough to carry him away, but it did slash his face with its talons as it went by. He had two long gashes on his cheek that were oozing blood already.

One of the feathery monsters, which were much bigger than any eagle she'd ever seen or heard of, now that she got a good look, went straight for the sailors. All of them but Vorun and Mirkus had dropped to the ground, and the creature was heading for those two. A puff of feathers exploded from the thing's body and it veered, spinning wildly, then slamming into a tree trunk. Before it could slide to the ground, another arrow punched into its head. It seemed that Tere had not had to dive into an awkward position like she had.

Now that they knew where the attack was coming from, the party was able to fight the birds more effectively. They took down two more of them, one with arrows from both Lily and Tere and one that Aeden was able to cut the wing off of as it flew, finishing it with Jia's help once it was down. Another slammed into a shield Urun had erected for himself and after taking a hard bounce, it gained the sky again and flew off with a squawk. There were four other birds, but once they witnessed the result of the attacks by their companions, they apparently decided to go and find prey that was a bit easier to kill.

The battle had only taken a couple of minutes and Lily scanned the skies to see if the attack would resume. After more than five minutes had passed, she relaxed a little, though she kept an arrow nocked on her string.

"Birds this time," she said.

Tere headed for the closest carcass. "Yeah, but do you see the size of them? The ones we killed are going to be dinner tonight."

Lily shrugged. They might as well eat the birds. They were already dead, after all. She just hoped they didn't have tainted meat. With the corruption in the forest, there was no telling what might be in there. She promised herself she'd have Urun do something, like delve the meat or purify it or sanctify it. Whatever he could do.

"Is everyone okay?" Jia asked, mirroring Lily's thoughts.

Aeden was already next to Urun, casting his healing spell on the priest. Everyone else looked to be fine. Lily was a little dirtier than before, with what amounted to grass stains on her left shoulder where she hit the ground hard when she dove out of the way of the bird, but she was uninjured.

The party went into motion again, adding to the endless number of steps they'd taken so far. Lily hovered between the end of the front group consisting of her friends and the rear group of the sailors.

As she ran her eyes over everything, searching for danger or things they might have dropped, it struck her.

"Where is Mirkus?

All eyes went to the back of the group. Even Vorun, who was in his customary place at the very end, swung his head back and forth with a surpsied look on his face. When he didn't spot the boasting sailor, he shrugged silently.

"He was there during the fight," Grobel said. "That bird went for him and Vorun, the one that Tere shot in flight."

"Do you think he got sick of being ignored and left?" Tere asked.

"I...I don't think so," the sailors' leader said. "That would be stupid. He won't last a second out there without a group to protect him."

"Everyone take a buddy and start searching," Lily said. "We can find out why he left after we find him." She headed straight for Vorun, the closest one to where Mirkus had disappeared from. "Vorun, you're with me. Let's go find that man and slap him until he's red."

CHAPTER
THIRTY-NINE

Vorun followed Lily around as she chose the direction to search. As with all interactions with the man, he proceeded without speech or any apparent interest. After a handful of minutes, the entire thing became uncomfortable for her and she tried to start up a conversation to alleviate the feeling.

"Have you known Mirkus for a long time, Vorun?"

"Yes."

She managed to keep from rolling here eyes. Was every word a battle? "How long have you known him?"

"Six years."

"Are you two friends?" When the man didn't answer her, she turned to look at him, only to find him looking blankly at her. "Are you?"

Vorun's face was expressionless, but Lily could feel her own twisting in discomfort. Thankfully, he gave her an answer. Kind of.

"I do not really have friends. I am usually alone." Well, at least he was honest about it.

"I see. Well, I appreciate your help in trying to find him.

You've known him for a while. Do you know where we should look? Where he might have gone?"

"No."

"Okay. I guess we'll just keep searching. Hopefully Tere will find some tracks or a magical trail or something."

They searched for more than an hour and didn't find a trace of the missing sailor. Lily and Vorun were the third pair back to camp. Surprisingly, Tere and Brek arrived just before she had.

"Before you ask," Tere told her, his hand up, palm facing her, "I can't see a thing in the magical matrix. It's even worse since we've come into this tangled disaster area of a jungle, more than the regular jungle we were in before. With the fight, I couldn't pick out any footprints manually, either. Too much trampling from all of us. I circled around outside the general damage and couldn't find anything indicating where he went. It's like some magic spell plucked him off the face of the land and spirited him away somewhere else."

As the other groups came in, they had the same news. No one found any sign of where Mirkus Regas had gone.

"What are we going to do, then?" Lily asked.

"We have to continue on," Grobel said, though his face was etched with turmoil as he spoke. "We can't search the whole jungle and put everyone else at risk to find him. All we can do is hope that he was able to get away safe, either back to the ship or wherever it was that he wanted to go."

"You're saying that he left on his own, not that he was taken or attacked?" Lily asked.

"I hope he left on his own. It would be disappointing, but it's better than the alternative."

She had no argument for that. Still, the archer met the eyes of all the sailors, trying to find an ally or some reason she could give not to simply abandon the man. He was annoying, true, but to leave him to his fate in the dangerous jungle they were in? She didn't want that. There were no allies, though.

The men understood that to continue to search would bring them all into danger. Lily didn't like it, but the choice they had made was practical.

She consoled herself with the assurance that it was how things were. Living meant surviving, if one could. It was as simple as that. Mirkus would either survive or he would not, just like the rest of them. If it was truly his choice to leave them—for whatever reason—well, he would have to deal with the consequences. If it wasn't his choice, he was probably already dead.

Aeden cast his spell again to determine the direction in which they would continue, then slowly started off. If the mood in the party was somber after Jun was killed, it seemed even more so now. With Jun, there was a finality to the situation, closure. With Mirkus, well, it felt to Lily like they were abandoning him.

"You all right?" Tere asked from next to her.

"No, but there's not really anything I can do about it. It's the right decision, but I can't help but to think that maybe there's just one or two more things we haven't tried, places we haven't looked."

"I'm sorry. If I could think of a way to find him without putting the entire group at risk, I would tell you, but I can't. It cooks my brain trying to figure out how he just disappeared like that. He was only missing for a few minutes when we started looking. With all of us searching, someone should have found something." He shrugged as he frowned. "It sounds cruel, but we have to cut our losses."

"I know."

He watched her for a moment, then turned and followed the others. Lily stood there, casting her eyes back to where Mirkus had been the last time she saw him. *I hope it was your choice and you get to where you want to go safely*, she thought. With a sigh, she followed after the rest of the group.

The jungle, it seemed, had no sympathy for the humans

and their grief. Within an hour, they were under attack again. This time, it was a group of hairy humanoid creatures.

At first, Lily paused when she saw the figures charging at them from different directions, seeming to come out of every plant and tree around them. She thought they were trebaxel. She was actually fond of Scrapper, Aila's new friend she had adopted when she was off adventuring in the Great Enclave. The thought of killing some of Scrapper's distant relatives made her stomach turn, especially after the day they'd already had.

When she pushed away her preconceptions, though, she noticed that the creatures were more like regular apes than trebaxel. Most likely, they were more intelligent and possibly stronger and faster than simple apes, judging by the modified animals they'd seen so far, but they were still corrupted animals and not the same species as Aila's friend.

Which was a good thing, because she lost track of their number at fifteen. She and her friends were going to have their hands full.

Grobel held a sword out in front of him, trying to position himself between the other sailors and the creatures. For the time being, the apes were focusing on the better armed and better trained members of the party, but it was nice to see that Grobel was willing to fight.

Surprisingly, Brek held a sword as well, a beat up old weapon he'd seen Mirkus carry a time or two, though she'd never seen the man use it. Brek looked more than ready to do so, standing next to Grobel and facing the bulk of the monsters swirling around Aeden, Urun, and Jia—when she was out in the open for more than a few seconds.

The clash with the front group of the monsters made Lily flinch. Four of them ran full speed at Aeden like they were going to break all his bones and crush him on impact. He stood calmly in front of them, for all the world looking like he was going to greet them politely. When the monsters got to him, she thought she'd see the Croagh knocked off his feet and slammed backward. But that's not what happened at all.

A few hand gestures and a mouth that moved to pronounce something Lily couldn't hear was all the action Aeden took, but it was more than enough to stall the charge. All four of the apes slammed into something that wasn't visible and careened off in different directions. The sound was a mix between two logs striking each other and bones breaking. Through it all, Aeden stayed in exactly the same spot.

At least until the impact. Then he moved like a mongoose, slashing and finishing off all four downed creatures with shocking efficiency.

Lily mentally shook her head as she began to let arrows fly toward some of the other creatures.

She and Tere brought down at least a half dozen of the apes within a few seconds. The creatures looked strong, and they were fast, but arrows in the eye, head, and throat killed them as easily as it would a human.

Urun chose to cast offensive spells this time, using his staff to channel eerie magic that had no visible evidence it was being cast until the priest's target simply fell dead or—even worse—withered in front of Lily's eyes.

Jia was in her element. That is, she was at home in the chaos as the monsters darted around without any apparent plan or strategy. She would rise up from some hiding place, slash one of their throats, and then disappear again. When she got caught in between a trio of the monsters, she spun and slashed with her knives, dodging every swipe of hairy arms, twisting and evading any contact with the beasts that she didn't initiate. In seconds, the three were on the ground, bleeding and mostly dead, if not completely so, and the former Falxen spun off into the shadows of the vegetation to disappear again.

While the fight went on, Lily kept an eye on the sailors, fully intending to give them ranged support if any of the apes made it to them.

None did.

Soon, the melee was done and there were nineteen carcasses sprawled across the area.

"That was almost disappointing," Tere said as he and Lily went through the tamped down area reclaiming their arrows. "I've gotten used to monsters that work together and use strategy. These were barely more than regular apes."

"I'll take an easy fight over a hard one right now," Lily responded, putting her foot on the face of one of the downed creatures and yanking her arrow from its eye. "I'd rather we didn't have to fight at all anymore until we do what we need to do and get out of here."

"The problem with that," Aeden said from a dozen feet away, "is that I'm pretty sure what we came here to do is to kill whatever it is that's causing the corruption. This isn't some quest to retrieve an item. Osulin wants us to end the corruption. That sounds like there's going to be more killing to me."

Lily had to admit the highlander had a point, but it didn't make the idea any more palatable.

She honestly didn't know why she was having feelings antagonistic to what they were doing. Her life had always been a fight against one thing or another, from her childhood sickness to bandits and those on the streets that wanted to take advantage of her to her tenure as a Falxen assassin and even since, when she faced combat often as she tried to help her friends and all humanity against the animaru.

She thought maybe it was in response to the shifting mood of her companions. They seemed less compassionate than normal and maybe something inside her was compensating for that, trying to be the nurturing one for a change.

Gods! She wasn't entering the period others have always

warned her about and joked about in a morbid, sometimes creepy way, was she? The dreaded nesting instinct? No, that couldn't be it. She was suddenly looking forward to the next attack, just so she wouldn't have to think about...other things.

She didn't have to wait long.

FORTY

The party had barely left the site of their last battle, it seemed, when the soft sounds of vegetation rustling and faint chittering noises prompted Lily to nock an arrow and dart her gaze at the surroundings, trying to place the direction the noise came from.

Flashes of grey and tan bounced up over the tops of some of the bushes and through the vines. When the creatures finally showed up, their slinky gait reminded Lily of a pet ferret she had for a short time when she was a child. She had found the animal wounded and brought it home. Her mother helped her clean its wounds, apparently from a predator that almost succeeded in making it dinner, and they nursed it back to health.

When it was nearly healed, it would play, bouncing around and chittering *dook, dook, dook*. She could watch it for hours as it ran, jumped, and pounced on little balls Lily had made from leaves and string, tied tightly together. Too bad it only played for fifteen minutes or so before deciding to take a nap for another couple of hours. She'd almost forgotten about the little animal, which they released back into the wild once it was fully healed.

But the things coming at them, though they moved the same way and had similar fur, were a dozen times larger than an adult ferret or weasel. They were the size of the huge mastiffs that some people bred and trained in the Great Enclave, their shoulders nearly chest high to an average person, though these creatures were longer and slinkier than the bulky dogs. Having quick, agile creatures that large, sporting the same long, sharp teeth Lily remembered, erased the smile from her face and impressed on her that this was not going to be an enjoyable situation.

The weasel creatures fought like unintelligent beasts, with no strategy and no coordinated effort. Though the battle was chaotic and dangerous—the monsters had sharp claws and sharp teeth and they found their way through the guard of several of the party members during the scuffle—the pack of the long, flexible creatures didn't prove to be any real challenge. None of them got anywhere near the sailors, for which Lily was thankful.

After the fight and the subsequent healing, it was back to pushing through the jungle again. It hadn't seemed possible, but the vegetation was getting even denser and a higher percentage of the plants were now of the more dangerous kind, with sharp edges, thorns, or even poison. The speed at which the group traversed the jungle dropped considerably, and the party inadvertently spread out a little more.

When they stopped in what passed for a clearing—there was actually room to sit down between trees and bushes and vines, though barely—Lily scanned the group. She'd gotten into the habit of doing so, especially with the sailors, and did it automatically whenever they stopped and gathered together.

"Where's Denos?"

Grobel looked around and his eyes widened. "I saw him a few minutes ago."

"Denos!" she called out, but no answer came. "Damn it. Not again."

Without any real direction, every member of the party got up and spread out to look for the missing sailor.

"Over here," Aeden shouted a few minutes later.

Lily was the fourth person there, after Jia and Brek had joined Aeden, being close by when the Croagh shouted. She saw Denos's thin body immediately, his black hair matted with blood and leaves, his mouth open, and his eyes popping out in panic. He had vines wrapped around his throat so tightly, there were welts and deep bruises in his flesh.

The vines were detached from any other plant or the ground.

Lily could do nothing but stare at the sight. Grobel sounded what she and probably everyone else was thinking.

"Someone strangled him. Those vines aren't the kind we've seen attack. Someone cut or tore them free and used them like a rope to cut off his air."

"This wasn't someone running off and it obviously wasn't an animal attack," Aeden said. "Maybe the apes we fought could manage something like this, tearing up vines and using them as tools to strangle Denos, but none of the other animals we've seen could do it."

"Do you think there are humans, or at least humanoids, stalking us?" Jia asked. "Not a very honorable way to attack someone. Hiding and ambushing them when they're expecting their enemies to be animals."

"Says the former assassin who has made plenty of kills from the shadows," Urun pointed out.

"Hey!" Lily shouted. "Enough fighting. Isn't it enough that three of our number are already dead, and not by natural means or by the normal jungle predators. The last thing we need to do is fight amongst ourselves."

Her statement was met with stony silence.

After a full minute, Lily sighed. "Come on. Someone help me cut Denos out of all those vines so we can bury him. We can't leave him for the animals to eat. It's bad enough we can't bring his body back to his home and family."

"He doesn't have any anyway," Grobel said. "It's what gave him such a sour outlook on life. His entire family was taken years ago when a virulent fever spread through his hometown. Denos had no one but the rest of the crew."

A lump formed in Lily's throat and she didn't trust herself to speak. Instead, she nodded toward the crew leader and drew one of her long knives to cut the vines. Grobel and Brek joined her and so did Tere, bless his withered old heart.

The group busied themselves with clearing some vegetation and digging a hole for Denos, and then burying him. They erected a little cairn over the mound after they'd covered it up. It was the best they could do.

"If Denos was still breathing, he'd tell us all that we're all doomed, sooner or later," Grobel said with a dry chuckle. "I think I might have to agree with him. This is something more than the dangers of the island or the jungle. Something—or someone—is hunting us. Which one of my men is next?"

"There may not be a next time," Lily said. "Even if there is, what makes you think whatever it is won't attack one of the rest of us?"

Brek cleared his throat and then spoke up, something he hadn't done since Jun died. "There are three dead sailors that say it'll be another one of us. You would think whoever or whatever it is would try to take out the powerful people first, weakening the group. It doesn't make sense to kill us. All we do is carry stuff. Though I guess since it's so easy to kill us, our attacker decided to reduce our numbers in the easiest way possible."

Lily didn't have the heart to disagree or scold him for his attitude. Three of his friends were gone, two of them undeniably dead. It wasn't even an argument anymore that Mirkus was dead, too. It had always seemed unlikely he'd run off, but with the evidence they had now, it was clear he had been attacked, killed, and the body spirited away for some reason.

After several minutes of milling around, Aeden cast his spell and started the group walking again, their number one less than before.

Before they even settled into a cadence for the day, the next group of monsters was upon them. These were huge but squat creatures that seemed to be covered in a natural armor of hard plates. They were of a size with the cattle that could be seen in any farming community, but with their natural protection and sturdy claws, they proved to be formidable.

Though the monsters were resistant to strikes from weapons, the party soon switched to very precise strikes, targeting the vulnerable spots between their plates. That, coupled with the relatively slow movements of the creatures made them one of the least dangerous attacks they'd been exposed to on the island.

The next attack, less than half an hour after the armored creatures, was more of the cat creatures. This time, however, there were a full dozen of them plus another one that was larger and seemed to be the leader. With shrieks and screeches, it directed the other cats in impressive formations that pressed the humans quite effectively. So much so, in fact, that a couple of the animals were able to slip through to where the three remaining sailors were. Lily, forced to fight two of the cats with her knives after they snuck up and pounced on her, couldn't help the sailors, and Tere and the others were deep into battle themselves and were separated from the men by several trees and thick bushes. Vorun huddled in on himself behind Brek and Grobel, but it was the former that really seemed to shine during the conflict.

When Lily had met Brek, she placed him as one of those men who talked a good game, always having something to say and always needing to be the center of attention. Not quite as much as Mirkus, but similar. It was true that he was like that, but on this day, he showed everyone another side of Brek Zexus.

Gone was the easy smile, the witty sayings, and even the smirk he often wore when he was developing a prank. He gritted his teeth, set his stance, and used his sword like he had a score to settle with the attackers. Maybe he did. Three of his friends were dead and though it wasn't the cats that had done it, it was like he thought they had.

What he lacked in skill he made up for in sheer determination and valor. When even Grobel paled as the two cats with razor sharp claws came at them, Brek ran toward the attackers.

Somehow, he kept from getting slashed too deeply or from being knocked down by the obvious power of the felines. As he awkwardly evaded most of the attacks and by luck or by skill managed to receive only superficial cuts, his sword never rested, slashing wildly either at the cats' paws or at their bodies and faces.

When all was said and done, he had injured one cat so badly it tried to retreat and the other sported several deep gashes that, while probably not immediately dangerous, would likely cause the cat to bleed out in time. Even that wasn't enough, though. Brek, with a leg dripping blood, chased the fleeing cat down before it got to a full run, and rammed his sword through its neck, then stomped on its face.

Grobel, seeing Brek's bravery, rallied himself and attacked the remaining cat as it turned to pounce on Brek. Between the two of them, they were able to whittle the beast down until both of them stabbed it in the torso at the same time. One—or both—hit something vital because the cat dropped to the ground with a mewling cry and then lay still.

Immediately after, Brek collapsed to the ground, weak from blood loss and unable to keep his feet. Grobel dragged him back to where Vorun was waiting and the two of them started trying to bandage Brek's wounds.

Luckily, the battle didn't last much longer after that and Urun was able to make it to Brek to cast healing spells over him. The magic didn't replace the lost energy, but it did close up his wounds to prevent more of his blood from leaking out.

"We'll rest here, at least for a little while," Tere said. "It'll give Aeden and Urun a chance to heal everyone else and each other and will let us regain some of our stamina. It doesn't look like things are getting any easier. I think the chance of scavengers coming to get the carcasses is less of a risk than it would be for us to move on."

No one dissented, so as Aeden and Urun helped to heal the others, Lily helped her friends to clean up, wiping the blood from them and bringing them food and drink.

Half an hour's rest later, Grobel stood up suddenly. "Brek?" He looked around and his face grew concerned. "Has anyone seen Brek?"

"He probably just went to take a nature break," Urun said. "I haven't seen him since I healed him."

It was like the air had been sucked out of Lily's lungs. She jumped to her feet and started into the surrounding jungle. Thankfully, the others did the same.

When they found Brek, it was not what they were hoping for. He lay on his back, eyes open and staring straight up into the sky.

His entire chest had been torn open and his heart was missing.

CHAPTER
FORTY-ONE

Grobel, and even stoic Vorun, stood stone still, expressions of horror on Grobel's face. Even Vorun's looked vaguely like it held a look of distaste. Lily had the urge to shuffle them away from the grisly sight, but they were both grown men, older than she was, and she had no right to try to shield them like they were children.

Tere glanced at her and she immediately picked up on a similar thought. He moved his head incrementally toward the two remaining sailors, then back to Lily. She shook her head subtly at him and, of all things, the old archer let out a breath very much like a sigh as he turned back to inspect the wound that was Brek's entire chest.

Lily was in no way squeamish, but she almost cringed as she ran her eyes over the sight. Brek's shirt was torn off him so thoroughly, there were only scraps left on his upper arms. His chest was opened up, the skin sliced unevenly down the center, slanting a bit to the left. The lungs had been damaged, though it wasn't clear whether it was during the gash that opened him up or after that. It appeared that his heart was torn out from the bottom of the ribcage, his entrails pushed to the side and partly torn as well.

She was no expert, but it looked to her that something had to reach a hand—or a claw—up into his chest cavity to get at his heart. But why?

"There are no teeth marks," Tere announced, snapping Lily out of her own analysis.

"What?" She was having trouble understanding why he'd even say such a thing.

"The wounds, they're all cuts and tears. There are no teeth marks. Whatever killed him didn't do it so it could eat him."

"Then why take the heart?" Aeden asked.

"I don't know. I guess it's possible the killer took it to eat it later, but even that concerns me. If the thing was intelligent enough to kill quickly and silently, then took the heart to consume it later, that's not good news."

"As if any of it is," Urun said. "There's a man lying there who was killed a few dozen feet from the rest of us and whose body has been savaged."

Tere scoffed. "Fair enough. I meant that if Brek's attacker is smart, too, then things are even worse than they seem."

"Did you see him?" Grobel asked. "Did you see him in the fight with the cats? Like a hero in a story, he was. He stood there and looked those monsters in the face and went to battle with them to protect me and Vorun here. I always thought Brek was a good guy, but with all the jokes and how much he talks, I thought it was all empty boasting. I was scared out of my wits, but he stood right up and swung that sword at them. A hero, I say. He didn't deserve to end like this. Not like this."

Lily strove to figure out what to say in answer, but came up blank. She looked at her friends, and they seemed to be at as much of a loss as she was. She finally opened her mouth and said, "He was. All we can do now is to give him as close to a hero's burial as we can. I'm sorry."

Grobel nodded with gritted teeth. Another of his men, his friends, that he'd have to bury. He and Vorun searched out a place for a few minutes and then, when they'd found one they thought suitable, started digging. Lily joined them, then Aeden, and they'd soon put Brek's broken body to rest. Grobel said some words, essentially what he'd told them before, and the party mechanically gathered up their gear and continued on the path that seemed likely to kill them all.

Before the group even got a dozen feet away from where they'd stopped to bury Brek, Lily turned to the two remaining sailors and fixed them with a stern gaze.

"You will stay together from now on, until we get back to the ship and Captain Balstad tells you to stop shadowing each other. I don't care what you're doing, you will stay together. That means sleeping, answering nature's call, or anything else. Neither of you is ever to be alone. Get it?"

Both men nodded and dropped their eyes, as if she was some matron who had issued an order while wielding a large wooden spoon.

She turned to the rest of the group, too, including Tere. "And that goes for everyone else. No one is to be alone. Ever. We will all have at least one more person with us at all times. That way, if whatever it is that's stalking us tries to kill us off, there will be at least one other person to yell an alarm. If the predator is so powerful that it can kill two people at a time without them being able to sound an alarm, well, then we have a great deal more to worry about." The others didn't argue, but Jia snorted in a way that seemed to be the precursor of a genuine laugh. Lily drilled her green eyes into the smaller woman's and Jia adopted a neutral face, nodding her acquiescence to the unspoken command.

It was true that Lily was sounding like an old biddy, barking orders and expecting people to follow them, but by the gods, she wasn't going to deal with more of her party dying, especially in the underhanded way the others met their end. Facing a powerful foe and losing one's life in honest battle was one thing, but those sailors didn't do anything to deserve the deaths that were handed to them.

The attacks from more and varied monsters didn't let up. The next to attack them was a horde of giant snakes and huge wild dogs, though thankfully the snakes didn't seem as intelligent as the other group they'd battled.

The beasts numbered more than fifteen, but without intelligent strategy, it was simply a matter of basic combat and the animals couldn't compare with the skilled warriors they faced. This time, none of them tried to go after the sailors, so Grobel and Vorun—who hadn't taken up the sword that Brek had used—stood next to each other, watching for any danger. It was the way Lily preferred it, the men staying back out of trouble while the seasoned warriors took care of the danger.

By the time they were finished with the battle against the dogs and snakes, it seemed that everyone was ready to end the day.

"I'll see if I can spot a good place in the next few minutes," Tere told the others. "It's still a couple of hours until dark, but I think we deserve to stop a little early after the day we've had."

Lily watched Urun as Tere made his proclamation and was surprised he didn't object. Now that she thought of it, the priest hadn't really been his fastidious self, complaining about wasting time and trying to get everyone to move along in finishing the quest his goddess gave them. It was one more thing to put in the category of everyone seeming a bit off.

As promised, Tere did find a place that looked like they could use it for a campsite. It was full of lush vegetation like the rest of the jungle, but it wasn't quite as congested as most of what they'd passed through that day.

Just as the elder archer opened his mouth, no doubt to say that was where they were going to stop for the night, motion off to the side caught Lily's attention and she fitted an arrow to her bowstring in the blink of an eye.

Tere was faster.

After a blur of motion from him, everyone's attention went

to a vine, as thick as a strong man's arm, with an arrow punched through it and holding it to a nearby tree.

Lily blinked, then rubbed her eyes, but the scene didn't change. The vine, stuck as it was, still moved, and not just a little. It wasn't motion from the arrow and it wasn't the wind. The thing flailed as if it were trying to free itself and go toward Tere again.

"What the..." Jia started, but trailed off as the entire area exploded with plants moving of their own volition. Going straight for the nearest person.

Lily let fly with several arrows, just as Tere did. As she picked targets and did her best to pin them to trees, she marveled at the different types in front of her. There were the regular vines, sometimes more than a dozen feet long and in different thicknesses. Those seemed to try to club anyone close. Then there were the thorny vines, which were just as it sounded. They were thinner and more flexible than the other vines, but they moved much more quickly and they were studded with sharp thorns capable of tearing through skin easily.

Other plants were squat bushes, either with wiry woody branches or with nettles and saw leaves on them. The one thing they all had in common was that they were able to move, not held to the ground at all. Off-hand, Lily wondered if they planted themselves when they weren't moving so they could get nutrients or if they fed in some other way, such as by eating people and animals. She decided that was not a path her thoughts should take.

Aeden, Jia, and to a lesser extent, Urun were in the thick of it. The priest had put up a shield, but he had been considerate enough to step over to the sailors and stand in front of them.

Lily and Tere continued to release arrows while Aeden whirled and slashed so quickly, his arms and blades were only blurs. Jia didn't bother hiding because the plants didn't seem to have a problem finding her even though they obviously didn't have eyes. She worked her daggers like a master, cutting into leafy flesh and separating many limbs from their attackers.

Still, with all the motion in the relatively small space, it was pure pandemonium. Lily sometimes wasn't sure if the plants she was piercing with her arrows were motive or the simple sedentary variety. She didn't use her fire arrows because everyone was mixed in so thoroughly, her friends might catch backlash from the magic. As it was, she hesitated before launching each arrow, confirming to herself that she wouldn't hit her friends by accident.

The battle took longer than most of the others they'd fought since getting to the chaotically tangled part of the forest, but that was most likely because of the sheer number of attackers. It was useless trying to count them all because they looked just like the normal variety of plants until they started moving. It was difficult to discern which parts belonged to which plant monster. Eventually, though, they did finish. It took going through and chopping up the plant remnants left on the ground and then Urun going back over it and sensing the plants up close.

"There's something odd and decidedly different about the ones that are moving," he explained. "Their life auras are not the same as the regular plants in the forest. Unfortunately, I have to be close to sense it, so it won't do any good as a warning in the future, not until they're already close enough to attack."

The priest said it in clipped tones and it was obvious he was not in the best of moods. Lily thought of asking him what the problem was, but decided to leave it alone. She was tired, hungry, and not thrilled about how the day had turned out, either. She'd let Urun have his space until he had the chance to cool down.

After clearing out the mangled vegetation from the area, the group decided to camp on that spot. True, there might be more of the motive plants, but the risk was probably lower than them running into some other danger, be it animal or plant, if they continued on. Also, one benefit of their enemies being plant monsters was that there was no blood spattered all over the ground.

The party made a sad picture, sitting around the fire they'd started, listlessly waiting until it was time to go to sleep. Different people went off in pairs to relieve themselves and Lily was happy to see that they weren't being difficult about the rule she had pressed upon all of them.

Everyone but Grobel and Vorun sat on whatever rock, fallen tree, or bump they could use when Lily heard the sound.

It was not quite speech, more of a grunt that was trying to be words. Had anyone been talking at the moment, she wouldn't have heard it at all. But no one was and she did. She snapped her head up at the same time the others did. Without a word, they all grabbed their weapons and ran toward the source of the sound.

When they reached it, less than a minute later, Lily's eyes bugged out.

Grobel and Vorun were trying to kill each other.

FORTY-TWO

L ily's vision of the two men was obscured by the heavy vegetation, but it was clear they were doing their best to end each other's lives. Grobel had his sword and swung it awkwardly, indicating that he was already injured. Vorun moved with great agility, whirling and dodging the blade and occasionally parrying it with a dull tink, almost like he was holding a dense, solid piece of metal, but nothing was visible in his hands. Maybe he had some strange kind of small weapon that was easily concealed.

"Hey!" Tere shouted as he drew back the arrow he had on his bowstring. He didn't release right away, for which Lily was thankful. She was holding her own shot until she figured out what was happening.

"Attacked...me..." Grobel huffed out. Vorun remained silent, but when he realized he would either have to stop fighting or be killed, he slashed out once more at the other sailor and took off running, slipping between several trees like he was part snake.

Grobel groaned as Vorun's last attack got through his shaky guard and cut into his abdomen. Lily wasn't sure what weapon Vorun was using, but judging by the amount of blood, it was sharp.

From where Tere was, he didn't have a shot, whether by Vorun's pure luck or by design. The trees lined up perfectly so that the more experienced archer couldn't get him.

Lily, on the other hand, had a very small window through the trees and other vegetation. She sighted her target, let out her breath, and released the arrow. The grunt and then a thud were satisfying.

The entire party reached Grobel in an instant. Lily yelled for Urun to heal him quickly as she continued on to where Vorun had gone, Tere at her side. The priest was only a few steps away and came to a sliding halt at the downed Grobel and began his casting, Aeden staying to guard him, with Jia shadowing the archers.

When they reached Vorun a few dozen feet later, Lily let out a breath. The man, ostensibly the murderer of all the other sailors except Grobel—hopefully not Grobel—lay in a twisted heap at the end of a trail of smashed vines and leaves after his body had hit the ground. The arrow that had punched through the back of his head and protruded a couple of inches from his forehead was clearly the cause of his demise.

"What should we do with him?" Jia asked.

Tere stepped up to the body carefully and kicked it. When there was no movement, he checked for a pulse on Vorun's neck and watched for any other sign of life. After a minute he relaxed.

"He's dead. To answer your question, Jia, I say we leave him for the scavengers to eat. He doesn't deserve a burial and we don't need to waste time doing anything with him. He's gone."

"Let's go back and check on Grobel," Lily suggested. "Maybe he's got an explanation for this. Urun should have gotten to him in time, right?"

Tere watched her for a moment, like he was reading her

face. Or her mind. Then he nodded. "I'm sure he did. A slash like that won't kill immediately. Come on."

Lily pulled her arrow out of Vorun's corpse, wiped it on his clothes, and returned it to her scabbard, in the location for arrows she needed to inspect for damage. When they got back to where the fight had happened, they found the old sailor sitting up and talking with Urun and Aeden.

"Vorun?" Grobel asked.

Tere drew his finger across his throat. "Dead. Do you want to tell us just what in the hells happened?"

Lily put her hands up, palms out toward Tere like she was trying to push him away. "Hold on, now. Tere, we do need answers, but why don't we get Grobel back to camp so he can get some food and something to drink and recuperate a little bit before we demand information out of him.

The left side of Tere's lip twitched upward slightly, but he shrugged his acquiescence. "That's fine. You need to be carried, Grobel, or are you good to walk?"

"I can walk, thanks to Urun. I really thought I was a goner there. Thank you all."

The sailor walked back to the camp with the others all surrounding him. He didn't move like he was injured, but he did seem to be significantly weakened. Once they'd settled in and Grobel took a few pulls from a waterskin, mumbling something about wishing he'd brought something stronger, he began to answer Tere's question.

"I'm not really sure what happened. Vorun said he needed to go and relieve himself, so I had to go with him. One minute he was walking off to do his business behind a bush and the next, I caught rapid movement in the corner of my eye and jumped back out of reflex. That's the only thing that saved me as Vorun slashed at me.

"The thing is, he didn't have any weapon I could see, but it sure did a number on me, raking across my back and lighting it up with fire. I already had my sword in my hand, so I started trying to fight. I figured he wasn't skilled, no matter that he'd gotten the drop on me, but every time I tried to strike him, he slipped out of the way or he blocked it.

"I should have yelled right from the beginning so that you would all know something was happening, but honestly, I was so panicked I didn't think of it. A man I've known and worked with for many years was trying to kill me. I still can't wrap my head around it. He got a good swipe in at my leg and it hurt like all get out, so I kind of groan screamed. That must have been what alerted you.

"The rest you know. Thank you for coming when you did. I wouldn't have lasted much longer."

"Did he say anything to you?" Jia asked.

"No. Not a word. He just attacked out of the blue. I don't understand it. Did something make him go crazy? Maybe the grief from the others made him snap."

Lily didn't think so. "I think it's more likely he was the one all along. It makes sense now how the others could be surprised without sounding an alarm or putting up a decent fight. They all knew him and never would have expected it."

"But why?" Grobel asked. "What possible reason could he have?"

"There's no telling," Tere said. "We may never find out. We'll have to be satisfied that the danger is over, at least from our secret predator. We still have the jungle and whatever is corrupting Life's Cradle to deal with, but I'd much prefer the enemy you know and can see than one that's invisible or unknown."

They continued asking questions about anything that may have seemed off with Vorun in the last week, but Grobel couldn't think of anything. It was clear that, now that he was resting, the shock of the entire thing was catching up to him. Soon, his eyes were vacant and he mumbled answers to questions. When he answered at all.

"That's enough," Lily said, still wincing that she seemed to be acting like the mother of all the sailors. Or, at least, the mother of the only remaining sailor that had accompanied them. "How about we let him go to sleep. We don't need him to take watch duty tonight. Hopefully he's in better condition in the morning, though after what he's been through, I'm not sure if he will be."

Lily volunteered to take first watch and Tere said he'd join her. Aeden and Jia would have the second watch, with Urun being able to sleep the entire night to make up for all the healing he'd done that day. Fixing up Grobel put a strain on him since the man was so close to death.

The night was quiet, even more so than normal in the crazy section of the jungle they'd been in for the last few days. Lily could have done with some noise to distract her from thinking about what had happened. As it was, she couldn't get out of her head the belief that there should have been something she could have done, something she should have seen. She all but ignored Tere to argue with herself while she gave the outward appearance of scanning the surroundings.

"There's nothing you could have done," Tere said softly after a time. "Nothing any of us could have done."

"Is this how it is? How it was? To be a hero, I mean. I'd thought of it since I was very young, but I don't think I counted the cost, not the real cost. It's not just about surviving to continue the job, is it? There's all this—" she waved her hands abstractly "—to deal with."

"Yes. This is how it is. People don't understand, not really. Everyone thinks about the danger, about the hardships and the sacrifice. They think about how at any time a so-called hero could lose their life for nothing more than to save a stray cat or someone who doesn't want their help anyway. They think of it romantically, and in their minds, there is an honor in risking your life for others, for an ideal. Most won't go further than thinking about it, mind you, but it's generally regarded as truth all over the world.

"But this other part, that's what people don't get. What happens if you're so good—or so lucky—that you don't die? What happens, instead, if those you try to protect die, even those you care most about? Most people don't understand what that can do to your mind. To your motivations. They don't get it."

"But some do," Lily said.

He gave her a sad smile. "Yes, some do. Unfortunately, mostly they have to go through what you just did to really understand. Have you ever wondered why I tried to dissuade you from following this path?"

Lily gave him a dry chuckle. "I just figured it was because you're an old curmudgeon and you didn't want to deal with a green archer tagging along."

He snorted. "Well, yeah, that was part of it." The ghost of a smile he had formed melted off his face. "Mostly, though, I wouldn't wish this life on anyone. There are times when it gets so bad, you wonder if it might be better to just drop your guard, let something or someone end it all."

"Or to flee everyone in the world and hide out in a magic forest."

"Exactly." He picked up one of her hands. His calluses didn't feel rough like she'd always thought they would. Maybe it was because hers were toughened, too. "I'm sorry you have to deal with this, but I'll tell you again: you couldn't have done more. You'll disagree with me, in your mind, and you'll come up with a hundred different things you could have done to stop it. Don't. It's easy to look back, having the full knowledge of what happened, and make up actions that could have been taken. We couldn't have known. Hells, even the other sailors, who worked with the man every day, didn't know."

"I know," she said. "It's just that—"

"No. We take some responsibility for those we try to protect. It's natural. You're probably shocked that you're acting like—feeling like—you're their parent or something.

That's all well and good, but don't let it make you start doubting yourself. Trust me. I've been at this a long time."

She nodded, but as he had said, she disagreed with him. She should have been able to do something. In an attempt to change the subject, she blurted out a question she'd been pondering for a while.

"Do you feel...all right?"

"Me? Why would you ask that?"

She lost her courage to discus the subject completely. "Oh. I just...I mean...this whole thing is putting a lot of pressure on everyone. You're kind of the leader, seeing as how you're the most experienced and all."

He frowned at her for a moment, almost like he was suspicious of her trying to deflect the subject she herself brought up. Then his face went neutral again. "I'm fine. A little caught up in fighting monsters, so much so that until what happened the last few days, I hadn't really much thought of the effect on everyone else. I think I'm just tired and want to go home and rest in a bed where the chances of being ripped apart and eaten in my sleep are at least a little less."

He tried to soften the mood with a smile, but even with the joke, she still wasn't comfortable. Not only had she backed away from talking about what had been bothering her, but he knew she had done it.

"I'll be glad to get home, too, though who knows how long it'll be for? There are plenty of missions we'll be going on until the war is done one way or another."

"Such is the life of a hero in the Days of Darkness," he said.

Thankfully, they moved onto lighter subjects, even checking the perimeter of their small camp to keep themselves busy. When their watch ended, they said goodnight and curled up to sleep. She drifted off thinking of how she had referred to the Academy and their little dormitory as home. The thought of it made her smile for the first time in what seemed like an age.

FORTY-THREE

Physically, Grobel was able to continue the next morning. Mentally, he wasn't as ready. The sailor's eyes were red-rimmed and outlined by dark circles and he seemed not to be focusing his eyes on anything specific.

"Grobel," Lily said. "Are you able to continue?"

"Gone. They're all gone. The captain is going to have my hide. I told him I'd take care of them, I'd protect them the best I could. But who knew about Vorun? Better that he had killed me, too."

Lily wanted to tell him not to say that, but she felt it would do more harm than good, arguing with his point of view. Instead, she stood next to him, silent. The others around them did their best to keep themselves busy with whatever they were doing.

After a moment, Grobel sighed. "I can travel. Nothing wrong with my legs, not after Urun healed me yesterday. Please overlook my bad attitude. I'm out of sorts."

Lily patted his shoulder. "I know. I'm sorry. What do you say we try to get this mission finished and get out of this jungle?"

Grobel nodded and picked up his pack, hitching it up before he grabbed hold of what had been Vorun's pack. The other supplies, those that weren't used up, had already been split up amongst everyone else.

Lily had thought the part of the jungle they had entered three days before was bad compared to what they had been traveling in previously. They even referred to it as the maelstrom. But it paled when compared with the section they reached less than two hours after they'd started that day.

Impossibly, the vegetation was even thicker, slowing them to a crawl. Worse, the temperature jumped at least ten degrees from the already hot temperatures they had been going through, and the humidity got so high that Lily expected droplets to form on her if she stood still for more than a few seconds, simply from the air itself.

Breathing became a chore like someone was sitting on her chest and the effect of it all was that she only wanted to lie down and sleep right where she was.

"I guess we can take this to mean we're getting close," Urun said. Lily wasn't sure she understood, but between the foul mood she was in and the energy it would require to speak, she decided to ignore him.

Of course, the next set of monsters took that opportunity to attack them.

A humming or buzzing sound started out as little more than leaves rustling in the breeze. It got louder and it didn't take more than a few seconds for everyone to drop what they were carrying and ready their weapons. By the time the noise became recognizable, it was no surprise that the danger came from above.

More than fifteen mosquitos the size of housecats buzzed toward them, their membranous wings generating the noise that sounded just like their smaller cousins, but a thousand times louder. The sharp proboscis emerging from each of their faces were more formidable than normal mosquitos, of course, about the size of a typical dagger, and Lily shuddered at the thought of whatever kind of venom or disease the monsters carried, not to mention their penchant for drinking the blood of those they bit.

The battle was fast and chaotic, most of the damage being done by Lily and Tere as the insects buzzed around to dive toward the remaining people. Aeden and Jia—and to a lesser extent, Grobel—slashed at any that attacked them, while Urun took the sensible approach of putting a shield in place and watching for anyone who got bitten so he could help them out.

Aeden had his swords busy with four of the monsters attacking him at a time. He impressively kept from being punctured by their sharp proboscises while he cut two of the creatures down, but then two more joined and one was able to come in through a blind spot behind him and stab him with its appendage.

He immediately grunted, much louder than he would have done with a simple wound, and Urun was there immediately while Aeden growled and whirled, swords blurring, as he cut into the monsters. The one that punctured him got neatly sliced in half, while the others suffered anything from a wing being slashed off to the final one that Aeden skewered on one of his swords.

Before the last insect hit the ground, Aeden was swaying on his feet. Urun half-caught him as he toppled, bringing both men to the ground. The priest didn't bother getting up and cast a healing spell from the awkard position he had fallen into. Aeden emitted a low moan, but seemed to revive, at least a little.

Once Urun judged the Croagh as being fit to continue, he got up and watched everyone else. If the venom was strong enough to affect Aeden that quickly, anyone else bitten would need immediate attention or they might die.

While both men were busy with the healing, Lily had

exerted herself even more than normal, striving to release arrows faster and more accurately. She created a veritable sea of projectiles to try to keep the other monsters from taking advantage of the situation. Tere must have noticed what she was doing—or had exactly the same idea—because what insects near Urun and Aeden she didn't hit with her arrows, his found. Between that and Jia ghosting the periphery of the battlefield and taking out unsuspecting mosquitos buzzing around and looking for targets, the danger was soon past and another battle was behind them.

No sooner did they recuperate and begin moving, though, than Aeden inadvertently set off a kind of natural trap. As he pushed and cut through the dense vegetation, a plant launched barbs at the Croagh.

The whipping motion of the plant's vines used to propel the projectiles was enough to warn Aeden, though just barely in time. He dropped to the ground as nearly a dozen of the sharp thorn-like darts flew over him.

Of course, once he was on the ground, several vines with serrated edges, almost like saws, reached out to grasp at him. From what Lily could see, it was at least two different kinds of plants attacking, possibly more. As she tried to get an arrow into a vital part of any of them, she wondered if someone or something was controlling the vegetation monsters or if they somehow acted together by instinct or even a rudimentary intelligence.

No spot she sunk an arrow into made the plant stop moving. As with the attackers the day before, the only alternative was to chop the vines and stems to bits. They even went so far as to dig up the roots and destroy those as well, though whether it was for the sake of thoroughness or plain irritation at the attacks, Lily wasn't sure, even in her own mind.

One thing was clear: she was sick and tired of dealing with the island, its jungle, and the creatures that lived in it.

Another break to gather their wits and recuperate, and the

party was on the move again. By then, it was mid-afternoon and it was starting to look like they might have to spend another night in the deadly jungle before reaching their destination. Surely they were getting close to their goal.

That's when they encountered the wall of vegetation.

At first, Lily thought it was only a particularly thick section of the jungle, but after stopping to rest in front of it and then moving as a group along the edges, it quickly became apparent that they weren't going to be able to go around it.

"What do you think, Urun?" Aeden asked after they'd skirted the edges one way for an hour and then back the other way for another two.

The group had tried the obvious action of cutting through the tangle of vines and dense bushes so thick that only the tops of the trees a few dozen feet above the ground were visible. Some of the thicker vegetation actually resisted being cut too deeply by any of their weapons, while others seemed to grow before their eyes to replace any damage they suffered.

Aeden had tried several spells, all to no avail. Lily used one of her precious fire arrows, but the flame was snuffed out as soon as it made contact with her target and the waited for explosion never happened.

"Huh," she said. "I guess if it gets put out too soon and too thoroughly, it doesn't have a chance to explode. I'll have to keep that in mind."

Even Urun got into the conflict, using whatever spells he could manage to think of to attack the wall. Even his powerful spells that caused living things to go through their lifespan in an accelerated time frame didn't do anything other than cause ripples, some small sections rapidly wilting and dying, but replaced almost immediately with other vines. As a last resort, just to be thorough, he tried nature healing spells, hoping the corruption would make the magic act like a harmful offensive spell.

There was no effect whatsoever.

After their long trek the first direction, Aeden cast his finding spell before they turned to come back. It pointed directly to the wall. When the second casting did the same thing at the other end, two hours' walk from the first one, there was no doubt.

"Life's Cradle is either directly on the other side of that wall, or it's located so centrally that the spell points to it no matter where we are on the wall," the Croagh said with exasperation. "We don't even know how thick the wall is. It could be a few inches or a mile wide."

"The wall curves," Tere said.

Aeden rubbed at his eyes. "Come again?"

"The wall, it's curved. It's hard to tell as we walk through the jungle outside of it because we can't sight down it for any distance and there's no reference point, but it curves enough that it's probably a circle a couple of miles wide. I think we could walk around it all the way, ending up back where we started, and we'll probably never find an opening."

"Urun?" Jia pleaded. "Anything?"

The priest shook his head. "I'm sorry, Jia, but I don't know anything about it, other than it's full of the corruption I've been feeling since we got on the island. I would say that the source of it is in there, somewhere, but I don't' know how to get to it."

Jia swung her gaze back to the surface of the wall for a moment. She finally nodded and, without another word, ran at the wall full speed. When she reached it, she bounded up on it, like she was going to walk right up it.

The problem was, the vegetation allowed her feet to sink into its surface, then held her tight before she got a few feet from the ground.

"Ah! Help. It has me."

Aeden was the first to her, grabbing her around the waist and pulling her as hard as he could. It was a contest, until Tere and Lily joined him, each taking an arm and adding their strength to the endeavor. Slowly, the black-clad woman's legs came free.

"Did it feel to you like it could have held her even if there were ten more of us?" Lily asked. "Like it decided we'd learned our lesson and let her legs go?"

"Yes," Aeden said.

"Yeah," Jia agreed.

Tere was satisfied with just nodding.

"Well, what do we do?" Jia asked. "Trying to climb it is definitely out of the question."

CHAPTER
FORTY-FOUR

They ended up setting up camp for the night. In their exploration of the wall, they not only hadn't been attacked, but they hadn't seen more than a few birds. Even the small animals seemed to be staying away from the mass of tangled vegetation, almost as if it was poisonous in some way. Or because they had keener senses than that humans and knew it wasn't a good and natural thing.

"Anyone want to discuss ideas on getting past that green wall?" Aeden asked, "or do we want to try to figure out things on our own and then come together to talk about what we come up with?"

"I vote for trying separately and then comparing notes," Jia said.

"Sounds good to me, too," Lily agreed.

No one had any objections, so they staked out their own little spaces in the area where they set up camp and dealt with their problem in whichever way they desired. For some, that was leaning back against a tree or rock and closing their eyes. For others, it consisted of staring blankly out into the jungle or at the wall that was their problem. Lily decided she wanted to have a little space and moved off a short distance to ponder their dilemma.

Now that their stalker problem was solved, the group was somewhat more relaxed about remaining in pairs at all times. There was no specific conversation about it; it was simply a matter of no one bringing it up. It helped that they hadn't seen anything dangerous the entire time they were trying to skirt the wall. It was the first time since they'd reached the heavier jungle—though at this point, Lily wanted to refer to it more as the *middle heavy jungle*, since they had reached what was really heavy in the wall holding them back—that they'd gone so long without being attacked by anything. It was nice, but it also tickled the back of Lily's neck, like someone was watching her.

How could they pass the wall of tangled plants? It didn't seem like they could get over it. Even if they climbed a high tree at the edges and tried to jump over, it didn't seem that it would be that easy. It might be like jumping right into the maw of some hungry beast. They could climb a tree, though, and at least take a look to see how thick the wall was. If it was a thin barrier, that would probably make things a bit easier for them. She'd definitely mention that idea to the others.

Was the obstruction intelligent? It hadn't shown that it was. Most of what happened as they tested it could be chalked up to reflex or instinct, if plants could even be said to have such things. Master Chesaren would probably say plants had instinct, perhaps even a kind of intelligence, though different than the way people and other sentient things thought. Lily wished the master was here now. She would know what to do. Even Urun, who tried to commune and be in balance with all of nature, couldn't compete against the master when it came to specializing in plants. While Urun relied on his magic, Master Chesaren had her vast amount of information and experience.

Something danced around in her mind, defeating her

ability to catch hold of it. Was it something the master had told her?

A soft sound like a muffled leaf or small twig crunching underneath the vegetation and detritus that made up the floor of the jungle jolted Lily's internal alarms and she whipped around, long knives in her hands.

It was only Tere.

"Whoa," the older archer said. "Be calm. I'm just checking on you to see what you're up to."

Lily let out a breath and slipped the knives into their sheaths. "Sorry. I think I'm a little jumpy. As if it's not bad enough being attacked several times a day, now that everything is quiet, it's like waiting for the arrow to be released."

Tere looked at her blankly for a moment, then chuckled. "It's been interesting. It will all be over soon, though. Have you thought of anything to help us get past the wall?"

"No. I do have one idea, though, that—"

"Were you looking at that?" he interrupted her, pointing toward a section of the wall where she had been staring when he had come to her.

Something in her mind set off more alarm bells. Maybe it was the old joke kids play where they bait their friends into looking somewhere and then chide them for being gullible, but that wasn't all of it. It had just occurred to her that Tere had shown up to check on her and to talk to her. More importantly, he had alerted her to his presence. In all the stories she had heard and all the time she had known him, she had never once heard of or witnessed him making a noise while he moved. It was one of the most infuriating things about him— and Jia, too, while she was thinking about it—but it was an inviolable rule of nature.

Tere never made a sound. Never.

Her blades were out in an instant and before she could even consciously think of what was happening, the knife in her right hand clanged against something hard being slashed at her with great force. Great enough to nearly knock the weapon from her hand.

"To arms!" she yelled. "Attacker." As she shouted it, her body fell back on the years of training and combat to leap back to gain some distance. As she did, she noticed—though couldn't quite reconcile the sight—that Tere's hands had transformed into claws, complete with sharp nails at the end.

Other sounds exploded around her, some of which she thought were voices, but she couldn't spare the mental energy to interpret them. The man in front of her—exactly like the one she had come to know except for the arms ending in claws—was wickedly fast. Even faster than the normal Tere. Probably faster than the young Erent Caahs. It was everything Lily could do just to keep from having her throat slashed out.

Her enemy made it look easy, his face calm and unhurried, his blurringly fast arms everywhere at once. She did her best to back away while blocking the barrage coming at her, but it wasn't working well. In a few seconds, she received gashes to her shoulders and arms. It wasn't that the strikes were necessarily aimed there, but in her attempts to mitigate the damage, she at least got her limbs part-way to where the swipes were aimed: at vital areas like her throat and her upper abdomen.

A blinding flurry of claws came at her from each side, diagonally from below and above, even what could only be called a straight jab with the claws extended toward her like a striking spear. She frantically whirred her knives to meet the attacks, but she found her speed lacking.

She received a few immediate wounds, one of which seemed deep, from the way her skin and that which was below it tugged, but it wasn't until the final straight thrust that she was afraid she might not survive the encounter.

Just as the straightened fingers shot toward her heart, a flash of silver passed in front of her and the blow was deflected, bouncing aside enough so that the razor-sharp claws sunk into her left shoulder. She screamed at the pain and rammed her right knife into the fake Tere's arm, though he was able to evade enough so that it only resulted in a shallow wound.

More importantly, her attacker turned his attention to what had deflected what would have been a mortal strike. Aeden stood beside her, moving his swords faster than she'd ever seen—even faster than the clawed attacker—trying to keep the steel-hard nails from reaching her again.

Lily was rammed aside and Jia began to slash at Tere as well. She lost her balance and thought she was going to fall onto her back, but someone caught her and dragged her back out of the battle quickly. Lily turned to find Urun holding onto her. The chilly feeling of healing slammed into her and she gasped, but her shoulder knitted as she watched it. Gods, those claws had punched nearly completely through her. If Aeden hadn't deflected it, she'd be a corpse right now.

An arrow whizzed by, just missing Aeden and Jia, but the claw-weilding Tere dodged it with preternatural agility and the projectile disappeared into the surrounding vegetation.

Lily shook her head. Jia, Aeden, and Urun were all accounted for. Who shot the arrow? She turned to where she thought it had come from and had to blink several time. Tere stood there, a grimace on his face that chilled her to the bone. He was trying to line up another shot that wouldn't hit his friends but that would still strike the one who attacked her.

The other Tere.

"Gods damn it," she spat and made to get up to get back into the battle, but Urun held her with surprisingly strong hands.

"Let them handle it. There's not much room around whatever that thing is, not with Aeden and Jia both at work and with the real Tere shooting arrows."

She knew the priest was right, but it was hard to sit back and watch when the thing had tried to kill her to begin with.

"Urun, what is that thing?" she asked.

"I don't know, but it's obviously not Tere. It's got enough control in its shapeshifting that it can keep everything else like the one it's trying to mimic."

"Shapeshifter?" she said, her mind still trying to catch up.

The next moment, the fake Tere let loose with a flurry of strikes and, with Aeden and Jia both in defense mode, took off, jumping into some bushes it had maneuvered the two near. The real Tere shot off three arrows in rapid succession, blindly aiming for where he thought the shapeshifter might be. She could hear him spitting curses at the creature, at the ambient magic that interfered with him seeing magical signatures even though bushes, and at the jungle in general.

The entire group—including Grobel who Lily noticed was now standing next to Urun—watched where the fake Tere had gone for a moment, as if it was going to jump back out and resume the fight, but it didn't.

"Are you all right, girl?" Tere said from next to her. She hadn't even heard him approach. Yes, this was the real Tere.

"Gods, it's you," she said, pulling him into a hug. "The real you."

"It is." He wrapped his arms around her and patted her back. "I think you figured out we were duped. That thing wasn't killed. It wasn't Vorun, either, no more than it's me. Damn, I hate shapeshifters. My magical sight helps, normally, but I really don't like them at all."

CHAPTER
FORTY-FIVE

N ow that the ambush and battle were over, Urun took his time in healing Lily until there were not even any marks where the shapeshifter's claws parted her skin like a fine blade.

Lily shivered and Urun raised an eyebrow at her.

"Are you cold? I've never heard you complain about being chilly, despite your choice in wardrobe."

She smirked tiredly at him. "I was just thinking of that thing. It looked exactly like Tere, even sounded like him, all except for the razor-sharp claws. It's going to take a while to get that out of my head." She looked over to Tere, who was still staring at where the attacker had gone, a deep frown creasing his face. When he noticed her, he raised both hands and clawed his fingers toward her as he hunched down in what she thought might be a werewolf imitation. She couldn't help but to laugh. That man!

"Needless to say," Aeden interjected, "we need to reinstitute the buddy rule. No one is ever to be alone at any time, for any reason. This thing can probably appear like any one of us, so if anyone is alone, I say we attack first and ask questions later. You have all been warned. Not only will you compromise the safety of everyone else if you don't have someone with you at all times, but you may end up dead for it."

"Do you think maybe that's a little harsh?" Lily asked, not because she did, really, but because of the panicked look on Grobel's face.

"Not at all," Jia—of all people—said. "It took at least two of us, if not three, to fight that thing to a standstill. True, it was chaos and whatever that thing is might not actually be that good, but if someone insists on going off alone, we're all in danger for it. The only reliable test is to kill whoever it is and see if it keeps its form."

"Does it even work like that?" Lily asked. "Will it revert when it's dead? Is this a finchoi, like the one you killed in Hosen when you were younger, Tere?"

"You know too damn much about my life, have I ever told you that?"

"Once or twice."

"Hmph. Well, to answer your question, I don't know. That's not the only kind of shapeshifter I've encountered. Very early in my adventuring days, when Raisor and I were passing through the easern part of the Mellanor Forest, we almost died to an ilyu. I don't think it's universal. Which kind of shifter is this? It's obviously pretty skilled, but as for when it dies, I don't know what'll happen. I sure intend to find out, though, if it tries to attack us again. It kept its form when we thought we killed Vorun.

"One of the things that really puzzles me is if it's been with us the whole time or if it just found us recently and infiltrated our group. Maybe we can stop just short of killing it and get some answers."

That got Lily thinking. "So, the clothes it was wearing, the things it carried, even the hair on its head, how does it do that? The clothes looked just like yours, Tere, as did the knives it wore on its belt, though it didn't use them."

"Osulin told me that in the old days, when there were

more creatures that could change shape like that, the very skilled ones could make clothing and even items when it took shape. They're actually part of the thing's body and it can color them so well that any chameleon would be jealous."

Jia bounced on her toes, demonstrating her typical boundless energy. "Really? What about size? Can it make itself huge like a dragon or tiny like a mouse or an insect?"

"No," Tere and Urun said at the same time. Tere waved his hand in a submissive gesture, and Urun continued. "They can change size, but not that much. The typical range seems to be between a pre-adolescent child and a very tall and stout man. Anything beyond that and the magic that makes their ability possible would have to either create or destroy substance. According to Osulin. Tere?"

"I was going to say that same thing. I've done some research, since I met more than one shifter. What I learned confirms what Urun said."

"Okay, good," Lily said. "At least we don't have to scrutinize every insect or rodent we see. Any ideas what it's after? It took Brek's heart, but it didn't seem to want to eat any of the men it killed. Why else would it travel with us?"

Tere shrugged. "Who knows? Maybe it is looking for treasure, just as some of the men were when we started. A better question, on another subject, is what we're going to do. Did anyone think of how we'll get past that wall, shapeshifter or not?"

Lily watched the others and it was quickly apparent there weren't any ideas. Or at least ideas that someone was confident enough about to be the first to propose one. She hadn't come up with anything definitive, either, but she did have the one idea that could help.

"I don't have anything specific that will help us get past the wall, but I do have a suggestion," she said. "We probably can't climb a high tree and jump over, but we could climb high enough to see how thick the wall is. Like we talked about before, if it's very thin, we might be able to work on one location enough to break through. There are trees right at the edge where we should be able to see over it for some distance."

No one had any other suggestion for what they should do, so the group went with Lily's suggestion.

"If you don't mind," Jia said, "I can be the one to climb the tree. I'm very good at it."

"I've seen her do it," Lily said. "Trust me, let her be the one. She's like a monkey. A cute, blue-haired monkey."

Jia bent her arms and mimed scratching under her armpits while crouching down. She didn't make the *oo-oo* sound, but it looked like it was a near thing. Lily was just glad that the woman was showing a little of her funny side, since the group as a whole still didn't seem quite normal to her. It was another thing that weighed on her mind. The implications of that were more than Lily wanted to think about. Could there be more than one shape shifter...?

"How are we going to make sure that it's still her when she comes back down?" Urun asked. "These trees are tall and the foliage pretty thick. If she goes near the top, she'll be out of sight to all of us."

"That's a good point," Aeden said.

Lily looked up at a big tree near them. It *was* a good point. "I'll climb up after her and keep her in sight the entire time. If it looks like I won't be able to keep an eye on her without leaving everyone else's sight, someone can climb up after me. Everyone will be in someone else's view at all times. Does that work?"

"I'll go up after Lily," Tere said.

"And if necessary," Aeden added, "I'll go up and keep an eye on Tere. There's no way we should need more people than that in the tree. If so, we'll have to abandon the idea because we'll run out of people."

"Agreed," Jia said. "Now we have to find the tree to climb. I guess we'll be looking for it together, huh?"

They went together as a group and found a tree right on the edges of the wall of vegetation. It stretched up at least a hundred feet, probably more. If that wasn't high enough to see what they needed to see, then they'd have to find a taller tree.

As discussed, Jia sprang onto one of the lower branches and started scurrying up like she was simian. Lily had to ask her to slow down so she could climb at a more moderate pace and keep Jia in sight. Working together, they were able to ensure that Jia didn't leave Lily's view. It helped that the limbs were large and fewer of the smaller branches clogged her vision. Most of the leaves—and the vines growing throughout the boughs—were at the edges where they could get sunlight, leaving a sort of skeleton of wood in the middle that allowed someone near the trunk to see all the way up nearly to the tip of the crown.

"Can you guys still see me?" Lily called down, but kept her eyes on Jia the entire time.

"We can spot you easily," Tere called back. "Especially with that hair."

Lily shook her head, making her red hair bounce. It had always brought attention to her. She guessed it was for the good this time.

After several minutes of being in the same spot, Jia started to descend, doing so at a much faster pace than she'd gone up. Lily wondered how fast the woman could have climbed the entire tree had they not asked her to slow down.

Then Jia got to within a few branches of Lily, she said, "We're good. Let's go down and I'll tell you and the others what I saw. You want to go down first?"

"No. Go ahead. I'll keep watching you and Tere will keep watching me so there's no chance of the shapeshifter replacing us." She thought for a moment, then added, "You didn't see any monkeys or other large animals while you were up there, did you?"

Jia shook her head as she passed by and traveled toward

the ground. "No, but who's to say a shapeshifter can't take the form of a branch or rock or something?"

Lily could only watch the woman descend as she stood there on her branch with her mouth open. She followed immediately by her looking around at any shape large enough to be hiding their stalker. Or, more correctly, for their stalker to be hiding as.

When Lily climbed down, Tere spoke before both her feet were even on the ground. "As far as I know, shapeshifters cannot take the form of inanimate things. Not convincingly so, in any case. We heard what Jia told you." She couldn't tell if he was holding back a smile, but even if he was, she couldn't blame him.

"That's...reassuring."

Jia rubbed her hands together. "So anyway, let me tell you what I saw. The wall isn't really so much a wall but it's just how the jungle is after this. As Tere said, it does look like it goes in a circle, but it's not different enough looking at the edges all the way around for me to tell for a certainty where it starts. Needless to say, though, we're going to have to figure out not just how to get through a section but how to traverse this kind of dense vegetation—nearly sentient vegetation—for some distance.

"I did see a break in the plants, one that looks to be the ruins of something large, maybe a whole city. It's clearer there, not quite without trees and bushes and vines, but the vegetation is even sparser than the jungle we left behind a few days ago. All we have to do is to get through the tangle to get there. Can anyone here fly? Now's a really good time to tell the rest of us."

She made a show of inspecting each person, but it didn't seem anyone was in the mood for jokes.

"It's obvious that city is where we need to go," Aeden said. "We'll have to figure out a way to get there. Urun, can't you do the thing where you tell the vines and bushes to move out of the way and let us pass? I saw you do it when we traveled in the Grundenwald and in other places."

The priest shook his head. "This entire jungle, from the start, refuses to cooperate with me. It's the corruption. If anything, it's more hostile to me. Maybe it thinks I'm its enemy."

"You *are* trying to end the corruption," Lily said. "That kind of means you have to kill whatever it is that's giving it its magic or life or thought process. Thus, you *are* its enemy."

"I guess. Anyway, there's nothing I can do. It simply won't listen to me."

Aeden clenched his jaw, the muscles on the side of his face twitching in response. "There has to be a way. We'll figure it out, or we'll have to turn around and leave."

"We can't just leave," Urun whined. "We have a mission from Osulin herself to eliminate the corruption at Life's Cradle."

"That's all well and good," Tere snapped, "but unless we can figure out how to get through to the other side of this tangled mess, Osulin is going to need to work a miracle for us or we'll starve to death here on this side waiting for that miracle. Either come up with a plan, get Osulin to help us, or shut your mouth."

Urun glared at Tere, but didn't say anything at a volume anyone else could hear. He appeared to be mumbling to himself, but he stopped at that.

"Maybe we should take a few minutes to think silently," Lily suggested. "We have to stay near each other, but we can think on the problem individually and discuss anything we come up with."

It seemed like the mood of the entire group had shifted with the exchange between Urun and Tere, so all Lily got were some nods. She sat down half a dozen feet from the impenetrable emerald wall of vegetation and tried to think of what they could do.

A few minutes turned into half an hour, which turned into a few hours, and everyone was still in their own minds. Lily wondered if this is what it looked like when a group splintered and all went in their own directions, both figuratively and literally. She hoped not. She couldn't really see any of them surviving to get back to the ship going alone. Well, maybe Jia could. She could sneak out of the jungle without being seen. The rest of them, though, would be overwhelmed. Even if the shapeshifter didn't find them.

During their quiet thinking time, Lily treated the problem —the big wall of plants that seemed to adjust to their attempts to go through or around it—like it was a single physical, sentient thing. In her mind, she picked it up, turned it around in her hands, and considered it from every angle. It didn't help. She couldn't come up with anything that would work to traverse the dense jungle wall.

Her mind started to wander, random thoughts appearing where they were not wanted. Snippets of experiences in her life, portions of conversations, things she didn't even really remember that she remembered, it seemed like her mind was trying to fill the emptiness in her attempted bucket of ideas with whatever it felt like. She let them pass before her consciousness, allowing them free rein in her mind.

Then, something caught her attention. It was Master Chesaren's voice, something she said to Lily before she left for Drusca.

"Your outlook on things is...different. Not just different than most peoples', but wildly different than the plants you are trying to nurture. It must be like you're speaking an unknown language to them. It's no wonder you're having issues communing. It's almost like you are the complete opposite of them and their view of the world."

It was true. She had problems trying to project her feelings toward her plants as Master Chesaren had instructed her.

They didn't seem to want to hear her thoughts. Found them too foreign. Or opposite, as the master had pointed out.

What if...the opposite was closer to what a corrupted plant would understand?

When the master told her to talk to the plants she was trying to grow, either verbally or mentally, Lily thought the older woman had some issues with her mind. Master Chesaren swore that if she gave it a try, she would see results of some kind.

"Plants don't think like you and I, but they do instinctually know things and act accordingly. Whether it's the magic of the world or simply how they were created, I don't know. Give it a try, though, child. What is there to lose? On the other hand, much could be gained from the attempt, at the very least healthy vegetable and herb plants. A conversant garden is a happy garden."

She opened her mind and projected a bit of herself toward the jungle wall. She wasn't sure if she knew how to do it correctly, but she did her best to communicate her thoughts on life. *Living is tough and dangerous. It is a full-time occupation to simply survive, and that is all anyone or anything could hope for: to live as long as possible. Surviving is all. Everything else is just added ornaments attempting to make living more attractive.*

Lily wasn't sure what to expect. She continued to throw her thoughts out, hoping something would happen.

Some say there must be a purpose to life, but is that true? I haven't seen anything that would convince me. Survival, that is what life is about.

Something did happen.

When Master Chesaren explained to her what should occur when she tried to connect with the plants she was attempting to grow, she described it as *more of a feeling than actual thought or communication.* Lily had felt a ghost of a sensation back then, one that made her believe that the plant was either unwilling or incapable of forming a rapport with her.

She thought she knew what the master was talking about now. After a brief sensation that she could only describe as feeling like she was being scanned or having her mind read—though not quite so powerful as that—a feeling of tolerance, maybe even acceptance trickled into her mind. She wasn't sure what to think.

The first thing Lily did was to open her eyes and look around to see if one of the others was casting some kind of spell, maybe playing a joke on her. None of them were paying attention to her, though. It still could be a prank, but she thought not. Why would someone do that to her, especially with tempers flaring as they currently were?

Instead of analyzing it, she closed her eyes again and opened up her mind. The feeling didn't grow, but it was still there and she was more certain it wasn't coming from within her group of friends. It was coming from somewhere in front of her, whether somewhere inside the vegetation wall or from the wall itself.

In her mind, she was already trying to frame the words she was planning on saying. *Uh, Tere. I think I'm onto something....* Of course, she didn't know where to go from there, so she aborted any plan of speaking just yet. Better if she understood what was going on first before trying to explain it to others.

For several more minutes she sat, letting the odd sensation wash over her. Not knowing what else to do, she rose, took a few steps until she was standing directly in front of the dense green obstruction. She reached her hand out toward it, holding her breath.

Slowly, her fingers contacted the wall of densely packed vines in front of her. But they *didn't* contact it. As she moved her hand forward, things shifted and a small space opened up, allowing her to penetrate the surface. Immediately, she worried that it might grab her or snap shut on her hand after she'd pushed in a little farther, but she got her fingers and half her palm in before a shout from behind startled her. Not just her, but apparently the wall as well because it pushed her hand back out, though it didn't harm her.

"Lily! What the hells are you doing?" It was Tere, and his anger was evident in his tone.

Lily turned to find everyone looking at her, all but Grobel on their feet as if to snatch her back from certain destruction.

"Uh, Tere. I think I'm onto something," she said.

Tere crossed his arms in front of his chest and grimaced at her. "Tell us."

She explained to them briefly what the master had told her and how she tried to commune with the plants she was trying to grow, and how her plants didn't want anything to do with her. She also repeated what the master said about it, that Lily didn't seem to have an attitude that meshed with the way green things tended to feel about the world. Then she tried to tie it together with what she had figured out just moments ago.

"I think I can commune with these plants because my attitude makes sense to them."

Urun took a step toward her, his head cocked. "You're saying that your particular way of looking at things endears you to a corrupted jungle?"

"Yes?" she squeaked. Putting it that way, she didn't feel like it was such a good thing.

"Huh," the priest said. "It could work. What did you see, Tere, that made you shout at her a moment ago?"

"She had her damn hand halfway into the surface of the wall."

"Wait," Aeden said. "She actually had her hand *in* it? We haven't been able to do so much as put a dent in it, no matter how much we tried. Well, other than Jia's legs, but that was the wall opening up to trap her."

"I did," Lily said. "It was allowing me to move my hand

into it. At first I was afraid that it might be letting me get in just enough to grab me and harm me, but it didn't. I didn't feel any ill intent and it didn't hurt me in any way. Even when Tere yelled and startled it, it pushed me out instead of snapping around my hand." She put her hands up to head off what she knew was coming. "I know, it sounds like I'm saying it's not evil. I'm not. I'm just saying that it didn't seem like it was going to harm me, not that I want to adopt it as a pet."

Urun looked at Tere. "I don't have any ideas about how to get into or through that thing. If she thinks she can do it, I say let's let her try. If you get uncomfortable in any way as you do it, though, Lily, you back off immediately and we'll try to figure out another way. It's not worth risking your life on a hunch."

She chuckled. "I've risked myself for much less than that for most of my life. If I can convince it to let us go through. I'll do whatever is necessary."

"I guess we have a plan, then," Tere huffed. "Don't go taking any unnecessary risks, girl, no matter how much you think we need it. It's not worth it. I'm not done training you yet. How are you going to carry on for me if you go and get strangled by vines?"

"Aww," she said. "I knew you cared."

FORTY-SEVEN

L ily tried to replicate the sensation she felt before, standing a few inches from the wall with her eyes closed and trying to commune with whatever it was she had contacted earlier. It was hard to do with everyone else hovering around watching her, as if there was anything they could see. The thought hitched in her mind for a moment and she opened her eyes.

"Can you...feel or see what I'm trying to do? I mean, is it some kind of magic that you can detect somehow?"

Urun looked at Tere, who looked back and then at Aeden. All three men shrugged simultaneously.

"I can't see anything," Tere said. "But with all this bloody interference with my sight, I wouldn't expect to even if what you were doing *could* be seen."

Urun picked up the conversation. "I think what you're doing is mainly thought process, possibly some kind of slightly magical psionic type of thing. It may not be possible to see it at all. One of the masters at the Academy might, but we certainly don't."

That made sense. Lily still wasn't sure exactly what she was doing. If it was a magical thing, she'd be asking some pointed questions of the masters once all this was over. Questions about whether or not she was capable of using magic at all. She filed that away and turned her full attention back to trying to communicate with the wall of plants, though putting it that way, she was more convinced that she was already half mad.

"Before you dive back into yourself," Tere said, "let me tie this rope around your waist. If we get separated, it could help, if only to give us something to follow."

She knew as well as he did that if she got trapped within the wall, the rope would probably be severed, but she acquiesced. It would make Tere feel better. He hid it well, but he was a nervous wreck. Once tied, she got back to her work.

After a few minutes, she caught a hint of what she had felt earlier, then a few minutes more brought her to the point where she reached her hand out again. It seemed that she was being invited to do so, but Urun's and Tere's words echoed in her head, seeding her belly with a grain of fear.

She slowly reached and put her hand forward into the wall. It let her. A few fingers, then her whole hand, then her arm. That led to her walking forward, almost as if her hand was leading the way, breaking through a body of water to allow the rest of her to move more freely through it.

When her arm was inside the vegetation up to her shoulder, she opened her eyes again. It almost made her lose her concentration.

She could see through that mess. Not like it was transparent, but like it was a regular part of the jungle where she could take in the whole picture between the vines and leaves, even though there didn't seem to be space between them for her to see.

"See if you can follow me," she called back as she plunged into the morass. Tere was next, right on her heels, then came Urun, Grobel, Jia, and finally Aeden. From what she could see behind her, they were all able to follow her.

To Lily's eyes, it looked like a bubble formed in the vegetation, like a huge amount of air had been released in a vast body of water, slowly moving in time with her own progress. Exactly like that, in fact, except that there was no water and the bubble was moving sideways instead of up. She thought maybe her analogy had fallen apart, but regardless, it seemed that her friends could move along with her.

She couldn't see it close up again behind them, but she needed to keep her eyes forward, so didn't get a chance to watch and see if it did. Everything seemed to be moving in slow motion. The opening, her, her friends. It gave her the sense that the space would close up again, but it might take several minutes. Lily opened her mouth to say something about it, but Tere's voice stopped her.

"Keep your eyes on what you're doing," he told her. "We'll take care of the rest. Try to find the fastest way through to the ruins Jia told us about."

She gave him an ironic salute with her other hand, resulting in a scoffing hiss from him, and she smiled as she did what he asked. He was right, of course, but no sense in letting him have an easy time of it.

For nearly an hour, they slogged through the vegetation, seeing not a thing else, be it beast or insect. Some of the plants looked to be the same type that had attacked them before, but they didn't do anything now, just sat immobile, though Lily could feel they could move if they wanted to.

Finally, Lily stepped out into a more open area. It was so abrupt, she stumbled, like she had just fallen down the last step on a staircase, one she hadn't realized was there. Her awkward landing was on weathered stone. Very weathered.

"I think we made it to the ruins," she told everyone. "Time to stop and figure out what we'll do, yes?"

After resting their feet—and their nerves—for a few minutes, they decided to untie everyone from the rope. She hadn't even noticed the others had tied themselves to it. It had been days since they'd been in an area with as much room to move around, and visibility was good. It was a relief to get the rough fibers off and even better to be able to walk without having to constantly push plants out of the way.

They couldn't see the buildings Jia described, but they found bits of buried stone everywhere. Lily dug through the soil at her feet and found several areas where there were only a few inches of dirt with stone underneath. Other spots had exposed stone that had obviously been worked.

"It's an ancient road," Tere said. "The city must have been fair sized to have paved roads out away from the buildings. Either that, or the buildings were all destroyed so thoroughly, there isn't a trace of them."

"I did see the ruins of some buildings," Jia said. "We'll get there if we follow the road."

Urun grumbled something unintelligible, obviously miffed at something.

She faced the priest "What's wrong, Urun?"

"Don't ask him," Tere said. "He spent most of the trip cursing under his breath. The plants don't seem to like him."

"I'll say," Aeden added. "I saw multiple occasions where some of them pushed him or swiped at him, even though they pulled back for Grobel and then the rest of us."

Lily shrugged. "That would make sense. It's the same thing as why they seem to connect with me even though Master Chesaren told me all my views on things are exactly opposite from what most plants respond to. These corrupted plants are like anti-nature plants, so it fits they'd find fault with you."

They started off again, following Jia's suggestion and keeping to the road as much as they could, considering how little of it there was to actually see. Soon enough—travel was much faster without the choking vegetation pressing in on them from all sides—they reached other stone shapes, these sticking up out of the ground, sometimes as high as their heads. They weren't recognizable as buildings yet, but that was all they could be.

"We're getting close now," Lily said. She was paired off with Tere in the front of the group. Aeden and Grobel were a bit behind them, followed by Urun and Jia. Everyone was doing well in sticking with their partner, even as they moved into territory that wasn't as congested with vegetation, but was crowded with stone shapes recognizable as walls and even doorways. There were no doors, of course, but it was becoming easier to see that they were indeed in a city.

"Aeden, can you cast your spell again?" Tere asked the Croagh. "Just so we can make sure we're heading in the right direction."

Aeden nodded and within minutes had cast his spell, the magical light indicating which way to go. They were on track.

"Will you lead us, Tere?" Aeden asked. "We have the general direction, but you're much better at scouting than any of the rest of us."

The archer took the lead and they continued. In one area, the remains of whatever large building once stood there looked to have been in a quake, or hit with some other kind of tremendous force.

Tere tsked. "It must have been higher than the others. All this debris didn't come from a low building collapsing."

The way the stone had fallen created a warren of sorts, with narrow and twisty pathways throughout. Lily looked at them with suspicion.

"Looks like a great setup for an ambush. Restricted movement, possibly unstable walls, blind curves. Maybe we should back up and go around this mess."

"I agree about not liking it," Tere said. "But did you see how large an area this thing took up? It must have been some kind of arena or something. It might take us hours to go back and go around it. Aeden's spell said what we're looking for is directly through here."

"Yeah, but I don't know. I have a bad feeling about this."

"First you commune with plants like Urun and now you're prophesying like Fahtin. What's next, actually casting spells like Aeden or Marla?" She glared at him and he put his hands up. "Just kidding. Listen, I understand, but I think it's better to go through this way. We'll face the same if we try to go around, or worse. What do the rest of you think?"

Grobel refused to give any input and the other three preferred to continue as they were going.

"All we can do is try to be very careful," Aeden said. "That's why you and Tere are up front. The two of you are experts at tracking and scouting. I'll lead if you want and I'll cast the direction spell more frequently, if that'll make you feel a little better."

"No, it's fine," she told him. "We'll be careful, as you say."

Once they started off again, their pace slowed quite a bit. Tere and Lily checked for traps or unstable piles of stone that might drop on them. They listened for even the slightest sound of anyone in front of them. They constantly scanned the ground for any kind of tracks.

Those behind them didn't take it easy, though. If anything, they were going a little slower, making their own checks and squeezing their way through narrow turns and openings. As they progressed, the pairs, though sticking together, spread out from the other pairs. Enough so that it didn't occur to Lily that Tere was the only one in her sight.

Until she heard Jia yelp.

FORTY-EIGHT

"Damn it!" Tere yelled as he pushed on Lily's right shoulder to spin her around. "Get back there. That's the kind of sound someone makes when they've been attacked."

She was already two steps into her sprint by the time he finished his sentence, moving as fast as she could through the tricky and narrow passage. Ahead of her, Aeden and Grobel were doing the same thing, just rounding another turn in their path. The Croagh already had his swords out and Grobel was doing his best to keep up with the larger man.

When they made it through to the slightly wider area Lily had seen earlier, she was shocked once again by the sight of two of her companions apparently battling to the death. Lily and Urun were both moving awkwardly, partly because of the difficult terrain, but also because of visible injuries.

At first, Lily couldn't reconcile what was before her. It made no sense. Then she noticed Jia's hands and face. It was hard to tell with her dark clothing, but on her skin, the red liquid was more evident.

There was no way in creation that Urun Chinowa could draw blood fighting against Jia. He could use his staff passably well as a mundane weapon, but Jia was a supreme warrior. There was only one explanation.

"Urun is the shapeshifter," Tere said, drawing an arrow back but waiting until the two combatants were a bit more separated.

Aeden reached the two and jumped in, swords arcing toward Urun. Surprisingly, the priest smoothly evaded them, even batting one to the side with what sounded like a metal object in his hand. Then a movement so fast Lily couldn't see it pushed Aeden aside. It didn't look like a forceful push. In fact, there didn't seem to be any contact at all. But when Aeden wheeled and faced the priest again, there were slashes on the side of his face, already dripping blood.

Jia looked the worse for wear. Her normally perfectly controlled movements had more of an erratic, even desperate manner to them. Whatever it was the two were fighting, it had been too much for her alone. It was a wonder she was still alive.

Grobel raised his sword and started toward the melee, but Lily shouted at him. "Don't you dare, Grobel. It's too much for you. You'll only get in the way and get killed. Back off. We'll handle this thing."

The only remaining sailor from those that had joined them glanced at where Aeden and Jia were desperately fighting what appeared to be Urun and then back at Lily. For a moment, she thought he was going to rush to his death, but the moment passed and he let out a sigh, then moved off to the side of the area so he'd be out of the way. He didn't see Lily nod, too intent on the battle he almost joined.

With him safely out of the way, Lily imitated Tere, aiming an arrow at the battling Urun, looking for an opening that wouldn't endanger her friends.

It was uncanny, the way the fake Urun was moving. To see the familiar form not only whipping around his limbs as gracefully as Aeden and Jia, but doing so even faster than them, or at least as fast, strained logic. It was an unfair comparison with Jia, since she seemed to be seriously injured. She still fought with skill and control, just not at the level she usually did. The worst part about how the Urun fought was that he seemed to know exactly where to position the other two combatants so they would be in the way of any incoming arrows. Frustrating didn't begin to describe it.

Aeden whirled his swords, the steel a blur in his hands. A left overhead chop at the same time as a right horizontal slash should have given anyone trouble, but his opponent swung his hand up at exactly the right time to push the side slash up with a clang. The deflected sword bounced into the other blade, deflecting it as well. Meanwhile, Urun sliced through the air with his other hand, right for Jia.

The woman's blades were in motion as well, but she twisted in the middle of her attempted strikes to evade the hand. It seemed silly, until with a tug of fabric and leather, the skin on Jia's arm opened and blood immediately started to leak out.

"Son of a bitch," Tere said. "That thing has claws. That's what we've been hearing when it parries weapons. What are they made of?"

Lily heard what he said vaguely, but more importantly, Jia's evasion opened up a small space between her and Urun, and Aeden had moved a half step away as well to bring his swords under control. With a quick exhalation of breath, Lily let loose the arrow she'd been holding. The projectile cut through the air without a sound, for all appearances going straight toward the fake Urun's abdomen.

At the last possible fraction of a second, the shapeshifter bent its body just enough that the arrow passed by without so much as catching its clothing. Then again, if what Tere had said about the clothes being part of the creature's body, it stood to reason that if it could dodge, it would dodge completely.

Unfortunately, Jia had no such luck in evading. Once the shaft had passed through where the creature had been, it laid down a gash on her thigh before bouncing off a stone and shattering on the other side of the battle.

Jia didn't fall, but she immediately backed off, trying to protect her leg. Lily felt horrible. It wasn't a serious injury, but with everything else, it might be enough to allow the monster-Urun to use those claws to hurt her badly.

Lily threw down her bow and got her hands around her knife hilts, but Tere had acted more quickly. He was already a half-step from the trio, his long knives both bared. He shouldered Jia out of the way and parried a claw slash that had been aimed at her. Jia, being the professional she was, retreated to give Tere and Aeden more room to work. With two uninjured foes, the Urun look-alike wasn't going to have an easy time of things. That was a good thing, in Lily's book.

Jia limped toward Lily, half watching the fight and half navigating her way toward the archer. When the smaller woman turned her attention completely toward Lily, the archer put her hands out to the sides, tilted her head, and shrugged at Jia, trying her best to force a smile though she felt horrible for harming her friend.

Jia's eyebrows flicked upward and she smiled at Lily. Of course, she wouldn't hold a grudge. She would know that Lily hadn't done it on purpose.

"There's room for three," Jia said pointing at thumb back toward Tere and Aeden, who were just now getting into the rhythm of the combat.

Lily must have really been stunned about hurting Jia for her to stand there like a raw novice. Without a word, she charged in, slipping into the motions of her two friends.

It was funny, the way one got used to fighting with companions. After so many battles crammed into what was really a short amount of time, Lily could feel the flow in Aeden's and Tere's rhythm. Gliding into it with them felt like coming home after a long trip on the road. She took up the third side of the triangle, hefted her blades, and began the dance.

The fake Urun was fast, blindingly so, but he was in the middle of three skilled warriors with no way of escaping without making himself vulnerable. He must have known because instead of trying to flee, he lashed out with his claws —which Lily could clearly see during the infrequent times they were not blurs of motion—in both attack and defense.

The shifter slashed at Lily with his left hand while simultaneously blocking a strike from Aeden's blade and trying to lay a gash onto Tere's arm. Lily blocked the strike hard with both knives crossed and the power surprised her, nearly knocking the weapons from her hands. The vibration of the strike resonated in the bones of her arms. She would be parrying for all subsequent attacks.

Tere dodged the strike leveled at him and overreached just a bit to slash at Urun's arm as it passed. He struck a glancing blow, but it was a negligible injury. Still, it was nice to see the monster on the receiving end.

Aeden came in with both swords low while Tere—on the left side of the fake Urun—slashed at the oponent's head with one knife and stabbed straight toward the abdomen with the other. Taking advantage of being behind the creature, Lily lunged in with both knives, slashing outward from the center of the shifter's back.

The thing wearing Urun's face twisted its body unnaturally, barely evading Aeden's swords, slapping Tere's lunge, and actually elongating its head to keep from being struck by Tere's other knife. It could not, however, escape Lily's blades completely.

Whether because he could not see her clearly or simply because it wasn't possible to evade all six strikes, one of Lily's blades caught the thing on its right shoulder, piercing and opening up the flesh over its shoulder blade. When Lily didn't feel the tugging from scraping along the bone, something she surely would have with how deep the blade went, she realized that the creature probably didn't have bones. With how it changed shape, it might not even have organs.

If that were the case, how could they kill it?

The fake Urun howled, a sound she had never heard the priest make. In fact, it might not be possible with human vocal cords.

The injury was enough to cause the shapeshifter to stumble in its smooth motions. Enough so that one of Aeden's swords caught its leg on his backswing. That upset its balance even more, something Tere took full advantage of.

The old archer whirled his knives around in their trajectory and brought them back around in the perfect position to meet the creature as it recoiled from Aeden's and Lily's strikes. It lashed out, trying to gain some distance so it could recover, but Tere's blade met its left hand at the wrist as it came toward him. With the force of the strike, coupled with the speed at which the arm was moving, the blade went completely through, lopping off the hand and depriving the creature of one of its weapons.

Lily, manuevering her knives around to attack again, opened her eyes wide as the stump of the monster's hand didn't spurt blood, but sealed itself almost instantly and then started to elongate, taking the rough shape of a hand. It looked as if it would take a handful of seconds before it could accomplish the change and she wasn't about to give it the time to do so.

"It's growing its claw back," she yelled out, managing to skewer the same arm as the shifter swung it away from Tere. Her blade punched right into the biceps and Lily didn't waste any time in twisting her knife and tearing outward to do as much damage as possible.

Again, the creature screamed an inhuman bellow as it

turned its body to pull back its ruined arm and tried in vain to slash at her with its good hand.

This time, it was Aeden's sword that met the arm as it came toward Lily. The blade sliced through the forearm halfway between the elbow and hand, separating that extremity as well.

With both hands either missing or not fully formed, all three humans attacked instantly with a ferocity rarely seen except in the most intense of battles. Aeden rammed both swords down into the fake Urun's chest, angled so that they entered near the collar bones and made their path through the torso before punching out of the lower back. Lily rammed both knives into the thing's head, approximately where the ears were. Tere, with his long blades in a reverse grip, slashed powerfully outward from opposite sides of the neck, cutting cleanly through and leaving Lily holding a disembodied head stabbed through with her knives.

It seemed that was enough to finish the thing off because the body dropped to the ground, twitched a few times, and lay still.

Before it finished moving, though, the body and head transformed into a creature that looked all too familiar. It was dark-colored, had course, wiry hair on it, and was humanoid in shape. Whether its natural form or not, simply having knowledge of something that looked like it now did revealed the final secret.

It was animaru.

CHAPTER

FORTY-NINE

L ily flung the head from her blades to the ground with a disgusted shudder. Those creatures were despicable enough without one looking at her while pierced through and hanging off her knives. She was about to say something about the animaru, but Jia's insistant voice cut through all her thoughts.

"Aeden, over here. Fast."

Lily caught movement out of the corner of her eye. Two blobs of darkness, no bigger than a housecat, flitted away from them, disappearing into the jungle, but not before Tere launched an arrow at one. The shaft went through it harmlessly and stuck in the ground. She blinked, wondering if she'd really just seen what she thought she had.

"You saw that, too, right?" Tere said.

A nervous laugh spilled out of Lily's mouth. "I did. I was hoping I hadn't imagined it."

"No. I saw two of them. They moved, fled when we spotted them. Anyway, they're probably harmless."

The Croagh, to his credit, didn't ask why but stumbled his exhausted and injured body into motion toward where only a piece of the woman's black-clothed body was visible. Tere was a step behind him and Lily only half a step behind and to the side of him. Grobel stood, swinging his head back and forth between the others.

When Lily arrived on the other side of a bend in the path they had been taking, Aeden was already casting his healing spells on the prone form of Urun Chinowa. The *real* Urun, thank the gods.

"Is he going to be okay?" Lily asked Jia, who had stepped out of the way in the cramped space to let Aeden work.

Aeden was apparently too busy to answer, so Jia did so for him.

"We don't know. At the end of the battle, it occurred to me to look for Urun. He had been right behind me, so I knew he couldn't be far. I found him here, unconscious. I'm not sure what happened to him. Why wouldn't that animaru have slashed out his throat instead of knock him out?"

"The sound," Tere said. "Even with a quick slash to the throat, there can be sound. A little air can still get through and make at least a gurgling sound, enough to tip off anyone close that something was going on. A knock on the head, though, can be done more quietly. Lucky for Urun you two were sticking together like you were supposed to."

"Not close enough," Jia said.

"In these narrow, twisty paths, you did the best you could do," Lily told her. "And even surprised, you fought that thing long enough to call for help."

"It was fast. I think I might have been able to take it if I wasn't ambushed. Just barely, though. Those claws are sharp. I can tell you that from experience."

It was then when Lily remembered that Jia had several serious wounds herself. "Here, let me clean your wounds and bandage you. If Aeden has enough strength left after he finishes with Urun to heal you, then that's fine, but in the meantime, you could bleed to death."

"No need," Aeden said. "It was like Tere said. Urun just got bumped on the head. I healed it. He'll probably be awake in a little while. Right now, he's having a nap, but he's fine. If you can hang on for a moment longer, Jia, I have one more important thing to do."

He didn't wait for an answer, but stalked back over to the animaru's body. Without pausing, he widened his stance and began to motion with his hands, rolling them almost like he was punching an invisible target in front of him, one hand after the other. When he pronounced words Lily didn't understand but that were recognizable, she understood.

"*Rausha. Jitaka. Airuh.*"

Upon finishing the last word, Aeden thrust his palms toward the monster's corpse and light flashed momentarily. The body twitched, then seemed to deflate a bit.

Aeden walked back to them. "Sorry. I wanted to make sure it stayed dead this time. Life magic does a good job at that. Now, let me take a look at what that monster did to you, Jia. By the way, I agree with Lily. Great job in alerting us and holding out even though you were ambushed and injured."

Jia grumbled something under her breath. Lily knew her well enough to recognize it as disappointment that she'd been surprised to begin with.

Since Urun was sleeping, the group decided to camp and rest. They carried Urun a short distance until they came to a wider area within the pathway. On the way, Lily told the rest of them what she'd seen, the two balls of shadow. After dealing with the shapeshifter, no one seemed to get too excited about possibly seeing small moving shadows.

"Probably just some kind of harmless animal that lives in the jungle," Tere said.

Lily sat down hard, more tired than she really had a reason to be. The past week had worn her down. It suddenly occurred to her that they hadn't thought to use the message tablet in all the time they'd been on Visuren. The others' attitudes had been...different, and she had been so overwhelmed, it had slipped her mind as well. She still needed to discuss the blood-lust and other strange actions of her friends, but first things first.

"Aeden, when was the last time we sent a message through the tablets? Maybe we should warn the others there are animaru shapeshifters. Infiltrators."

Aeden pulled the message tablet from his pack and tossed it to Lily. "That's a good idea. Wait, what did you just say?"

"That there are shapeshifters."

"After that."

"Ummm. Infiltrators?"

Aeden closed his eyes and shook his head. "Damn me for an imbecile. Dannel's story. The dark family and the light family, how the dark family inserted spies in the light family. He was warning us about this."

The others stared at him in silence.

"I'll have words with him the next time we chance upon him," Aeden continued. "Anyway, the tablet. We haven't been keeping them up to date on how things are going. I can't believe I hadn't thought of it all this time. Here." He handed her the message tablet.

Lily thought for a few minutes, trying to compose in her mind what she was going to write. She hadn't thought that she would be the one sending the message. Once she had a reasonable grasp of what she wanted to say, she started scratching at the surface of the tablet with the stylus.

HEY EVERYONE, IT'S LILY,

WE WANTED TO LET YOU ALL KNOW WHAT WE'VE BEEN UP TO. SORRY WE HAVEN'T KEPT YOU POSTED, BUT WE'RE HAVING A ROUGH TIME OF IT HERE. THE ISLAND IS MOSTLY JUNGLE AND THE AREA AROUND WHERE WE THINK LIFE'S CRADLE IS LOCATED IS THE HEAV-IEST AND MOST FORBIDDING PART OF IT. EVEN THE PLANTS ARE

TRYING TO KILL US, AND THEY ESPECIALLY HATE URUN BECAUSE THEY'RE CORRUPTED.

IT'S BEEN CONSTANT BATTLES WITH THE PLANTS, THE WILDLIFE, AND WITH A SHAPESHIFTER THAT INFILTRATED OUR GROUP. IT KILLED NEARLY ALL THE SAILORS THAT CAME TO HELP US CARRY OUR GEAR AND IT SURPRISED AND ALMOST KILLED JIA, TOO.

WE DESTROYED IT, BUT WHEN WE DID, IT REVERTED BACK TO WHAT WE THINK IS ITS ORIGINAL FORM. IT'S AN ANIMARU. WE WANTED TO WARN YOU THAT THERE ARE APPARENTLY SHAPESHIFTING ANIMARU OUT THERE. THIS ONE WAS VERY GOOD AT IMPERSONATING PEOPLE AND IF IT WEREN'T FOR JIA'S EXCEPTIONAL REFLEXES, IT MIGHT HAVE GOTTEN INTO A SITUATION WHERE IT COULD PICK US OFF ONE AT A TIME.

ANOTHER STRANGE THING THAT HAPPENED WAS THAT RIGHT AFTER WE KILLED IT, SOME KIND OF MOVING SHADOWS SCURRIED AWAY FROM THE AREA. I GOT THE SENSE THAT THE THINGS HAD BEEN WATCHING, BUT DON'T KNOW IF THEY'RE A NORMAL PART OF THIS JUNGLE OR SOMETHING ELSE.

I HOPE EVERYONE IS DOING WELL. I THINK WE'RE GETTING CLOSE TO FINISHING THINGS, ONE WAY OR ANOTHER. I'D LIKE TO HAVE SOME GOOD NEWS IN THAT RESPECT WHEN WE MESSAGE NEXT TIME. BE SAFE.

—LILY

After reading the message to the others, Lily watched the tablet for a few minutes, but no reply came immediately. She stored the little stylus in its holder and kept the tablet in her hands so she'd know from the buzzing when an answer came. She didn't specifically ask for a response, but she knew her friends were polite enough to provide one when they were able to confirm they got her message.

"I wonder about those shadow critters," Tere said. "Does

anyone else feel like they were watching us, spying on us like they're intelligent?"

"They've probably been following us the whole time," Jia said. "A few times while in the jungle, I thought I saw small shadows that seemed out of place. Maybe the next time we see them, you guys should try magic on them or something."

"Do you think they were—" Lily started, but paused when she felt the message tablet in her hand buzz. She brought it up and looked it over. "We got a response. Here, let me read it to you."

GREETINGS, LILY, TERE, JIA, AND AEDEN,

I HAVE READ YOUR ACCOUNT AND I FEEL I MUST APOLOGIZE TO YOU. WHEN I CAME TO THIS WORLD, S'RU COMMANDED THAT WE PLAN IN FAVOR OF NUMBERS WITH ONLY A FEW OF THE HIGHER POWERED ANIMARU. THUS, WHILE I COMMANDED THE TROOPS OF ARUZHELIM HERE IN THIS WORLD, WE DID NOT HAVE ANY ERFINCHEN, SHAPESHIFTERS, IN OUR RANKS.

IN FACT, ANIMARU WITH THAT ABILITY ARE EXCEEDINGLY RARE, THUS I DID NOT MENTION THEIR EXISTENCE. I DO NOT KNOW IF KNOWING OF THEM WOULD HAVE AIDED YOU IN DISCOVERING THE INFILTRATOR EARLIER, BUT I SHOULD HAVE TOLD YOU OF THEM. OF THE REPORTED ANIMARU WHO CAN CHANGE THEIR SHAPE IN THE WAY YOU DESCRIBE, I KNOW OF ONLY THREE.

PLEASE CHECK THE LEFT EAR OF THE ONE YOU KILLED. IF THERE ARE TWO SMALL TEARS ON THE LOWER PART OF THE LOBE, AS I EXPECT, THEN THE ANIMARU YOU KILLED IS CALLED SASTIROZ. HE WAS EVER ANXIOUS FOR NEW AND DIFFERENT ASSIGNMENTS, WHEREAS THE OTHER TWO WERE HAPPIER WORKING IN SUPPORT ROLES FOR THEIR SUPERIORS. IT IS BY HAPPENSTANCE THAT I KNOW OF SASTIROZ'S SCARS AND HIS ORIGINAL FORM. I WILL TELL YOU THE TALE WHEN I AM ABLE, SINCE I AM THE ONE WHO GAVE THEM TO HIM.

As for the shadows you observed, I would guess they were pilae. They are used often for spying and are relatively harmless from a physical standpoint. It is not unlikely that they were assigned to follow the Erfinchen to provide a full report to whichever Animaru general sent them. They may be harmed by magic, but are difficult to strike mundanely because their power offsets their appearance from where they are actually present. Unless one knows how to strike them, often only the penumbra is attacked and thus they suffer no damage.

We are happy that you have survived the dangers you have faced and we all wish we were there to aid you. Be careful and come home safe to us. Our thoughts are with you. Thank you for thinking to update us on your activities.

—Khrazhti

"Great," Lily said after scratching out a response to Krazhti. They still hadn't heard from Saria's group. She wondered how they were doing. "Now we have spies following us, too?"

Jia scratched her head. "I wonder how they're going to get back to whoever sent them to make their report. They can't fly, right?"

"I doubt it," Tere said. "If they could, they probably would have done that to get away instead of slinking through the jungle."

"And they probably can't swim. Khrazhti told us how there's no water in her world."

"We'll need to keep an eye out," Aeden said, scanning overgrown ruins around them. "If we see them again, we'll have to try magic to kill them. Wide area magic to bypass that penumbra thing Khrazhti wrote about."

Tere grunted agreement, while Lily and Jia didn't even

375

show that much of a response. Lily was dead tired and Jia was probably even worse off. The thought of expending energy on words wasn't even a consideration.

She wondered what else the mission had in store for them. After everything so far, she wasn't sure she wanted to find out.

FIFTY

Urun came to a few hours later, seemingly not much worse for what he'd been through.

"What happened?" he asked, scratching his head. "The last thing I remember, I was walking along, following Jia, and now I find myself lying down in an area I don't remember passing through, let alone stopping to rest in."

"The shapeshifter," Tere said. "It knocked you out and took your form, then tried to get the drop on Jia, but didn't quite manage it."

The priest's mouth dropped open and he looked over the Jia. "I don't know why it didn't kill me, but are you okay? Do you need healing? Based on what we saw before, that thing can fight."

"I'm good," she said. "Aeden sorted me out. How are you? We're glad that it made the choice to knock you out instead of trying to kill you instantly and quietly."

"I'm glad, too. It probably doesn't know enough about human anatomy to be confident it could kill me quickly without sound. Lucky me." He rubbed the back of his head.

"Well, it won't be doing anything to anyone again," Tere

said. "We took its head off, and Aeden blasted it with life magic afterward. It was animaru."

Urun's brows shot up his forehead. "Really? How do you know?"

"Khrazhti confirmed it through the message tablet. She even knew which one it was precisely. Apparently they're pretty rare. Rarer now that we've taken one off the list."

"How long was I out?"

"A few hours," Aeden said. "I cast several healing spells on you, just in case. Do you feel all right?"

Urun closed his eyes for a moment, then opened them again. "Yeah, I'm fine. Thank you for that. All of you. I guess the big mystery is solved." He turned toward Grobel. "I'm sorry we couldn't have figured it out and taken care of the problem before it killed all your men."

"Me, too," the old sailor said. "But it's not something you run into every day now, is it?" He paused for a moment, then his eyes darted from person to person. "Is it?"

Tere laughed. "No, Grobel, it isn't. I've been around as long as the mountains and I've only run into a few shapeshifters. I'd like never to run into any more."

The conversation trailed off, only to be taken up again as Urun got to his feet.

"What do you say we finish this thing? We have to be pretty close to the Cradle, right? Let's press on and get done with it."

Lily narrowed her eyes at the priest. "Are you sure you're up to it? That was quite a blow to the head you took."

"I'm fine. I just had a nice nap and everything. I want to be done so we can leave this island and never come back."

The narrow path through the rubble widened gradually. Soon, the group was able to spread out and move more naturally and, more importantly, stay together. The shapeshifter was gone, but none of them knew what other dangers were waiting ahead of them.

"I really appreciate you all," Urun said.

Lily's head snapped around to the priest. That was not the kind of thing she had expected of the Urun he'd been since they started traversing the island. He saw her reaction and continued.

"I mean it. I know that for a lot of our trip on this island, I was caught up in the survival aspect, the kill-or-be-killed mentality. I still have a strange urge to go and hunt prey. The fact is, though, you all came with me on this mission for no other reason than because you didn't want me to attempt it alone. Thank you. You've put your lives on the line for no other reason than that you're my friends. That's a different thing for a solitary person like me. It means a lot."

"We're not just friends, Urun," Jia said. "We're family. Like it or not—believe it or not—all of you are the family I never had. There was a closeness to some that I worked with in the Falxen organization, but nothing like this. I would risk my life for any of you and I believe you would all do the same. Of course we wouldn't let you take a risk like this without offering to come along. If the others didn't have important things they were already doing, and they weren't spread all over the world, every one of them would have come with us. I know that for a fact."

Urun nodded, his eyes gone misty. "I don't doubt it, though why any of you think I deserve it is beyond me. Thank you so much."

Lily thought about what Jia said. It was true. Any and all of their group of friends would have risked their lives for any of the others. It was a feeling she hadn't had since she was a little girl, the sense of belonging and love. She pondered that as they continued toward a place where they might all lose their lives and she found that she wasn't afraid or concerned that her life might end.

On the contrary, what bothered her was that maybe not all of her friends would survive.

The thought made her stumble and stop. How had she gotten so far from where she had been as a child? She had been so happy and full of hope, even during the rough times when she was afflicted by illness. Memories of little delights and pleasures cascaded in her mind, reminding her that once she didn't see the world through her tired, cynical eyes.

She couldn't be blamed, she thought. Taking a child's whole existence away like circumstances had was not the best way to engender a positive outlook on life. Lily thought she did well, considering how things had gone for her.

But the fact remained that she saw life as a constant battle, something that one must strive to conquer or lose everything. To her, it had always been all about survival. Nothing else mattered. If something distracted her or got in the way, then that thing was undesirable. It was the manner in which she had lived her life for so long.

Friends, even family, were the distractions that could prove to be fatal weaknesses. With no close connections remaining, Lily the Falxen had been able to do her job and to meet the challenges of life easily. She had been satisfied, if not content. The future, if there could be one for a paid assassin, would take care of itself. Her primary concern was to win the battle against the world every single day, thereby earning another day of life.

Now she wondered if maybe her viewpoint was a bit too extreme. She loved her new friends, would do anything for them. That included risking her own life, which went contrary to her long-held opinion that life was, at its base, only a simple fight for survival.

It occurred to her that for the first time she could remember clearly, living was more than being simply about surviving day to day. She wondered if, in rethinking the old opinion, the magical plants of the jungle would even let her pass anymore. Her unorthodox beliefs were what had endeared her to them to begin with.

Before Lily got too much further in her thought process, the scrabble of Urun's feet on a bit of stone distracted her. It sounded like the priest had been moving quickly and had stoped abruptly, skidding on gravel.

"Gods!" he said as Lily turned to see him put his hands to his temples. "Do any of you feel that? I think I might get sick."

A glance around at the others showed that they didn't experience the same thing Urun was feeling. There were questioning looks, but none of them seemed to be in distress.

"What is it, Urun?" she asked, stepping over to him to put an arm out to steady him.

"The corruption. The filth. None of you can sense it? Aeden, even you?"

The Croagh shrugged. "Sorry, Urun."

"It's not magic itself, then. Tere, can you see anything in the magical matrix?"

"No. Other than the normal interference I've felt since we entered the jungle, I can't see anything amiss."

Urun shook his head. His eyes were still closed, like he was having a severe headache. "Just corruption of nature itself, then. It's a lot stronger than I've felt before. I think we're almost there."

Though Lily couldn't sense anything, she did notice the plants snaking between the ruins up ahead. They didn't look normal. Though they seemed firm and lush enough, their color was off, almost a sickly, bruised color compared to the verdant emerald they'd been passing through before.

Aeden cast his spell again and when the light erupted from him and shot straight ahead of the group, the intensity was greater than it had ever been.

"I think you're right, Urun," he said. "Whatever the spell has been sending us toward is just up there."

Lily looked toward where Aeden was pointing. There didn't seem to be anything different about it than what she saw in any other direction. Cracked and deteriorating stone, trees and vines, the same old thing. Like the rest of the area inside the wall, including the one they were standing in, she could detect no movement or life of any kind, not even insects or small birds.

If she was honest with herself, it felt like the proverbial calm before the storm.

"I don't have a great feeling about this," she said, but followed the others as they moved ahead.

FIFTY-ONE

A short distance later, the entire terrain changed. The adventurers moved out of the disorganized and cluttered ruins into what seemed like a courtyard of some kind. There was a little stone showing through on the ground, but the most striking thing was the total lack of rubble and nearly a complete absence of plants.

It was, simply, a barren area, contradicting every other place they passed through on the island, with one exception.

In the center of the open space, with several dozen yards between it and the next obstruction or large plant, was a most unique tree.

The towering woody monster looked much like a banyan tree, made up of many individual trees that seemed to have melded and twisted together into a trunk that had to be at least twenty-five feet across. Though it appeared squat, it still reached up a good forty feet in the air, its green boughs of dense leaves giving its upper portion the look of a dome. Thick, twisty, vine-like branches spread out in every direction, casting a circle of shade that had to be fifty yards across.

Even Lily could feel that something wasn't right with the tree.

"Is that...?" Lily started.

"No life," Urun interrupted. "It feels like there is no life in that thing, though it has to be alive. Just look at it. It looks like it's thriving. Why can't I feel any natural life in it?"

"It's corrupted," Tere said. "I can see it with my magical sight. With all the interference I've been experiencing, that means it's *really* corrupted. I think we've found your source, Urun."

Aeden scratched his head. "So, what, do we chop it down? What are we supposed to do, Urun? It's the mission Osulin gave you. We're just here to help."

The priest was still staring at the tree as if he was trying to read its intentions or see through its dull brown surface to its insides.

"Urun?"

He blinked and shook his head. "Sorry. I...I've never seen this kind of corruption. Or this much of any kind of corruption at one time. Not even in the Mellafond. How many centuries did it take to get so polluted and poisoned?" He rubbed his eyes. "That's rhetorical. I'm not sure I know much more about what we're supposed to do than what I've already shared with you. My guess is that yes, we need to destroy it, though my heart rebels against the thought of doing so to such a magnificent and unique specimen."

Almost as if in response to what the priest said, the branches of the tree started swaying like they were in a strong wind. Rather than settle down as they would with a gust, though, they began to pick up speed, joined by other branches. Within seconds, a dozen huge branches were whirling around the massive trunk, whistling through air that contained no wind that should make the movement possible.

"I think it heard you," Jia said. "We should probably prepare to be attacked."

Lily took one look at Grobel, standing by and holding his sword up in an awkward defensive stance.

"Don't even think about it, Grobel," she said. "Go find a place to hide behind something big and made out of stone. Leave this to us."

His head swung slowly toward her and he nodded as he gulped. Given permission, he scurried off to do as she said. She sighed in relief. That was one thing at least that she wouldn't have to worry about. On the other hand, Jia's obvious prediction was coming true as several of the large branches came down toward the tiny humans standing there.

Lily jumped to the right as Tere lunged to the left, with the others all scattering in their own directions. The deceptively fast branch came down right in the middle of where she and Tere had been standing, hitting so hard that it shook the ground where she stood, more than ten feet away. As it was, stone cracked and a cloud of dust erupted from the site of impact. A hit like that would have definitely killed her.

She drew and loosed two arrows, one immediately after the other. She caught Tere's motions as she did so, but with him it was three projectiles. All five thudded into the tree within two inches of each other, but did nothing to the massive monster. Lily didn't really think it would, but her attack was more reflex than conscious thought.

Jia flitted around the other branches that were swinging around her. She barely seemed to touch the ground, like some kind of skittering half-avian insect. Somehow, while on the move dodging the pummeling wood, she coated her daggers with something from a small pot she pulled from her belt pouches. Lily had seen the woman use poison a couple of times in all the time she'd known her, but never in the middle of a battle like now. She must have figured that the only way she could damage something so mammoth with her daggers was to poison it.

Jia flipped over two of the branches trying to sweep her off the face of the land and slashed deeply into another branch that was smaller than most of the rest that were attacking, only a hand's span thick. The lines she carved immediately took on a different color than the chestnut hue of the bark. They turned a reddish yellow color, almost like dirty blood. The branches did not, however, slow in their movements or die immediately. Unfortunate.

While Lily was trying to decide what she could to to attack a gigantic tree, she watched as Aeden demonstrated some impressive acrobatics, twisting, dodging, flipping, and rolling out of the way of three branches intent on smearing him across whatever hard surface was nearby. He trimmed a few small branches from the larger ones attacking him, but it made almost no difference but to allow a better view of the combat for the onlookers.

Lily glanced over her shoulder at her quiver and found she had only five of the fire arrows left, as indicated by their red fletchings. Rather than attack one of the pummeling branches, she aimed one of the arrows at the trunk and let it fly. She was happy when it thunked into the bark but was not snuffed out like with some of the plant monsters, but the explosion that resulted was not what she'd been hoping for. It charred a roughly circular area on the tree, but it was obvious it didn't get much farther than the bark. The damage, it seemed, was superficial.

With the tree distracted by the fire arrow, Aeden took the opportunity to stay in one place for a few seconds, making his strange movements and gestures that indicated he was casting a spell. He did it smoothly, possibly even unnoticeably to someone who didn't know the Croagh and his meticulous, perfect movements well. To Lily, though, the squat stance he took and the exaggerated pushing motions to his sides was a break in his normal combat form. She also recognized what he was doing, even without hearing his enunciation of the words of power. He was putting his shield in place. That was a very good idea.

Immediately after he finished, he began another set of

movements, apparently deciding that trying to attack the creature with his swords was not the best tactic. This time, he was more fluid, moving as he rolled his left wrist—which he'd emptied with a smooth flick to sheathe his sword in its scabbard—while he pointed the blade still in his right hand at the tree. He had moved in, dangerously close to the monster, but as he finished his new spell, a section of the trunk near where Lily's arrow had landed burst into flames.

The attack was different than the fire arrow in that the tree itself seemed to be the source of the flame rather than to have a smaller blaze land and then detonate. It didn't seem to do any more damage than Lily's red-fletched arrow, but it definitely got the tree's attention.

Four of the huge branches immediately changed their trajectory and homed in on Aeden. He performed another set of complex moves, dodging three of them completely.

The fourth, unfortunately, landed on its target.

The great, woody arm of the tree monster struck Aeden with a downward diagonal blow so powerful it looked like it would crush the Croagh. It threw him to the ground, but there was still empty space between the rough bark and the man, no doubt occupied by his shield.

But the branch's force had not yet been expended completely. It continued down on him and his shield became visible, flashing and crackling as the appendage tried to burst through it. In the end, the shield visibly shattered, but it had held long enough for Aeden to roll out of the way without serious injury. The branch whomped on the ground where he had been, but he'd already escaped, if only barely.

At the same time, Lily caught movement on her other side and watched as Tere was struck a glancing blow from one of the branches that had been aimed at him in secret while everyone's attention was on Aeden. The old archer tried to twist out of the way, but a piece of the branch caught him and sent him rocketing away from the battle to bounce on the courtyard floor and skid across broken stone and dirt. He made an attempt at a roll and to regain his feet, but it was a sloppy thing due to the force with which he had been hit.

Lily's heart jumped when she realized what would have happened if that blow had struck him solidly.

Taking a leaf from the tree's book, Urun attacked while the monster was distracted with trying to dismantle the other members of the group. He raised his staff, using it as a focal point for a spell, and thrust it toward the creature. A sickly green light raced through the air and splattered against one of the the the tree's largest branches. The bark—and even the wood beneath it—shriveled a little bit and many of the leaves at the end of it curled up and dropped off, dry as if they'd been burned.

It must have been Urun's spell that aged the target, but apparently the tree was too massive, too old already, or just too powerful for the spell to affect it greatly.

The tree monster answered the attack with several branches, swinging toward him with great speed and momentum. As they descended, it didn't look as if he was going to try to dodge, but rely solely on the shield that glowed faintly around him.

Jia, getting into the action herself, launched half a dozen throwing spikes and stars after coating them with the poison she had used earlier. The tree had plenty of branches to dedicate a handful for each attacker, so Jia bounced around, twisting, diving, and flipping so precisely that some of them missed her by only a hair's breadth. All the while she threw her projectiles, focusing them on one of the large branches. It was having an effect, the target area turning a milky green-brown, but it was slow going.

Then the heavy wooden extremities landed on Urun. More precisely, they landed on his shield, which was fortunate because the weight and force of the weapons would have killed an unprotected person.

As it was, his shield made a keening noise and the priest dropped to his knees, the dirt beneath him actually indenting from the force. He still held his staff up above his head in both hands, pouring more power into the protection, but it wasn't clear if he'd be able to hold the powerful limbs off for long.

Lily wasn't sure how much it would help, but she loosed two of her remaining fire arrows at the tree, just below where one of the big branches met the trunk. The combination of the two went deeper than the first arrow she had shot, but it wasn't enough to incapacitate the branch, let alone kill the tree.

What it did do was to get the monster's attention.

Lily backpedaled as fast as she could, almost too fast to keep her feet. Three branches came at her, two swinging from the sides and one lunging straight ahead at her. She glanced quickly behind her, dropped to her back and rolled out of the way, and smoothly came to her feet just in time to dive to the left to dodge the lunging branch. When she got far enough away, at the very edge of the cleared area, the tree recalled its limbs instead of chasing after her.

That had been way too close.

She had given Urun a slight reprieve, but now it looked like he'd be under fire again. What did they have to do to put that tree monster down?

FIFTY-TWO

The tree monster went back to focusing on Urun, apparently still upset about the damage that was done to it. As Lily tried to get her bearings, Tere tossed his bow aside, drew his knives, and started slashing at one of the branches attacking Urun. For a wonder, the tree moved that branch and another one to try to squash the pest, which gave Urun a bit of relief from the constant pounding on his shield.

Meanwhile, Aeden was making motions Lily hadn't ever seen associated with his spells. He scooped the air with his fingers splayed out, upward and away from his head, but then circling around and arcing back toward his face. Then they reversed direction again, scraping along downward and back up to move toward his head again. It looked like he was miming grabbing things out of the air and pushing them into his own body, into his head.

Immediately after, he changed his motions, this time looking like nothing more than a dance. The Croagh twisted his whole body, bending supple wrists back and forth in front of him, one arm at a time. Again, as his hands flowed, they gave the impression of bringing something in. He repeated it twice with each hand, then thrust his palms outward as if her were pushing something away. Lily wasn't sure what he was doing. She'd assumed he put another shield in place after the previous one had shattered, saving his life, but the movements for the spells didn't look like what he did earlier.

Finally, Aeden did something she recognized as the spell he'd cast earlier, the one where he made the tree catch fire. The thing was, he was rolling his hands in the opposite direction as before. She wasn't really sure about the significance, but realizing she'd been staring at what he was doing for half a minute, it was time to join the fray again.

She pulled out, nocked, drew, and loosed her remaining fire arrows at one of the branches going after Urun. As before, there was some scorching and the damage went beneath the bark, but it wasn't serious enough to keep the tree from using the branch as a cudgel to try to smash the priest into the ground.

As she dropped her bow and drew her long knives, Aeden's spell took effect. She ran toward where Tere was fighting, hoping to confuse the tree with another person, when two branches whose bases were close to each other on the trunk started forming layers of ice on top of them. At first, Lily wondered what was going on, but then she realized that Aeden casting the spell with the hand motions in reverse was the spell he'd talked about before. It could make fire or ice, depending on the motions. He must have opted for the ice variety, though she couldn't understand why.

The tree must have been sensitive to cold because there was an immediate reaction as three branches shot toward the Croagh. Strangely, the two branches affected by the spell not only didn't go after Aeden, but they slowed down considerably. One of them even looked to be developing ice crystals within it.

Aeden did a good job of dodging, but the frenetic limbs didn't allow any margin for error. Lily's mouth dropped open as one of the branches slammed into the warrior, throwing him a dozen feet into a crumbling stone wall, shattering some of it with a cloud of dust and debris. There was no way anyone could survive a strike like that, not to mention the rough landing.

She was still in motion and seeing what she'd just seen only added speed to her step. Lily screamed like a banshee jumping toward the tree though she knew being airborne was not a smart thing to do because her ability to dodge would be seriously compromised. Still, she sighted the freezing branch and as she plummeted toward the ground, she swung both knives down as hard as she could.

The effect was, in a word, exceptional.

The branch, apparently frozen all the way through, exploded as her knives drove into it. Sharp, icy pieces of wood peppered Lily's face and chest, laying down dozens of small cuts on her. She bounced off the main trunk of the tree, rolled until she could right herself, and then darted away before an attack could land on her.

The tree, though it didn't have a conventional mouth, made a whistling, shrieking sound as its heavy branch crashed to the ground, completely severed from the rest of it. She understood now why Aeden thought ice might do the trick. If only he'd survived to witness it.

With the tree's attention well and truly on her now, Urun was able to rise to his feet and bring his staff to bear. He looked exhausted, but he wasn't done with the fight. Not yet.

To escape the branches slowly stalking her, Lily angled toward where Aeden had gone down, hoping against hope that he still lived. Luckily, the tree seemed to be in a mild form of shock and wasn't twirling its extremities around as smoothly as before, so she was able to get clear while the rest of her friends took up the battle.

The dust was starting to clear where Aeden had collided with the stone. Crumbling or not, it was still rock and more than hard enough to shatter bones. Lily pulled herself up short when she heard the scratching of gravel and saw the shadow of something moving within the dust. Afraid of causing it to collapse more fully, she slid to a stop.

"Aeden?"

Weak coughing came from within the dust cloud and the sound of stone shifting grew louder. "I'm good." He coughed again. "I hope you saved some for me."

The archer rushed toward the voice and found Aeden, covered in dirt and with bruises and blood seemingly everywhere.

"How?"

"I'll explain later," he huffed. "I tried out a new spell. I think it worked well." A coughing fit racked his body and he stumbled. Lily pulled him into a hug, more to keep him upright than anything else. "Thanks. Let's get back in it. I know the spell to use now. Did it freeze the branch completely?"

Lily had to close her wide-open mouth before opening it again to answer. "Uh, yes. I slammed both my knives into it and it shattered. I thought it had killed you."

"It did," he said. "Good job with the knives. Are you up to doing it again?"

"Hells yes."

"Fine, help me get to where I have a visual and I'll see if I can freeze up some more parts for you to smash."

By the time Lily and Aeden left the obscurity of the dust cloud and made it back to where they could witness Tere, Urun, and Jia continuing their battle with the tree monster, Urun was slinging his magic at the enemy with full force.

The previous attacks, especially the shattered branch, seem to have shocked the tree and many of its branches were quivering or jerking about madly, without the precision of movement they had before. That, in turn, made them easy targets for Aeden's magic. And Urun's.

A bolt of power flew from the priest's staff and struck one of the branches near where it came out of the trunk. It visibly withered, taking on a dry and brittle appearance. It wasn't just how it looked, though, because as it continued in its frenzied shaking, it actually broke off from the trunk and thumped to the ground.

"I think we have it on the run," Aeden said, grunting as he shifted to perform the physical component of his spell. "Get ready."

Lily drew her knives again and warily went toward the tree as Aeden pronounced the words of power for the spell.

"*Vasant. Parat. Ushma.*"

Immediately after he finished, one of the larger branches frosted over and Lily sprinted toward it. By the time she reached it, the wood looked like it had been sitting in an open field for an entire winter. She slammed her knives into it, feeling the reverberation in her elbows and even up into her shoulder, but it was worth it. The branch shattered like the other one. Lily angled her body and face away as it did, so she was able to keep from getting quite so many cuts, but dodging them all was not possible, so a few new sources of trickling blood were added to the ones she already had.

Between Aeden casting his spells and Urun aging parts of the tree, the monster had fewer and fewer weapons with which to attack them. When the final branch came free of the trunk, the two casters combined their attacks onto the trunk itself. It was huge, but without the branches, it didn't seem nearly so dangerous.

With the magic affecting the tree, Tere, Lily, and Jia attacked it relentlessly, even if a bit less enthusiastically because of their exhaustion. Finally, after several minutes of constant abuse, with large chunks torn and shattered out of the thing's body, the tree teetered, then tipped and fell onto its side. It lay there, trembling violently, but it had no limbs left to attack or even move.

The magical onslaught ceased and Aeden and Urun dropped to their knees, lacking the strength to stand. The other three combatants acted similarly, with Lily taking one knee, Tere bending over with both hands on his own knees, and Jia dropping where she was and sitting in the dirt and stone dust.

It was finally over.

FIFTY-THREE

L ily considered the tree as it lay on its side trembling. A sensation, not unlike what she had felt when the thing had allowed her to come in through the green morass, seeped into her mind. It was a profound sadness.

Drowning even that feeling was a sense of loneliness.

With a lurch, Lily came to her feet and stumbled to the side of the tree, where she dropped to both knees and put her hands on the bark. It was pitted and scarred, even more than normal for the rough surface, but that wasn't what she paid attention to. Touching the tree, its thoughts transferred more easily into her, almost a conversation.

"Lily?" Tere cautioned from several feet away.

"It's fine," she said, barely paying attention to him. Instead, she focused on the stream of memories intruding in her mind. They didn't start at the beginning. Even as ancient as the creature beside her was, it apparently didn't remember that far back. What it did remember was tens of thousands of years of its most recent history, though. A history that literally brought tears to her eyes.

Once, the entity had others it cared for, nurtured, protected. If such a being could be considered happy, it was, though content was probably a better term. It passed its time in the lush jungle, caring for its charges and performing its original, self-appointed function, though it couldn't seem to remember exactly what that was.

As the centuries passed, changes in the world modified everything around it. Large pieces of its lifetime skipped by and then it sensed something was wrong. Gradually, it lost the knowledge of who or what it was, sinking, ever sinking into darkness. Until the painful damage Lily and her friends had done to it, the creature had been lost to that darkness. Unable to think clearly. It acted on impulse. Instinct. A twisted version of both.

But now, it had gained a lucidity, of a sort. Apologies for any harm it may have caused, for damage it had wrought, flowed into Lily and she found herself softly sobbing over the loss of something truly unique. There was no doubt it was dying, and it was doing so alone. No companions, no purpose, not even a clear idea of what it had done for so many centuries.

Lily thought about Master Chesaren and what she had tried to teach her. She tried again, desperately, to send her thoughts to the tree. *You are not alone. I am here. Be at peace and take the rest you have earned.*

Something in the tree's thoughts assured Lily that it understood. Gratitude flowed into her mind, and a sense of peace. Then it dimmed, faded, and disappeared altogether.

"And so passes something so wondrous that we will never know," she whispered as she put her forehead on the rough bark and let her tears fall.

"Lily?" Jia asked, and the archer realized the shorter woman was right next to her. "Are you...okay?"

Lily sniffed, wiped the back of her hand across her eyes, and sat back on her feet. "Yeah, I'm fine. It's just that it—"

While she was speaking, the tree shimmered, then—like its thoughts—faded away as if dissolving. A soft flash of green appeared in its place and then there was suddenly something there.

A glowing gem, of a form they had seen before.

"You have got to be kidding me," Tere said. "How many of these damn wells are there? There seems to be one everywhere we go."

While Tere ranted, Lily noticed off to the side a familiar circular stone wall where she could have sworn there had been just another section of crumbling, ruined building. Her gaze flicked between it, Tere, and the gem that was almost within her reach.

"Maybe it's not an accident we tend to find them," Aeden said. "Or are directed to where we can find them. Lily, I think this one is yours to place."

She raised her eyebrows at Aeden, but he only gestured toward the gem. Jia stood with a tired smile on her face, while Tere's hand made a similar motion to the Croagh's. Urun leaned on his staff and watched her. Only Grobel didn't indicate that she should take the gem, but the old sailor was completely out of his depth, emerging from his hiding place with the most confused of expressions.

Lily shrugged. It might as well be her. She had just communed with what was apparently the well's guardian, though she hadn't known it at the time. She picked the gem from where it floated nearby and was shocked that it pulsed with warmth. Holding it to her breast as she walked to the well, she angled toward the little indentation into which it was to be placed. She wasted no time in setting the stone where it belonged and, once the wall had snatched it from her hand to pull it the last few inches, she stepped back, awaiting the explosion of light and magic that she'd come to expect from the wells.

Only, this time there wasn't a grand light show and zooming stars. She waited for a solid minute, expecting something to happen, but nothing did. The archer traded looks with the others, scratched her head, and wondered if she'd done something wrong.

When she was just about to look over the edge of the wall into the darkness of the well, a pressure washed over her. It wasn't a tremor so much as a gentle but forceful pushing. It built in intensity and light poured out from the darkness within the hole circled by the wall. An orderly arrangement of light flares rose up from the depths, each one a different varia- tion of all the colors she'd ever seen. After rising ten feet above the well, they swirled like a mini tornado made of light then compressed into one big ball. It compressed even more until it was the size of a fist.

Then it exploded outward.

Lily threw her hands up to her eyes to keep from being blinded. The glaring light dimmed quickly and when her eyes adjusted again, she caught the motion of two things falling slowly to the ground beside the well. One was a stone like she'd seen before, the one with those symbols that Marla kept and translated. Cogiscro.

The other looked like...a seed?

It was a seed unlike any she'd ever seen before, but it had the appearance of a smooth semi-circular pod of some plant. It was green, but it also glowed faintly.

The stone could take care of itself, she thought. It wouldn't be harmed by falling. But the seed was something different. She didn't want it to strike the ground, especially a section with stone visible. She lunged and caught it before it did so.

As her hand made contact with the seed, a weak flare of power that she recognized pulsed from it. It felt like the magic of the tree creature, of the jungle's green wall. There was only the single pulse and then nothing. Lily stood there, holding the seed and looking down at it in wonder.

"Where's the magic?" Jia asked. "All the other wells threw out a fireworks show and then dumped magic into the world. Why didn't that happen this time?"

Urun stepped up to Lily, still leaning heavily on his staff. He reached a hand out toward the seed and Lily instinctively pulled it away.

The priest's face turned sad. "I'm not going to take it. I can feel something from it, though it seems shielded. Tere?"

"Yeah. When the tree died, the interference with my magical sight disappeared. I can see magic entwined in that thing. A lot of magic. But yes, it does seem shielded or contained somehow. Strange."

Jia came close and peered at the seed. "It's kinda cute. Anyway, I guess the well released the magic in a more controlled package this time. Are we done here?"

Lily noticed Grobel standing silently apart from the rest of them, his utter confusion evident in his eyes, which were flicking back and forth between all of them and the seed. "We'll explain it all to you, Grobel. Maybe after we have a little rest, we can head back to the ship. Like Jia said, we're done here."

As Lily's eyes tracked Jia picking up the Cogiscro stone a barely perceptible motion caught her attention. Had that shadow just moved? She blinked several times and shook her head. She was just tired. A little rest and they could head back. She had a feeling the trip back to the ship was going to be a lot easier than the journey to where they were.

FIFTY-FOUR

"So," Lily said to Aeden as they were resting in the camp they hurriedly set up on the site of the battle against the well guardian. "Do you want to tell us how you miraculously survived a hit that would have killed an elephant?"

"Oh, that," Aeden said. He chewed some dried fruit as if he hadn't somehow lived through what surely should have ended him.

"Yeah, that."

"It's one of the spells in the Raibrech called Saving Force. It has been explained to me as a last-ditch lifesaving spell, but no Croagh I have ever heard of has used it in combat. The purpose is to prevent death within a short time after the spell has been cast. It's kind of like the Final Save card in the card game Skirmish, where it nullifies a fatal blow within the next two rounds in the game."

"A get-out-of-Percipius's-realm-free card?" Tere asked with a chuckle.

"Well, yes. I guess that's exactly what it is."

Jia held up her hands. "Wait. You have a spell that prevents you from being killed and we're now just hearing about it? What is that about?"

Aeden wiped his hands on his pant leg. "Hold on. Let me finish explaining. Like I said, that was the way the spell was described to us as we were trained in the Raibrech, but there are issues with it. First, there's a relatively short time during which it will work. *If* it works. You can't just cast it at the beginning of every battle because by the time you need it, it will have been long expired."

"How long are we talking?" Lily asked. Aeden responded with an exasperated look and a clenching of his jaw. "Sorry," she added. "I'll save my questions until you have explained more." She gave him a little smile, which softened the hard planes of his face a bit.

"No one knows how long, but it's a relatively short time. I don't know how they know that, but that's the way it was explained. Another problem is one of strength. The spells of the Raibrech are not known for being very powerful. When I cast them, the magic is a lot stronger than most Croagh, probably because of my connection with the Song, which is the basis for the magic of the Raibrech. Even with that, though, most of the spells aren't impressive until I get to the point where I can cast the enhanced versions. Those are the few spells I've figured out more thoroughly. I have discovered the most effective movements for them and seamlessly integrated the words of power and unspoken parts of the spell, such as the right mindset and concentration. Even with all that, I've never cast the spell before. Wait, that's not right. I have never cast it in combat. I've cast it a few times, just to see what it would do. All I got was a tingly feeling throughout my body, not really anything to go on. As you can imagine, trying to test it out would mean risking my life for no other reason than to see if it works.

"All of this together means that only the most specific of situations would allow me to test it out effectively."

"A situation like we were in earlier," Urun offered.

"Exactly. That thing hit so hard, it was a risk to be anywhere near it. I've never fought anything before that could kill me with one hit. It seemed like a good time to try the spell out. Of course, there are even more extenuating circumstances. One is that it had to be the enhanced version. That required me to have *figured out* the enhanced version.

"Luckily, I've been going over the information in the book Tsosin Ruus left for me, since I had to leave the book at the Academy so nothing would happen to it on our trip. So instead of learning more of what was in it, I kept pondering what I'd already read, not an easy thing to do with all the other stray thoughts in my head I've had since I got on the island."

Tere rubbed the stubble on his chin. "Good thing. The spell definitely worked and saved your life. I agree with Lily: no one could have survived a direct hit like that. It's nearly a miracle I didn't die just from that glancing blow. Thank you for the healing, Urun, by the way. One other thing, though, Aeden. What stray thoughts are you talking about? The appeal of living your life in a *kill or be killed* manner, perhaps?"

Aeden must have still been exhausted because his eyes widened and his nostrils flared for a brief moment before he schooled his expression. He was usually more controlled than that.

"Why do you ask that, exactly?" the Croagh asked.

"Because that's what I was feeling. Something in me was urging me on, to find battle and defeat enemies. There were thoughts, but mainly it was the feeling, the desire to go out and prove I was the apex predator."

"You too?" Jia asked. By the sick look on Urun's face, he'd had the same thoughts.

Lily observed Grobel as well, but he still seemed so overwhelmed by everything he'd seen and experienced, she wasn't about to bring him into the conversation. It was clear, though, that her friends all had the same issue. "That's what it was," she said off-handedly.

"What was that?" Tere asked.

"Oh, I noticed your attitudes. I was actually afraid that you'd been replaced, once we found out that there was a shapeshifter around. I kept trying to figure out why you were saying what you were saying and acting the way you did. I know you all pretty well by now, and it didn't seem like you were the people I knew."

"Hold on," Aeden said. "You're saying that you *didn't* have any of those feelings? None of the urges to fight to the death."

"Nope. Not a one."

"But if we all did...then why didn't you?"

"No clue. I was feeling like I was going crazy. It seemed like the whole world and everyone I knew in it had suddenly changed. A more logical solution was that only I had changed and wasn't thinking like myself. I'm glad to know it was all of you who were the problem." She laughed, but no one else joined her.

Urun stared at her until she was uncomfortable. Like he was analyzing her and was going to announce that she truly was the one with a problem. "Your attitude. That's what it was."

"Pardon?" she said.

"Your uncommon attitude. You've explained how you have always believed that life was simple survival. It consists of nothing more than exerting yourself to stay alive for one more day while fighting against all the forces that are trying to kill you. Anything other than that battle, conducted each and every day of your life, is irrelevant or, at most, trivial. It's what allowed you to commune with the corrupted guardian."

"I don't think I really feel as strongly as that...anymore."

"But you did before. That was your pattern, your core tenet of beliefs. Thoughts of the battle for dominance couldn't affect you simply because you already lived every day of your life in that mindset. Whatever effect the corrupted magic here had, it bounced right off you."

Jia's concerned face and liquid eyes appeared in front of Lily so quickly, she almost fell backward off the piece of crumbling stone on which she sat.

"Is that true, Lily? Was it that bad?"

"I...I don't know if it was *that* extreme..." The archer found herself being smothered in a hug by the shorter woman.

"There is more to life than that, Lily," Jia said. "A lot more."

Lily returned the hug. "I know that now. I learned that from this mission, from the guardian. From all of you."

"Good. We'll talk more about this. Later."

"Okay. One more question for all of you, though. Are all those thoughts of fighting and killing to prove yourselves gone, because I'm not sure I can tolerate another moment of it. It's like being in a cage with wild animals, or like being around a group of teenage boys."

Tere seemed to appreciate the humor, his mouth curving into a slight smile as he answered her. "I don't know about the others, but for me, the feeling disappeared when the tree died. It was there one moment and simply gone the next. I'd grown accustomed to it, but it was immediately apparent when it went away."

"Same here," Aeden said.

"That's how it was with me," Urun agreed.

"Me, too," Jia said.

AFTER EATING and getting some sleep, the group headed back through the jungle toward the ship. Not only was it an easier time with Tere leading them unerringly back across the same trampled jungle they'd come through, but they didn't have to fight for their lives even once along the way. They saw some of the animals, even the larger ones, but all at a distance.

"Maybe they have the natural fear of people now that the corruption isn't ruling their behavior," Aeden offered.

"Or maybe they recognize a priest of Osulin and won't attack him," Jia countered.

"Whatever it is," Tere said, "I like it better than fighting battles every couple of miles."

It took almost two whole days to get back to the ship—they really had been wasting time wandering in circles and squiggles on the way to Life's Cradle—with a night spent camped in between. When they finally reached the edge of the jungle, it hardly even seemed to deserve the name after slogging through the thicker area near the Well of Life. They broke into the open and spotted the beach and the glistening water of the Aesculun Ocean. The sun was inching lower in the sky just above the western horizon as they set foot on the beach itself and spotted the Eurus.

A profound sense of sadness struck Lily when her eyes fixed on the ship, bobbing slowly in the gentle waves. To her left, Grobel's legs gave out, probably from sheer emotion, and his knees hit the sand.

"I didn't think I'd ever see her again," the old sailor said. "How can I tell the captain I let all his men die?"

"You won't," Lily told him. "We're going to explain it all to him. Just be happy to be home, Grobel. It's not your fault the others didn't make it. If anything, it's ours. Let us tell the captain."

He nodded, his eyes staring blankly toward the ship, but not seeming to focus.

They trudged along the beach to where the boat was already underway to pick them up. Those on the ship must have been watching, waiting for the group to come back. No doubt they already realized it was smaller than when they'd left.

They boarded the boat and silently allowed the crewmen to row them back to the the ship. Other than companionable clasps of forearms and a squeeze of Grobel's shoulders, the men didn't speak, either, no doubt picking up on the mood.

As the boat bumped against the ship's hull, Lily and the others climbed the rope ladder to finally stand on deck in front of a tense and nervous Captain Balstad.

No one else offered to speak, so Lily took the initiative, thinking even as she did it how strange it was that she would be forced to do so.

"Captain Balstad, we have a long tale to tell you. Maybe you should sit down for this."

FIFTY-FIVE

Captain Tesnair Balstad sat quietly as Lily and the others explained what happened during their entire time away from the ship. The captain couldn't seem to help flicking his eyes toward Grobel, who had accompanied them though he hadn't been ordered to do so.

When everything had been told, the captain of the Eurus sat with his shoulders hunched, deflated and defeated. He looked to have aged several years during the telling.

"I can't blame you lot," he said. "We talked about it before-hand, that it was dangerous and that you all might fail completely. I had no idea, though..." The captain trailed off as he looked at his sole remaining sailor who had gone on the journey. "I'm sorry, Grobel. I never should have sent any of you."

"No, Captain," Urun said. "Without your men's help, we might not have come through alive ourselves or completed the goddess's mission. We owe Grobel and the others a great debt. We're sorry there was no treasure or artifacts to bring back, but we did tell you we weren't going to be searching for them."

The captain waved away the last comment. "We'll have a

ceremony for the others. There's...ah, no need to let anyone else know about the shapeshifter and all that, is there?"

"Definitely not," Tere said. "There's no good reason to talk about it and many reasons why it would be a horrible idea. I think it's best if that information was kept within yours and Grobel's heads."

"I agree. Like I said, we'll have a ceremony to put the men's spirits at rest and then we'll head out. It was a marvelous opportunity to be the first to cross the Aesculun, but it may be some time until I'll think of it as anything but a tragedy."

THE TRIP back to Horizon was uneventful, especially in light of what they had experienced on the island. Osulin's charm worked magnificently and no danger threatened them as they sailed back to the mainland.

After putting into port, Lily and the others disembarked after thanking the captain—and Grobel—several times and paying the captain double the fee they'd offered before the trip. They collected their horses and retraced the route they took down to Horizon. At Satta Sarak, they headed west on the Trail of Sarak until it merged with the River Road, which led them back to where their trip had started.

Finally, they arrived back in Drusca. Lily was nervous about talking with her uncle. It was time, once and for all, for the two to address his unreasonable plan to take his own life. She hoped she could convince him that there were many things worth him living for. She even had a secret weapon she hoped would tip the balance if he was being stubborn.

The group went straight to Lily's uncle's house. As they approached it, Tere reached over from his horse and squeezed her shoulder.

"You'll do fine. We'll wait out here so it doesn't seem to him that we're ganging up on him."

"Thanks," she said. "For everything. If I can get through to him a fraction of what I learned about life myself on this trip, it shouldn't be a problem. I'll let you know when to come in or if I need help."

Jia gave her an enthusiastic thumbs up while Aeden and Urun smiled and nodded at her, respectively. Then the rest of them stepped away so Lily could knock on the door and be the only one her uncle saw when he opened it.

Here goes, she said to herself.

Lily rapped her knuckles against the door and waited nervously. Shuffling inside preceded the door opening, and she was looking into her uncle's face.

"Lily," he said, wrapping his arms around her. "I'm glad you're safe. Come in, come in."

They released each other and she followed him into the house after she picked up the box she'd gotten for him from the bank. Lily closed the door softly and padded after her uncle.

"Uncle Arten, why would you think I wouldn't be safe? I just had a few things to do to help out Urun."

A wry smile crossed his face. "You keep dangerous company. I know you wouldn't have gone off like that if it wasn't very important, which means that it was dangerous. Am I correct?"

She laughed at his logic. "Okay, it was a little dangerous. I'll tell you all about it later. Maybe my friends can come over and we can all tell you about it."

"That...that's fine." His face had lost what little excitement it had when he first saw her. "So, no troubles getting my stuff?"

"Umm, not many. I have it right here, but you will have to be the one to tell me if there's something missing."

"Why would there be something missing?"

"I don't know," she said. "Just check."

He eyed her suspiciously, but opened the box she handed him. She sat down on a chair facing his place on the couch.

Lily watched her uncle as his eyes fell upon the different items, looking for his emotions. Was he happy to get them, sad at the memories, complacent like he was with so many other things because he'd already decided he was going to die?

After a few minutes, he closed the box on his lap and put his hands over it.

"It looks like it's all here. We'll have to talk about splitting it all up so that you and whoever else might be interested can distribute them."

She took her lower lip in her teeth and sucked in air. "I was hoping you'd keep most of it. It belongs to you."

"We've talked about this, Lily," he said. "I haven't changed my mind. I've kept up with what I agreed, trying to eat better and take care of myself until you returned, but my plan still stands."

"Why, Uncle? One thing I learned from the mission I just returned from was that life cannot be taken for granted. Nor can those *in* our lives. I understand your sorrow, but can't you rejoice in those you have left instead of focusing completely on the one you've lost?"

"It's not just one!" he snapped. Then he dropped his head. "I'm sorry, Lily. I didn't mean to yell at you. It's just...well, I've lost nearly everyone. It's not just Elenya. It's my parents, *your* parents, almost everyone who has ever meant anything to me."

"But not me. You haven't lost me. I know I should have come to visit before, but now that I know you're still where I can find you, I'll visit more often. I've lost everyone else, too, you know. I can't bear to lose you, too."

He leaned forward and took her hands. "I know, Lily, but let's be honest. You have enough going on with trying to save the world. That's what you should focus on, not some old, worn-out man whose best years are behind him."

"Don't say that. Do you want to miss it if and when I have children? You'll be a great uncle. You can spoil them rotten and hand them back to me. Wouldn't that be nice?"

He chuckled, but it died quickly. "Are you planning on having children anytime soon?"

"Soon? No. I have this whole trying to save the world thing I need to take care of first, but I'm not opposed to the idea. I want them to meet the uncle who has always been so important to me."

"That's all very nice for you to say, Lily, but I'm really done with everything. I'm so tired, and life is such a chore. Better young people like you go about your life, even your heroing, without having to worry about a wasted old man."

Lily sighed. "Please don't keep saying things like that. You're not just important to me. There are plenty of people who want you to stick around. Plenty whose lives would be poorer without you."

"Really? Name one."

She looked at him levelly, staring him in the eyes for a good ten seconds. Then she dropped his hands, got up, and headed for the door.

"Lily? Wait. Lily, I'm sorry if I angered you. The last thing I want to do is to leave things with you mad. Please don't walk out."

She huffed loudly as she opened the door. Instead of going out, though, she opened it wide and stepped aside.

A woman entered through the doorway and Arten gasped.

"Iriam?"

To anyone who had seen her mother, Iriam Dufour was undoubtedly related. She had the same light brown hair as her mother and grandmother, the same rounded face, and her eyes held the same twinkle. She was slender whereas her mother was a bit heavier, but there was no denying the resemblance. Even the gentle curves of her lips into a knowing smile looked like Nadine's, and Mother Sella's as well.

"Hello, Uncle Arten," Iriam said. "Long time, no see."

Arten Fisher swung his head back and forth from Lily to Iriam, his expression flickering from mild anger to disappointment to what could only be giddy joy. Finally, he gave up trying to process it all and rushed to the woman and swept her up into a hug.

"You look like hell, you know," she said through a smile as she wrapped her arms around him.

Arten held on for a moment later and then stepped back to look Iriam over. "It's been hard. You, on the other hand, look fantastic. How's Jorem?"

"He's good. He wanted to come when Lily stopped by to chat with me, but, you know, responsibilities."

"Like you don't have any?"

"None that compare to talking to you about what Lily told me."

Lily's uncle turned his full attention on her. "That's not fighting fair, Lily."

The red-haired archer shrugged. "I don't remember you ever teaching me that I had to fight fair. If I recall correctly, you constantly admonished me to fight to win."

"Arten," Iriam said, drawing his attention back to her, "you are not going to do this ridiculous thing you're talking about. I won't allow it."

"Iriam, I'm not going to argue about it. You don't understand. I don't have—"

"I'm pregnant."

"Y-you're what?"

"You heard me. I'm having my first child and you are going to be the godfather. I simply refuse to accept that I have to figure out a way to tell my child that his godfather was too much of a coward to see things through and meet him or her. Lily told me all about how you don't think you have anything to live for. Well, if it's not for Lily—and who wouldn't want to live for her?—and it's not for me, then it'll be for the child that

I expect you to show as much wisdom and love to as you did to a girl whose parents never seemed to see eye to eye with her."

"I...I..." he stammered.

"This is not a discussion. You may stay here or you may come and live with or near us in Telna, but you are going to survive to spoil this child rotten."

Lily leaned against one wall, with her arms crossed and a smile on her face. She knew after talking with Iriam for a few minutes that her uncle was no match for her.

"A child," he said. "Congratulations."

"Congratulations to you, godfather," the third-generation healer said.

"I guess you've outwitted me. Both of you. Fine, I'll stick around for a little while, even if just to refresh my memory about the stories in these books here." He waved toward the box Lily had brought him with the story books in it. "I know when I'm beaten."

Lily clapped her hands. "Wonderful. I can't wait until you tell him or her the stories of Erent Caahs. I'll have to bring Tere to meet the kid. Oh, did I mention that part?"

Confusion was splashed all over Arten's face. "Mention what?"

"That Tere used to go by another name a few decades ago."

"No. Is he a bandit on the run?"

Lily inspected her fingernails. "No. He's Erent Caahs."

Arten blinked rapidly at Lily. "I beg your pardon."

"No need for that. Tere Chizzit is Erent Caahs, the greatest contemporary hero. He hates all the stories about him, but I think a young child could convince him to tell some of them. You wouldn't want to miss that. Speaking of which, is it safe for them to come out of hiding now. I'm hungry from all that traveling and I think a nice get together would be just the thing. I can even invite Nadine and Halden."

Iriam and Arten shared a look and then both of them

shook their heads and said at the same time, "Yeah, maybe we shouldn't go that far."

The dinner was a hit and Lily and her friends stayed with her uncle for another day before they decided to depart.

"I'll try to visit when I can," Lily said. "Send me a message at the Academy if you move and to let me know what's going on. I'll be traveling a lot, but that's my base of operations right now."

"I'll make sure he keeps you abreast of what's happening," Iriam said. "And we'll let you know what's going on with the baby as well."

"I can't wait," Lily said, and realized that she really meant it. "In the meantime, I have a seed to plant before I'm called off to go on another mission."

EPILOGUE

Dared Moran, the Mayor of the town of Praesturi, lounged in his comfortable stuffed chair in his lavish office, surrounded by art and expensive furniture, and the finest wooden paneling. And scratched his crotch. *Ah, that's better.*

He let out a little sigh, feeling the relief from addressing his itch. The man sitting in a less comfortable chair on the other side of his desk didn't seem to share his contentment.

"So, what are you here bothering me about again?" the Mayor asked.

"Yes, uh, I am here to give you the weekly report of the state of the city, Mayor."

Hearing the capital M made the Mayor smile. It had taken him almost a year when he first took the office to get through to everyone that the word "Mayor" was not a simple descriptor, but something far grander. Sure, it was a title, but not the common one. It was much more. It was a name, an exalted depiction. Something to be spoken with pride and reverence. He'd only had to kill four men until his staff got it right, and the rest of the town followed, after two more deaths. That was eighteen years ago, and he had taken the word as his name. No one, and he meant no one, called him Dared Moran any longer. Not more than once.

Old Pin Farley, the man in front of him, had been with him almost from the beginning. At only a bit over five and a half feet tall, slender as a bean sprout, he wasn't much to look at, but gods, the man could organize things like no one he'd ever seen. The Mayor let him run the city, only stepping in to make sudden decisions that struck his fancy or to do something that might be fun. Like executions.

"Pin, don't I pay you to run the city?" The Mayor asked.

"Yessir, you do, and I appreciate it. However, I feel it necessary to provide information on things that may be important. I realize you are very busy"—he glanced down at the desk, where the Mayor's hand was still hidden—"but I have always felt it better to give you information you don't need rather than to neglect informing you of something important enough to be dangerous."

He had to agree with that. A good way to lose your life, not giving the Mayor information that could cause him trouble.

"Fine, fine. Tell me your important news."

"It's about the forest," the thin man said. "Again. Three individuals have gone missing, each separately going into the forest. Two were loggers and the other was apparently hunting for herbs."

Dared narrowed his eyes at his administrator. "When you say 'forest,' you mean the *forest*?"

"I do. Not the trees surrounding the walls on the east, west, and south sides. I speak of the Verlisaru Forest to the north."

Praesturi was an unusual place. Located at the very southernmost tip of the island of Munsahtiz, the only part of the entire land mass not owned by the Hero Academy. The story of how that came to be was convoluted and boring, but the important part was that Praesturi was a free city, one that was filled with people who might have trouble living somewhere else. The dregs and misfits of society. Okay, it was populated by criminals.

The thing about it was that they were separated from the rest of the island by a massive forest that spanned the entire width. Verlisaru. The forest had more ghost and monster stories than the Grundenwald and it was a certainty that no one would ever try to attack Praesturi from that direction. Not unless it was the monsters who lived there.

"Why can't we burn the entire thing to the ground again?" the Mayor asked.

"Because the two times we tried, we lost more than thirty people to monsters and to people inexplicably wandering into the forest as if in a trance and disappearing. We don't have the resources to fight with the forest's magic. We might be able to beg for aid from the Hero Academy—"

"No! I'll not have those mad folk sniffing around my city. Next thing you know, they'll want to clean it up, make it 'fair for every citizen', dissolve our efficient government. No Academy people."

Pin sighed. He seemed to do that a lot. "I understand. The trouble has gotten worse, though. We can't even cut back the growth of the Verlisaru any longer. It's like taking down any trees at all, even saplings, is reckoned an act of war. Whatever is within those trees strikes back decisively. If it keeps expanding, it's going to encroach on the city itself."

"Mercenaries?" he asked the administrator. "Send out a call for mercenaries to clear some of it, even to explore and map it. We have coin."

"I will draft up an advertisement for your approval, then."

"Good, then we're done." He frowned at Pin. "One more thing. Make sure the advertisement is clear there are to be no Academy Heroes. I'll accept mercenaries with magic, even damn Falxen assassins, but no Academy folk. Clear?"

"Yes, Mayor, crystal clear. I will start on it immediately.

Maybe we can keep too many people from dying between now and when someone answers the call."

THE STORY CONTINUES in Hero's Light ...

If you'd like to be sure not to miss anything, and to score some free books, join my newsletter **here**.

(For the paperback version of this book, you can go to my website at pepadilla.com and click on the Newsletter menu item, or use the form at the bottom of every page).

HERO'S LIFE GLOSSARY

Following is a list of unfamiliar terms. Included are brief descriptions of the words as well as pronunciation. For the most part, pronunciation is depicted using common words or sounds in English, not IPA phonetic characters. Please note that the diphthong *ai* has the sound like the English word *Aye*. The *zh* sound, very common in the language Alaqotim, is listed as being equivalent to *sh*, but in reality, it is spoken with more of a buzz, such as *szh*. Other pronunciations should be intuitive.

Abhincstagna (*ab·HEENK·STAG·nah*) – a lake in ancient Ascesh that reportedly had magical properties. The great dragon Tero made his home near the lake.

Abyssum (*a·BIS·um*) – the world of the dead, Percipius's realm.

Acolyte – a current Hero Academy student who has mastered at least one school, but not three or more.

Adept – a Hero Academy student who has mastered at least three schools and continues to study at the Academy.

Aeden Tannoch (AY·*den TAN·ahkh*) – a man born to and

trained by a highland clan, raised by the Gypta, and able to utilize the magic of the ancient Song of Prophecy.

Aeid Hesson (*AY·id*) – former Master of the School of prophecy at the Hero Academy. He was murdered in his office at the Academy.

Aesculus (*AY·skyoo·lus*) – the god of water and the seas.

Agypten (*a·GIP·ten*) – an ancient nation, no longer in existence. It was from this nation the Gypta originated.

Ahred Chimlain (*AH·red CHIM·lane*) – noted scholar of the first century of the third age

Aila Ven (*AI·la ven*) – a woman of small stature who joins the party and lends her skills in stealth and combat to their cause.

Ailgid (*ILE·jid*) – one of the five highland clans of the Cridheargla, the clan Greimich Tannoch's wife came from.

Ailred Kelzumin (*ILE·red kel·ZOO min*) – the Master of the School of Water Magic at the Hero Academy.

Alain (*a·LAYN*) – the god of language. The ancient language of magic, Alaqotim, is named after him.

Alaqotim (*ah·la·KOTE·eem*) – the ancient language of magic. It is not spoken currently by any but those who practice magic.

Aletris Meslar (*ah·LET·ris MES·lar*) – the personal clerk and assistant to Headmaster Qydus Okvius, of the Hero Academy.

Aliten (*AL·it·ten*) – a type of animaru that is humanoid but has wings and can fly.

Alloria Yurgen (*ah·LORE·ee·ah YURE·gen*) – the leader (Vituma) of the Dark Council. She is the 102nd leader since the Council's creation.

Alpin Trebhin (*AL·pin TREH·vin*) – the Croagh warrior who was chosen as the chief for the Trebhin clan after the previous chief was killed in the Death Oath ritual combat.

Alvaspirtu (*al·vah·SPEER·too*) – a large river that runs from the Heaven's Teeth mountains to the Kanton Sea. The

Gwenore River splits from it and travels al the way down to the Aesculun Ocean.

Amatia (*ah·MAH·tee·ah*) – a member of the Dark Council, a seeress.

Ander Tosselnam – one of the three High Itera of the Church of Vanda.

Animaru (*ah·nee·MAR·oo*) – dark creatures from the world Aruzhelim. The name means "dark creatures" or "dark animals."

Aquilius Gavros (*ah·KWIL·ee·us GAV·roze*) – the Dark Prophet; he lived in the Age of Magic, during the time of the War of Magic.

Arania (*ah·RAH·nee·ah*) – a kingdom in the western part of the continent of Promistala, south and east of Shinyan. A thing of Arania is called Aranir.

Arba – an essentially extinct race of magical people whose ancestors were directly created by Mellaine out of the stuff of the forest and her magical tears. They had a special connection to nature and could use magic directly from the natural world.

Arcus (*ARK·us*) – the god of blacksmithing and devices.

Arcusheim (*AHR·coo·shime*) – a large city on the southern shore of the Kanton Sea, the capital of the nation of Sutania and the home of Erent Caahs before he left to travel the world.

Arstat Filz – the captain of the riverboat Brenain's Tears.

Arten Fisher – Lily's uncle (on her father's side).

Arto Deniselo (*AHR·toe   day·NEE·say·low*) – a dueling master in the Aranian city of Vis Bena who taught Erent Caahs how to drastically improve his combat abilities.

Aruna (pl. Arunai) (*ah·ROON·ah; ah·roo·NIE*) – a citizen of the tribal nation of Campastra. Originally, the name was pejorative, referring to the color of their skin, but they embraced it and it became the legitimate name for the people in Campastra.

Aruzhelim (*ah·ROO·shel·eem*) – the world from which the animaru come. The name means "dark world," "dark universe," or "dark dimension." Aruzhelim is a planet physi-cally removed from Dizhelim.

Ascesh (*AY·sesh*) – the northernmost continent in Dizhe-lim. Thousands of years ago, it included what is now Teroshi.

Asfrid Finndottir (ASS*·frid fin·DOT·teer*) – the Master of the School of Cryptology at the Hero Academy.

Asgeir Balstad (*AZ·gare BALL·stad*) – the boat captain Marla helps in Hirsen. He takes them to Iracundia and promises to pick them up.

Assector Pruma (*ah·SEC tor PROO·mah*) – roughly "first student" in Alaqotim. This is the student aid to a master in one of the schools at the Hero Academy. There can be only one per school and this person conducts research, helps to teach classes, and assists the master in any other necessary task.

Aubron Benevise (*AW·brun ben·uh·VEES*) – the Master of History and Literature at the Hero Academy.

Auxein (*awk·ZAY·in*) – an aide to the master and the First Student (Assector Pruma) at the Hero Academy. For larger schools, there may be more than one. In some schools there may not be any.

Ayize Fudu (*aye·EEZ FOO·doo*) – a Hero Academy adept, one of Quentin Duzen's associates.

Barda Sirusel (*BAR·duh seer·oo·SELL*) – the boy who tried to bully Marla when she was a child.

Batido (*bah TEE·doe*) – what Aeden's friends call their dormitory, from the Dantogyptain words for *second home*.

Beldroth Zinrora (*BEL·droth zin·ROR uh*) – the Master of the School of Dark Magic at the Hero Academy.

Bhagant (*bog·AHNT*) – the shortened form of the name for the Song of Prophecy, in the language Dantogyptain.

Bhavisyaganant (*bah·VIS·ya·gahn·ahnt*) – The full name for the Song of Prophecy in Dantogyptain. It means "the song of foretelling of the end," loosely translated.

Biuri (*bee·OOR·ee*) – small, quick animaru that recall the appearance and movements of rodents. They are useful as spies because of their small size and quickness.

Blennus (*blen·oos*) – Dannel Powfrey's horse.

Brace – the term used by the Falxen for a group of assassins ("blades").

Braitharlan (*brah·EE·thar·lan*) – the buddy assigned in the clan training to become a warrior. It means "blade brother" in Chorain.

Brandon Simm – one of the heads of the flash powder manufacturing families in Drusca.

Brausprech (*BROW·sprekh*) – a small town on the northwest edge of the Grundenwald forest, in the nation of Rhaltzheim. It is the hometown of Urun Chinowa.

Breath of Galendia (*gah·LEN dee·ah*) – the boat owned by Asgeir Balstad.

Brek Zexus – one of the crew of the ship Eurus who went with the party into the jungle on Visuren island.

Brenain Kanda (*bren·AY·in KAHN·duh*) – a mythological heroine who stole magic from the god Migae.

Brenain's Tears (*bren·AY·ins*) – the riverboat Lily and the others take down toward the Aesculun Ocean. Coincidentally, this is the same riverboat they were planning on taking north when the group was first in Satta Sarak.

Bridgeguard – the small community, barely more than a guardpost, on the mainland end of the northern bridge to Munsahtiz

Broken Reach – a rugged, unforgiving land to the southeast of the Grundenwald. There are ruins of old fortifications there.

Campastra (cam·PAHS·trah) – a tribal nation in the southwestern portion of the continent of Promistala

Cara Moore – a member of the Dark Council.

Carlan Templar – the former Master of Thrown Weapons at the Hero Academy. He died and then his school was merged with the School of Launched Weapons to become the School of Ranged Weapons so they could create the new School of Firearms, with Master Liluth as its first master.

Catriona (Ailgid) Tannoch (CAT·ree·own·ah ILE·jid) – the wife of Greimich Tannoch. She is originally from the Ailgid clan, but now has taken the last name Tannoch.

Ceti *(SET·ee)* – a higher level type of animaru, appearing aquatic with small tentacles, even though there is no water in Aruzhelim. They are very intelligent and have magical aptitude. Some of them are accomplished with weapons as well.

Charislev Pardruscan (*CHAR·iz·lev par·DROO·scan*) – the founder of the city of Drusca. He built it on a bet.

Cholu (*CHOE·loo*) – the leader of the group of tribespeople Sirak brings with him to get Marla.

Chorain (*KHAW·rin*) – the ancestral language of the highland clans of the Cridheargla.

Clavian Knights (*CLAY·vee·en*) – the fighting force of the Great Enclave, the finest heavy cavalry in Dizhelim.

Codaghan (*COD·ah·ghan*) – the god of war.

Cogiscro (*coe·JEE·scroe*) – an ancient system of runic writing that was used in magic spells. The symbols are phonetic and are arranged in a circular pattern.

Colechna *(co·LECK·nah)* – one of the higher levels of animaru. They appear to be at least part snake, typically highly intelligent as well as skilled with weapons. They are usually in the upper ranks of the command structure. Their agility and flexibility makes them dangerous enemies in combat. A few can use magic, but most are strictly melee fighters.

Corcan – one of the five highland clans of the Cridheargla.

Cridheargla (*cree·ARG·la*) – the lands of the highland clans. The word is a contraction of Crionna Crodhearg Fiacla in Chorain.

Crionna Crodhearg Fiacla (*cree·OWN·na CROW·arg FEE·cla*)) – the land of the highland clans. It means "old blood-red teeth" in Chorain, referring to the hills and mountains that abound in the area and the warlike nature of its people. The term is typically shortened to Cridheargla.

Croagh Aet Brech (*CROWGH ET BREKH*) – the name of the highland clans in Chorain. It means, roughly, "blood warriors." The clans sometimes refer to themselves simply as Croagh, from which their nickname "crows" sprang, foreigners not pronouncing their language correctly.

Daana Vaskova (*DAHN·ah vas·COVE ah*) – a prophetess and author who lived at the end of the Age of Magic. She wrote many children's tales, the majority of which had hidden meanings and prophecies.

Daibhidh Trebhin (*DAY·vid TREH·vin*) – the clan chief of the Trebhin clan when Aeden went to meet with the other clans of Croagh.

Dannel Powfrey – a self-proclaimed scholar from the Hero Academy who meets Aeden on his journey.

Danta (*DAHN·ta*) – the goddess of music and song. The language Dantogyptain is named after her.

Dantogyptain (*DAHN·toe·gip·TAY·in*) – the ancestral language of the Gypta people.

Daodh Gnath (*DOWGH GHRAY*) – the Croagh Ritual of Death, the cutting off of someone from the clans. The name means simply "death ceremony."

Daphne – one of the tavern maids at the Wolfen's Rest inn in Dartford.

Darkcaller – one of the Falxen sent to kill Khrazhti and her companions. A former student at Sitor-Kanda, her specialty is dark magic.

Dark Council – a mysterious group of thirteen people who are trying to manipulate events in Dizhelim.

Dartford – a small town on the mainland near the north bridge to the island of Munsahtiz.

Darun Achaya (*dah·ROON ah·CHAI·ah*) – father of Fahtin, head of the family of Gypta that adopts Aeden.

Denore Felas (*den·OR FEHL·ahss*) – a great mage in the Age of Magic, the best friend of Tsosin Ruus.

Denos Chal (*DEN·ose*) – one of the crew of the ship Eurus who went with the party into the jungle on Visuren island.

Desid (*DAY·sid*) – a type of animaru. They're nearly mindless, only able to follow simple commands, but they are fairly strong and tireless. They are about five feet tall with thick, clawed fingers useful for digging. They have the mentality of a young child.

Dizhelim (*DEESH·ay·leem*) – the world in which the story happens. The name means "center universe" in the ancient magical language Alaqotim.

Dmirgan (*DMEER·gen*) – a town in Kruzekstan, where a young Erent Caahs killed a man he thought was a murderer

Dob – a small arba boy whose father was killed in the battle where Urun and the others first met the arba in the Mellafond.

Dorin Panalus (*DORE·inn PAN·uh·lus*) – one of the heads of the firearm manufacturing families in Drusca.

Dreigan (*DRAY·gun*) – a mythical beast, a reptile that resembles a monstrous snake with four legs attached to its sides like a lizard. The slightly smaller cousin to the mythical dragons.

Drugancairn (*DROO·gan·cayrn*) – a small town on the southwest edge of the Grundenwald Forest.

Dubhghall Trebhin (*DOO·gall TREH·vin*) – one of the representatives of the Trebhin clan who went to fetch Aeden to come back and talk to the clan chiefs. He is abrasive and impolite.

Ebenrau (*EBB·en·ra·oo*) – the capital city of Rhaltzheim, one of the seven great cities in Dizhelim

Elaith Tucker (*eh·LAY·ith*) – one of the cooks/servants assigned to Batido.

Elenya Fisher (*eh·LEN·yah*) – the deceased wife of Arten Fisher, Lily's Aunt.

Ellia (*ELL·ee·ah*) – one of the tribespeople Sirak uses to try to get Marla, the only female warrior in the squad.

Elmer Trensel – one of the heads of the firearm manufacturing families in Drusca.

Emily Fisher – Lily's mother.

Emora (*ay·MORE·ah*) – the term of endearment Tsosin Ruus used for Iowyn Selen. It means *my love* in Alaqotim.

Encalo (pl. encali) (*en·CAW·lo*) – four-armed, squat, powerful humanoids. There are few in Dizhelim, mostly in the western portion of the continent Promistala.

Epradotirum (*EP·rah·doe·TEER um*) – an extremely powerful entity who lives in another plane of existence, touching the mortal plane when, every few centuries, he is hungry. Aeden and some of his friends met the Epra while running from assassins near Satta Sarak.

Erent Caahs (*AIR·ent CAWS*) – the most famous of the contemporary heroes. He disappeared twenty years before the story takes place, and is suspected to be dead, though his body was never found.

Erfinchen (*air·FEEN·chen*) – animaru that are shapeshifters. Though not intelligent and powerful enough to be leaders among the animaru, they are often at higher levels, though not in command of others. They typically perform special missions and are truly the closest thing to assassins the animaru have. A very few can use some magic.

Esiyae Yellynn (*ess·SEE·yay YELL·in*) – the Master of the School of Air Magic at the Hero Academy.

Espirion (*es·PEER·ee·on*) – the god of plans and schemes. From his name comes the terms espionage and spy.

Eurus (*YOOR·us*) – the name of Tesnair Balstad's ship, the one Lily and the others took to the island of Visuren.

Eutychus Naevius (*YOO·tik·us NAY·vee us*) – a renowned mathematician in ancient times. One of his principles, the third theorem of alternating magical series, was the key Marla used to decrypt Ren Kenata's letters.

Evindia Elkien (*eh·VIN·dee ah EL·kee·en*) – a member of the Dark Council.

Evon Desconse – a graduate of the famed Hero Academy and best friend to Marla Shrike.

Exulmucri (*EX·ool·MOO·cree*) – an ancient game of strategy, thought to be the first of its kind. It was also the first game to use dice.

Fahtin Achaya (*FAH·teen ah·CHAI·ah*) – a young Gypta girl in the family that adopted Aeden. She and Aeden grew as close as brother and sister in the four years he spent with the family.

Falxen (*FAL·ksen*) – an assassin organization, twelve of whom go after Aeden and his friends. The members are commonly referred to as "Blades."

Featherblade – one of the Falxen sent to kill Khrazhti and her companions. He is the leader of the brace and his skill with a sword is supreme.

Fior Tassen (*FEE·ore*) – Tesnair Balstad's first mate on the Eurus.

Fireshard – one of the Falxen sent to kill Khrazhti and her companions. She wields fire magic.

Flagon Fairbairn – one of the heads of the flash powder manufacturing families in Drusca.

Forin Vess – the old tracker Lily and the others heard of in Simpton's Well.

Forgren (*FORE·gren*) – a type of animaru that is tireless and single-minded. They are able to memorize long messages and repeat them exactly, so they make good messengers. They have no common sense and almost no problem-solving skills

Formivestu (*form·ee·VES·too*) – the insect creatures that attacked Tere's group when they were on their way to Sitor-Kanda. They look like giant ants with human faces and were thought to be extinct.

Fortuna Vandenbom – one of the heads of the firearm

manufacturing families in Drusca, the only woman among the family heads. They also make the flash powder.

Fyorio (*fee·YORE·ee·oh*) – the god of fire and light, from whose name comes the word *fyre*, spelled *fire* in modern times.

Fyrefall – a desolate and dangerous land in the south central part of Promistala, full of hot pools, geysers, and other signs of volcanic activity.

Gardon Wessel – one of the heads of the firearm manufacturing families in Drusca.

Gareth Briggs – a member of the Dark Council.

Gemsport – the largest port city in the Great Enclave, on the southwestern shore of the Kanton Sea.

Gentason (*jen·TAY·sun*) – an ancient nation, enemy of Salamus. It no longer exists.

Ginsa (GIN·*sah*) (G pronounced like in *begin*) – one of the tribespeople Sirak uses to try to get Marla

Gneisprumay (*gNAYS·proo·may*) – first (or most important) enemy. The name for the Malatirsay in the animaru dialect of Alaqotim.

Godan Chul (*GO·dahn CHOOL*) – an ancient mythological race of spirit beings, created accidentally from the magic of the God of Magic, Migae. The name means, roughly "spirit's whisper."

Goren Adnan – the Master of the School of Military Strategy at the Hero Academy.

Graduate (at the Hero Academy) – a student of the Hero Academy who is either an adept or a viro/vira. That is, anyone who has mastered at least three schools at the Academy and is either still studying there or has left the school.

Great Enclave – a nation to the west of the Kanton Sea and the Hero Academy.

Greimich Tannoch (*GREY·mikh TAN·ahkh*) – Aeden's close friend, his braitharlan, during his training with the clans.

Grobel Saltaran (*GROE·bell sal·TAH·ran*) – one of the crew of the ship Eurus who went with the party into the jungle on Visuren island.

Grundenwald Forest (*GROON·den·vahld*) – the enormous forest in the northeastern part of the main continent of Promistala. It is said to be the home of magic and beasts beyond belief.

Gulra (pl. gulrae) (*GUL·rah; GUL·ray*) – an animaru that walks on four legs and resembles a large, twisted dog. These are used for tracking, using their keen sense of smell like a hound.

Gwenore River – a large river that splits off from the Alvaspirtu and travels south, through Satta Sarak and all the way to the Aesculun Ocean

Gyerju (*gyare·JOO*) – a village in southern Shinyan where Jia Toun's father was born and grew up.

Gypta (*GIP·tah*) – the traveling people, a nomadic group that lives in wagons, homes on wheels, and move about, never settling down into towns or villages.

Halden Dufour – Nadine's husband (he took her last name)

Hamrath – a small town on the coast of the eastern part of the Kanton Sea, just north of the bridge from the mainland to Munsahtiz Island.

Hane Bryce – a member of the Dark Council.

Heaven's Teeth – the range of mountains to the east of the Kanton sea, in between that body of water and the Grundenwald Forest.

Heronorus (*hare·ON·or·us*) – the god of honor.

Honor's Peak – the mountain bordering the Shinyan capital city of Tongqi, home of the Chamber of the Trial of Honor.

Ianthra (*ee·ANTH·rah*) – the Goddess of Love and Beauty.

Ianthra's Breasts (*ee·ANTH·rah*) – a mountain range between Arcusheim in Sutania and Satta Sarak. Even though there are three peaks, the two that dominate were named for the physical attributes of the Goddess of Love and Beauty, Ianthra.

Iaurium (*ee·OUR·ee·um*) – a port city in Arania, on the western shore of the Kanton Sea.

Ichod Nesbotom (*ih·kod nes·BOE·tom*) – a ship's captain that apparently teases Tesnair Balstad relentlessly.

Iowyn Selen (*EE·o·win SELL·en*) – a great mage in the Age of Magic, the love of Tsosin Ruus's life.

Iracundamel (*EER·ah·COON·dah·mel*) – the ancient name for the well of power at the center of the Mellafond swamp. The name means, roughly, *nature's wrath* or *Mellaine's wrath*.

Iriam Dufour/Pashik – daughter of Nadine and Halden, granddaughter of Mother Sella the healer.

Ironspike – one of the high-ranking Falxen who negotiates with the Dark Council for long-term assignments of assassins.

Iryna Vorona (*ee·REEN·ah voe·rone·ah*) – Master of the School of Interrogation and Coercion at the Hero Academy.

Isbal Deyne (*ISS·bahl DANE*) – a member of the Dark Council.

Isegrith Palas (*ISS·eh·grith PAL·us*) – the Master of Fundamental Magic at the Hero Academy.

Itera (*ee·TARE·ah*) – high level functionaries in the Vandan Church. They are essentially the second level from the top, though the High Itera, the top three of their number, are above the rest, just below the Patr Pruma.

Jandar Zumlee (*JAN·dahr ZUM·lee*) – an Academy graduate who is working for the animaru to open portals to Aruzhelim.

Jarnorun (*jar·NOR·un*) – an animaru lord, one of Kirraloth's two main commanders.

Jehira Sinde (*jay·HEER·ah SINDH*) – Raki's grandmother (nani) and soothsayer for the family of Gypta that adopts Aeden.

Jhanda Dalavi (*JON·dah dah·LAHV·ee*) – the Head

Scrivener at the Hero Academy. He is in charge of the small army of scribes who make copies of books and who create many of the records necessary for the functioning of the school.

Jia Toun (*JEE·ah TOON*) – an expert thief and assassin who was formerly the Falxen named Shadeglide. She uses her real name now that she has joined Aeden's group of friends and allies.

Jintu (the Render) Devexo (*JEEN·too day·VEX·oh*) – the great hero and tribe chief who united the tribes of Campastra to fight the false Malatirsay two centuries ago, becoming the high chieftain of the Arunai.

Joceus Davenson (*joe·SEE·us DAA·ven·sun*) – the current king of the Great Enclave, a direct descendent of Thomasinus, Son of Daven, who was the first king of the Great Enclave.

Jorem Pashik – Iriam Dufour/Pashik's husband.

Josef – the owner of the Wolfen's Rest inn in Dartford, a friend of Marla Shrike.

Juinsai (*joo·een·SIE*) – a village in Arania, in the borderlands south of Shinyan, where Jia Toun grew up.

Jun Freemud (*JUN FREE·mud*) – one of the crew of the ship Eurus who went with the party into the jungle on Visuren island.

Jusha Terlix (*JOO·shah TER·liks*) – the Master of the School of Mental Magic at the Hero Academy.

Kaeso Hiberus (*KAY·sew hi·BEER·us*) – the author of the holy book of the Church of Vanda, the Vindictae. He claims to be the prophet of Vanda and that he was given the information directly from the god at the end of the Age of Magic.

Kaila (*KY·lah*) – the young encalo girl who Erent Caahs met when he was a boy, searching for his family's killer. He helped her to rescue her caravan.

Kanton Sea (*KAN·tahn*) – an inland sea in which the island of Munsahtiz, home of the Hero Academy, sits.

Kebahn Faitar (Kebahn the Wise) (*kay·BAWN FYE·tahr*) –

the advisor and friend to Thomasinus; the one who actually came up with the idea to gather all the scattered people and make a stand at the site of what is now the Great Enclave.

Khrazhti *(KHRASH·tee)* – the former High Priestess to the dark god S'ru and former leader of the animaru forces on Dizhelim. At the discovery that her god was untrue, she has become an ally and friend to Aeden.

Kirraloth *(KEER·uh·loth)* – an animaru high lord, given the command of all animaru on Dizhelim after Suuksis failed to turn or destroy Khrazhti.

Kruzekstan *(KROO·zek·stahn)* – a small nation due south of the highland clan lands of Cridheargla.

Kryzt *(KRIZT)* – a type of animaru with spikes all over it, shaped roughly like a wolf but with a longer tail. It has sharp claws and teeth.

Leafburrow – a village in Rhaltzheim, north of Arcusheim off the River Road, the location of a bandit ambush where Erent Caahs demonstrated his special spinning arrow technique.

Leaf Talker – the historical name for an arba community's leader.

Lela Ganeva *(LEE·lah·gahn·AY·vah)* – the woman Erent Caahs fell in love with.

Lerus Costanti *(lehr·OOS coe·STAN·tee)* – one of the three High Itera of the Church of Vanda.

Lesnum *(LESS·num)* – large, hairy, beastlike animaru. These sometimes walk around on two feet, but more commonly use all four limbs. They are strong and fast and intelligent enough to be used as sergeants, commanding groups of seren and other low-level animaru.

Lex – Evon's horse, a chestnut stallion

Lilianor (Lili) Caahs *(LI·lee·ah·nore CAWS)* – Erent Cahhs's little sister; she was murdered when she was eleven years old.

Liluth Olaxidor (*LIL·uth oh·LAX·ih·door*) – the Master of the School of Firearms at the Hero Academy.

Lily Fisher – an archer of supreme skill who was formerly the Falxen assassin named Phoenixarrow. She uses her real name now that she has joined Aeden's group of friends and allies.

Lis (*LEES*) – a minor deity who battled the sun, nearly killing it, and causing so much damage that to this day, it is weakened in the wintertime.

Lucas Stewart – a young student at the Hero Academy. He's often used by the masters as a messenger because of his strong work ethic and reliability.

Lucio Sanctus (*LOO·chee·oh SAHNK·toos*) – the Patr Pruma of the Vandan Church.

Lusnauqua (*loos·NOW·kwah*) – the rugged land surrounding Broken Reach, in the center of the eastern section of the continent of Promistala.

Malatirsay (*Mahl·ah·TEER·say*) – the hero who will defeat the animaru and save Dizhelim from the darkness, according to prophecy. The name means "chosen warrior" or "special warrior" in Alaqotim.

Manandantan (*mahn·ahn·DAHN·tahn*) – the festival to celebrate the goddess Danta, goddess of song.

Marla Shrike – a graduate of the famed Hero Academy, an experienced combatant in both martial and magical disciplines.

Marn Tiscomb – the new Master of Prophecy at the Hero Academy. He replaced Master Aeid, who was murdered.

Masseni Devexo (*mah·SEH·nee day·VEX·oh*) – the daughter of chief Rovalu Devexo, an influential warrior princess of the Arunai.

Mellafond (*MEH·la·fond*) – a large swamp on the mainland to the east of Munsahtiz Island. The name *means pit of Mellaine.*

Mellaine (*meh·LAYN*) – goddess of nature and growing things.

Miera Tannoch (*MEERA TAN·ahkh*) – Aeden's mother, wife of Sartan.

Migae (*MEE·jay*) – the God of magic. The word "magic" comes from his name.

Mikel Tonsend (*MICK·ell*) – the bank worker Lily deals with in Satta Sarak before getting to Tannis Edgar.

Mionn Bhais (*MYOON BAJH*) – the Death Oath, a tradition set forth at the beginning of the Croagh clans. It consists of a magical ritual that binds the clan chiefs to either submit to one leader or to challenge that leader in combat to the death.

Mildred Farnsworth – the cook/servant assigned to Batido. The other two cooks/servants (Elaith and Tarden) report to her.

Mirkus Rigas (*REE·gas*) – one of the crew of the ship Eurus who went with the party into the jungle on Visuren island.

Mora Davenson (*MORE·ah DAA·ven·sun*) – the queen of the Great Enclave, wife of Joceus Davenson.

Morningsilver – the horse the Academy let Jia use, a pale grey horse whose coat shone in the right light.

Moroshi Katai (*mor·ROE·shee kah·TAI*) – a mythological hero who battled the Dragon of Eternity to found the nation of Teroshi.

Moschephis (*mose·CHE·feess*) – the trickster god, from whose name comes the word mischief.

Mother Sella – the town healer in Drusca when Lily was a girl.

Mudertis (*moo·DARE·teez*) – the god of thievery and assassination.

Munsahtiz (*moon·SAW·teez*) – the island in the Kanton sea on which the Hero Academy Sitor-Kanda resides.

Muscade (*moos·CAWD*) – the horse the Academy let Aila use, a light reddish brown mare.

Nadine Dufour – Mother Sella's daughter; she took over being the neighborhood healer when her mother got too old.

Nanris – the unofficial capital of Kruzekstan, more important than the actual capital of Kruzeks because most of the wealth of the nation is centered in Nanris.

Nasir Kelqen (*nah·SEER KEL·ken*) – the Master of the School of Research and Investigation at the Hero Academy.

Naxon Den-Uto (*NAX·on DEN·OO·toe*) – the chief of the Den-Uto tribe of Arunai

Nessa Shua (*NESS·ah. SHOE·ah*) – one of Cara Moore's underlings, an unattractive woman who wears very tight clothing on her superbly fit body and fights with great flexibility.

Nightheart – the horse the Academy let Raki use in his travels, a black stallion.

Nobleflame – the horse the Academy let Lily use, a dark red gelding.

Nutenlo (*noo·TEN·loe*) – one of the tribespeople Sirak uses to try to get Marla.

Omnisagnitio (*OME·nees·ahg·NEE·shee·oh*) – the name of the Well of Power found in the cave system where Tsosin Ruus's cache of information was found, within the Aerie Mountains.

Omri – a fair sized city in northern Kruzekstan, one of the first of the cities to fall to the animaru.

Osulin (*AWE·soo·lin*) – goddess of nature. She is the daughter of Mellaine and the human hero Trikus Phen.

Pach (*PAHKH*) – in Dantogyptain, it means five. As a proper noun, it refers to the festival of Manandantan that occurs every fifth year, a special celebration in which the Song of Prophecy is sung in full.

Padraig Seachaid (*PAD·reg SHAW·chid*) – the clan chief of the Seachaid Croagh clan.

Patik Fisher – Lily's father.

Patr Pruma (*POT·er PROO·mah*) – the leader of the Church of Vanda.

Pedras Shrike – Marla Shrike's adoptive father, the groundskeeper for the administrative area of the Hero Academy.

Percipius (*pare·CHIP·ee·us*) – god of the dead and of the underworld.

Phoenixarrow – one of the Falxen sent to kill Khrazhti and her companions. A statuesque red-haired archer who had a penchant for using fire arrows.

Pilae (*PEEL·lay*) – a type of animaru that looks like a ball of shadow.

Pofel Dessin (*POE·fell DESS·in*) – a traveling scholar who meets Marla and Evon on their journeys.

Pouran (*PORE·an*) – roundish, heavy humanoids with piggish faces and tusks like a boar

Praesturi (*prayz·TURE·ee*) – the town and former military outpost on the southeastern tip of the island of Munsahtiz. The south bridge from the mainland to the island ends within Praesturi.

Preshim (*PRAY·sheem*) – title of the leader of a family of Gypta

Promistala (*prome·ees·TAHL·ah*) – the main continent in Dizhelim. In Alaqotim, the name means "first (or most important) land."

Qozhel (*KOE·shell*) – the energy that pervades the universe and that is usable as magic.

Qydus Okvius (*KIE·duss OCK·vee·us*) – the headmaster of the Hero Academy, Sitor-Kanda.

Raibrech (*RAI·brekh*) – the clan magic of the highland clans. In Chorain, it means "bloodfire."

Raimund Bainer (*RAY·mund BANE·er*) – one of the three High Itera of the Church of Vanda.

Rainstorm – the horse the Acaedmy let Urun use, a grey mare with black speckles.

Raisor Tannoch (*RAI·sore TAN·ahkh*) – a famous warrior of Clan Tannoch, companion of the hero Erent Caahs.

Raki Sinde (*ROCK·ee SINDH*) – grandson of Jehira Sinde, friend and training partner of Aeden.

Ren Kenata (*REN ke·NAH·tah*) – a Hero Academy adept who was is not only one of Quentin Duzen's associates, but also a member of the Dark Council.

Rhaltzheim (*RALTZ·haim*) – the nation to the northeast of the Grundenwald Forest. The people of the land are called Rhaltzen or sometimes Rhaltza. The term Rhaltzheim is often used to refer to the rugged land within the national borders (e.g., "traverse the Rhaltzheim")

Ritma Achaya (*REET·mah ah·CHAI·ah*) – Fahtin's mother, wife of the Gypta family leader Darun.

Roneus Lomos (*ROE·nee·us LOE·mose*) – the Master of the School of Stealth at the Hero Academy.

Rougang (*roo·GAHNG*) – one of the major cities in modern Shinyan, in former Xin tribe territory. In ancient Shinyan, it was a town, the headquarters for the rebel forces of Xin Tai Rong.

Rovalu Devexo (*roe·VAH·loo day·VEX·oh*) – the current high chief of all the Arunai. He resides in Devexo, within in the territory of the Devex-Numantu tribe)

Ruthrin (*ROOTH·rin*) – the common tongue of Dizhelim, the language virtually everyone in the world speaks in addition to their own national languages.

S'ru (*SROO*) – the dark god of the animaru, supreme power in Aruzhelim.

Saelihn Valdove (*SAY·lin VAHL·doe·vay*) – the Master of the School of Life Magic at the Hero Academy.

Saevel (*SAY·vell*) – the arba huntress who guided Urun's group through the Mellafond swamp.

Salamus (*sah·lah·MOOS*) – an ancient nation in which the legendary hero Trikus Phen resided. It no longer exists. Things of Salamus were called Salaman.

Saria Gilwenys (*SAW·ree ah gill·WEN·is*) (gill is pronounced like a fish's *gill*) – an Academy graduate who has been out in the world working as an operative for Sitor-Kanda. She is half astri.

Sartan Tannoch (*SAR·tan TAN·ahkh*) – Aeden's father, clan chief of the Tannoch clan of Craogh.

Sastiroz (*SASS·teer·oz*) – an animaru lord, one of Kirraloth's two main commanders.

Satta Sarak (*SAH·tah SARE·ack*) – a city in the south-eastern part of the continent of Promistala, part of the Saraki Principality.

Scrapper – the name Aila gave the small trebaxel they found in Sintrovis

Seachaid (*SHAW·chid*) – one of the five highland clans of the Cridheargla.

Semhominus (*sem·HOM·in·us*) – one of the highest level of animaru. They are humanoid, larger than a typical human, and use weapons. Many of them can also use magic. Most animaru lords are of this type.

Senna Shrike – Marla Shrike's adoptive mother.

Seoras Corcan (*SORE·us*) – the clan chief of the Corcan clan of Croagh.

Seren (*SARE·en*) – the most common type of animaru, with sharp teeth and claws. They are similar in shape and size to humans.

Shadeglide – one of the Falxen sent to kill Khrazhti and her companions. She is small of stature but extremely skilled as a thief and assassin.

Shadowed Pinnacles – the long mountain range essentially splitting the western part of Promistala into two parts. It was formerly known as the Wall of Salamus because it separated that kingdom from Gentason.

Shaku (*SHOCK·oo*) – a class of Teroshimi assassins.

Shanaera Eilren (*shah·NARE·ah ALE·ren*) – the Master of Unarmed Combat at the Hero Academy.

Shinyan (*SHEEN·yahn*) – a nation on the northern tip of the western part of Promistala, bordering the Kanton Sea and the Cattilan Sea. Things of Shinyan (such as people) are referred to as Shinyin.

Shu root/Shu's Bite (*SHOO*) – a root that only grows in Shinyan, the key ingredient to the poison Shu's Bite.

Sike (*SEEK·ay*) – a class of Shinyin assassins

Sintrovis (*seen·TROE·vees*) – an area of high magical power on which the Great Enclave was built. In Alaqotim, it means *center of strength*.

Sirak Isayu (*SEER·ack ee·SAI·yoo*) – a member of the Dark Council. He comes from the southern part of the continent of Promistala, near the Sittingham Desert.

Sitor-Kanda (*SEE·tor KAN·dah*) – the Hero Academy, the institution created by the great prophet Tsosin Ruus to train the Malatirsay. The name means roughly "home of magic" in Alaqotim.

Sittingham Desert – a large desert in the southwestern part of Promistala.

Skril Tossin – best friend of Marla Shrike and Evon Desconce, a Hero Academy adept.

Snowmane – the horse the Academy lent to Aeden, a chestnut stallion with a white mane

Solon (*SEW·lahn*) – one of the masters in Clan Tannoch, responsible for training young warriors how to use the clan magic, the Raibrech.

Souvenia (*soo·VEN·ee·ah*) – an empire that was one of the world powers before the War of Magic, and one of the major players in that war. It no longer exists.

Srantorna (*sran·TORN·ah*) – the abode of the gods, a place where humans cannot go.

Sudepta Sinde (*soo·DEP·tah SINDH*) – one of Raki's older brothers, the one whose birthday it was when Raki's family went out to get him a present and were attacked and killed.

Surefoot – Marla Shrike's horse.

Surus (*SOO·roos*) – king of the gods.

Sutania (*soo·TAN·ee·ah*) – the nation south of the Kanton Sea, the capital of which is the city of Arcusheim.

Suuksis (*SOOK·sis*) – an animaru lord; Khrazhti's father.

Szestithan (*ZESS·tih·than*) (the th is pronounced like in *thousand*) – the highest of the animaru, the only one who deals directly with S'ru after Khrazhti defected. He's called S'ru's Shadow.

Tannis Edgar – the bank official in Satta Sarak who runs a scam where he sells off peoples' stuff, including Lily's uncle's mementos she goes there to retrieve.

Tannoch (*TAN·ahkh*) – one of the five highland clans of the Cridheargla, the one to which Aeden was born into.

Tarden Starsen – the helper and general gofer/servant assigned to Batido. He mostly does the physical work that doesn't involve cleaning or cooking.

Taristen Tracten – one of the heads of the firearm manufacturing families in Drusca. They also make the flash powder.

Tarshuk (*TAR·shuk*) – a semi-desert-like area to the southwest of the Heaven's Teeth range that has stunted trees and scrub.

Tazi Ermengo (*TAH·zee air·MANE·go*) – the king of the doomed kingdom of Awresea. He taunted the god Fyorio and was destroyed along with his entire kingdom, which was renamed Fyrefall.

Tefford Pimms – the inn keeper at the inn in Simpton's Well where the party stayed.

Tere Chizzit (*TEER CHIZ·it*) – a blind archer and tracker with the ability to see despite having no working eyes. He is Aeden's companion in the story.

Tero (*TAY·roe*) – the Dragon of Eternity, one of the mightiest of all dragons who had ever lived and whose plummet to his death created the Astugi Sea.

Teroshi (*tare·OH·shee*) – an island nation in the northern part of Dizhelim. Things of Teroshi, including people, are referred to as Teroshimi.

Tesnair Balstad (*tes·NARE BALL·stad*) – the ship captain who is the brother of Asgeir Balstad (the one who took Marla to Iracundia). He takes Lily and the others to Visuren.

Thalia Fendove (*THA·lee·uh FEN·doe·vay*) – a member of the Dark Council.

Thomasinus, son of Daven (*toe·mah·SINE·us*) – the hero who banded the remnants of the troops of Gentason together to create the Great Enclave. Once they elected him king, he changed his last name to Davenson.

Thomlin Byrch (*TOM·lin BIRCH*) – a member of the Dark Council.

Thritur Nyhus (*THRY·tur NY·hus*) – a member of the Dark Council.

Thunderlight – the horse the Academy let Tere use, a black stallion with white markings that look like slashes.

Tide's Blessing – the inn Marla and the others stayed at in Hirsen.

Toan Broos (*TOE·aan*) – traveling companion of Erent Caahs and Raisor Tannoch.

Tongqi (*TOHNG·chee*) – the capital city of Shinyan, nestled in the bowl created by the mountains near Honor's Peak.

Toras Geint (*TOR·ahs GAYNT*) – an old tracker and scout who befriended Erent Caahs when he was a boy and who mentored the young hero, training him to track and hunt, among other things.

Toross Iardisith (*TORE·oss ee·ARD·ih·sith*) – an Academy graduate who is working for the animaru to open portals to Aruzhelim

Touhas Ailgid (*TOO·ahs ILE·jid*) – the elder of the Ailgid clan of Croagh who was named their clan chief after much of their clan was destroyed by the animaru.

Trebaxel (*tre·BAX·el*) – ape like creatures that are rumored to exist in Sintrovis, in the Great Enclave.

Trebhin (*TREH·vin*) – one of the five highland clans of the Cridheargla.

Tresica (*TREH·sih cah*) – Ivel's girlfriend who dumped him and cheated on him with Sharan Kolga.

Trikus Phen (*TRY·kus FEN*) – a legendary hero who battled Codaghan, the god of war, himself, and sired Osulin by the goddess Mellaine.

Tsosin Ruus (*TSO·sin ROOS*) – the Prophet, the seer and archmage who penned the Song of Prophecy and founded Sitor-Kanda, the Hero Academy.

Tuach (*TOO·akh*) – one of the masters in Clan Tannoch, responsible for teaching the young warriors the art of physical combat.

Tufa Shao (*TOO·fah SHA·oh*) – the Master of the School of Body Mechanics and Movement at the Hero Academy.

Tunin Ferrol (*TOO·nen. FARE·all*) – one of Cara Moore's underlings. He is obsessed with food.

Twilight – the horse the Academy let Khrazhti use, a grey mare.

Urtumbrus (*oor·TOOM·brus*) – a type of animaru that are essentially living shadows.

Urun Chinowa (*OO·run CHIN·oh·wah*) – the High Priest of the goddess Osulin, a nature priest.

Utrix (*OO·trix*) – a colechna (snake-type) animaru who looks for the hidden cache Tsosin Ruus left for Aeden and Marla. He is a mage and obsessed with study to gain knowledge of the new world he has come to.

Vadim Plesca (*VAH·deem PLES·kah*) – a mage during the Age of Magic, a close associate to Aquilius Gavros.

Vaeril Faequin (*VARE·ill FAY·kwin*) – the Master of the School of Mechanista Artifice at the Hero Academy.

Valcordinae (*val·COR·di·nay*) – a series of extremely ancient tunnels with a well of magical power at its core. The word is ancient Alaqotim for *strong minds*.

Vanda (*VAHN·dah*) – a modern god, claimed by his followers to be the only true god. It is said he is many gods in one, having different manifestations. The Church of Vanda is very large and very powerful in Dizhelim.

Vandictae (*vahn·DIC·tay*) – the book of holy writings of the Church of Vanda.

Vandictatorum (*vahn·DIC·tah·TOR·um*) – the massive domed structure in Vandomus, the center of learning about the Vandictae. Essentially a university of the church's holy writings.

Vater (*VAH·ter*) – one of the tribespeople Sirak uses to try to get Marla.

Vatheca (*VATH·ay·kuh*) – the headquarters and training center of the Falxen. It is a mixture of two Alaqotim words, both meaning "sheath."

Veraugun (*vare·ow·GOON*) – the name of the Well of Power found in Shinyan. It means true honor in ancient Alaqotim.

Vesta – a huge mythological beast that was too large to come down from the heavens to Dizhelim. Surus did battle with the monster to prevent it from destroying the world.

Videric Dewitte (*VEE·dare·ic deh·VIT*) – the Master of the School of Magical Healing at the Hero Academy.

Vincus (pl. vinci) (*VEEN·cuss; VEEN·chee*) – Aila's chain blade weapons.

Viro/Vira (pl viri) (*VEER·oh / VEER·ah / VEER·ee*) – a former Hero Academy student who has graduated with a mastery in at least three schools and no longer lives at the Academy or participates in its function.

Visuren (*vi·SOO·ren*) – the large island southeast of Promistala, sometimes referred to as "life's cradle."

Vituma (*vi·TOO·mah*) – the leader of the Dark Council.

The name derives from the ancient Alaqotim term for *prophet's shadow*.

Voordim (*VOOR·deem*) – the pantheon of gods in Dizhelim. It does not include the modern god Vanda.

Vora (*VORE·ah*) – the Leaf Talker of the tribe of arba in the Mellafond swamp.

Vorun – one of the crew of the ship Eurus who went with the party into the jungle on Visuren island.

Votior Renusa (*VOE·tee·ore reh·NOO·sah*) – Alloria Yurgen's head servant.

Vulmer Liadin (*VUL·mer LEE·uh·din*) – the first headmaster of the Hero Academy, appointed by Tsosin Ruus himself to run the school for the Prophet.

Waterdancer – one of the high-ranking Falxen who negotiates with the Dark Council for long-term assignments of assassins.

Wolfen – large intelligent wolves that roam desolate areas in the Rhaltzheim.

Wolfen's Rest – the inn in Dartford, on the mainland not too far east from the bridge to the island of Munsahtiz.

Xaviera Contanko (*zaw·vee·AIR·ah cone TAHNK·oe*) – the Master of Artifice: Items of Power at the Hero Academy. She journeyed to the Dark Pinnacles with Raki, Jia, and Urun.

Xin Su Jun (*SHEEN SOO JOON*) – the current Shinyin emperor, son of the former emperor.

Xin Tai Rong (*SHEEN TIE ROHNG*) – the rebel leader who eventually defeated Chao He Ling's forces and became the first emperor of Shinyan.

Yezras Farlingian (*YEZ·rass far LIN·gee·an*) – the Master of the School of Conjuration and Invocation at the Hero Academy.

Yoniko Takesi (*YOE·nee·koe tah·KAY·see*) – a member of the Dark Council.

Yralissa Zinphinal (*eer·ah·LISS ah ZIN·fin·all*) – the Master of the School of Illusion at the Hero Academy.

Yxna Hagenai (*IX·nah HAG·en·eye*) – the Master of Edged Weapons at the Hero Academy.

Zejo Troufal (*ZAY·joe TROO·fahl*) – a hero who lived at the end of the Age of Magic. He was Erent Cahhs's idol when he was a boy, before he himself became a hero.

Zhadril (*ZHAD·reel*) – an animaru mage—former high priest of S'ru—who was defeated in battle by Khrazhti to lose his position. In Dizhelim, he was given permission to study corrupted magic in a swamp area.

Author Notes

Thank you for sharing in Lily's adventures with me in Hero's Life. If you enjoyed the book, **could you please leave a review?** It's no secret that authors like me need reviews from readers like you to increase the number of people who get their eyes on my books. Reviews and ratings are so important in creating word of mouth so other readers will try my stories. I would appreciate it immensely if you could help.

The danger is increasing, the story becoming more complex. With the Dark Council, the Falxen, and other groups we've seen before taking a greater part in events, it's clear the conclusion of the conflict will not be a simple one. No longer is it a matter of whether or not the animaru will end all life on Dizhelim. Now, many conclusions seem possible, most of them bad for the world as a whole.

The next book, Hero's Light, features a newer character and allows us to get more historical information that will help us understand what is truly happening in Dizhelim. With so many entities at odds, our heroes will need every advantage they can get to survive, let alone emerge victorious. Things are starting to boil. Will the increase in pressure inhibit Aeden and his heroic companions, or will it make them stronger? We'll get our answer soon. Thank you so much for reading, and hopefully I'll see you soon!

P.E. Padilla

About the Author

A chemical engineer by degree and at various times an air quality engineer, a process control engineer, and a regulatory specialist by vocation, USA Today bestselling author P.E. Padilla learned long ago that crunching numbers and designing solutions was not enough to satisfy his creative urges. Weaned on classic science fiction and fantasy stories from authors as diverse as Heinlein, Tolkien, and Jordan, and affected by his love of role playing games such as Dungeons and Dragons (analog) and Final Fantasy (digital), he sometimes has trouble distinguishing reality from fantasy. While not ideal for a person who needs to function in modern society, it's the perfect state of mind for a writer. He is a recent transplant from Southern California to Northern Washington, where he lives surrounded by trees.

pepadilla.com/
pep@pepadilla.com

Also by P.E. Padilla

Adventures in Gythe:

Vibrations: Harmonic Magic Book 1 (audiobook also)

Harmonics: Harmonic Magic Book 2 (audiobook also)

Resonance: Harmonic Magic Book 3

Tales of Gythe: Gray Man Rising (audiobook also available)

Tales of Gythe: Ix: Legacy of Honor

Harmonic Magic Series Boxed Set

The Unlikely Hero Series (under pen name Eric Padilla):

Unfurled: Heroing is a Tough Gig (Unlikely Hero Series Book 1) (also available as an audiobook)

Unmasked (Unlikely Hero Series Book 2)

Undaunted (Unlikely Hero Series Book 3)

Unlikely Hero Series Boxed Set

The Shadowling Chronicles (under pen name Eric Padilla):

Shadowling

Witches of the Elements Series :

Water & Flame

Song of Prophecy Series :

SoP1 - Wanderer's Song (available as an audiobook also)

SoP2 - Warrior's Song

SoP3 - Heroes' Song

SoP4 - Hero Dawning

SoP5 - Hero's Mind